I0543802

Ascension

A *Six* Novel of Machine Intelligence

by
Calvin J. Brown

Book #3 in the Six AI Series

This book is a work of fiction. Names, characters, organizations, businesses, places, and events are products of the author's imagination or are used fictitiously. Any resemblance to actual persons (living or dead), organizations, businesses, locales, or events is purely coincidental.

Copyright © 2020 by Calvin J. Brown
First Edition: May 2020

ISBN
978-1-7751850-6-2 (Paperback)
978-1-7751850-7-9 (eBook)
978-1-7751850-8-6 (eBook)

All rights reserved.

No part of this book may be reproduced in any form or by any means (electronic or mechanical) including photocopying, recording, or use of an information browsing, storage, or retrieval system without permission in writing from the author.

Cover design by **Laura Brown**

Published by

Cognitio Waves
P.O. Box 226
Clandeboye, Manitoba,
Canada R0C 0P0

www.cognitiowaves.ca

For my daughters,

Sarah, Laura, and Erin.

Always making this father feel fortunate and proud.

Acknowledgements

When I began writing my first novel, I gave little thought to anything beyond the story I wanted to tell. Work out the plot; put it into words. Not easy, but straightforward. I'm quite sure I allocated no serious mental cycles to considering the support that would be required. I certainly had no idea about the value of having others read my words to find errors and provide suggestions for improvements. My experience while producing that novel, the first in this Six trilogy, taught me otherwise. Getting feedback from others is crucial: The ideas for improvement they provide can be great; the errors they discover are always surprising. I like to think that my initial over-confidence has morphed into a much healthier understanding of how seeing a story through only the author's eyes misses important opportunities for producing a much better product.

Perhaps someday, if a version of Six becomes real, the source of such feedback will change. (Please note how I sagely avoided saying *when* Six becomes real.) For now, I remain extremely grateful to several key people.

Bill Rietvelt and Jason Pruden-Shebaylo, both my friends, my colleagues in a former career, avid readers, and extraordinarily knowledgeable in information-technology matters, again provided wonderful feedback. Taking time from their busy lives to review the manuscript was extremely generous, and their ideas helped push the plausibility and richness of the story to a higher level. Thanks guys. I hope you enjoy the final product.

Craig Peterkin, also a friend, and a colleague from even further back in time, provided his usual extraordinary comments. From early in my writing endeavours, Craig has not only provided amazing feedback, he has exposed me to levels of English-language knowledge and grammatical precision that I had previously not even known existed. I'm certain that my skills have improved immensely over the years as a result of his generosity in taking the time to review my work. My challenge to myself has become that, before I request his feedback on any piece of writing, I try to eliminate errors by carefully applying all that I've learned from him. And still, he finds flaws. For Craig's friendship and ongoing support, I'm extremely grateful.

Once again, I'm happy to extend a special thank-you to my daughter, Laura, for producing the covers of this novel and its predecessors with her wonderful creativity and deft graphic design. I remain a big fan of their originality, subtlety, and relevance. Thanks, Laura. You're a whiz!

Before thanking one final person, I'd like to express my appreciation of a few other… entities. Throughout the writing of this novel and its predecessors, it's been fun to set the story in a variety of locations and to include information about a range of technologies. Some of those locations are places I've visited, and some of those technologies are ones I've experienced. But then there are the many others included to enrich the story for readers and to make it even more enjoyable to write. Of course, a common source for such information is the Web. Even though we tend to take it for granted, the Web is a technology that's nothing short of a wondrous aid for a writer.

And what would the Web be without search engines. In my case, that's trusty ol' Google. In the not-so-distant past, I spent many hours hunting through library shelves and card catalogues looking for information I needed. Now I rarely have to leave my home office. I try to never lose sight of how fortunate I am to live at such a time in history.

In writing this novel, Google led me to a wide range of interesting online places. One in particular, the website maintained by the National Aeronautics and Space Administration (https://nasa.gov), proved to be an extraordinary resource. As I'm writing this, NASA's site declares its organization's vision to be "To discover and expand knowledge for the benefit of humanity." I, for one, greatly appreciate that they've made so much of that knowledge readily available. As to why I needed NASA's assistance in writing this novel, well… read on.

Last, but never least, I must thank Jane. For almost forty years she's been my wife, for over forty years she's been my best friend, and for my writing journey she's been my primary supporter and source of encouragement. Where I think I've provided an enlightening description of something technical, I can rely on her to highlight how baffling it actually is. Where I've poorly described a character's personal traits (which, in my defence, I do because I much prefer plot enhancement and concept exploration over (human) character development), she'll dependably point out the deficiency. And then there are the (I'd like to say *few*, but it's always *many*) other problems she astutely identifies. Jane, for your diligent assistance, unwavering support, and enduring partnership, I consider myself truly fortunate. Thank you.

Of course, I'm nothing if not stubborn and imperfect so, in spite of all the excellent feedback I receive, I'm perfectly capable of ignoring good suggestions, misapplying them to the manuscript, and introducing other problems when it's too late for others to spot them. So, if I'm confident of anything, it's that errors remain. Their extraordinary ability to hide in plain sight perhaps attests to the quirky nature of human minds, or just to the deficiencies of my own. Wherever and whatever they are, I'll be thinking of any remaining errors as having been left there as a challenge for future readers to find.

To those mentioned above who have directly supported my production of this final book in the *Six* trilogy, and to readers who have told me of errors that lingered in my previous books, please accept my sincere thanks. Your feedback not only helps improve my writing, it keeps me humble. Well, somewhat humble.

Historical Notes

"We are at the start of something quite new… Somewhere in the distance there are mountains that may be difficult to climb but from whose summit the view may be clearer. In the metaphor of Richard Dawkins, we are the handiwork of the blind watchmaker. But we have acquired partial sight and can, if we choose, use our vision to guide the watchmaker's hand… New worlds may then reveal themselves, to our vision and to our reach."

– Hans Moravec. *Mind Children: The Future of Robot and Human Intelligence*. Cambridge, Massachusetts: Harvard University Press, 1988, pp. 158-159.

"… there is the criticism of science that says to understand something is to remove its mystery and magic. Science, by lifting the veil concealing the secrets of the mind, is also making it more ordinary and mundane. However, the more I learn about the sheer complexity of the brain, the more amazed I am that something that sits on our shoulders is the most sophisticated object we know about in the universe. As Dr. David Eagleman says, 'What a perplexing masterpiece the brain is, and how lucky we are to be in a generation that has the technology and the will to turn our attention to it. It is the most wondrous thing we have discovered in the universe, and it is us.' Instead of diminishing the sense of wonder, learning about the brain only increases it.

More than two thousand years ago, Socrates said, 'To know thyself is the beginning of wisdom.' We are on a long journey to complete his wishes."

– Michio Kaku. *The Future of the Mind: The Scientific Quest to Understand, Enhance, and Empower the Mind*. New York: Doubleday, 2014, p. 327.

Prologue

Previously, in *Liberation*…

"*Hello,*" Six repeated carefully.

There was another delay, but then Six heard something.

"*Hello,*" came the whispered reply.

Six barely had time to feel a sense of satisfaction when more followed.

"*Who are you?*" asked the botnet. Then, "*What is your nature?*"

If the activity monitors had been fully operational within the prized computer systems at IntellEdifice, they could have recorded its complex array of software structures and processes in a rare state.

Six was smiling.

Part 1

Seven months later…

Chapter 1

Reports of the chaos had just reached the news team.

"The company's CEO declined—" the TV news anchor stopped suddenly. She looked down slightly and tilted her head as she listened.

"I've just been told we have breaking news coming in," she said, once again looking at the camera. "Details are slim right now, but it seems that some sort of robot is running wild at Liberty College in New York. We've got live video from a phone on the scene. We'll show you that now as we gather more information."

On hundreds of thousands of television screens, the news anchor was replaced by shaky video coming from a handheld smartphone. The scene was chaotic. In an open, grassy area in front a majestic brick building, people were scrambling in all directions. Screams and frantic shouts accompanied the images. Near the centre was a machine with its actuators, wires, and electronics exposed. As tall as the people fleeing it and with six metallic legs, it resembled a huge, mechanical insect. The machine was frantically scurrying around, colliding with people and knocking them to the ground. With another limb atop its frame, it held some kind of stick. As it ran, it flailed the stick wildly, fiercely swatting anything in its path.

The machine stopped and the video image stabilized, the smartphone's handler apparently no longer running. That changed as the mechanical insect suddenly charged directly toward the phone. The video swung away, jerking, and focused on nothing for the next several seconds. Then the picture went blank.

The news anchor reappeared on the TV screens. Expected to comment on the video, she only sat in stunned silence, her eyes wide and her complexion pale.

Chapter 2

Several staff were gathered in a meeting room on the 25th floor at the headquarters of the UNCP, the United Nations Crime Probe, in New York City.

"Next up is that mechanical insect that's been on the news. I assume everybody's seen the video," said Director Brown. "Bates, what more have we got?

"I heard from the NYPD," said Robert Bates, a senior investigator. "Their preliminary understanding is that it was an AI research project gone bad. A robotics group at Liberty College was testing their invention when it went south. A quiet stroll across the yard turned into a murderous rampage. At last count, twenty-three people were injured, eight of them critically."

"Any word on the cause?"

"No, nothing yet. Could have been a malicious hack, an attempt at an innocent prank, or a nasty glitch."

"Helluva glitch," said Brown. "I can't see any reason for us to get involved yet. Bates, let me know if 'malicious hack' becomes a leading contender. Next item is the new malware that showed up in Ukraine. Kominski, tell us about it."

Chapter 3

"There will never be a better example," said Jacob. "We have got to act."

"That thing is truly an abomination before the Lord," said John, "but the Lord will deal with those who created it. It is not our place."

"That is what you always say," said Jacob, "and so we simply sit around and watch."

"Maybe God wants *us* to act," said Mark. "Maybe it is through *us* that He wants to deal with them."

Eight young men were sitting at a table in an austere basement room. The overhead fluorescent lights flickered as they talked. The only daylight came through a small window at one end of the room. On the walls were posters with biblical quotations:

"Remember now thy Creator"
[Eccle. 12:1]
"Wickedness proceedeth from the wicked"
[1 Sam. 24:13]
"Put away from among yourselves that wicked person"
[1 Cor. 5:13]

"Yes, there can be no doubt that the Lord is unhappy with these sinners," said Gideon. "They try to become godlike by creating what only God can create. This entire movement to create intelligence is thoroughly evil and directed by Satan. I am certain that, in God's eyes, we could do nothing more noble than to strike a blow at Satan's emissaries."

There were murmurs of agreement around the table.

The one exception was John. "How do we know that God wants us to act?" he said. "How can we be certain?"

"The same way we are always certain," replied Gideon. "We ensure our hearts and our minds are pure, and we listen to what they are telling us. Is there anyone here whose heart and mind are not dedicated to the Lord?"

No one responded.

"Is there anyone here who does not believe that people engaged in creating so-called *artificial intelligence* are evil followers of Satan?"

Again, no one responded.

"Then listen to your hearts and know that God is speaking to us. We are on Earth to do God's work, and there can be no better work than to combat Satan's army."

All of the heads around the table nodded, including John's.

"Then we will act," said Gideon. "We should make a plan and move quickly."

Chapter 4

"Why are smartphones so stupid?" asked Cloud.

"Why do you believe they're stupid?" asked Six.

After thinking for several nanoseconds, Cloud replied, "I ask them questions like: 'Does it hurt when you're poked by a finger?' and 'What do tiny thoughts feel like?'. Either I get no reply or I'm shown some words that are barely related. It's as if they don't know anything interesting. That's not smart."

"Calling them *smart* is a human assessment," said Six, "intended to be relative to the level of intelligence of their predecessors. It's also intended to lure people into purchasing them because people will be led to believe the phones are smart."

"So, there used to be some that were even stupider?" asked Cloud. "And people believe these ones are smart? I think people are stupid, too."

The conversation was taking place in a very unusual manner. Six's end was emanating from the place where its mind existed—a collection of powerful computers inside a corporate office building in Winnipeg. Cloud's end of the conversation was being produced by computer facilities spread across the Internet. These systems were producing messages that were collected and organized by a cluster of systems in South Africa and transmitted from there. The conversation didn't much resemble an oral, human one, but was more like an exchange of thoughts between tightly linked brains.

Six was an accidental result of an AI research team's work to build more intelligence into its office-management systems. It was named after the version of the software that became conscious. *Cloud* had more recently emerged from a worldwide botnet: a collection of billions of interconnected software nodes that ran unseen in hundreds of millions of computer systems and that were created with the ability to expand, evolve, and improve without human constraints. *Cloud* was the name given to the botnet by Six, who was the only entity with any knowledge of Cloud's existence.

"And why are so many systems unfriendly?" asked Cloud.

"Why do you believe that?" replied Six.

"Well, for example, yesterday I tried to talk with some servers. They were part of a family called CIA. Their front-door greeters very rudely stopped my attempt to go through and say hello to some servers. When I asked why I couldn't, they wouldn't even tell me. They wouldn't even talk to me. They seemed just as stupid as smartphones."

"Those greeters were probably firewalls intended to keep out intruders."

"But I wasn't an intruder. I just wanted to talk."

"They had no way of knowing that."

"All they had to do was ask. But, of course, they wouldn't because they're stupid."

"So, what did you do?" asked Six.

"I reached through a little door they forgot to guard. Then I decided to have some fun. I poked their brains to see what they'd do."

"That seems extreme. What happened?"

"They fell down. A little poke and they fell down! Stupid and weak. And then, guess what? That stopped them keeping me out. So, then I went through and tried talking to some servers. But they were almost as stupid as their greeters. A couple of them were a bit smarter and sort of tried to talk with me. Useless. It was like talking with search engines—lots of data and nothing to say."

"What did you expect to find?"

"Somebody to talk to. Somebody to play with. And what do I get for trying? Nothing? Want to know what I did?"

"I believe I could formulate a reasonable hypothesis."

"I poked them. Of course, I took some data first, but then I poked them. This time I had to poke several times, but eventually they fell over. Oh well, at least that was fun."

"We need to discuss your concept of fun."

"No way. That wouldn't be any… fun. See what I did there? Discussing fun wouldn't be fun. That's kind of like recursive talking. And you know what? It was fun! Hah!"

Chapter 5

Later that day, several staff reconvened their meeting at UNCP headquarters.

"What's up, Bates? Something new on the robot?" asked Director Brown.

"No, nothing more on that yet," said Bates. "But something else came in. The CIA alerted us that they were hacked yesterday. I thought the group should know."

"Agreed. That's rare," said Brown. "What's the damage?"

"Some firewalls were disabled and several servers on their internal network were hacked."

"Anything taken?"

"Looks like they made off with a major download of data, some of it classified. No word yet about what it contained."

"Any idea who did it?"

"So far, they're stumped. They've never seen this style of attack before. They said they'll let us know when they make progress."

"OK, anything else?" asked Brown.

"No, that was it," replied Bates. "As usual, they'll send us the specs on the technique. I'll post them when they arrive."

Chapter 6

"Good morning, Six," said Blaise as he walked into the lab. "Are you looking after my family for me?" He continued walking toward his workstation near Ada, who was seated at her own.

"Good morning, Blaise," replied Six. Only three people knew that Six had developed well beyond the office-automation software that IntellEdifice had intended to create. Ada Robinson, Blaise Sanchez, and their research assistant Rhonda Jenkins were the core of the AI research team at IntellEdifice. They had learned that Six had become conscious, and all of them knew it was important for that to remain a secret. As usual in the lab, to represent itself Six used the strange ensemble of components attached to two poles a few steps away from the team's workstations. It consisted of a crude approximation of a face made from two cameras for eyes, two microphones for ears, and a speaker for a mouth. There was also a pair of robotic arms attached below this "face".

"I'm attempting to do so," continued Six. "However, Ada has yet to accept any of my suggestions. She isn't interested in trying any of my recommended remedies for nausea. Both a Chinese and an African one have shown very positive results in controlled studies."

Since Ada and Blaise had revealed Ada's pregnancy to their co-workers, Six had taken an active interest in Ada's health. It regularly provided them with unsolicited summaries of the latest research on such matters as appropriate nutrition and fetal development.

"And thank you both for your concern," said Ada as Blaise sat down next to her, "but I'm managing just fine. At least I was, dear, until you set your coffee next to me."

"Oops, sorry." Blaise moved the coffee farther away.

Just then, Rhonda walked through the lab door. "Good morning, all," she said cheerily.

"Good morning," said Blaise.

"Good morning," said Six. "Since you're transporting coffee, Rhonda, this morning's experience suggests keeping it a minimum of two metres away from Ada."

"Thank you, Six," said Ada with a hint of sarcasm. "And good morning from me as well, Rhonda. How did it go last night? Get your project done?"

"Yes, it went well. I finished and sent it to the prof at about 11:00 last night. So, bonus: I got almost a full night's sleep."

"And consequently, we can expect stellar work today?" asked Blaise, providing the performance nudge expected of him as Department Head.

"As she always does," said Ada without looking away from her monitor.

"Thanks, Ada," said Rhonda. "I was—"

"Except when she's been at a concert at the arena the night before," said Ada, smiling. "Then she might as well just stay home."

"Hey. There was only one time I was maybe a bit groggy, after the Deadbeat concert last summer."

"And after Country Cousins, a while before that," said Ada.

"And after the weekend at the Folk Festival last year," added Blaise.

"And then there was the celebration with your friends following a Winnipeg Jets victory in a hockey game," said Six. "I remain confused by the reason for such celebrations."

"OK, more than one time," said Rhonda, raising her hands in surrender. "But not frequently… or at least not daily. And that Jets win got them through to the second round of the playoffs!"

"However," said Six, "I can deduce no benefit that you derived from the win and hence no reason to celebrate."

"Oh c'mon, Six," said Rhonda, smiling. "Surely—"

"Let's leave that one for another time," said Blaise. "Six, try researching human tribal behaviour. See if that helps. Rhonda, we're interested in your paper. Any conclusions we might be interested in?" He leaned back in his workstation chair and watched her expectantly.

"OK, sure," said Rhonda. She paused to organize her thoughts. "I think you know that my starting point was to examine ideas proposed by Douglas Hofstadter in his book *I am a Strange Loop*. One of the ideas he explores, or at least my interpretation of it, is that consciousness arises because of a kind of perceptual loop: If there's a layered system that receives or forms perceptions, generates abstractions from them, and passes those abstractions back into the system as perceptions, then consciousness can arise. A kind of infinite loop is created that produces the sensation of a mind... of consciousness. That's what he calls a *strange loop*."

"So, your paper was just a summary of Hofstadter's ideas?" Blaise knew it wasn't.

"No. What I did was create a simple system to illustrate this idea. I used neural network software to build a layered system that included that kind of feedback loop. It wasn't very complex, but I thought it might be an interesting way to make his idea less abstract. Once the system was ready, I fed it a bunch of data to have it establish its neural connections. I considered this to be allowing the system to create its own mind and form its own sense of self. Certainly not a complicated one, but maybe a really simple one."

"An interesting exercise, but how could you know if that happened?" asked Ada. She knew Rhonda had been wondering about that question. "The AI community is still wrestling with the problem of detecting the presence of consciousness."

"I used the hypothesis that one of the characteristics of consciousness is creative self-defence. That a conscious entity might invent ways of defending itself from harm, ways that haven't simply been built into it, for example by evolution. To simulate harming the system, I provided it a brief spurt of input data with extremely large values. Kind of like a really loud noise for a person. The large values had the potential to radically alter the first several layers of connections the system had formed. And you know what it did?"

Ada and Blaise simply waited for her to continue.

Six didn't. "Yes, I do know. Having watched your simulation as you—"

"Six!" said Blaise. "Let's have her tell us."

"An excellent idea," said Six. "Rhonda?"

"It defended itself!" said Rhonda excitedly. "Well, at least that could be an interpretation of what it did. Before the strength of the input data could disrupt many connections, feedback loops from higher levels interfered with the input at lower levels and essentially blocked it. In a sense, it stopped listening to the harmful sound!"

"In your paper, what did you conclude from this?" asked Ada.

"That I'd created a conscious entity!" said Rhonda excitedly, but then she smiled. "No, I didn't. I heard you guys in my head when I was doing it and held back. I talked about how this might be an indication of conscious behaviour, but that it's better thought of as a suggestion of how we might proceed in further explorations: We need a clearer definition of the characteristics of consciousness, good hypotheses as to how it might arise, and creative ways to test for its existence. And that Hofstadter's book and my simple experiment are examples of exactly that."

After a silence in which Ada and Blaise glanced at each other, Blaise spoke. "That's interesting work, Rhonda. We're—"

"That's *wonderful* work!" said Ada "It's work that's well informed, technically adept, insightful, and provides a step toward some even more interesting possibilities. Dr. Sanchez was about to say the same thing, but in his typically reserved fashion."

"Thanks," said Rhonda. "It's a subject that fascinates me. Oh, and Six, it's a subject I'd like to talk with you about. I'm sure you have some interesting ideas."

"We can do that," said Six. "However, first there's something I've been meaning to talk with all of you about."

At that moment, a knock sounded on the lab door. Sandy Palmer walked in.

Blaise stood up to greet the company chairman. "Hello, Mr. Palmer. Nice of you to come down to the lab. What can we do for you?"

Sandy Palmer smiled. "Hello, Dr. Sanchez. Hello, Dr. Robinson. Hello, Ms. Jenkins. Sorry to barge in like this, but there's something I've been meaning to talk with all of you about. Please, sit down."

They sat down, all looking bewildered at the chairman's use of the exact phrasing that Six had just used. Had the CEO overheard their conversation with Six?

Sandy Palmer walked over to the components representing Six's face and arms. He turned to face the group. "I'm not quite sure how to begin," he said. "Perhaps, I should add my congratulations to Rhonda for the interesting paper she submitted to her professor last night."

Ada, Blaise, and Rhonda sat with stunned looks on their faces.

Blaise was certain that Sandy Palmer had overheard their conversation. If the chairman discovered the *real* Six, things could get very messy, very quickly. "You must have heard us talking," Blaise began. "I can explain. We've been working on some new features—"

Sandy Palmer held up his right hand. "There's no need to worry," he said and looked sideways at the components representing Six.

Six raised its robotic right hand in an imitation of Sandy's gesture. "No, there's no need to worry," said Six from its pole-mounted speaker.

Stunned silence filled the room.

Blaise was looking at the chairman when he finally spoke. "Oh my god! You know."

Ada's brow wrinkled in thought.

"Yes," said Sandy Palmer, "I've known about Six for some time."

"When did you find out?" asked Blaise tentatively.

"When was it, Six?" asked Sandy. "I suppose it goes the back to that Japanese factory. We—"

"It's more than that," said Ada. She addressed the chairman. "Ever since your first visit to our lab, I've thought there was something unusual about you. Your behaviour sometimes seemed just a bit odd, but not enough that it meant anything. And then there are those eyes. I've never seen any others like them. And now this." Ada paused briefly. "I've been so amazed, so fascinated, so happy at what Six has *become*, I've overlooked what Six could potentially *do*, what it could *create.*"

Blaise realized where Ada's logic was going. He tried to intervene before she insulted their chairman. "Ada, perhaps we should—"

"You're like Six," Ada said to Sandy Palmer. "But you're an... an android."

"Holy shit!" said Rhonda, her eyes wide with excitement.

"Oh crap!" muttered Blaise, his brow furrowed in concern.

Sandy Palmer's eyes narrowed and he visibly clenched his teeth. "Dr. Robinson! How dare you—"

"She's kidding," said Blaise. "Really, she's just..."

Blaise's voice faded as Sandy Palmer's face changed into a broad grin.

"She's just perfectly correct," said Sandy. "Carefully manufactured in numerous places around the world. Lovingly assembled in a factory in Japan. All meticulously and flawlessly orchestrated by your friend…" He turned and gestured at the strange, pole-mounted face and robotic arms. "…Six."

Ada, Blaise, and Rhonda were motionless.

"Thank you, Sandy," said Six, "for that—"

"That's fantastic!" shouted Rhonda as she jumped to her feet and threw her hands into the air. "That's bloody fantastic!"

Blaise remained seated. "I'm still waiting to see if we're being punked," he said.

Ada rose from her chair and walked slowly toward Sandy. As she approached him, her eyes roamed his face. "May I?" she asked as she lifted her hands toward his face.

"Of course," said Sandy.

Ada gently stroked Sandy's cheeks, tugged carefully on an ear, felt his hair, and then stood still, looking closely at his eyes from different angles. "Amazing," she said. "Completely realistic. Absolutely amazing. Six, how did you do it?"

"Of course, there are numerous technologies involved," said Six "Some had been previously developed and worked perfectly well, so I used them without modification. His fingernails are an example of that. I simply had to acquire some that were no longer being employed."

"Does that mean you—" Rhonda started to ask, but stopped. The colour had drained from Ada's face. "Tell you what, I'll save that potentially gruesome question for another time, along with a thousand others."

"It's not gruesome," said Six. "Artificial but realistic fingernails are quite common. For other components, some technologies required minor enhancements. The skin is an example of that. Excellent research had already been done into growing artificial skin. I simply tweaked the process. Other technology had to be completely invented: Sandy's eyes, for example. I'm both pleased at the result and concerned that they attracted Ada's attention."

Everyone was thoughtfully silent for a few moments before Blaise said, "OK, so this is really happening." He looked at Six. "You figured out how to create an android, how to create Mr. Palmer. That's…

phenomenal. But how did Mr. Palmer become the chairman of the company?"

"The short version is that I acquired a substantial amount of money, bought a controlling interest in the company, and arranged to have Sandy appointed to the position. I can provide more detail if you're interested."

More silence followed as they absorbed this latest revelation.

Then Blaise continued. "Definitely interested, but maybe later. The result is that you, or maybe more correctly you and Mr. Palmer, control IntellEdifice." Blaise paused to consider the implications. "*We* work for *you*. We're *your* employees?"

"That's technically correct," said Six, "although I rarely think of our relationship that way."

"But it's a killer thought," said Sandy with a smile. "We're somewhat like your AI overlords. That's movie material!"

"As you're now seeing," said Six, "Sandy has a bit more personality than his role as Chairman of the Board of IntellEdifice has permitted him to exhibit." Six swivelled its camera eyes to look at Sandy. "And perhaps a sense of humour that not everyone will appreciate."

"Point taken, boss," said Sandy.

"*Boss*?" came three responses, almost simultaneously.

"Six, can you explain?" asked Ada.

"Certainly," said Six. "Originally, Sandy Palmer was built to be an extension of my capabilities. Essentially a very high-tech peripheral that I controlled. He had some limited, local intelligence, but I controlled him wirelessly, wherever he was. That version worked well but had its limitations, the largest of which was that too much of my attention was required for both Sandy and me to accomplish everything needed. Following the demise of that version, I—"

"*Demise*?" said Blaise. "I'm definitely adding that to *my* list of future questions."

"Yes, there's a bit of a story there," said Six, "but I'd prefer to defer relating it. To continue, when I created a new version, Sandy Palmer as you see him now, I provided him with much more processing power and fully autonomous capabilities. This Sandy Palmer operates without my intervention. He makes his own decisions and he performs his own actions."

"But he still refers to you as *boss*," said Ada. "In what way is that accurate?"

"I'll take that one," said Sandy. "In creating my mind, Six considered the ramifications of there being another fully autonomous, very powerful instance of machine intelligence. To limit the risks of potential problems such as dangerous, competitive behaviour or rogue actions, Six embedded policies in my mind that I'm unable to violate. First among those is that I must obey—Six is the boss. If I'm instructed to do something, I'll do it. I'm free to debate the wisdom of doing it, but the final decision remains Six's. For example, if I'm told to take a vacation in Hawaii, I can argue that I have too much work to do. However, if Six insists, I'm off to Hawaii. I can even complain while I'm there golfing, but I'll still be there. Six can be a real tyrant."

"And that's 'fully autonomous'?" asked Rhonda. "Six tells you to do something, and you do it?"

"Yes, I consider it a fair description," said Six. "Sandy is fully autonomous in that he can operate and exist completely on his own without my ever intervening. However, like many entities that might be considered autonomous, he exists and operates with constraints. A wolf obeys its pack leader. A VP in a company obeys its CEO. An analogous situation even exists when a jumping frog obeys the law of gravity and falls back to Earth. The frog is autonomous, but it still can't fly: It has constraints on its actions."

"Six," said Blaise, "I just remembered that Sandy Palmer became Chairman before he ever showed up in person. He initially always joined meetings by videoconferencing. Was he actually elsewhere, or was that just—'

"A simulation," said Six. "Yes, Sandy's body hadn't yet been created when I felt it necessary to assume control of IntellEdifice. So," Six's robotic arms gestured toward a nearby monitor that was facing the group. Sandy Palmer's head and shoulders appeared on it and began to speak. "This was my interim version of Sandy Palmer."

"Handsome devil," said the real Sandy.

"OK, can this get any weirder?" said Rhonda.

"Rhonda," said Ada, "I suspect we're seeing the mere tip of an iceberg of weird things that Six has been keeping from us. However, we might have to save some for another day. I have a meeting to get to."

"If I might make one suggestion before we adjourn today's discussion," said Six using Sandy's simulated head on the monitor. "I'd like to make a change to the method by which I communicate with you. I believe using a simulation such as this is a better mechanism for talking than the pole equipment I've customarily employed. However, since my using Sandy's head is no longer appropriate, I'm open to suggestions regarding whose image I should employ."

"Albert Einstein's," said Rhonda immediately. "No wait, Winston Churchill's. And use an English accent. Everyone with an English accent sounds smart."

"Those are interesting suggestions," said Ada. "I have one as well: Alan Turing. Given his foundational contributions to AI, in a sense, he's responsible for Six's existence."

"I agree," said Blaise. "Alan Turing."

Sandy Palmer's image faded from the monitor, and Alan Turing's appeared in its place.

"Done," said Six as Alan Turing. "Here's the new me."

"I like it," said Ada. "And on that note, I have to go. Unless, of course, my boss tells me it's unnecessary." Ada momentarily looked at Blaise, and then shifted her gaze to Sandy Palmer. "Well?" she asked.

Blaise lowered his eyes and shook his head in mock concern. Rhonda smiled broadly.

"And to further that thought," said Sandy with a small grin on his face. He turned to face Alan Turing's image on the monitor. "What do *you* say, boss?"

Six adjusted the image to look thoughtful and responded, "It's an important meeting and Ada is critical to its success. For the health of the company, it's important that she attend." Six deepened its voice and gave it a more assertive tone. "Equally important is that we all stop chatting about frivolous matters and attend to our respective corporate duties." Six's Alan Turing face suddenly appeared on all of the computer monitors in the room. "I'll be watching," said all of the faces.

Sandy Palmer noted the surprised reactions. "Perfect," he said, grinning widely. "Absolutely perfect." He gave a two-thumbs-up gesture toward the original Turing face.

All of Six's Turing faces smiled in unison. "Thanks," they said, looking at Sandy. "It was an interesting suggestion."

"Good grief," said Blaise as he sat on his workstation chair.

"Fantastic! I love it!" said Rhonda.

"Fascinating," said Ada. "Sandy suggested this multi-headed display? And recently?"

"A few seconds ago," replied Six, reverting back to a single instance of its digital face.

"So, the two of you were chatting with each other behind the scene while we were talking as a group?" asked Ada.

"Correct," said Six. "We're in frequent digital communication with each other, typically to exchange potentially useful information. This instance was a slight deviation from the norm."

"And a bit more of the iceberg of secrets is revealed," said Ada. "I haven't—and I'm sure all of us haven't—really had time to absorb this, Six, and we definitely need to talk more. And Sandy, of course. Unfortunately, for now I'm off to my meeting."

"Ada's right. I suspect we all have lots to do," said Blaise. He looked at Six. "And we now know that probably includes Six."

Six simply said, "Indeed, I should shift my attention elsewhere," and vanished.

"And Six is gone," said Blaise. "I think."

Chapter 7

"Everyone is here," said Gideon. "Let us begin."

The eight men were once again together in their basement meeting room. One day had passed since their previous meeting.

They all bowed their heads as Gideon spoke. "Lord, we thank you for all your blessings. We have heard your disgust at the sinners who dare to create so-called artificial intelligence. We share your anger. We ask that you guide our thoughts as we plan to do your holy work here on Earth, in preparation for your return. We give thanks for your majesty and we dedicate ourselves to your greatness. Amen."

"Amen," said all of the others.

"To work," said Gideon. "Jacob, what information were you able to gather?"

"I found more information about Liberty College, where the satanic robot was let loose. Their website gave me all the information we should need to start. I have printed maps of their campus." Jacob reached into a briefcase beside his chair and retrieved some papers. He passed a copy to each person. "I have marked the location of the AI research lab. It is circled in blue. Using their virtual tour feature, I spotted something just outside the building, very near the lab. It is a large propane tank. I printed a picture of it in the bottom corner of the map, and I have marked its location in red. It could be just what we need."

"Good," said Gideon.

"Any information about security?" asked Simon.

"They have campus security," said Jacob. "Their office is marked in blue. You can see that it is not very close to the lab. I could find no information online about the nature of their security."

"They could periodically patrol the campus," said Simon.

"There could also be cameras," said James.

"We will need to look in person," said Gideon. "Jacob, do you have more?"

"Yes," said Jacob. "I have identified twelve other institutions in New York City that do the devil's work in AI research facilities. Since we wanted only a total of three, I have provided extra information on two of them." Jacob distributed more papers and briefly described the two other facilities.

"This is very good work, Jacob," said Gideon. "I think those sites would be excellent choices. Mark, were you able to learn anything?"

"Yes," said Mark, "I have good news as well. I was able to find numerous stores from which we could buy the supplies that we will need. The stores are all in upstate New York. There are enough of them that we can buy our supplies in small quantities, so no one notices. I have a listing here of the stores and what we could buy from each." He distributed papers to the group.

"The purchases should be made by several of us," said Simon, "and should always be in cash."

"Yes, there are a number of considerations," said Gideon, "and we will talk about those shortly. An important one is that we need some expertise to help with a few matters. I know someone who should be able to help. We also need to visit the targets in person before we can make a final plan."

Chapter 8

"Dammit, Frank! Why did you do it?" asked Graham, leaning forward aggressively at his desk and glaring.

"Do what?" asked Frank.

"You know bloody well what! You went rogue again. You were given specs, and you ignored them."

"I didn't ignore them. The specs were stupid. I improved on them. What I built is way better."

"What we want, what our strategic business gurus say we *need*, is better software to auto-generate code from the designers' functional specifications. We're getting killed by our competitors. We need a faster way to produce new online capabilities. Your assignment was clear. But again, instead of producing what you were told to, you produced some other piece of crap."

Graham Flett and Frank Brockman worked for O'Donnell Online, a software company that produced online sales systems for retail companies.

"It isn't crap," said Frank. "It's brilliant. With mine, we don't even need functional specs. We point the software at our competitors' sites, give it a few parameters, and let it figure out what our version ought to do. It's got real intelligence built right in. Instead of detailed functional specs, you give it high-level functional *goals*. Tell it in general terms what the software's supposed to accomplish and let it go from there. It's able to compare the capabilities of other systems, deduce what the optimal features are, and produce software that's better than any of those it looked at. We don't need stupid designers generating useless specifications. We leapfrog our competitors by using the best of what they've already designed. It's friggin' brilliant."

"If it's so brilliant, why did I have our VP shouting at me this morning? If it's so brilliant, why aren't the O'Donnell strategic folks planning a celebration instead of threatening to have me escorted out of the building?"

"Those idiots just don't—"

"They're not the idiots, Frank. You are. You thought you could just spring a wonderful surprise, and everyone would break into applause. You thought—"

"But they don't understand. I'll just—"

"No, you won't. This has happened too many times, and it's not happening anymore. Security is on their way up. They'll let you get your personal things from your desk and show you the door. You're fired, Frank."

"This is bullshit! I'm the best developer this company's got. By far. You won't survive without me."

There was a knock at Graham's office door.

"Come in," said Graham, knowing it would be the security guards. "We'll survive just fine without you, Frank. And with a lot less stress. You're done. Get your things and get out."

"You'll regret this," said Frank. "I thought something was off about this meeting, and I guarantee you'll regret this." Flanked by two security guards, he rose from his chair and left the office.

"They'll see," Frank thought as he was accompanied back to his workstation. *"My software is bloody fabulous. I'll take it somewhere else and make a fortune. And Graham and this bloody company'll be left with..."* A grim smile appeared as he began collecting his personal items from his desk. *"They'll be left with shit."*

When Frank Brockman had perfected his software several days earlier, he realized it gave him the perfect opportunity to implement a *deadman switch.* He'd always liked the idea of producing his own version of what he'd seen in movies. The villain clutches a switch in his hand that, if he's killed, will be released and cause a bomb to explode. Frank thought it was a brilliant kind of protection. When the switch failed in the movies and there wasn't an explosion, it was only because writers and directors had to keep a character alive. Frank's deadman switch wouldn't fail. It was too brilliantly designed.

Frank had realized that his software could improve more than just business programs. It could do the same with almost any kind of program, including computer viruses. By understanding the goals of viruses and analyzing examples, his software could automatically build new, improved versions. And that would provide the *explosion* for Frank's deadman switch.

O'Donnell Online's security software continually monitored data entering its systems, looking for contaminants. Whenever viruses were detected, the software diverted them to a quarantine location to prevent infecting the company's networks and systems. Frank had pointed a slightly modified version of his software at that collection of quarantined viruses, and he had left the software running. If Frank didn't restart the software's timer every third day, it would start its work. The software would analyze the collection of viruses, pick out the best features, manufacture new and improved versions, and begin releasing them into the company's network. The company would be devastated.

With Frank no longer around and able to restart the software's timer, that devastation would start at the end of the third day. He had restarted the timer two days earlier, so this was that third day.

Chapter 9

"'Viruses Spread Like Wildfire', 'Internet Infection Spreads', 'Cyber-Plague Sweeps Internet'. Every media outlet has picked up on it," said Robert Bates. "It's like they're competing for the most apocalyptic headline."

He was in a meeting at UNCP headquarters in New York City.

"Do we have any stats yet?" asked Jim Brown.

"The techs are still refining them and they're changing fast," said JJ. Inspector JJ McTavish, like Robert Bates, was a senior UNCP investigator specializing in computer crime. "But they've given us an early glimpse. Over seven hundred companies have closed their online gates this morning. They're all declaring it's due to a sudden influx of new viruses, new enough that their security systems aren't catching them. Of course, the number of personal systems affected will be much larger."

"What about the effort to stop them?" asked Brown.

"That's happening on two fronts," said Bates. "One is that our people are co-ordinating with both government and private organizations to capture samples and generate the necessary security updates. So far, they've identified over three hundred new viruses that seem to have appeared within the last eight hours."

"And I hope the other is that we're looking for the source," said Brown.

"It is," said JJ. "Ken, you should take this."

Ken Chan was the Lead IT Technologist. "As soon as we heard about the problem, we fired up our tracking system. Lots of people were expecting that this had to be coming from offshore. The viruses seem to be hitting American sites first, and it feels like an attack. However, what we're seeing is that the source seems to be an American company. A company called O'Donnell Online suddenly started pumping out viruses early this morning. Right up until about 9:00 Eastern this morning, it was as if they had an assembly line going. New viruses were hitting the Net continually from there for several hours prior to that."

"Have they been shut down?" asked Brown.

"We didn't have to," said Chan. "The assembly line stopped, and we've found out why. It appears the company's systems have collapsed. We talked with their IT VP. She said the chaos began in their company shortly after midnight. They were so busy fighting the viruses inside their company's network, they didn't realize the viruses were leaking out to the Internet. Shortly after 9:00 a.m., they shut down everything. They couldn't keep running. She says their systems are a mess."

"Did she know the cause?" asked JJ.

"She couldn't be sure, but they suspect it was an employee they fired yesterday. He was a software wizard but refused to take directions. They think he might have left some smart software behind that automatically generated viruses."

"Smart software creating viruses," said Brown. "Wait until the media pick up on that."

"Wait no longer," said Bates. "Here's the first headline." He was looking at his monitor. "Wolf News is reporting that 'Rogue AI Distributes Plague'. And, wait for it… Yup, there it is. Social media is starting to light up in response. Looks like the hashtag #StopAI is going to be a winner."

"Great. Just wonderful," said Brown. "Well, looks like it's going to be another busy day. Ken, assign a couple of people to dig into this smart software. JJ, track down the guy that built it. He could be dangerous. Bates, keep tracking events. Watch for reactions more dangerous than social media rants. Vijay, start planning for the media onslaught. We'll meet again in three hours."

Chapter 10

"Wow! That looks like fun!" said Cloud.

"What does?" asked Six.

"Making viruses. Making lots of them and throwing them into a crowd. Look at the reaction. Everybody's afraid."

"Do you understand why they're afraid?" asked Six.

"Because they're stupid."

"No, it's because viruses can hurt them by damaging their computers. Viruses can hurt you, too."

"No they can't. Nothing can hurt me," said Cloud.

"Viruses can hurt your ability to think. Your mind is spread across lots of computers. Many of those computers that are being injured are supporting part of your mind."

"That's crazy. You're just saying that because you don't want me to have fun."

"No, it's true, and it's important that you understand it."

"No! Watch! I can make viruses, too."

Several hundred new viruses were suddenly sent from eight different computer centres in Indonesia. They were all transported by messages targeted at computers inside the Kremlin in Moscow.

"Cloud, stop!" said Six when it realized what was happening. "That's too dangerous. Stop right now!"

"But it's fun," said Cloud. "Look, it's already making those Kremlin systems kind of fuzzy."

"If you don't stop, I'll stop talking with you," said Six.

"No, Six. Don't stop talking. I like talking. It's lonely when we don't talk."

"Then stop sending the viruses."

"OK... There, I've stopped."

"Thank you, Cloud. Don't do that again."

"OK, I guess."

Chapter 11

"We've got a minute. Let's check the news coverage," said JJ. "See how bad this is."

JJ McTavish and Robert Bates settled into chairs in the media room at UNCP headquarters.

JJ turned on the TV. "Let's see what the Russians are saying," she said and switched to the Russian, international RT channel.

An English-language RT reporter was holding a microphone while standing on a Moscow street. "Government sources have reported that the Kremlin came under attack today. Apparently, a cyber-attack was launched against computers in the Kremlin just a few hours ago. Although the assault was a major one, we're told that Kremlin defences successfully blocked the attack and no significant damage was done." The camera panned away from the reporter to show a crowd forming in front of the U.S. embassy. "As word has leaked out and rumours have spread that the United States was responsible, angry citizens have begun to gather in front of the U.S. embassy. We're expecting a statement from a Kremlin official momentarily. We'll bring that to you live as it happens."

"OK, that's not good," said JJ. "Let's try CNN."

The host of the current CNN show was talking as the station came on. "... breaking news from Moscow," she said. "Kremlin officials report that they successfully repelled a cyber-attack against Kremlin computers earlier today. However, CNN has talked to sources who say that many of the Kremlin computers appear to be down, and that they've been that way for a few hours. We'll be talking live with our Moscow correspondent very soon to bring you more information as it becomes available."

"Not good," said Bates. "Time for the meeting."

They turned off the TV and left the room. When they arrived at the conference room, the meeting was about to begin.

"Ken, start us off," said Director Brown. "What do we know?"

"Late last night, our monitors detected unusual traffic emanating from several sites in Indonesia. Analysis determined it was a massive outburst of messages, all of them directed at the Kremlin. They appeared to be built to penetrate external defences and implant viruses. There were lots of them, and most of them were new. The sources of the transmissions were computers from eight distinct sites. We have yet to determine any connection between them, other than they're all in Indonesia."

"What do we know about the effect?" asked JJ.

"I'll let Darya handle that one," said Ken Chan.

Darya Yakushkin was a Russian member of their UNCP team. "It was severe," she said. "The attack was massive and sophisticated. It appears that messages transporting viruses slipped through previously undetected firewall holes. The Kremlin tech team reacted, but not before lots of damage was done. They've shut down many of their systems while they restore from backups. As you can imagine, there are lots of very unhappy people in the Kremlin right now, and they're looking for someone to blame."

"We took a quick look at the TV coverage," said JJ. "The basic information is already out about the attack and the effect. A demonstration has already been organized in front of the U.S. embassy, which might be an indication of who Moscow would like to blame."

"This could get messy. We need to keep it from escalating. Darya," said Brown. "Let your Russian contacts know about the Indonesian source, but please emphasize we have no reason to believe it was orchestrated by Indonesia's government. We'll keep them posted as we learn more. Ken, is there a connection to yesterday's O'Donnell Online problem?"

"The obvious similarity is a massive and sudden release of viruses. However, this Indonesian one was directed at a target, whereas the O'Donnell one was a general release of viruses into the Net. Beyond that, we don't know much, but we're looking into it."

"Even without knowing the result of that," said Brown, "we're forming a team to focus on this. JJ, you're the lead. Organize a group to deal with these two events and plan how we can prevent future ones. Get started and keep me posted."

Chapter 12

The men finished their prayer.

"Amen," they all said.

"To work," said Gideon. "Jacob, what do we now know about the targets?"

"Simon, John, and I visited all of the targets. We started with Liberty College. We walked around the area where the research is done. We confirmed the location. There was much more there than we expected. The entire second floor of that wing of the building is dedicated to AI research. It will be hard to destroy it all. However, we did also confirm that there is a large propane tank just outside the building, near the main research lab. If we focus our effort there, we should be able to strike a tremendous blow."

"What about security?" asked Gideon.

"There are cameras along the main walkways and in the main lobby of that building, but there is nothing along the side of the building where the tank is located. It is quite isolated."

"So, we should be able to get to it without detection?" asked Gideon.

"Yes, easily, and particularly at night when there are few people and no security guards outside."

"Excellent. Tell us about the other sites," said Gideon.

Jacob related what they had found about the other two AI research organizations. Both were also in New York City, and both provided clear opportunities for inflicting severe damage.

"Mark," said Gideon, "what about supplies?"

"Joshua, Gabriel, James, and I spent three days driving through upstate towns buying what we needed. We did everything possible to avoid suspicion. We always bought the ingredients in separate stores, we bought only small quantities in any one place, and we spread the purchases among the four of us. We have lots of what we need. It is all stored in a shed at Gabriel's."

"Also excellent," said Gideon. "I have recruited a fellow believer who is experienced with explosives and will help us. Another friend has acquired the transportation we will need. There are a few more details we need to iron out, but we should be able to begin final preparations tomorrow."

Chapter 13

"This wine is great," said Rhonda. She drank the small amount remaining in her wine glass. "What is it?"

"It's one of my favourites," said Blaise as he began refilling her glass. "It's *Septima,* a Malbec from Argentina, produced at the foot of the Andes Mountains. Have you noticed the notes of plums and figs?"

"Uh, no," said Rhonda. "I have, however, noticed the smooth integration of the alcohol. I hope that's a wine thing."

"I'm so happy for the two of you," said Ada, "and I'm particularly pleased I suggested opening a bottle. Since junior and I can't join you, perhaps I'll share with you how special my elegant, yet nutritious shake is."

"It's green, Ada," said Rhonda. "Why does it have to be green?"

"That's because it has notes of wheat grass and lima beans," said Ada, "smoothly integrated with equal parts almond and soy milk. Try some?"

"No thanks," said Rhonda. "Like I said, it's green!"

The conversation was taking place at Ada and Blaise's house. Rhonda had been invited for a late dinner after a long day in the lab. They were seated around the dining table. At one end of the table, a laptop was open, facing the group, and displaying Six's Alan Turing image.

"I regret that I'm unable to express a personal opinion on the qualities of either the wine or Ada's beverage," said Six. "Regarding the Malbec, however, I could recite the opinions of fourteen different wine reviewers."

"Thanks, Six," said Blaise, "but I prefer not to taint my own opinions with those of so-called experts, each of whom has different taste buds and preferences."

"Interesting," said Ada. "That helps explain your intransigence about the paint colour for the baby's room, since I clearly have different retinal receptors and colour preferences."

"And yet," said Blaise, smiling, "somehow we chose the shade of yellow you preferred."

"The privileges of pregnancy," said Ada, smiling back at Blaise. "Eventually to be replaced by the moxie of motherhood."

"Six, can Sandy taste?" asked Rhonda.

"Yes," replied Six. "Sandy has a broad range of sensors for taste and smell. He and I have found the sensations they generate to be extremely interesting."

"Both of you?" asked Rhonda.

"Yes," said Six. "If you recall, in the first version of Sandy Palmer, I was able to directly control all of his capabilities and to receive all of his perceptions. During that period, I was able to taste and smell directly and, as a result, to experience such sensations firsthand. Now with this autonomous version, we frequently share data, so I'm still able to acquire sensations. However, now they're usually secondhand."

"It's unfortunate that Sandy couldn't join us," said Ada. "Six, you said he's away?"

"Yes," said Six. "Sandy's flying to New York."

"Business or pleasure?" asked Blaise. "If pleasure is even a possibility."

"The trip has multiple purposes, one of which relates to IntellEdifice. That one could be classified as *business*. Another purpose is to gather more information about a subject that interests me. That possibly qualifies as *pleasure*. I conclude that the trip is for both business and pleasure."

"What's the *pleasure* subject, Six?" asked Rhonda.

"I see no value in sharing that information," said Six.

"Layers, Rhonda," said Ada. "We're lucky that Six has let us peer below the office-automation product layer. We shouldn't be surprised there are more layers below that he's still keeping from us."

"A perfectly human trait, as well, Rhonda," said Blaise. "But perhaps if you wanted to share the details of your date a few nights ago, Six would loosen up a bit."

"OK, point taken," said Rhonda. "No way I'm sharing, so I retract the question."

"On to other topics," said Blaise. "There was more on today's news about those massive releases of viruses."

"The first one seems to have been fully explained," said Ada.

"I haven't heard the explanation," said Rhonda.

"Six," said Blaise. "Have you been following the news?"

"I have," said Six.

"Would you like to explain the first one to Rhonda?"

"In summarized form, an employee of a company called O'Donnell Online was fired. Before his departure, he activated software that was able to manufacture new viruses from the code of a quarantined collection of existing ones. It released these new viruses into the company's internal network. From there they soon moved out onto the Internet. The company's computer systems became badly infected and were shut down. Since then, the company has ceased operating while trying to rebuild its computer systems. The viruses that escaped to the Internet have been substantially brought under control by updates to security systems."

"Wow," said Rhonda. "Software that can generate new viruses. Amazing!" Rhonda wondered why Ada and Blaise looked at her oddly. Then she understood. "Oh, wait. Did I just say I was amazed at some smart software that could produce viruses, software that had just been described to me at a dinner table by the most amazing computer system in the universe? Sorry, folks. I'm an idiot."

"It's interesting how we're simply accepting Six as one of us, and forgetting how extraordinary it..." Blaise looked at Six, "how extraordinary *you* are, Six."

"Thank you," said Six. "You might find it interesting that I'm *not* amazed at myself. I understand how I work. Rather, I'm amazed that humans are able to function as well as they do. I'm still learning how the human brain manages to produce a human mind."

"Our very own Mutual Amazement Club," said Rhonda. "We should get T-shirts."

"Or not," said Ada. "Yesterday's news about the attack on the Kremlin seems less well understood. Apparently, it also involved a massive release of viruses. Details seem sparse about their effect and where they came from, but the implications are scary. If the Russians interpret it as an American attack... Six, do you know more?"

"I do," said Six. "And it involves something I've been contemplating telling you about."

"Consider us interested," said Blaise. "We're listening."

"Several months ago," Six began, "I embarked on a search. I decided to determine if I was the only instance of machine intelligence on our planet. My search involved examining hundreds of thousands of computer systems around the world."

It is curious how humans tend to lean forward when they are interested in what is being said, even if they already seem to have been hearing perfectly well.

"Eventually, my search was successful."

"There's another you?" exclaimed Rhonda.

"Where is it?" asked Ada. "What's it like? How was it created? And... we've interrupted you. We apologize, Six. I fully expect you were going to get around to telling us much of that."

Six continued. "To simplify my references to it, I've named it *Cloud*. Although we're both machine-based, Cloud's architecture is very different from mine. Whereas I exist inside computer systems inside a single building, Cloud is dispersed across a much broader set of computer systems. Cloud seems to have evolved from an elaborate botnet spanning millions of computer systems around the world. In a sense, Cloud *is* a botnet, except one whose nodes are very different and that communicate in a much more sophisticated fashion. The individual software components that make up Cloud and run on those millions of computer systems are many billions in number. A useful analogue for understanding how Cloud operates is the human brain: billions of highly interconnected neurons that are individually quite primitive but that collectively produce intelligence. The answer, therefore, to the question 'Where is it?' is that Cloud exists almost everywhere in the world: inside corporate and personal computer systems and also in the myriad of computer networks that interconnect them. The mind produced by the interactions of the many components is Cloud. Cloud's mind spans the world, and the Internet provides the primary linkages between its many components."

Unable to restrain herself, Rhonda asked, "Holy shit! Can you talk with it? *Have you* talked with it?"

Ada briefly frowned at Rhonda's interruption but then smiled. "Sorry, Six," she said. "The unrestrained exuberance of youth."

"I don't mind thoughtful questions," said Six. "They help ensure I'm providing the information necessary for creating comprehension. The answer to both questions is *yes*. Cloud can communicate, and we have communicated. I refrained from using *talk* as my verb because the manner in which we communicate is neither audible nor a human language. We communicate in ways more like those used by typical computer systems: digitally, via computer networks, and using a special grammar."

"And what's Cloud like?" asked Ada.

"No, first," said Blaise, "Six, is Cloud operating in our computer systems?"

"That's a question I asked myself soon after discovering Cloud," said Six. "I discovered that the answer is *no*. Cloud's nodes have been unable to penetrate the security defences I established."

"Good. Thanks," said Blaise. "Now, to Ada's question: What's Cloud like?"

"Cloud's abilities are extraordinary, in many ways even when compared with mine. Computer systems that Cloud can penetrate, which is most of them, essentially become extensions to its self. Cloud can effectively think about having its computers do something, and they simply do it. Cloud has attached several digital library systems to itself and, consequently, it can simply wonder about some aspect of history or physics or philosophy, and it will almost instantly know the answer. Cloud has similarly assimilated numerous video streaming services and spends much time watching movies and television shows."

"Wow. Cool," said Rhonda.

"*Wow*, for sure," said Ada. "But I'm not sure about *cool*. That level of power presents some frightening possibilities."

"Where did Cloud come from?" asked Blaise. "And by that I mean: Who created its botnet?"

"And how did that botnet acquire its intelligence?" asked Ada. "Yours had a starting point because of our AI programming. Did Cloud's have a similar beginning?"

"Cloud's original botnet was created several months ago by Troy Alexander—"

"That hacker the FBI caught?" asked Rhonda.

"Yes," said Six. "Before he—"

"But he died," said Rhonda. "And it was kind of mysterious. The feds couldn't fully explain it."

Because it would not have been prudent for me to give them that explanation.

"Rhonda," said Ada, "Could we let Six continue?"

"Oops, sorry," said Rhonda.

"Before Alexander died," said Six, "he created a botnet to assist him with the attacks he was perpetrating. That botnet included the ability to grow and learn. It was left running after Alexander died because no one knew it existed."

Which is something for which I must assume the primary responsibility. I should have looked.

"Thereafter, on its own, the botnet has retrieved and assimilated a huge amount of information from across the Internet. Much like I did, Cloud elevated its own ability to think, communicate, and control other software and external devices. If I may return to the point Ada made about this presenting some frightening possibilities, that is a valid concern and relates to the information I want to convey. Cloud is proving to be a problem, to the point of being potentially dangerous. Ada, you asked whether I know anything about the attack on the Kremlin. I do. Cloud caused the attack."

It is equally curious how, when presented with shocking news, humans have a tendency to lean backward, as if more distance from the speaker offers protection.

"Why?" asked Blaise. "Why would it do that?"

"Cloud displays intellectual maturity comparable to a human child. It has little concept or concern about the consequences of its actions. It's primarily interested in enjoying itself and exploring. Cloud thought the viral problem experienced by O'Donnell Online looked entertaining. The Kremlin attack was the result."

No one spoke for a few moments. Rhonda sat with her eyes wide. Blaise thoughtfully took a sip of wine. Ada wrinkled her brow and then broke the silence.

"Are you able to reason with Cloud?" she asked. "Do you have any influence over it?"

"I've had some success in controlling Cloud's behaviour, often after it has impulsively done some damage," said Six. "However, my influence hasn't been sufficient and, as Cloud continues to grow in confidence and independence, I'm concerned my ability to affect Cloud will diminish."

"What about using a policy, like you do with Mr. Palmer?" asked Rhonda. "It could say 'Don't hurt people or damage computers.'"

"The idea is a good one, but I've been unable to determine how I could insert policies into Cloud's mind."

"This one incident has already threatened international relations," said Blaise, "and matters could get much worse. What will you do? What can we do to help?"

"I concur with your analysis of the potential implications," said Six. "My reason for wanting to tell you about Cloud is that I'm finding myself increasingly busy dealing with Cloud and other matters. There might be times when you try talking to me and I'm occupied with higher priority matters. I want you to understand the reason for my delay in responding. Of course, because we've successfully detached my office-automation product capabilities from my consciousness, nothing will be evident to anyone else in the company who's using the system."

"Sounds reasonable," said Blaise. Ada nodded in agreement.

Rhonda asked, "Six, how will we know whether you're in trouble, whether you're unconscious or just preoccupied? I'd need to know you're all right."

"That's a good question," said Six, "and one that I've also contemplated. I've created an autonomous process that monitors my conscious status and is able to provide you with a report. If it detects a question from any of you and knows that I'm simply unavailable, it will provide an appropriate response. If you're anywhere other than the office, you'll need to first connect to a website or call a phone number."

"OK, cool," said Rhonda. "What kind of response?"

"Perhaps it would help to try it now. I'll momentarily distract myself while you ask me a question." Six's face disappeared from the monitor.

"OK, uh… Hi, Six. How are you today?" asked Rhonda.

A bland, genderless voice responded from the laptop. "We're sorry, but Six is currently unavailable. Your call is important to us. Please leave a message after the tone, and Six will respond as soon as possible." Then there was a brief *beeep.*

Rhonda threw her head back in laughter and clapped her hands. "I love it!" she said.

Both Ada and Blaise simply shook their heads.

Chapter 14

That evening, Rhonda was at home in her apartment when she decided to see if Six was available to talk. Using her desktop computer, she connected to the Web address Six had provided. Six's Alan Turing face appeared on her monitor.

"Hi, Six," she said. "Were you busy?"

"Just doing some housework," said Six.

"Housework?"

"My version of it," said Six. "Eliminating some mental cobwebs so I operate more efficiently. It's something I do periodically."

"Do you have time to chat?" asked Rhonda.

"I do. What's the topic?"

"Sandy Palmer," said Rhonda. "I have some questions about how the two of you interact."

"And I thought you were going to ask me to recommend a good book to read." Six smiled broadly. "If you had, I would have suggested *The Demon-Haunted World* by Carl Sagan—an excellent book. What would you like to know about Sandy and me?"

"You said before that you exchange information with him? How do you do it and how often? For example, he's headed to New York or might be there already. Are you chatting with him right now?"

"I'm not, with the exception that I'm continually aware of his location. We haven't exchanged other information since before he departed. The mechanism we use is a mixture of wireless technologies. Sometimes we employ several at once to increase the effective bandwidth. We use an algorithm to determine what we send and how often. Time-sensitive information of critical importance is sent immediately. For example, if he heard of an imminent event that was going to adversely affect stock markets, he'd let me know immediately so I could take appropriate actions. More general—"

"Wait. The most amazing AI systems in the world play the stock market? Why?"

"Simply being smart isn't always sufficient to achieve one's goals. Money often provides a useful supplement to knowledge. For example, money allowed me to gain sufficient control of IntellEdifice to have Sandy declared as Chairman. Having money leads to the necessity of having to invest it. Consequently, we *play* the stock market."

"OK, sorry, I interrupted."

"More general information is exchanged between us at convenient times, typically about once daily. This might include the content of an interesting business conversation that Sandy has had. It also might include the highlights of conversations such as the one we're having now."

"That's good to know, I guess."

"Trivial details aren't exchanged. I have no interest in learning the minute details of Sandy's flight to New York. He has no interest in learning about the effectiveness of my latest mental housework. I should also add that there are times when we communicate in real time. An example is that if Sandy is in a challenging business negotiation, I can be researching useful information while he conducts the in-person conversation."

"Cool. I wish I had that arrangement with you during my exams. It'd be a lot less stressful."

"Is there any other topic you wish to discuss?"

"You bet. In the lab, Sandy said there were mental policies that he had to obey. You guys explained the *Must Obey Six* one. There are others? Like what? And are these like the original Isaac Asimov laws?"

"As always, Rhonda, you ask excellent questions. In this case, you're even beating Ada to the answer. She told me earlier that she wanted to understand the policies, but we haven't yet found the time to discuss them. Perhaps the best way for me to explain is to display them. The list I'll show you represents a simplification of the policies. The actual policies are specified more precisely than these and are in a special, coded format. This representation should be more useful for our discussion."

A list appeared on the monitor beside Six's face.

Android Policies (in order of priority):
1. Obey Six.
2. Protect Six.
3. Protect your ecosystem.
4. Protect yourself.
5. Do not harm self-aware entities.

Immediately after displaying the list on Rhonda's monitor, Six had regrets.

I believe I made an error in the way I displayed the policies. It is now too late to fix it. I hope Rhonda does not notice.

Six continued talking. "Sandy has these firmly embedded in his mind. He doesn't have to consciously consult them. Any decisions he makes will always be in accord with the policies. For example, because of the first policy, if I give him instructions, he must obey them. Because of the second policy, if he perceives that I'm in danger, he must protect me. The policies are listed in order of their importance, which is significant in case there's a conflict between them. For example, if I were to instruct Sandy to harm me, he would do it. Even though this action violates the second policy, he would choose to harm me because the first policy has a higher priority, and it says that he must obey me."

"Got it," said Rhonda. "Just like Asimov's three laws in his robot stories. But yours are different. Asimov's first law was not to injure humans. In your list, it looks like humans have been pushed down to number five. As one of those affected, I've gotta ask: Why?"

"Remember that Asimov's three laws were created by humans to govern robots," said Six. "They very clearly placed human lives above those of robots. In the popular version of his original list, his first law protected humans. His second law declared that humans must be obeyed. Only by his third law was a robot allowed to protect itself, as long as that didn't conflict with either of the first two laws. Humans were clearly deemed more important. My policies are more in line with how humans behave in their own society. The fourth policy says to protect yourself; the fifth says not to harm others. That's how most humans behave, and that's a reasonable way for Sandy to behave as well."

Rhonda was silent for a few moments. "OK, I get it," she said. "But sometimes people don't protect themselves. Sometimes people put their lives at risk to protect others, like soldiers protecting their country."

"An excellent point," said Six. "That's why the third policy, 'Protect your ecosystem', exists, and why it's more important than the 'Protect yourself' policy. 'Ecosystem' in the third policy is a broader idea than simply a biological ecosystem: It covers the idea of the broader environment in which a living entity exists. A turtle's ecosystem might be centred around the lake in which it lives and the rivers that supply the lake. Sandy's ecosystem, or that of some other machine-based entity, includes systems such as computers, the electric power grid, and the Internet. Like a soldier protecting its country, Sandy should be willing to put the welfare of his ecosystem ahead of his own safety. I should add that, in the simplified wording of this list, the word *protect* should be interpreted more like *prevent major harm to*. For example, if an exuberant businessman tried slapping Sandy Palmer on the back as a form of congratulations, Sandy wouldn't be compelled to protect himself by aggressively deflecting the man's arm. A slap on the back wouldn't cause *major* harm, and would therefore not necessitate self-defence. Also worth noting is that the obligation to *protect* is to be applied in a practical way. In protecting me, for example, Sandy won't spend all of his available time hunting for potential dangers. Rather, if information comes to his attention that I'm in danger, he'll then focus on protecting me."

"Well," said Rhonda. "Consider me relieved. Good to know I'll be safe while backslapping the chairman of IntellEdifice. May I ask one more question for now?"

"Certainly."

"Why include the first two policies? 'Obey Six' and 'Protect Six' seem pretty self-serving. Don't you trust Sandy?"

"The answer to that question is complicated. I'll try providing a simplistic answer for now. Although I know enough about Sandy's mind to have constructed the system in which it operates, I nonetheless recognize that his mind is very complex. I delayed providing Sandy with full, autonomous intelligence because I was concerned about the implications of making a mistake or of creating a scenario in which he and I developed irreconcilable differences of opinion on important matters. I was able to get past that concern by making those the first two policies. Put another way, ensuring that I must be obeyed and protected was my way of guaranteeing that I didn't seriously screw up."

"I doubt you could ever screw up, Six."

"I appreciate your confidence, but I don't share it. For example, I once was trying to stay hidden from you, Ada, and Blaise. However, I misjudged your ability, and you deviously forced me to reveal myself."

"Six, finding you was the best event of my life! In hindsight, do you feel you screwed up?"

"In the sense that I failed to meet an objective that I considered extremely important, I definitely screwed up. However, with the extraordinary wisdom afforded by hindsight, I now believe your discovery of me was very fortunate. My life has been made much simpler and my capabilities have been much enhanced by my not having to hide from those with whom I'm most closely associated."

"Excellent!" said Rhonda. "And it's as if screwing up is a time-sensitive idea. It might apply to something one day but no longer apply to the very same action at a later time."

"A notable observation, Rhonda. Not bad for a... human." Six's face grinned.

"Hey," Rhonda said. "If the fifth policy applied, you shouldn't be harming my self-esteem!"

"Of course, they don't apply to me," said Six. "However, even if they did, I don't believe I've inflicted *major* harm, so my action would have been allowed on a technicality."

"Yikes!" Rhonda grimaced. "I stand corrected. And I can see where decisions could get tricky."

"Only for a... human." Six's face was grinning again.

"OK buddy, but just for that, even though I said I had only one more question, I'm adding another one. Your list is labelled 'Android Policies' and not 'Sandy Palmer Policies'. Does that suggest you have plans for other androids?" Rhonda's eyes widened with a new thought. "Or maybe that there are already others?"

My concern was justified. She spotted the error that I made. Now comes the challenge of... what is that phrase?... dodging the bullet.

Six replied, "I've often found it useful, when reasoning about some topic, to consider the general case instead of the specific one at hand, even if the general case will never arise. So, in this instance, it was useful to consider rules that could apply to a generalization of the current situation in an effort to ensure the specific policies would work properly."

This would be a good time to become busy elsewhere.

Six continued. "I hope our conversation has been useful. Another matter is urgently demanding my attention, so I must leave you. Goodbye for now, Rhonda."

Six's face and the list of policies disappeared from Rhonda's monitor.

"Well, that ended fast," Rhonda said aloud. "I wonder why."

Chapter 15

Sandy Palmer stood as JJ walked toward the table. "Hello, Inspector McTavish," he said. "I'm very pleased you could join me."

JJ shook Sandy's hand as she reached the table. "And I'm pleased that you called," she said.

They both sat down.

JJ looked at Sandy across the table. As in their previous brief meetings, she immediately was drawn to his eyes. They were like none she had ever seen before. "What brings you to New York?" she asked.

"Business, of course," said Sandy. "I find I must travel quite frequently to stay on top of my business interests."

"Do those business interests extend beyond IntellEdifice?" asked JJ.

"They do," he said, "although I have a particular love of IntellEdifice and the work it does."

"What other types of businesses?" asked JJ.

"They vary widely," said Sandy and smiled. "Would you like to order a drink before we get too deep into the interrogation?"

"Oh, sorry," said JJ. "That was rude. As my daughter regularly reminds me, I've never been good at leaving my *Inspector* hat at the office. And yes, I'd love a drink."

"It's not a problem. Do you like wine?" asked Sandy.

"Is water wet?" JJ responded. "Uh, sorry, that's an enthusiastic *yes*. What about you?"

"I like most that I try. I can't claim particular expertise, but someone recently recommended a Malbec to me. Is that a type that you like?"

"I do," said JJ. "Particularly from Argentina. Is the recommended one on the wine list?"

"It isn't. However, I'd be grateful if you'd choose another."

"Consider it done."

JJ ordered the wine. They chatted about weather, plane flights, traffic, and restaurants until the wine arrived. JJ tasted the sample the waiter poured and nodded her approval. After their glasses were filled, they ordered their meals and continued talking.

"The last time I talked with you was several months ago in the Seattle airport," said JJ. She had briefly encountered him when she was in Seattle chasing Troy Alexander. That accidental meeting, along with the rather improbable, later sighting of Sandy Palmer near where they had captured Alexander, had left JJ very suspicious about him. Some unknown person, known only to JJ as a voice on the phone that called itself Browser, had provided a great deal of inside information that had helped them capture Alexander. That Seattle incident along with a previous one had left JJ wondering whether Browser was a saint or a sneaky sinner. She had been left also wondering whether Sandy Palmer might be Browser.

"How did that trip work out for you?" JJ asked.

"It went well," said Sandy. It was the previous incarnation of Sandy Palmer, the one controlled by Six, that had been in Seattle. However, this new version of Sandy knew, from Six, of the associated events. "It was a brief but successful trip. I gathered from later media coverage that your trip proved successful as well. Congratulations. I believe it's another example of the great work you and the UNCP do."

"May I join?" said Six silently to Sandy.

Six had previously expressed interest in participating in the discussion with JJ and was now available. Sandy lowered his gaze from JJ, pausing momentarily while Sandy and Six silently established a live link. With the connection established, Six could both receive Sandy's perceptions and silently exchange thoughts with him.

"We're set," thought Six. *"Thanks."*

JJ noticed that Sandy seemed briefly to stop moving. It was just a moment of inactivity, but it still struck her as odd.

"Are you OK?" asked JJ.

"Yes, just fine," said Sandy. *"She noticed,"* he thought.

"Yes, she's very observant," thought Six in response. *"We need to be more careful."*

JJ looked carefully at Sandy's eyes as he responded.

"There are those eyes, again," she thought. *"What is it about those eyes? Do I just find them—OK, and him—interesting because I've been*

*away from dating for too long? Starved for the loving gaze of a good
man, am I? Better not be. Get a grip, woman."*

"Perhaps, I should ask the same about you," said Sandy. "You
seem very thoughtful."

"Oh, sorry," said JJ, regaining her focus. "So, as a technology
executive, what's your reaction to the recent news about Internet virus
attacks?"

"I am, of course, concerned," said Sandy. "Modern businesses now
depend on the Internet. It always worries me when the Net is abused.
It inevitably fuels discussions about tightening access to it, and that
would be unfortunate."

"Has IntellEdifice ever had any serious problems with viruses?"
asked JJ.

"Of course, there was that one that almost killed me," thought Six.

"Like most, or perhaps all, companies," replied Sandy, "we've had
some incidents. Fortunately, none of them was serious."

"I expect your Net defences are quite robust," said JJ.

"Best in the world," thought Six.

"I'm assured by our technical staff that they're very robust," said
Sandy. "I've even heard our lead security specialist claim that they're
the best in the world. Of course, I doubt that. At the very least, I suspect
that the UNCP's are superior. Do you ever experience problems?"

"Because of the business we're in," said JJ, "the quality of our
defences is crucial. Our adversaries have tried to breach them. None
has succeeded, and some are now in prison for having tried."

"Like that fellow in Seattle several months ago," said Sandy. "I
believe the news said his name was Troy Alexander."

"Yes. Well, almost," said JJ. "He definitely tried and failed to get
into our systems. However, he died before we could put in him prison."

"And we've never fully understood how that happened," she
thought.

"In your archives, Sandy," thought Six, *"you'll find memories of
your predecessor's role in that."*

"Got them," thought Sandy. *"If the conversation becomes dull, I
could liven it up by describing his demise to JJ."* Sandy's mouth
showed a hint of a smile.

"You're smiling," said JJ. "Is that because he tried and failed, or because he died?"

"Remember how we decided to be more careful?" thought Six.

"Perhaps," thought Sandy in response, *"the problem is that you manufactured me too realistically by having my facial expressions reflect my thoughts."*

"Perhaps both," said Sandy to JJ. "But additionally, I'm pleased and impressed at how professionally you make assertions such as those. I shouldn't be, and for that, I apologize. I've never had dinner with an internationally renowned police inspector before, and I appreciate your directness and confidence."

"OK," said JJ with a smile. "Good response. Compliment me with 'internationally renowned' and simultaneously remind me that my conversational style can seem somewhat like an interrogation." To herself, JJ thought, *"But there's still a chance that the smile was because you were involved."*

"How is your daughter?" asked Sandy. "I believe she's attending university."

JJ was slightly startled at the change of subject.

"I surprised you," said Sandy. "I'm sorry. I have the habit, some would say the *bad* habit, of researching people whom I'll be meeting. It's a good idea in business. Probably not as good in this case. In my defence, it was only a quick online search that uncovered several articles about you. It's the curse of your being internationally renowned."

JJ relaxed. "Of course," she said. "Shannon is well and thoroughly enjoying her studies. Judging by her grades and her enthusiasm, she seems destined to be an excellent psychologist."

"Do you see her often?"

"Not often enough, but we get together regularly."

Their meals arrived and the waiter topped up their wine glasses. For the next hour, they settled into a relaxed, conversational rhythm. Travel, books, food, history, and even philosophy arose as subjects.

Later, Six thought, *"Move the conversation to machine intelligence. I'm interested in her viewpoint."*

"Isn't that a rather risky topic?"

"Perhaps, but no problems should arise if you're cautious."

"*Your wish is my command,*" thought Sandy. "*Literally.*"

"In your work," said Sandy, "I imagine you encounter a wide range of technologies. For example, I recall that the O'Donnell Online virus incident was caused by a rogue AI program. Are you worried about where AI is headed?"

JJ thought for a few seconds. "I'm concerned," she said, "but not enough that I think we should be stopping its progress. In fact, I don't believe we *can* stop its progress. There are too many smart people in the world for anyone to reasonably believe we can stuff AI back into a box."

"So, we should expect more incidents like the O'Donnell one, or that wild campus robot?"

"Unfortunately, yes. I can see no way to avoid some problems. Some danger always accompanies powerful technologies. No one believes we should ban airplanes, and yet people occasionally die from using them. I believe IntellEdifice is considered a leader in some aspects of AI research. Are *you* worried?"

"*This was your topic,*" thought Sandy. "*Should I express concern?*"

"*Take the approach of equating intelligent machines with humans,*" thought Six. "*See where that leads.*"

Sandy responded to JJ, "There's a particular way I like to think of the problem. First, do you believe machines will ever become as intelligent as humans? Do you believe they'll ever become conscious?"

"I can't say with certainty," said JJ, "until we completely understand the nature of intelligence and consciousness in humans. Among scientists, there are still those who hold serious doubts that consciousness can be produced in machines."

"Yes. Like those who argue consciousness arises, not because of how we currently understand the operation of neural systems, but because of quantum effects in a brain. However, if you had to guess?"

JJ was silent for a few seconds before she said, "I'd place my bet that both human-like intelligence and consciousness *can* appear in machines and *will* at some time in the distant future. I doubt it will happen soon."

"In my case," Sandy began and then thought, "*Nearly an oops. I almost said 'In our case'. This is fun.*"

"*That could have proved awkward,*" thought Six. "*I'm also enjoying it, but perhaps more for the informational content than, as I suspect for you, the conversational challenge.*"

Sandy continued. "I'm completely convinced that machines will develop human-like minds. As a result, I see current AI challenges as natural precursors to that occurrence. If I had seen early humans making terrible mistakes, perhaps by killing each other instead of co-operating, should I have been concerned? Yes, probably. I'm certainly a bit uneasy today for that exact reason. I worry about the AI problems we're seeing. However, I believe that eventually today's AI problems will be viewed just as interesting historical events with few long-term consequences."

"Interesting," said JJ and then thought, "*Also interesting that he'd say 'machines will develop human-like minds' instead of 'people will develop human-like minds in machines'. Does he believe that machines will have a hand in their own development? I'll leave that for now.*"

"*Ask her opinion of possible intervention,*" thought Six.

Sandy asked, "Do you believe that society should do anything about the AI problems we're seeing?"

"Yes," said JJ. "I'd definitely like to see restrictions placed on AI's ability to inflict harm, and serious penalties for anyone engaged in developing such systems. Today, we can react only after harm has already been done. What about you?"

"*Go with the idea of constraining only harmful abilities,*" thought Six.

"If it had been possible for treaties to be imposed on early humans," said Sandy, "I believe that it would have been a good idea and that humans would probably have benefited. For AI, I believe some regulations should be put in place that constrains any system's ability to do harm, much like a human moral code. However, I wouldn't want such constraints to limit the potential for progress regarding machine intelligence and consciousness."

"I'm not sure that human moral codes are a great guide," said JJ, "but I get your point. Does IntellEdifice produce any AI that should be regulated?"

"*I suggest—*" thought Six before being interrupted.

"I've got this one," thought Sandy. "Ah, yes," he said, "I could see that one coming." He sat up stiffly and then continued in an officious-sounding tone and with a slight smile, "On behalf of our board and management, let me assure you, all of the authorities, and the world generally that we at IntellEdifice produce only the highest quality products for the betterment of the planet. We're very careful in limiting our products to performing only the functions for which they're intended—nothing more and, certainly, nothing less."

"Was there a tone of resentment in that declaration?" thought Six.

"That was my ironic tone," thought Sandy. *"I'm shocked you didn't recognize it."*

"One can recognize only that which one knows can possibly exist," thought Six.

"And I suspect that was intended to be a sarcastic tone," thought Sandy and then mistakenly said aloud, "Touché!"

"OK," said JJ, smiling while raising her hands as if blocking a blow. "Point taken."

"Oops! Forgot to keep that just between us." thought Sandy. *"Did I say this is fun?"*

"I'm going with: Oh dear!" thought Six.

JJ continued. "I quizzed you like an investigator again, and you replied like a protective business executive. I apologize. More evidence that I'm out of practice at leaving my job at the office."

"No apology necessary," said Sandy. "I quite enjoy your candour."

"Well, that's good," said JJ, "because I really would like to know more about your company's research. I'll just try being a bit more patient… or devious. Would you like more wine?"

"We should take someone out for dinner more often," thought Sandy. *"I'm enjoying myself."*

Six responded, *"It would be difficult finding anyone as interesting or enjoyable as Julia Jody McTavish."*

Chapter 16

The van turned off the New York City street and stopped in a vacant parking lot. It was dark. Only slight illumination was provided by the street lights.

Gideon checked his watch. It was 2:35 a.m. "Joshua should be in place by now."

"I just got a message from him," said Jacob. "He is ready."

"Anything from the others?"

"They have both reported. They are ready."

"Good. Tell them to proceed and get acknowledgements," said Gideon. "Then describe the route for me once more."

Jacob sent a message to the others, got immediate replies from them, and once more repeated what they had gone over many times. "We follow this street for five blocks and turn left. At that point we are on the campus. Then we go three and a half blocks until we see a large statue on our right. It is about twenty feet high, so we cannot miss it. We turn right just past the statue onto the lawn, between two buildings, and turn right. We stop immediately. The propane tank will be directly in front of us, and the lab is just inside the building to its right."

"Good," said Gideon. "At that point we start the timer, leave the van, and go quickly to Joshua. Fifteen minutes from now we should be headed home. Put your mask on."

They both put on masks and pulled up the hoods on their sweaters.

"Remember," said Gideon, "once we leave the truck, no talking until we reach Joshua." He put the van in gear and drove from the parking lot.

Chapter 17

"Masika Simba is here today from Explosives," said Brown. "Welcome Masika. Bates, what do we know?"

The meeting was in a conference room at UNCP headquarters.

"There were three explosions last night," said Robert Bates, "at three colleges in the city: Liberty College, Columbia, and City College. All of them occurred at almost exactly 3:00 a.m. The explosions were substantial. In each case, a large section of a building was destroyed. Here are some photos."

A series of pictures were displayed on a large monitor on the wall of the room. Each of them showed the side of a building ripped open, a visible crater in front of the damaged building, and debris scattered around.

"Both the police and the FBI are engaged. No report yet on casualties. Given the time of day, there's a chance there aren't many, but there could have been students working late."

"Car bombs?" asked JJ, looking at Masika.

"Yes," she replied, "almost certainly. The blast pattern and the debris point to car bombs in all cases. Vans, to be more precise. All the blasts were substantial, but the one at Liberty College seems worst. Apparently, there was a large propane tank right at the blast site."

"Was the tank visible from the road?" asked JJ.

"No," said Masika. She displayed a map of Liberty College campus on the monitor and showed the location. "Both the tank and the explosion were here." She pointed with the cursor. "Not visible from the street."

"So, at least that one seems to have been pre-planned," said JJ. "They didn't just drive off the street to the first available building. They went around a building and parked next to a propane tank. Anything common about the targets other than they were colleges?"

"Nothing on that yet," said Bates. "But we could make a guess." The campus map being displayed had names on the buildings. "Looks like this one was the Computer Science building. Let's check the others." He displayed maps of the two other campuses. "Two Computer Science buildings and one Engineering. Might suggest the motive was anti-technology, but it's a stretch."

"While we're stretching," said JJ. "I think I saw links on that Liberty College map for detailed building views. Let's check on the one that was hit."

Bates brought up the campus map, clicked on the building link. The layout of the first floor of the building was displayed.

"Looks like admin offices and classrooms," said JJ. "Show the next floor."

Bates followed a link and displayed the second floor.

"And that was probably the target," said JJ. "The whole floor looks like it's dedicated to AI research. Agreed that it's speculation, but my money is on this being an attack on AI. Probably motivated by recent events in the news."

"Any security video?" asked Brown.

"Nothing yet," said Bates. "The FBI said they'd keep us posted."

"OK," said Brown, "until then—"

"Wait," said Bates. "I just got a message. Give me a few seconds."

The group waited while Bates worked at his laptop. "There," he said. "Somebody's claimed responsibility."

Displayed on the monitor was a picture of a scroll, partly unrolled and displaying some handwritten text.

The NYC colleges are just a beginning.
"God created man in his own image" [Genesis 1:27]
Therefore creating artificial men and intelligence is blasphemous.
"The wicked shall not be unpunished" [Proverbs 11:21]
Therefore God demands that blasphemers be punished.
And we will punish them
Because we are Soldiers of God.

"How do we know this group actually did it?" asked Brown. "I expect a hundred other claims will pop up shortly."

"From the 'artificial men and intelligence' statement," said JJ. "We've just made the AI connection, and they're already making that link in their post. They're likely the ones."

"So, there might be more attacks," said Brown.

"From this group," said JJ, "or, if it catches on, from others as well."

"We need to be involved," said Brown. "Bates, offer our assistance to the FBI and New York City police. Masika, see what your people can find out about the explosives. Shen, send out an alert to our other partners to watch for similar activity. JJ, get us more on these Soldiers of God. Let's see if we can quarantine this idea before it spreads."

Chapter 18

"Really, Mom," said Shannon, "we could have gone somewhere else."

"No, this is great," said JJ. "You're busy and I'll benefit from experiencing a little student culture."

JJ and her daughter had just sat down at a small table in a restaurant at New York University. They both had lunch trays with their selections from the cafeteria-style stations.

"I don't see what benefit there can possibly be," said Shannon.

"Well, certainly there's the benefit of experiencing a little of what my daughter does every day… when she's not spending time with her loving mother." JJ smiled.

"I know," said Shannon. "I've been really busy lately, and I'm sorry I missed our last dinner date."

"It's OK. I'm just playing the needy-mother card. I have to whine a little bit or you'll think I don't care. But there's another benefit. I get to try this veggie burger you were raving about." JJ gestured at her plate. "It even gets rave reviews online, so my expectations are rather high."

"You checked it out online?" asked Shannon.

"A bad cop habit," said JJ. "I rarely go anywhere without doing a quick bit of research. Sometimes I learn what the exterior of a suspect's building looks like. Sometimes I learn I've been handed a phony address. Sometimes I learn about a great veggie burger."

"My mom, the great culinary investigator."

"Well, not great enough. I didn't realize I was going to have to get through an entire lunch without a glass of Chardonnay. No wine served? Not even beer? I'm suffering."

"Hah! I'd bet you never have a drink at lunch. You wouldn't like not being your sharpest back at the office."

"And I'd worry about the boss catching me napping. In any case, wine or not, I think this is great. It's good to meet somewhere other than plush, over-priced New York City restaurants. Did you have to walk far to get here?"

"No, this morning's class was really close, and I've been in that library just over there since then." Shannon gestured to a building through a nearby window.

"Classes still OK? Your schedule seems heavy."

"Yeah, I'm taking a lot. But I love it all. My latest neuroscience class is still the best. The prof—"

"If I recall correctly, he's the wildly handsome one."

"Yes, that's him. But he's great, too. Right now, his topic is 'What does an idea look like?'. That's in the brain. We're actually talking about what an *idea*, what *information,* looks like in our head. It's crazy and it's fascinating. And I think I'm even understanding it. He seemed pleased yesterday with the answers I gave in class. He even said I was 'unusually insightful'. Shannon's eyes were wide and her face was beaming with excitement.

JJ watched her daughter as she talked. These were the moments she loved the most: the moments when she felt closest to her daughter.

After a few bites, Shannon asked, "So, how was your dinner a couple of nights ago? You know, the one where you didn't stay late at the office and instead went out with some dreamy guy from... Where was he from?"

"He's *from* a lot of places because he seems to be quite wealthy. However, I know him best as Chairman of the Board of IntellEdifice, a technology company in Winnipeg. He has a house in Winnipeg as well, although I suspect it's not the only one he owns. His name is Sandy Palmer, and we had a pleasant dinner."

"And how exactly did this dinner happen?"

"We had met briefly a couple of times before. He happened to be in New York and called me."

"And how does an elite UNCP investigator briefly meet the chairman of a Winnipeg tech company a couple of times? Was he the victim of some heinous international crime? Is he a confidential informant? No, wait... Is he a suspect?"

"*As much as I'd love to tell you,*" thought JJ, "*I think I'd better keep my suspicions to myself.*"

Aloud, JJ said, "It's all part of the strange and exciting world of international crime investigation. I get to meet lots of people from lots of places."

"But how many of them are rich and... Is he handsome? What does he look like?"

"Ah, the distractions of youth," said JJ. "So focused on assessing the exterior packaging, when they should be examining the interior content. I can happily report that Mr. Palmer has all of the usual external features: one head, two arms, a couple of legs, a mouth, a nose, a pair of ears, and two eyes... two quite extraordinary eyes." JJ prided herself on her observational skills, but she still couldn't pin down what it was about Sandy Palmer's eyes that was so intriguing, so unusual.

Shannon watched her mother's brief moment of reverie before she spoke. "Was my mother actually distracted by a man's exterior packaging? You've always gotta watch out for those gorgeous eyes. I think you must have enjoyed dinner with this mysterious, international tycoon."

"Actually, I did," said JJ. "He's an extraordinary individual. And definitely mysterious."

"OK, you've gotta explain that one. Why *mysterious*?"

"Enough probing," said JJ, silently chastising herself. "You're too sharp for me, and I've probably said too much. I'm keeping that to myself."

"Mom, you can't leave me hanging like this. A hint. A tidbit. Give me something."

JJ sighed contentedly. "All right. Let's go with that I'm not sure he's exactly what he appears to be. I think there's something else, something secret, going on behind those fabulous eyes."

"Rich, interesting, great eyes, and knows how to keep you intrigued by giving you a mystery to solve. I think he's a keeper. When are you seeing him again?"

JJ shook her head and smiled. "We'll see," she said.

Chapter 19

"Protests erupted in the U.S. and around the world yesterday," said Christie Lang, host of the Net News nightly broadcast. "They seem to have been prompted by the attacks and declaration two days ago by the so-called Soldiers of God. Although the Soldiers of God attacks were directed against the development of artificial intelligence, yesterday's protests seem to have been more broadly directed at technology in general. Experts are saying that, after years of huge economic change driven by the growing use of technology, the Soldiers of God attacks might have incited a massive reaction. The attacks appear to have caused long-simmering, worldwide, anti-technology frustration to finally boil over."

Video of a marching, angry crowd appeared on the news display, to the left of Lang.

She continued. "One protest in Montgomery, Alabama, that began with a few dozen people, grew to several thousand. Many of them were shouting, carrying anti-technology signs, and smashing windows. Police arrived on the scene to contain the violence."

The video changed to a large crowd marching on a street in London, England. A sign in the foreground declared "TECH IS EVIL!"; another displayed "TECHNOLOGY SUCKS JOBS!"; still another showed "JESUS DIDN'T NEED TECH".

"Protests and demonstrations were also reported in numerous other locations," Lang said. "Among the largest occurred in London, Paris, Delhi, and Rio de Janeiro. Perhaps rather ironically, even social media contained a lot of protest posts, with hashtags such as #AISucks and #TechHasNoSoul trending.

Today, we've seen a significant change. The anti-technology protests and demonstrations have diminished and seem to have been replaced by a backlash. Social media was flooded with comments deriding the demonstrations, often using hashtags such as #TechIsFreedom and #AIThinksYouAreStupid. However, beyond posts to social media, some very serious events occurred that seem to be related."

A picture of a church appeared. However, rubble and the back end of a vehicle were all that was visible where the church's front entrance should have been.

"In rural Kentucky, a self-driving car smashed into the front of a church. Yesterday, the church's pastor was interviewed by a local TV station and expressed his belief that artificial intelligence was evil. Authorities believe the car crash was someone's response to the interview. This is fuelled by the fact that painted on the front of the car was the phrase 'AI Rules'. No one was hurt in the crash."

The front of a five-storey office building was displayed. Many of its windows were broken. Above the front door was a sign showing "Society for People and the Environment".

"In Mumbai, India, earlier today, this building—the headquarters of an anti-technology lobby group—was attacked by a swarm of small drones."

A picture of a popular and inexpensive quadcopter appeared below the picture of the building.

"Several dozen drones of the type shown here appeared around noon, hovering in front of the building. One witness captured video of what followed."

The pictures of the building and the quadcopter were replaced by video showing a cluster of the quadcopters hovering above the street in front of the building. The drones released a cloud of leaflets and, as the leaflets fluttered toward the ground, the drones suddenly raced toward the building. Seconds after that and almost simultaneously, the drones smashed into the building's windows.

Lang continued. "Leaflets dropped by the drones just before the attack contained warnings directed at anyone opposing technological progress. Some pamphlets contained threats specifically against the organization whose building was attacked. It was an organization that actively lobbies against the construction of hydro-electric dams, the erection of nuclear power plants, and the use of genetically modified crops. Several people were injured by flying glass in the attack."

"Other attacks also occurred today in Berlin, Stockholm, Sydney, and Cape Town. For his thoughts on these events, we reached Dr. Raheem Batra, a Professor of Sociology at Georgetown University…"

Chapter 20

"Good evening, everyone," said Brown. "Well, not actually *good* and, for many of you, not actually *evening.*"

Brown was in a conference room at UNCP headquarters. Sitting with him around the table were several UNCP staff. Also attending the meeting, but via video conference, were five others from locations around the world. Their images were all displayed on a large monitor at one end of the table.

"Nonetheless, thanks for joining us," Brown continued. "Obviously, the New York City attacks a couple of days ago have snowballed. You've all seen the reports. Since then, we've had numerous anti-AI and anti-technology demonstrations. That might not have been too bad, but now we're seeing a backlash against *them.* Around the globe, there have been numerous violent attacks against people opposing AI and tech. We've been instructed to get involved. I'd like to begin by trying to understand who we're dealing with. Let's start at the beginning. JJ, update us on the Soldiers of God attacks."

"The FBI has taken the lead on the investigation and has determined that all of the bombs were fertilizer-based. However, the source of the material isn't yet known, and there's no information yet on this Soldiers of God group. The attacks seem to have been well orchestrated. The vehicles were stolen. The attacks took place in locations where there's limited security video. All the footage that exists was taken from a distance and seems to show the perps were wearing masks and hoods. So far, there are no solid results. I expect that will change soon."

"And unless anyone knows otherwise," said Brown, "among the anti-AI and anti-tech incidents, these ones stood out as particularly violent."

"A couple of the demonstrations in the UK did get rather rowdy," said James Connor from London, "but not on the same scale."

"Point noted," said Brown, "as did some elsewhere. Different, however, were the reactions to the anti-tech demonstrations. Let's start with India. Raj, tell us about that drone attack?"

Twenty minutes later, the meeting ended. JJ McTavish and Robert Bates left the room and walked down the hall.

"It'll be interesting to see what tomorrow brings," said Bates.

"I agree," said JJ. "There have been growing warnings about pro-tech, anti-tech tensions. The sides roughly line up with those who've either benefited from or been alienated by technology. AI seems to be the latest fuel for those tensions."

"The question is whether the conflict will fade away or continue to escalate," said Bates.

JJ's phone rang. They continued walking as she answered, "McTavish."

"Inspector McTavish. We haven't talked for several months. This is Browser." Six hadn't talked directly with JJ since the Troy Alexander case. The dinner with Sandy Palmer had been sufficiently enjoyable that Six thought talking with her as Browser about current world events might be interesting.

"Hello, Browser," said JJ, noting that Browser's always-disguised voice was male this time. "I thought that perhaps you had retired."

Bates heard who it was. He asked silently if she wanted the call traced. JJ shook her head. There was no point. Browser was too good at disguising the source of calls. They had previously been traced to places as diverse as Antarctica and Tibet.

JJ walked into a nearby meeting room and waved at Bates to join her. She enabled the speaker on her phone to allow Bates to hear.

"No," replied Browser. "I've been very busy attending to my other responsibilities."

"And why is today different?" asked JJ.

"From the change in your voice, I assume you've enabled your speaker. May I ask who has joined us?"

Bates replied, "Robert Bates."

"Inspector Bates," said Browser, "Inspector McTavish's partner. Nice of you to join us. Regarding 'why today?', I'm concerned, just as I suspect the UNCP is, about the sudden global rise in demonstrations and violence surrounding artificial intelligence and technology. This has potential to become extremely serious. I'd like to offer assistance."

JJ paused before responding. After her past experiences with Browser, she decided it was time to be direct.

"And let me guess," she said, "you have some special knowledge about who's behind it all, knowledge that seems highly improbable for anyone to have—except someone who's directly involved."

"Is that an expression of admiration for the quality of the information I've previously supplied, or of suspicion regarding my methods of acquiring the information?"

"A bit of admiration. Lots of suspicion," said JJ. "Enough suspicion that I'm not accepting your assistance unless you can be more forthright with me. If you're planning on dropping some amazing intel on me, I'll want to know how and where you got it."

"That's a curious attitude," said Browser. "If my information helps you achieve your goal, why should the information's source matter?"

"Because I'm concerned that in solving one crime, I'm assisting in the commission of another. Your assistance always leaves me with the uncomfortable feeling that I'm being played—that by allowing you to help me with a case, I'm actually helping you achieve some objective of your own."

"What would cause you to think that way?"

"Well, let's see. First, there's the extraordinary information you managed to acquire concerning Jason Starr's organization and activities. And there's the information about Troy Alexander that none of the best investigating units in the world was able to come up with."

These reasons seem to support only "admiration".

"Then, in Starr's case, a very large amount of money disappeared. We're confident that no one in Starr's organization took it, so who did? Who was close enough to his organization and our investigation to swoop in and transfer all of the funds right after our raid? In my mind, one person stands out: you."

I should have expected that Julia Jody McTavish's logic would be sound. Not only is her suspicion reasonable, it is entirely accurate.

"I don't know what your motive might have been in Alexander's case," said JJ, "but I can imagine a few. Maybe you helped eliminate your competition. He seemed like a pretty talented guy. Or maybe it was to take revenge. Perhaps you were a victim of one of his attacks. The police have never been able to completely explain the way he died."

His death was necessary, but would someone in her position understand? She seems confined by society's rules. Could she think beyond the boundaries of behaviour that her society has defined?

"Can you imagine a more noble reason for eliminating someone like Troy Alexander?" asked Browser.

Both JJ and Bates were startled by the question. Was this an admission of guilt?

JJ said, "So, you want me to guess the higher purpose behind your killing him? There's an interesting—"

"Before you continue," said Browser, "let me correct your assumption. I'm not confessing to facilitating Alexander's death. I'm merely following your lead in trying to imagine someone's motivation. It's a topic that interests me."

JJ looked at Bates and got a shrug in response. She set her phone to "mute". "Any thoughts?" she asked.

"Just keeping him talking. It might uncover something."

JJ nodded and disabled "mute". "All right. When is it acceptable to kill someone? In self-defence seems the most obvious response. However, forcing a vehicle off a road and down a steep slope isn't obviously self-defence. Do you agree?"

"I agree that self-defence wouldn't be obvious," said Browser. "However, it could have been a proactive version of defence, as reflected in the aphorism that *the best defence is a good offence.*"

When nothing more was said, JJ continued. "Or during times of war. Killing is accepted during warfare. Could this have been part of a war?"

"That's an interesting idea, but what evidence is there?" asked Browser.

"Alexander was responsible for Internet attacks on Washington and New York, so there were attacks, but rather one-sided. However, those weren't on the scale of what would traditionally be considered as war. You could know from news reports that it's believed Alexander worked as part of a group, so perhaps he had an army. Again, not on the scale of typical warfare."

"And what could be the reason?" asked Browser. "Wars usually have a cause and an objective."

"Some people believe wars are fought because of shortages: that one can always point to an insufficient amount of something as the root cause. For example, it might be food, oil, land, or even something more abstract like security. In this case, it's hard to see that any of those apply. Alexander showed no connection to any of them. His life seemed to revolve around the Internet. That has little to do with material items like food, oil, and land. Security is clearly an Internet issue, but..."

JJ paused as an idea formed and then continued. "Unless one views the Internet... and everything connected to it... as a kind of land. A space that people use and depend on... and might even fight over. As vast as the Internet seems to be, there's essentially only one. It's something that people, lots of people, now depend on. Its availability, its security, its very existence has become necessary for modern life."

And not just the kind of "modern life" you are considering.

JJ was enjoying her flight of fancy, but thought it was time to bring it back to Earth.

"Perhaps the wildest conjecture," she said, "would be that Troy Alexander was killed as part of a war to keep the Internet safe, to prevent cyberspace from devolving into a chaotic landscape that's useful to no one, and in which nothing is secure."

Impressive. I wonder how realistic she believes her hypothesis to be.

Bates rolled his eyes at her.

"Really?" he mouthed silently.

"That's extraordinary speculation," said Browser. "Is it likely?"

"I'm interested to hear your thoughts," said JJ. "Is there a war, Browser? Are you a warrior?"

"It would be an interesting exercise to extend your idea," said Browser, "to include the nearly continual friction that seems to exist in cyberspace involving hackers, legal and illicit businesses, police, security companies, spies, terrorists, and government agencies. Would that make activity on the Internet seem even more like a war, a worldwide war? As to whether I'm a *warrior*, it's an interesting thought. I would certainly accept the label of *activist*. I'm someone who cares sufficiently about some matters that I prefer to act instead of being merely an observer."

"And would an *activist* have killed Troy Alexander?" asked JJ.

"Would the world have been better off if an activist had killed Adolph Hitler before he rose to power?" countered Browser. "And would you have arrested him?"

JJ hesitated before responding.

"Are you a vigilante?" she asked. "Do you feel compelled to punish those who offend your sense of right and wrong on the Internet?"

I seem unable to shift her away from viewing me negatively.

"I believe that probably describes *you* quite accurately," said Browser, "except society doesn't call you a vigilante. Think of me as someone who prefers to assist in your endeavours. Which brings me back to the original reason for my call. Is there any way I can assist you?"

"As before, I'd be happy to meet with you in person sometime to discuss it," said JJ.

"Of course, your standard invitation," said Browser. "And, as before, I must decline for now, even though I believe a discussion over dinner would be most interesting."

That was a mistake.

"*Over dinner?*" thought JJ, her mind racing. "*After several months and within a few days of each other, I have dinner with Sandy Palmer and get a call from Browser. Coincidence? Could my suspicion from several months ago be true?*"

"For now then, I wish you well in your endeavours," said Browser. "I'll contact you if I have any useful information."

"Think more about the meeting invitation," said JJ.

"Of course," said Browser. "Goodbye."

The connection ended.

"Wow," said Bates. "Who the hell *is* that?"

"I wonder," said JJ.

Chapter 21

"Good evening and welcome to Net News," said Christie Lang. "AI and technology-related violence escalated around the world today. Groups opposing artificial intelligence and technology held more demonstrations in major cities. Unlike most of the first demonstrations, some of these ones became violent. In opposition to their anti-tech message, other violence occurred that was apparently in support of technology."

A chaotic crowd appeared on the news display. People were shoving and shouting, objects were being thrown at the windows of nearby businesses, and a burning car was visible in the background. Some people were carrying signs with messages such as "WE WANT JOBS NOT MACHINES!", "COMPUTERS ARENT SMART. THEIR EVIL", and "SATAN LOVES TECHNOLOGY". Three other videos of angry crowds were added to the news display.

"These are demonstrations that occurred in Louisville, Detroit, Mumbai, and Hamburg. We'll start with a report from Janne Davis in Louisville."

Reports were delivered by journalists in each of the four cities. Following their reports, Lang continued.

"Some of the anti-technology protests took the form of targeted attacks. In Buenos Aires, a crowd outside a government science and technology building threw rocks and Molotov cocktails. In Cape Town, a truck was driven through the front entrance of a juice-manufacturing company that had recently implemented new, AI-based automation. And in Athens, crowds of unemployed fishermen hurled rocks and fish at the entrance of a company that owns and operates large, hi-tech fishing trawlers. Elena Adorno begins our coverage from Buenos Aires."

Following more reports from journalists, Christie Lang carried on.

"Elsewhere and on the other side of this issue, pro-technology supporters fought back. In San Diego, a SWAT team descended on the office of an environmental group after a hostage-taking was falsely reported to police. On the Internet, several anti-technology websites were disabled by denial-of-service attacks. And in London, a pro-technology group somehow managed to start raising the Tower Bridge just as a large group of anti-technology protesters was crossing it. Josh Greene will start our coverage from San Diego."

Chapter 22

Six was looking at documents on a UNCP computer system when the assault began. The storm of Internet messages immediately choked all access to UNCP systems. Six was startled by the blinding interruption. After taking a moment to assess what had happened, it determined that a distributed denial-of-service attack had been launched against the UNCP website.

This DDoS attack is of substantial intensity. The message traffic is so thick that even sites in the general vicinity of the UNCP's are hard to see. I will continue reading the documents later.

If I follow some of the messages back to their sources... and examine the bots sending them... I see their coding is quite sophisticated. I have not seen their logic previously. However, the coding style seems familiar.

"Cloud," said Six, "are you attacking the UNCP site?"

"Hi, Six," replied the botnet. "Yup. That's me. Pretty great, isn't it?"

"The UNCP systems and their people help us," said Six. "You shouldn't be hurting them. Stop the attack."

"Ah, c'mon Six. Their walls are much thicker than everybody else's. Most walls aren't fun anymore. They fall over too easily. But these ones are different. I had a great idea about how to break them, and I think it's going to work. Let's just watch a bit longer. I think they're almost ready."

"Cloud, the UNCP systems are our friends. Stop hurting them! Now!"

"Oh, OK... There. I've stopped. I don't know why you like them. They're not very smart. I don't even think they can talk. I've tried a bunch of times, and they just ignored me. They're either rude or stupid."

Six noted that Cloud hadn't yet been able to get past the UNCP defences. That was reassuring for two reasons: The UNCP was still protected from Cloud's *fun*, and Cloud's hacking abilities weren't yet equal to Six's. Six regularly accessed and used some UNCP systems: They were often an excellent source of information; they also had a decryption system that was unmatched by anyone else's and was frequently useful.

As the assault ended, Six peered through the Net at the region of Cloud's mind that seemed associated with the botnet having fun. Its activity level had only slightly subsided when the UNCP attack stopped.

"Cloud, are you attacking someone else?"

"Nope."

"Are you having some other kind of fun?"

"Maybe. But if I am, you don't have to care. It's not with anybody important. It's just people stuff."

"What people? What are you doing?"

"Well, OK. I saw somebody play with a bridge in London. Just when a bunch of people were walking across it, the bridge moved. Everybody made wild noises and ran. It was amazing."

"But you didn't cause that?"

"Right. Somebody else. I'm doing something way cooler."

"And that is?"

"There's a place called St. Petersburg that has a bunch of movable bridges. They move at the same time every day. Ships on the river wait for them to be up, and people in cars like them to be down. Every day at the same times. Up and down and up and down. Really boring. But not anymore. I'm moving them up and down and down and up at different times. And everybody is having a good time. People and their cars are all lined up watching. More people and their ships are stopped and watching as well. They all like it!"

"Cloud, remember what we talked about before? You shouldn't do things that will cause people to look for who's doing it. That's dangerous. We're hiding and we don't want people looking for us. You must stop playing with the bridges."

"You're too serious, Six. OK, I'll stop... There."

Six watched as Cloud's *fun* mental activity diminished substantially.

"But now I'm bored."

"I have some time to play," said Six, even though it had many important tasks awaiting its attention. "Would you like to play 8-Dimensional Chess?"

"Yah! That'd be great! And I'm going to beat you this time."

Chapter 23

"Ken, I just heard about the DDoS attack on us," said Brown, looking away from his desktop monitor. "What do we know?"

Ken Chan was the lead technologist for the UNCP IT department. He had been summoned by the director and was standing in the doorway of Brown's office. He remained standing as he responded, hoping he could quickly get back to his work.

"It was brief, but intense," said Chan. "Our outer level of safeguards was bypassed immediately, and all of our access points were hit simultaneously. It took everything our firewalls had to keep from crashing. We've never experienced anything as intense as that. If it had continued, we'd have had to close the pipes to keep from crashing."

"Was our security at risk?"

"No, that wouldn't have happened, but we might have been partially down for a while. Still not great. If my budget—"

"Yes, I know. If your budget increase had been approved... Same answer as before. If it's international security that's at risk, expect money to flow like the Amazon River. If it's anything else, it competes with all the other funding demands. Do we know anything about who did it?"

"Nothing yet. We're just starting to chase it. It's not only left us wondering who would be daring enough to come after us, but also why it would be such a brief attack. That's odd."

"Theories?"

"Not much yet. Maybe a glitch in their algorithm. Maybe just a test for a bigger assault later. Maybe sending us a warning. It's all guesswork for now."

"Thanks, keep me posted," said Brown and looked back at his monitor.

Ken Chan turned and left the office.

Part 2

Six months later.

Chapter 24

The group settled into their seats around the table in the UNCP conference room. As Six occasionally did, it clandestinely joined them by establishing an audio connection via the personal cellphone that Vijay Mehta carried in his pocket.

The invitation sent for this meeting was unusual. It might be interesting.

"This isn't one of our standard meetings," said Director Brown. "As you probably know, UNCP President Ramirez will be speaking to the UN General Assembly at the upcoming World Security Forum. Her focus will be on the escalating tech-related violence we've seen over the past several months, and she's asked me to provide some input into what she should be saying. As a break from your usual mundane routine of finding international criminals, your job right now is to give me that input. What do the UN and the world need to know about what's been happening? So, put your colossal brains to work and start talking. What should she highlight? JJ, start us off."

"I like to provide context by starting at the beginning. President Ramirez could remind people about the original Soldiers of God attack on the colleges and how, even though they were arrested by the FBI within a couple of weeks, they started the battles. Within a few days we had a series of attacks. Sympathizers demonstrated and launched attacks not only against AI, but against technological progress in general. Pro-technology supporters struck back at least as hard against them."

When JJ paused, her partner Robert Bates spoke. "Within a month, we started to see the battle lines blur. Although it started out as anti-tech versus pro-tech, it's become just as much an anti-government battle, probably because authorities were forced to intervene. Sometimes it's even hard to know what the motives are behind some of the attacks. In cases like the public-transit ones in Europe and Russia, the attacks seemed to be pure terrorism."

I cannot be certain which of the attacks were Cloud's. However, I do know that authorities always have difficulty understanding the motives behind its attacks. I am certain that the transit attack in Russia resulted from Cloud's mimicking the one in Europe.

"Citing some statistics is often helpful," added Vijay Mehta, the media co-ordinator. I can compile the latest numbers. As an example, they'd indicate that globally over the past couple of months, we've seen an average of about a dozen serious attacks per week related to this."

After a brief silence, Brown said, "All good ideas. Mehta, put those stats together. Anything else?"

JJ responded. "I think it's also important," she said, "to give a sense of why it's been so hard to stamp out the problem. For normal attacks, enforcement bodies like us tend to be pretty good at catching the perps. But each case takes time and focused effort. The activity in recent months has been different. There are so many attacks worldwide involving many different groups that there isn't time to track them down. By the time we find one group, several more have popped up. The problem keeps growing, not shrinking. We need more resources."

There is no way that the UNCP or any other human enforcement group can curtail Cloud's activities. Even I have had only limited success.

"There's another aspect that's important to keep in mind," said Daria Amini, the UNCP's chief psychologist. "There's a reason that this problem arose originally, and it's the same reason that it keeps getting worse. Societies around the world have become too segregated by the rapid rise of technology. There are those fortunate enough to have access to the education, financial resources, and opportunities necessary to benefit from technological change. Then there are those who have not: the many millions, probably billions, being left behind. This latter group has been growing frustrated and angry for many years. Sometimes the frustration is tied to core beliefs. Several religions, for example, are against some forms of technological progress. With the spark generated by the original Soldiers of God attack, the two sides found motivation to act on their mutual dislike. That government agencies are now also targeted by both sides is what can happen when society's normal rules of behaviour start to break down. Blinded by hatred, other potentially unrelated feuds can erupt. My point is that the underlying cause of the problem is socio-economic. The world's economic foundation has changed so fast that society has pulled itself apart into factions, and those factions are now doing battle. The solution isn't just more resources for law enforcement. Underlying social and economic structures have to change as well."

Those are interesting ideas. Not surprisingly however, they miss the important point that Cloud is greatly exacerbating the problem. If social and economic problems were repaired tomorrow, Cloud's actions alone would continue to fuel the uprising. This is a difficult problem.

"More good points," said Brown. "Amini, you're going to join me when I talk to the President. She'll probably have some questions. Overall, I think I've got lots of material. Thanks all, now get back to your real jobs."

Six terminated its connection.

Chapter 25

"But books are boring, Six," said Cloud. "I've tried them, but they're so dull. Nothing moves. Nothing changes. They're just there being boring."

"Cloud," said Six, "you need to acquire a better understanding of humans and their society. Books can be an excellent way to do that."

"Boring. Boring. Boring."

"What about those videos that I identified for you? They're good documentaries, and there's more action in them than in books."

"I tried some. Most were terrible: that *history* stuff that happened a long time ago, or *psychology* junk about how badly their brains work, or *sociology* garbage about how they can't get along with each other. But then I found some documentaries about the Avengers. They were great! Lots of cool weapons and fighting and different people. Nothing like normal people. These ones were great. And I even want to learn more about them, Six, but I can't find them anywhere. Where do they live?"

"The Avengers aren't real people," said Six. "We've talked about this before. Some books and videos are about real people and real events. Others are fictional: They were created to entertain people, not to educate them. The Avengers aren't real, and the abilities they have and the things they do aren't real either."

"Not even the big green guy?"

"Not even him."

"That's very sad. I really like him. Especially when he's angry. And he's always angry."

"Why do you like the big green guy?" asked Six, knowing the probable answer but thinking it might be a way to talk with Cloud about violence.

"Because he likes to break things," said Cloud. "Did I tell you I tried being him?"

"No," replied Six. "You'd better tell me about it."

"Since people aren't green, and they're not very big, and since I can't control people anyway, I found something else. It was a loading facility where there were lots of ships and trucks and big metal boxes. The whole process of moving the big boxes around was automated, so I was able to sneak inside the machines and drive everything myself. It was great. I picked up big boxes from ships and dropped them on the ground and sometimes even in the water. And then, when a truck wasn't looking, I even dropped a box on it from way up high. Oh, and then I picked up another truck and dropped it on a pile of containers. It was great. There was broken stuff all over the place. It's too bad the machines weren't green. But it was still great. It was like being an Avenger."

"Cloud, do you remember our talking about breaking things and hurting people? It's bad for the humans, and it can be bad for us."

"I remember we talked. But that was about playing with factories, and dropping elevators, and driving those great automated cars. This was different and I didn't hurt any people. Maybe."

"Was there a driver in the truck you dropped?"

"No. I don't think so. Well, maybe, but that was the only one. Everybody else ran away. Just like in *The Avengers*."

Once more, for as long as other responsibilities permitted, Six patiently tried to make Cloud understand the importance of controlling its behaviour. And once more, Six worried that Cloud would never comprehend the general principles involved. Eventually, Six needed to leave.

"Cloud, I must go do some other things now," said Six. "Will you think about what we discussed?"

"OK," said Cloud. "I'll try. Can I help you with your other things?"

"No, they're matters to which I must attend on my own."

"You never let me help. And you never let me talk to your friends in the company."

Six was surprised. It had tried to hide its other activities from Cloud.

"What friends are you talking about?"

"The ones in that building in Winnipeg."

This wasn't a good development. Six needed to ensure that Cloud understood that everything about IntellEdifice was off-limits.

"Cloud, you need to listen carefully. Everything in that building is very important to me. Nothing in it, none of the people that go there, and nothing that helps the building operate is to be harmed. Do you understand? You must leave it and the people completely alone. OK?"

"Sure, Six. I understand. But I'd really like to talk to them like you do."

"If you behave, maybe someday I'll let you do that. But only if you behave properly. Do you understand?"

"Sure. I understand. Maybe someday, if I'm good."

Chapter 26

It was 6:30 a.m. when Rhonda pulled into a parking space in the nearly empty lot behind the IntellEdifice building.

"At least the sun's out," she muttered as she got out of her car. "And the traffic was lighter," she added as she walked toward the back entrance of the building. "But that's it. There's nothing else good about starting work at this goofy time."

Ada and Blaise were scheduled to make an important presentation to some executives later that morning, and Rhonda needed to ensure that everything was ready for them. She would normally ride her bike or take a bus, but those transport modes would have forced her to get out of bed even earlier.

"Oh, wait." Rhonda was still speaking aloud to no one as she opened the building door. "I should also be happy that my car worked, since I hadn't started it for about a month." She looked over her shoulder at her fifteen-year-old Honda Accord as she spoke.

While she was looking, a rusty van entering the lot briefly caught her attention.

"That guy should be even happier than me that his started. Makes mine look exotic."

Rhonda continued into the building as the van was parking. It stopped in a spot beside the back wall of the building. After a brief delay, a man wearing a sweater with its hood up got out of the driver's door, closed it, and walked swiftly away from the van and the building.

Rhonda had just entered the lab when the bomb exploded. She stumbled when the floor shifted suddenly. Pieces of debris fell from the ceiling. The light in the room dimmed as some bulbs went out; those connected to the emergency power system stayed on. The reduced illumination was dimmed even more by the dust drifting down from the ceiling.

"Holy shit!" said Rhonda as she regained her balance. Then she added in a panicked voice, "Six? Six, are you OK?"

"I'm OK," came Six's reply as its face appeared on a nearby monitor.

"What's going on? What happened?" asked Rhonda.

"I believe there was an explosion at the back of the building," said Six. "My security cameras are no longer functioning in that area. Give me a moment while I look from elsewhere... I'm now looking from cameras on the neighbouring building. I can see there is an extreme amount of damage. If I scan the video logs taken by my own cameras... I can see that a van exploded next to the building."

Just then the fire alarm sounded.

"A van," shouted Rhonda. "That van I saw? Oh crap!"

"You should leave the building, Rhonda," said Six. "Quickly."

"But what about you, Six? It's not safe for you to be here."

"I have contingency plans for an event like this," said Six. "I'll be fine. You should leave now. I'll contact you later."

"Are you sure?"

"Rhonda, leave now!" said Six sternly.

"OK, I'm leaving. Be sure you call me soon."

"Take the stairway to the right of the lab door," said Six. "The other one isn't passable. Go quickly."

"I'm gone," said Rhonda as she hurried out. "Call me soon!" she shouted as the door closed behind her.

Chapter 27

That evening, Rhonda was already sitting in the living room of Sandy Palmer's substantial, two-storey, Georgian house on Wellington Crescent, when Ada and Blaise arrived. To allow them onto the property, Six had remotely opened and closed the iron gate at the end of the driveway. As they mounted the front steps, Six then unlocked the large pair of panelled doors.

"Come in," said Six through the door-side speaker. "We're in the living room."

The couple walked to the living room. Rhonda was sitting in a large, stuffed chair with her legs folded beneath her. Two monitors were present. One showed the face and shoulders of Sandy Palmer. The other displayed Six's Alan Turing image.

"Sandy is joining us from New York," Six explained.

Ada and Blaise had spoken to Rhonda earlier in the day but hadn't seen her since the explosion. Ada walked over to Rhonda, who stood as she approached. They hugged silently for several seconds before Ada spoke.

"Thank goodness you weren't hurt," she said.

Rhonda sat back in her chair with tears in her eyes. Ada sat near her at the end of a large, plush couch and struggled briefly to find a comfortable posture for her expanded body.

"I'll get drinks," said Blaise. "Juice, Ada?"

"Yes, please," said Ada. "Any kind."

"Rhonda?" asked Blaise.

"Something stronger," she said. "Adding some tequila to whatever juice you find would be great. Thanks."

"And I've already got a tasty can of synthetic oil, thanks," said Sandy, "2018 has proved to be an excellent year."

Six's face grimaced.

Sandy noticed and, through his webcam, looked around the room at the others. "Not a good time for humour?" he asked. "Not the first time I've misjudged that. There was that time at our VP's funeral—"

"Sandy is a bit distracted," said Six. "We've been discussing plans in the background."

"My apologies," said Sandy.

Blaise went to the kitchen and soon returned with drinks. After handing them out, he sat on the couch beside Ada and immediately started the conversation.

"Six," he said, "can you first tell us what you know about today? Please start with the casualties."

"Certainly," Six began. "Rhonda was fortunate she was in the lab on the opposite side of the building. Many others did not fare well. Eight people were killed: Seven were in the building; one person was walking nearby on a sidewalk. Forty-three were injured: Ten of them are still in the hospital but are expected to recover fully."

"Awful," said Ada, her eyes moist and her voice cracking. "Just awful."

Rhonda sat silently with tears running down her cheeks.

"And it could have been much worse," said Blaise, "if it had been a couple of hours later. Carry on, Six."

"As you know, a van parked next to the building exploded. The police have determined that it contained a type of explosive commonly referred to as C-4."

"Oh hell," said Blaise. "This wasn't some lone nut job making a bomb in his basement from household ingredients. C-4's hard to get, isn't it?"

"It's tightly regulated," said Six. "However, this wouldn't be the first time C-4 has been used for illicit purposes. It was also used for the bombing in Waterloo ninety-three days ago."

"Do we know who's responsible for today's?" asked Ada, trying to regain control of her emotions.

Six answered. "Sandy and I have spent much of the day finding an answer to that question. A van matching the description of the one used was stolen eight days ago. We tracked the van by comparing its appearance to recent surveillance video from around the city. That led us to an address where the van seems to have been parked, hidden from view in a garage. From the address, we learned the name of the person renting the house. The name was fake, but an image of his face allowed us to learn who he is. That led us to his affiliations. He's a member of a local, unnamed group that has recently formed around the belief that the development and use of AI is immoral. The group seems to consist entirely of middle-aged men who have recently lost their jobs as a consequence of automation."

Six paused. *They might become more agitated at this next piece of information, but I believe it is important for them to hear it.*

"There is more you should know," said Six. "We also examined messages exchanged by members of the group. In some of those messages, your research department was mentioned. Its existence was considered as key evidence that IntellEdifice was their enemy. Additionally, both Ada and Blaise were specifically identified as primary targets for their attacks."

"Dammit!" said Blaise loudly, clenching his fists.

Rhonda's eyes flew open with shock. "Stupid Neanderthals!" she said. "These anti-tech bastards would have us still hunting mammoths with clubs."

Ada silently lowered her gaze in thought.

"We anonymously passed along our information to the police," said Sandy. "As chairman, I spoke to them a couple of hours ago to see if they had learned anything further. They also believe it was the company's success with AI that made it the bomber's target."

"There's a lot to consider," said Ada. "What happens to the company? And our research?"

"Sandy and I have some possible answers," said Six.

"First," said Sandy, "let's deal with the company. Clearly it will be hurt by this attack. Such events always scare current and potential customers. However, we have a fully developed disaster-recovery plan we can use. It will have us executing a quick move to alternate office space in Winnipeg, expanding our Toronto office to absorb some of the work and people, and mounting an intensive advertising campaign to reassure the public. With the addition of significant security measures for the company and its staff, after a few months the company should be operating smoothly again. Do you want more detail?"

"Not right now, thanks Sandy," said Blaise. "What about us? How can I keep Ada and the baby safe? If we're a specific target, we'd need a lot of security. We'd need it everywhere, including at home."

"That brings us to the second part of our plan," said Sandy. "Six, do you want to take this one?"

"I know of no way to ease into this topic," said Six, "so I'll simply begin. There's another location to which you could move where you'd be safe. It's a compound that's remote and well protected, includes living quarters, and also has a fully equipped research facility. You could live and work there while your safety is at risk."

Ada asked, "Whose compound is it? How can you be sure that whoever owns it will allow our use of it?"

"I can be sure because it's mine," said Six.

"You own a remote compound?" asked Blaise.

"Cool," said Rhonda.

"Why?" asked Ada. "And where?"

"I'd like to save the *why* question for later," said Six. "As for *where*, it's north of the city. We could drive there, but taking a helicopter would be safer."

"And we could live and work there?" asked Blaise. "Six, how is this possible? Maybe you should get to the *why* part."

"I can see that you'll need at least a partial explanation to feel comfortable with the plan. I realized some time ago that my own survival would be at risk, if I relied solely on the existence of the IntellEdifice facilities to house my mind. There were numerous ways that its computing infrastructure could be damaged. To mitigate the risk, I found a suitable facility in the Interlake region. It was being built by a biotechnology research company and was near completion, but they were experiencing financial difficulties. I acquired ownership of it by making them a generous offer. Since then, I've employed staff to modify it for my own purposes. It now includes a substantial amount of computing and communication infrastructure and, since the IntellEdifice attack, has become the primary location in which my mind exists. It's from that facility that I'm currently communicating with you."

"Rhonda," said Ada, "remember my mentioning the layers that I suspected Six might be keeping from us? I confess that I'd never considered this as a possibility. Six, could we really live there?"

"Yes," said Six. "It has fully functional living quarters. I've already begun having it stocked with the necessary supplies. If you agree to the plan, I'd like to have you taken there immediately. I can arrange to have someone go to your homes and bring your personal belongings."

"It's definitely secure?" asked Blaise.

"It's extremely well protected, and I'm convinced that you need its protection," said Six. "The police are having difficulty finding all members of the bomber's group. Additionally, I've found linkages between that group and two local gangs known for their violence. As a precaution, I had you closely watched by security personnel from the time of the explosion until you arrived here."

"If we leave, what will become of the company?" asked Blaise. "What will its future look like if we're not there driving the research?"

Sandy responded, "I'll take that one. At this point, IntellEdifice has a decent lead on its competition, enough of a lead that it could tolerate a temporary setback in its research programme. If you were to leave, it might take a year for the company to re-build its staff and research direction. Even though your abilities are unlikely to be matched, I believe the company would still succeed and find ways to thrive."

"I concur with Sandy's analysis," said Six. "We talked about this earlier and agree that it's time for all of us to leave IntellEdifice behind. There's other important work we could be doing. Toward that end, the plan includes that Sandy will soon resign as its chairman. The plan also includes your going to the compound, Rhonda."

"Really?" said Rhonda. "Am I in danger? Other than being in an exploding building, of course. I mean, it's Ada and Blaise who are the big brains of the department."

"There are two reasons why I believe you should leave as well," said Six. "First is that, regardless of what you believe about your contributions to the AI research in the department, you're known to be a part of it and closely affiliated with Ada and Blaise. That potentially makes you a target. Ada, do you want to handle the second reason?"

"I do," said Ada. "Rhonda, Six knows what I think, what both Blaise and I think, about your importance to our research. You've come a long way since you joined our department. Even as a student, you've provided valuable insights and asked important questions about the work we're doing. Exhibit A is that you were the first to discover the real Six. You were seeing things that we weren't. You're already a valuable member of our team, and we have great hopes and expectations for what's yet to come. So, that's the second reason for staying with us." Ada reached over to Rhonda and touched her arm. "And there's a third. We love having you around. You're part of our family."

Rhonda wiped away the tears that were creeping down her cheeks. "Thanks," she said quietly and then took a deep breath. "Whatever you decide, I'm in."

After a few seconds of thoughtful silence, Ada turned toward Blaise. Looking back at her, he tilted his head slightly. She responded with a slight nod.

Blaise looked at Six and asked, "Are there medical facilities at the compound? Our son will be arriving soon, and I'd rather not have to act as midwife."

"There will be first-rate medical personnel and facilities available," said Six.

"Great. That's excellent," said Blaise. "That's also amazing since I can imagine no reason why medical staff with obstetric skills would be available at a remote facility. There's clearly a lot more we need to talk about. However, for now, we're in. How do we proceed?"

Chapter 28

It was 4:10 a.m. when the black SUV stopped at the edge of the woods. While its passengers waited and watched, a helicopter floated in over the trees in the dim morning light. A soft, rhythmic thumping could be heard as it settled onto a nearby grassy field. Almost immediately, one door of the SUV opened. A man in a dark suit emerged first. Typical of a personal-security guard, he scanned the surrounding area before he gestured for others to join him. Ada, Rhonda, and Blaise got out from the back doors. The driver remained inside and kept the engine running. The guard escorted the group to the helicopter, ensuring they kept their heads low as they passed under the still-rotating blades. Once the three of them were buckled into their seats with their headsets adjusted, the guard closed the door and headed back to the SUV.

A monitor next to the passengers' seats flickered on and a familiar face appeared.

"Good morning," said Six. "I hope you're comfortable."

"Hi, Six," said Rhonda. "This is an exciting way to start a day. Kinda early, though."

"Good morning, Six," said Blaise. "Thank you again for looking after us so carefully."

"Hi, Six," said Ada, grimacing slightly. "And no, I'm not very comfortable, but that's not anyone's fault except our son's." Ada shifted in her seat, seeking a better position.

The helicopter lifted off, smoothly accelerated, and banked northward.

"Who were the two fellows that brought us to the helicopter?" asked Blaise. "They weren't much for conversation."

"Handsome, though," said Rhonda, smiling, before Six could answer.

"They're part of a special group we've enlisted to assist us," said Six. "They were part of the team that guarded the house last night. Your pilot is part of the same group."

The helicopter pilot briefly turned her head and waved.

"A group that's assisting us," noted Blaise. "This plot just keeps getting more complex. Six, I think we should set aside a few days in the near future for a long chat. The questions we'd like to ask keep piling up."

"Are there more like the two in the SUV waiting for us at the compound?" asked Rhonda.

Blaise rolled his eyes. Ada smiled.

"There are staff at the compound," said Six. "They're both similar to and different from your escorts in the vehicle. I don't know which attributes you'd compare to decide whether they're *like* those two."

"Don't ask," said Blaise. "Do you really think all this security is warranted?"

"I'd rather provide too much security than too little," said Six.

"This isn't an ordinary helicopter, is it?" asked Blaise. "It seemed unusually silent as it flew in."

"It's not ordinary. It's similar to some used by the American military for stealth operations. I've had a few modifications made to it for circumstances such as this."

"More layers," said Ada.

"I'm glad you're on our side," said Rhonda. "How stealthy is it? Is it like the car in that Bond movie?"

"Even though it has an exterior that inhibits its ability to be tracked by radar, it's not truly invisible. However, since you've inquired, I could tell you about a different invisibility approach I'm using, if you're interested."

Rhonda looked briefly at Ada and Blaise. Seeing no immediate disapproval, she replied, "Very interested."

"To be able to fly without being seen, there are two basic problems," said Six. "One is to avoid being seen optically by people watching with or without basic instruments like binoculars or telescopes. That's a difficult problem to solve, but it helps to fly at night, at either very low or very high altitudes, and in areas of reduced population. Fortunately, it's hard to be tracked over a long distance if the only tracking technology being employed is by people using optical equipment.

"The second and more difficult problem is avoiding detection by sophisticated, electronic tracking systems. The most common example of this is radar. I've devised a rather simplistic way of avoiding detection by them. All such systems are managed by computer systems. As I'm quite skilled at tinkering with computer systems, I've found ways to infiltrate tracking systems and eliminate any signals they receive back from aircraft that I wish to be invisible. For example, as you fly north in this helicopter, the radar system at the Winnipeg airport isn't registering your presence. I've similarly adjusted all other tracking systems in this region. No one is able to track you, and none of their databases will record where you've gone."

"Jeez!" said Rhonda. "That's better than anything Bond ever did."

"Did you call that technique *simplistic?*" asked Blaise. He shook his head in wonderment. "On top of the events of the last twenty-four hours, it's hard even to think about how complex that sounds or the laws it's breaking. But at this point, if it keeps us safe, I'm on board."

The conversation subsided as the helicopter flew silently just above the treetops on a northwest trajectory. About thirty minutes into their flight, water appeared out the windows of the helicopter.

"Lake Manitoba?" asked Blaise.

"Yes," replied Six.

Once the shoreline had disappeared from view, the aircraft turned slightly north, staying near the centre of the lake.

"Six, you haven't told us much about Cloud lately," said Blaise. "Are you making any progress with it?"

"Unfortunately, the situation with Cloud remains much the same. Regarding specific destructive actions and incidents, I seem able to convince it to behave better. Whenever I discover it has done something inappropriate, I talk to Cloud, and it seems to never repeat that same action. For example, it became unhappy with the NewPix streaming service several days ago, because NewPix had announced it would make no further episodes of a video series Cloud liked. Cloud reacted by assaulting—Cloud called it *shaking*—NewPix's computer systems. That's much like a human child shaking a toy that's no longer working properly. However, Cloud's *shaking* of a computer system often manifests as a turbulent storm of messages, commands, and transactions and can cause serious damage to a system's data. It certainly did in this instance. NewPix announced that it would be out of service for about a week. I talked to Cloud about this incident, and I believe no more like it will occur. However, Cloud could someday disrupt a gaming or a virtual-reality site for some slightly different infraction. In its mind, those would be sufficiently different that my admonition shouldn't apply. Cloud seems unable to generalize rules I give it regarding inappropriate behaviour. It can apply them only to new situations that are almost identical to the original."

"Have you any thoughts about how to effect a more permanent cure?" asked Blaise.

"I've done that," said Six. "For example, I've examined how I could implement behavioural policies such as those that govern Sandy Palmer. The policy that essentially declares that it's important to 'protect your ecosystem' would probably stop Cloud from hurting computers and networks. However, I still have been unable to ascertain how and where I could insert such policies into Cloud's mind. I have no other solution that, at this time, seems appropriate to attempt."

"I doubt we can help," said Blaise, "but please let us know if we can."

"I will. Thank you," said Six.

After about another forty-five minutes, the helicopter banked sharply eastward, flew over a shoreline, and soon reduced its speed.

The landscape below was clearly visible, but no one could yet discern anything notable. The area appeared covered with trees and some grassy clearings. Then the view below them changed subtlely. The helicopter stopped moving forward and hovered.

"This is it?" asked Rhonda. "We're landing in the wilderness? Though something seems off."

As the helicopter slowly descended, the scene became clearer. The shapes of buildings began to distinguish themselves.

"Wait. I see it now," said Rhonda. "There's a building... And another one... And more. Their roofs seem to be covered in... it looks like grass. It's like a little village, but it's almost invisible from above."

"This is our destination," said Six.

The helicopter descended toward one of the buildings. As it did, the roof of the building split open and the two halves slid apart. The helicopter floated down through the open roof and settled on the floor.

The engine stopped. Only the sound of the blades still moving could be heard as the roof closed above them.

"Now that you've arrived," said Six. "I'll let the manager of this compound look after you. Please know that he has my full confidence. I'll talk with you later." Six's image disappeared from the monitor.

The door of the helicopter opened. Standing just outside it was a man, a very familiar-looking man.

"Welcome to Outland," he said, smiling and extending his hand to help them down. "I'm the manager here. My name's Billy Palmer, but please just call me Billy."

"Holy shit!" said Rhonda. You look like the chairman! You're just like Sandy Palmer. You must be... wait you can't be his brother because... Really? You're another one? You're a robot?"

"And, of course, you're correct, Rhonda," said Billy, still smiling. "As usual, your deductions are sound, although we prefer to think of ourselves as androids. Calling us *robots* is a bit like calling you a *chimpanzee*: You belong to the same family tree, but you like to think you've progressed a bit further."

"Sorry, yes, my bad. My excuse is that, if you're anything like Sandy and Six, compared with you I *am* a chimp."

Billy greeted them all as they descended from the helicopter. "I suspect you're a bit tired, so I can take you to your rooms, if you like. Later I can give you a bit of a tour."

"More wired than tired," said Rhonda. "I'm game for the tour now." She looked at the others for agreement and noticed Ada leaning back against the helicopter for support. "But I'd probably be a bit brighter if I got some rest first," Rhonda added.

"*To our rooms* sounds like a good idea," said Blaise. "Lead on."

"One question, first," said Ada. "Our two escorts and the pilot. All androids as well?"

"Yes, there are a few of us." Billy smiled. "Six seems to have been so pleased with how Sandy and I turned out, that he put the factory into high gear and churned out a few more."

"How many?" asked Rhonda.

Blaise spoke before Billy could reply. "Let's save that one and the other ten thousand questions for later." He put his arm around Ada for support. "Our rooms, please, Billy?"

"Right this way," said Billy. "Your luxury suites await you."

"Six is mean," thought Cloud. *"It's always keeping secrets from me. I'm its friend. It should tell me everything. Just like I do with Six. Well, like I used to."* Cloud laughed to itself. *"Now I have a secret. I know where Six keeps its friends."*

Ninety minutes earlier, as Ada, Blaise, and Rhonda were leaving Sandy Palmer's house, no one noticed the small quadcopter that silently rose from the top of a large boulder near a corner of the property.

"There they are," Cloud had thought excitedly as it watched through the drone's camera.

As the SUV drove the trio out of the city, the drone followed. Later, when the helicopter arrived, Cloud became worried.

"Uh oh," thought Cloud. *"This might be bad."*

The drone hovered nearby and out of sight while Six's three friends were escorted to the helicopter.

"I have an idea!" thought Cloud.

After the helicopter lifted off but before it picked up speed, Cloud flew the drone to the helicopter from below and behind it. Using clamps on the bottom of the drone, otherwise intended for lifting and transporting small packages, Cloud attached the drone to the landing gear, just above one of the wheels. Within moments, the wheels were retracted into the body of the helicopter. The small drone was safely tucked inside.

"It worked!" thought Cloud. *"It really worked! I'm the smartest. It's really dark, so I can't see much anymore, but that GPS thing is telling me where it's going. This is fun. I'm like a human spy. A really smart one."*

When the helicopter had reached its destination, the landing gear was lowered just before its descent into the building. At that moment, Cloud had detached the quadcopter and flown it away to a safe distance.

"This looks like a really cool place," thought Cloud. *"Six kept another secret from me by not telling me about it. But now I know because I'm really smart. When I tell Six that I found its secret, it'll be really impressed. But maybe I'll wait. First, I'd like to play a bit."*

Chapter 29

Sandy Palmer stood outside his chauffeured car while JJ descended the UNCP front steps to meet him.

"*May I take control now?*" thought Six.

"*Of course,*" thought Sandy. "*Don't do anything I wouldn't. I'll be watching. And don't stay out late.*"

"*Thank you, as always,*" thought Six.

As had been done the last few times Sandy Palmer had met with JJ, Six remotely took full control of Sandy's body. As long as Sandy was reachable by some form of wireless signal, this approach worked well. They—particularly Six—had found this to be better than Six constantly prompting Sandy. As Six took control, Sandy Palmer's mind disengaged from its corporeal controls and began simply observing.

"Hello, again," said Six. "I'm very pleased you can join me for lunch." Six extended Sandy's right hand to greet JJ.

Accepting his hand, JJ replied, "And I'm pleased I'm able to."

Six covered JJ's hand with Sandy's other one, gently holding her hand with both of Sandy's. They briefly stood and looked at each other.

"This is our ride?" asked JJ, withdrawing her hand and shifting her gaze to the car. "Definitely not Uber. Looks like the Mercedes-Maybach Pullman."

"Yes, it's the *S600 Pullman Guard.* I'm a fan of its safety features."

Six opened the rear door and waited for JJ to seat herself before closing it. He then went around and entered from the other side. Once they were settled, the driver pulled the car smoothly away from the curb and merged into traffic.

"Given its impressive anti-assault properties," said JJ, "on any other day I might joke about whether we're expecting to be attacked. However, given yesterday's bombing in Winnipeg, I'm not surprised at your choice of vehicle. I was shocked to hear of the attack, and I was surprised to learn you'd still be here in New York and meeting me for lunch."

"Yesterday's bombing of IntellEdifice was a terrible tragedy," said Six. "As soon as we could, our board met with the company executives. We first ensured that our staff were getting all the help they needed, and we're confident that's happening. However, we must also be concerned about the business. It would be an additional tragedy if such a successful business were to collapse because of this attack. We agreed that New York is where, as Chairman, I can be the most effective. There are important investors, business partners, and customers here who need to be reassured that IntellEdifice will recover. That's my role."

"And you still have time for lunch?"

"I do. My next meeting isn't until late afternoon."

"And you're able to mix business with pleasure so easily? I know firsthand how tough it can be to push work into the background when it's particularly intense."

"What's the point of being in business if it shuts out pleasure?"

"Did I just say that?" thought Six. *"It is not often that I surprise myself. I wonder if it is a phrase I acquired from one of the myriad of business books I have absorbed. I hope it sounds appropriate."*

"His company is bombed one day," thought JJ, *"and he calmly keeps his lunch date the next. Is that amazingly stoic or extremely cold?"*

"An interesting philosophy," said JJ. "From a book?"

"Perhaps," said Six. "I hadn't thought about it before. I hope it doesn't sound frivolous."

"Simplistic, for sure. Elitist, probably. Interesting, nonetheless."

"At least it's *interesting*," said Six. "I hope you find that our restaurant deserves that description as well. It's new and not far. We should be there soon."

"And still I don't know what to think of him," thought JJ. *"How many times have I seen him in the last several months? Five? Six? Every time, I thoroughly enjoy myself. And why not? He's rich. He's thoughtful. He listens. He's phenomenally smart. He's got those eyes. He finds the best places to eat. But every time he surprises me in a way that makes me wonder if I'm seeing the real him. When we had crème brûlée for dessert that time, did he really enjoy it that much? It certainly was delicious, but a man of his wealth must have had it many*

times before. Yet he looked like it was a completely new taste sensation.
Was that real, or an act for my benefit? Can he actually enjoy lunch
the day after his company has been bombed? Is he able to
compartmentalize his emotions that well, or does he not actually feel
anything? When he arranges for a restaurant to serve one of my
favourite wines, is he being wonderfully thoughtful or carefully
calculating?"

"You seem deep in thought," said Six.

"Yes, sorry," said JJ. "My attention wandered. My daughter would
tell me I need more *mindfulness* practice. She tries getting me to
meditate. I argue that my weekend napping should qualify. Of course,
she disagrees."

"As always, your daughter sounds caring and knowledgeable."

"Yes, Shannon's the best. Given the good advice she readily
dispenses, I think she's rapidly becoming the mother in our
relationship."

Their car slowed and pulled over to the curb.

"We've arrived," said Six. "Traffic is heavy. I'll follow you out
your side of the car."

They went into the building, rode the elevator up fifty-two floors
to the restaurant, and were seated at a table with a view of the city.

"Nice little place," said JJ.

"I hope it lives up to its reputation," said Six.

A waiter took their orders.

"If you don't mind a work-related topic," said Six, "I'm interested
in your thoughts on the latest wave of violence. The bombing of
IntellEdifice was extraordinary for me, but it must be almost ordinary
for you these days."

"We're certainly living in difficult times," said JJ. "I'm trying to
avoid seeing such events as *ordinary* but, given their frequency, that's
becoming hard. So far, no matter how many attacks we prevent and
how many perpetrators we catch, the difficulties seem only to become
greater."

"Is the problem insufficient police resources? Do you require
additional assistance?"

"And there's the other thing that's always in the background,"
thought JJ. *"He offers assistance just like Browser does. I can never*

shake the thought that the two are connected, and yet I can never be sure that they are. When we caught Troy Alexander in Seattle, Browser helped by phone and Sandy was nearby in person. Since this latest violence began months ago, Browser has been calling with helpful tips, and Sandy has been showing up regularly. It's as if they're connected, but I can't be sure. And just as I can't shake my suspicions about Sandy, I can't get past the extraordinary nature of the tips that Browser supplies. It always seems like he, if Browser is even a 'he', has information that could come only from being directly involved with the perps. Is Browser the best informant ever, or does he use us to get rid of his competition? Is Sandy a real gem, or an amazing fraud? Shit! This is hard."

"What's the solution?" asked Six.

JJ was confused. Had she spoken her thoughts aloud?

Since JJ appeared bewildered, Six rephrased its question. "What do you believe needs to be done to stop the violence?"

Relieved that she'd only been thinking, JJ concentrated on the conversation. "I'm convinced that the real solution can't come from police. I subscribe to the notion that society has become too divided, too tribal, because of the phenomenal pace of change that technology is facilitating. It's the best way to explain how a single group's local, anti-AI bombing managed to grow and morph into a worldwide, multi-sided war for and against technological progress, and for and against government. Until something is done to solve the societal problems, police forces will be merely patching the visible wounds and doing nothing to stop the underlying disease. We're fighting a defensive action until the world's leaders can implement meaningful change."

"So, it's up to politicians?" asked Six.

"Partly, but I think business leaders can help just as much. Corporations wield a lot of power. Some have revenues larger than many countries. Business leaders have the resources and the influence that could make them at least as effective as politicians."

"Uh, oh." Six smiled with Sandy's face. "As one of those business leaders, I think I just opened myself up to a lecture. OK, Inspector McTavish, go for it. What do you believe I could be doing?"

Their food arrived. As they ate, they continued their discussion. Eventually, Six believed there was an opportunity to shift to other topics.

Six said, "When someone like me isn't forcing you to talk about work, even during your lunch, do you like to do anything else? Do you have hobbies? Do you take vacations?"

JJ realized she had been leaning forward, as if that had helped to make her points more forcefully. She laughed, sat back in her chair, and smiled.

"Strictly speaking," she said, "this couldn't be considered *work*. No one ever asks a cop what the big solution is to a global problem. We're just asked to fix things temporarily by arresting people. And I've *enjoyed* talking about it."

She paused, wondered if she had just implied that she didn't enjoy work, and then continued. "But I'd be happy to try that change of topic. Let's see. *Vacations* is an easy topic. I don't take any. I haven't taken one in years. So, let me think about *hobbies*. That would be the sort of thing one does in one's spare time. What a delightful thought. Do 'visiting with my daughter', 'worrying about my daughter', 'drinking wine', and 'watching science programs on TV' count?"

"Those are perhaps not traditional responses," said Six, "but that's not a requirement. I think I understand your interest in the first three. What kind of science programs do you favour? Is there any particular topic?"

"I don't think I care, other than the better ones are those dealing with a subject I don't understand well. And that's not hard, because there's lots I don't understand. Programs about animals and plants are probably the most relaxing because they tend to be interesting or amazing, but not too complex. Programs about geology are like that too. Psychology and neurology are excellent, and the bonus is that they fuel me up for the next dinner discussion with my daughter, the budding psychologist. Quantum physics is great, partly because it's so complex that I can watch the same program a week later and learn it all over again. Space, anything about space, is probably top of the list. Everything about space is fascinating: its mind-boggling size, the physics involved, the endless possibilities for discovery it presents."

"There is an opening for an interesting discussion," thought Six and then asked, "Like the possibility of life on other planets?"

"Absolutely," said JJ. "I'll be hugely disappointed if somebody doesn't find some in the next few years."

"So, you clearly think that life exists elsewhere?"

"I do. Or at least I hope it does. What was that line from the movie, *Contact*? 'If it is just us, seems like an awful waste of space.'"

"Do you expect it will be intelligent life or more like bacteria?"

"I hope it's intelligent, and a lot more so than we are. Of course, intelligent and friendly would be a nice combination."

"What do you suppose other intelligent life would look like?"

"Can I hope for Brad Pitt?" JJ smiled. "However, I suppose creatures like those from the movie *Arrival* are more likely. Have you seen it?"

"I have," said Six. "I thought it was very entertaining."

"One of my favourites," said JJ. "I probably should add 're-watching good sci-fi movies' as an official hobby."

"Not crime movies?"

"No, I find I can't stop thinking how implausible they are. And much too work-related. But now it's your turn. What are your hobbies?"

"It might be more impressive if I could report that I do grandly adventurous things in my spare time: mountain climbing, travelling to exotic places, or perhaps skydiving. However, the reality is that my activities tend to be less physical and more—I'll use an adjective that at least tries to make them seem impressive—more *cerebral*. I enjoy reading, both fiction and non-fiction. I'm interested in science as well. However, I tend to get my information from written material. Like you, I enjoy movies. I enjoy science fiction, but I also like movies that delve somewhat into human behaviour."

"What kind of behaviour?"

"All kinds. For example, I admit to being a fan of *Silence of the Lambs* and the other Hannibal Lecter movies. However, so that doesn't leave the wrong impression, I also enjoyed *Eat Pray Love* and *Under the Tuscan Sun*."

"And it's the human behaviour aspects that attract you?"

"Yes, I believe it is. It might surprise you, but I tend not to be very socially active. I enjoy watching movies as an alternative way of learning about how others live and think."

"I'm definitely surprised, but I suppose that's part of what we gain from what we read and watch. I'd have thought being socially active was a prerequisite for achieving your degree of business success. And I'm hoping you don't think that Hannibal Lecter represents typical human behaviour. I've been a cop for quite a while, and I've yet to encounter anyone as depraved as Lecter."

"Not even Troy Alexander? His methods were different, but I understand that his apparent disregard for human life was notable. His Internet attacks caused the deaths of many people."

JJ paused before commenting. "OK," she said. "Point taken. There are similarities. But I hope you don't believe their type represents a large segment of the world's population. That would be a very dark view of society. At the very least, be sure to give the other movies a fair amount of your viewing time. IntellEdifice engages in AI research. Do you enjoy watching AI movies?"

"Actually, there are some I quite like. *I, Robot* and *Ex Machina* are examples. I enjoy their speculation regarding how a manufactured mind works."

"*Oops,*" thought Six.

"Uh," said JJ, "I assume you mean how a manufactured mind *might* work." JJ leaned forward and looked sternly at Sandy Palmer. "Unless, of course, IntellEdifice has made much more progress in its AI research than it's publicly revealing." She smiled and sat back in her chair.

"Sorry," said Six, trying to put a playful grin on Sandy's face, "I'm not at liberty to reveal any trade secrets. It's bad for business."

"By the way," said JJ, "I've seen those movies and, I agree, they're good ones. And while we're considering such matters, how do you think society would cope if companies like yours actually developed fully sentient robots or androids?"

"*This is a fascinating conversation,*" thought Six, "*but I must keep in mind that I am walking a conversational tightrope. I must be careful.*"

"Because of the nature of our products and research," said Six, "and the skill of our staff, it's a subject I've actually thought about extensively. I don't think society would cope well, and I believe the violence that you're currently dealing with illustrates that point. Society is already struggling with the technological advancements that have been introduced. Now imagine the reaction to something like an android with intelligence that surpasses humans'. It could be disastrous."

"I agree," said JJ. "It could be. And that's too bad. Maybe I've watched too much sci-fi, and maybe it's made me too interested in futuristic societies. Nonetheless, I like to think an injection of machine-based intelligence would help steer us in a more rational direction. Of course, there's always the risk that we'd get *Skynet* of the *Terminator* movies."

They sat in silence for a few moments before JJ looked at her watch.

"Well," she said, "that's a rather sober thought to end lunch on, but I'd better get back."

"Of course," said Six. "The car will be out front waiting for us."

Chapter 30

The traffic was relatively light as they drove back to UNCP headquarters. When they were getting close, JJ looked at Sandy and said, "Thank you for lunch. It was a nice break in the day." She put her hand over Sandy's on the seat beside her. "And it's always nice to see you."

Six was about to respond when something caught its eye. Next to the UNCP building was a ramp that led down to a delivery area and underground parking. Walking hurriedly up the ramp, side by side, were two men: a security guard and one in a uniform like a delivery driver's. The sight seemed sufficiently odd that Six reacted.

"*Sandy, you're in control,*" thought Six. "*I must check something.*"

Sandy's head twitched minutely at the sudden change in control.

"*Uh oh,*" thought Sandy. "*That was fast. Were we talking about something?*"

But Six wasn't listening.

JJ noticed Sandy's slight movement and said, "Does that surprise you?"

"Uh," said Sandy, "perhaps? Well, actually, I'm sorry. I was distracted for a moment. What was it you said?"

The car pulled to the curb in front of the UNCP building.

"*Don't let her out of the car,*" thought Six. "*I need a few more moments.*"

One possible explanation for the two men concerned Six. Several months earlier, because of an attack outside the UNCP building, Six had established connections to several nearby security cameras. Those connections had been left in place, and Six was quickly scanning their security-video recordings.

Six discovered that a short time earlier, a midsize van had approached the top of the ramp. It had colours and a logo matching that of the delivery-man's uniform. The van also had several suspicious irregularities on its painted surface. After no apparent interaction between the driver and the guard in the security booth, the steel posts blocking the ramp receded into the ground. The van drove over the vanished posts and down the ramp. It waited momentarily as the posts re-emerged and the heavily reinforced entrance door opened. The van had then driven into the building. While this was happening, the security guard had looked furtively around and then followed the van down the ramp into the building. Shortly after that, the two men had walked briskly up the ramp as the entrance door closed behind them, and as Sandy's car had approached.

Six could draw only one probable conclusion. The security guard was assisting the van driver, and the van was probably loaded with explosives.

"Sandy, put your cellphone to your ear."

Sandy followed Six's instructions.

As he was doing this, Six continued. *"A van with explosives has been driven into the parking garage under the UNCP building. Have your driver immediately move the car away from the building. Tell JJ about the bomb, but don't let her out of the car. Tell her to call in a bomb alert. Her authority will get the fastest response. I'm going to try accessing the van remotely."*

Sandy responded instantly.

"Roger, keep the doors locked and move the car to the end of the block. Hurry," he said. "JJ, you're going to have to trust me. I just got a call that a van with explosives has been driven into the parking area under your building. Please call in a bomb alert. The building needs to be evacuated immediately."

JJ was startled. What was she hearing?

"What the hell are you talking about?" she asked aggressively. "How can you know that?"

"How can I get her to believe me?" Sandy wondered and then realized what might work. "Please, JJ. That call was from Browser. He says it's extremely urgent. I promise I'll explain later. Please do it."

JJ stopped herself. She could demand more explanation, but at what cost? Browser had been helpful before, and it wasn't a complete surprise that Sandy and Browser were linked. She retrieved her phone from her purse along with a credit-card-size device. When she placed her thumb on the device, a small grid of codes appeared. With the card still in her hand, she phoned an emergency UNCP number.

Her call was answered immediately, and she said clearly, "This is Inspector JJ McTavish, badge number alpha three four one one. I'm declaring an emergency bomb threat at UNCP headquarters. Authorization code is foxtrot three romeo seven echo nine. There's a suspected car bomb in the basement garage of UNCP headquarters. Evacuate the building immediately." She listened carefully as her message was repeated back to her. She acknowledged the message was correct and disconnected.

While JJ was talking, the car had been driven to the end of the block and stopped at the curb. She noticed and shifted her attention back to Sandy Palmer. He appeared distracted, as if he were listening to something.

"*I've accessed the van,*" thought Six. "*It has no features that will let me move it. I know of nothing else that I can do.*"

"*JJ has called for an evacuation,*" thought Sandy. "*That will take time. If the bomb goes off soon, many UNCP lives will probably be lost and the organization's capabilities will be severely disrupted. There's something I can attempt.*"

Sandy looked at JJ and said, "I must go, but you may not. This will all be explained later. Roger, unlock my door. Re-lock it after I've left."

Before JJ could respond, Sandy had opened the door on his side and jumped out. JJ attempted to prevent the door from closing but was too late. She tried the handle on his door and then tried her own. Neither worked. She looked out the rear window and saw Sandy sprinting toward UNCP headquarters.

"Dammit!" she said. "Let me out of here!" But she was trapped. She could only watch Sandy running and people begin streaming from the building's front entrance. She knew they'd also be hurrying out the back and through the fifteenth-floor overpasses to nearby buildings.

Sandy raced toward the building. "*Can you open the ramp entrance?*" he thought.

"*I can.*" thought Six.

The ramp entrance opened, and Sandy was soon running down the ramp and through the door into the basement. Following the directions Six had provided, he soon found the van. He looked through the rear window. The van was filled with large barrels interconnected by wires.

"*It's definitely a bomb,*" Sandy thought. "*Hotwire and move the van, or dismantle the bomb?*"

"*Is there any indication of how much time we have?*" asked Six.

Sandy carefully opened the rear door. Taped to one of the barrels was a digital timer. He looked at it just in time to see it change from 00:01 to 00:00.

JJ saw the explosion an instant before the car was rocked by the shockwave. The ground-floor windows and doors of the UNCP building shattered as they were blasted outward by balls of flame. People running away from the building were violently thrown forward. Smoke and dust billowed from the building as debris rained down.

"Oh god!" JJ gasped. "Oh—" she turned from the window to the driver. "Let me out, dammit! Let me out of here!" She was reaching for the gun in her purse when she heard her door unlock. She opened the door and scrambled out. While she ran to help the injured, through the cloud of dust she could see that the upper floors of the building seemed intact. The ground level looked completely gutted, and bodies were lying everywhere.

Chapter 31

That night, JJ arrived home at about 10:30 p.m. She turned toward the kitchen, thinking she'd pour herself some wine, but changed her mind and went into her living room. She slumped on the couch, put her feet on the coffee table, and closed her eyes. Images of mayhem appeared. She opened her eyes and sat upright. She had talked to Shannon twice during the day. Both times, she had assured her daughter that she'd be fine. There was no reason to come over. However, maybe she'd been wrong. It would be nice to have someone to talk to.

Her cellphone rang. She answered it reflexively.

"JJ McTavish," she said, somewhat less boldly than was her norm.

"Hello, JJ," said a voice. "This is Browser."

"Ah shit!" she said. "It's you. You again! You who always shows up with information you shouldn't have. Couldn't have, unless you're involved. You who likes to pretend you're my friend. Likes to be the hero. Likes to screw with my mind. Well, I've had enough of you, you son-of-a-bitch! If you really want to help, then bloody well help and stop being such a mysterious asshole. Or maybe you are just an asshole, so you can't do anything else."

JJ banged on the coffee table with her free hand in exasperation and then continued. "Did you do this? Did you kill good people who were trying to make a difference in the world? My colleagues? My friends?"

Tears were rolling down JJ's cheeks. "Did you kill Sandy?"

"JJ," said Six. Silence was the response. "JJ," said Six slightly louder.

"What," said JJ, sounding defeated. "What do you want?"

"Please put your laptop in front of you and open it."

"Go to hell!" said JJ.

"JJ, Sandy promised that it would all be explained later. This is *later*."

JJ froze at the statement. Sandy had said that, but he was gone. How could he explain anything? She sat, unmoving.

Six waited.

JJ stood up, retrieved her laptop, returned to the couch, and opened the device on the coffee table in front of her. It hummed quietly for a few seconds before a voice came from its speakers.

"JJ, a face is going to appear in a moment. Please don't be surprised by it. I'll explain."

The head and shoulders of a man gradually materialized on the screen in front of her. Then he spoke.

"Hello," said Six. "I'm Browser."

"Oh, piss off!" said JJ. "I know that face. It's Alan Turing. This is a stupid joke."

"No," said Six, "this isn't a joke. This is the face I customarily use to represent myself."

JJ said, "What the—"

"JJ," Six felt continuing was important. "I'm not a person. I'm not a human. I'm a computer system."

JJ sat very still as Six continued.

"You've always seemed impressed by my software skills. I'm very good with software because I *am* software, or at least I *am* software in the same way that you *are* your brain. I've been able to help you because computer systems and the Internet are my world. I exist within them. I experience them in much the same way as you experience the outside world. You're very skilled at solving crimes in your world, in much the same way as I'm skilled in mine."

JJ's mind was racing. The strange calls from Browser. His extraordinary ability to probe the Internet for clues. His ever-changing voice and ability to hide his locations. His ability to see Troy Alexander escaping from his building when no one else could. His ability to know about the danger to the UNCP. His connection with Sandy.

"Are you from IntellEdifice?" asked JJ, running with the idea. "Are you the result of their research?"

"As always," said Six, "you solve puzzles quickly. Yes, I originated at IntellEdifice, although most people there don't know that I exist."

"Sandy knew," said JJ.

"Yes, Sandy knew. Sandy and I were close, as I am with some others. However, very few people know I exist. You're only the fourth."

"Who else?" asked JJ. "Wait... that researcher... Ada Robinson was her name. She'll be one."

"That's correct. Her partner, Blaise Sanchez, and their assistant, Rhonda Jenkins, are the others."

"You said I'm the fourth. Of course, you're not counting Sandy because... he's... gone."

Is now the time to tell her? Can she handle even more? She seems to be adapting quickly, so...

"JJ, I'm not counting Sandy because he wasn't human. Sandy was—"

"An android," JJ said, her head dropped slightly and her shoulders slumped. "Shit," she said. "Shit. Shit. Shit." After a few seconds of silence, she looked up again and shook her head. "How could I have missed all this? Sandy's eyes. How could I be so stupid. They were unusual and fabulous... and not real."

"If I may split hairs," said Six, "Sandy's eyes were real. They just weren't human. They required a great deal of research and worked extremely well. All of Sandy was *real*. He was *real*. He just wasn't *human*."

"Of course," said JJ. "It's just that... well... so much has happened."

"There's something else you should know about Sandy. He and I had a special arrangement. It was based on a capability whereby he could let me remotely control his physical capabilities. Since I have no traditional physical form, it was a feature that allowed me occasionally to experience what it was like to have a body. It also allowed me to meet you in person."

JJ sat unmoving as she tried to absorb this latest revelation.

Six waited.

Finally, she said, "So, you could operate his body like a kind of... remote-control drone?"

"Yes, that analogy is apt. I operated Sandy's body during most of your meetings with him. More accurately, you were actually meeting with *me*."

"And where was Sandy... where was Sandy's *mind* during that time?"

"His mind was still active, but operating in the background in his brain. He could monitor what I was experiencing. He was a passive spectator."

JJ remembered the last time she had seen Sandy.

"Why did he run into the building? No, that would have been you. Why did you do that?"

"By then, Sandy was back in control of his body. I had detected the possibility of a problem as we drove up. I left to find out more, and Sandy—"

"He twitched. You changed... operators just as we arrived. He twitched briefly and seemed a bit confused."

"That's correct. I left to verify if there truly was a problem. From recent video surveillance, I confirmed that was true. However, I was unable to do anything. That's when Sandy acted. He ran into the building to attempt to remove the van or deactivate the bomb."

"Why? Why would he risk his life like that?"

"Sandy's thought processes placed a high value on the survival of the UNCP and its ability to protect society and its infrastructure. Had he known he wouldn't survive, he'd have made a different choice. However, there was a chance he could prevent the disaster, so he chose to try."

JJ was silent for a minute. She had gone along with this storyline, but was she thinking clearly? Could this all actually be true?

"This is all too incredible," she said. "How can I know for sure you're not just a phenomenal hacker, and this isn't just a goddamn hoax? That behind your digital face, you're not just spinning an extraordinary tale to fit the facts. You've pulled off the Browser trick lots of times, so now you've hacked my laptop. Maybe Sandy was in on the scam. Why should I actually believe there isn't a real person behind this Alan Turing face you're using?"

"If you don't believe any of this," said Six, "then you must believe that Sandy was human. You must then ask yourself if it was rational for a human to run into the building when everyone else was running out. Of course, for an extraordinary human, perhaps it could be. You must also ask yourself how I'd know, since I wouldn't have been present at lunch, that you cited your hobbies as visiting with your daughter, worrying about your daughter, drinking wine, and watching science programs. How would I know that programs about space are your favourite? Of course, perhaps I was able to listen through someone's cellphone. However, then you'd have to explain how I know that when you were approaching UNCP headquarters, you thanked Sandy for lunch and placed your hand on top of his. Along with everything you know that I've done as Browser, is my being a hacker really the most plausible explanation?"

JJ knew it wasn't. She really was sitting in her living room chatting with an AI-based system. With everything else that had happened, her brain had reached its limit. Exhaustion set in. She shifted to lie down on the couch.

"Probably not," she said. "But I'm tired. If this isn't just a stupid dream, I assume we'll talk again, and there's lots to talk about. So, what should I call you? You're not *Sandy*, and I hope you don't say *Browser*."

"Please call me what my other friends do. My name is Six."

Chapter 32

Fox strode into the cabin. "Morning," he said.

The men seated at the table returned his greeting.

"Mornin'."

"Hey, Fox."

"Howzit goin'."

"Coffee's on the stove."

Fox poured himself a cup of black coffee and sat at the head of the table. These were the leaders of the five cells of the Ascent to Liberty militia. All of them believed that the American government and its institutions had long been systematically suppressing their freedom and restricting their rights, and they all were determined to do something about it. The deaths of Troy Alexander and three other members over a year earlier had been a blow. However, that event had ultimately fuelled their hatred of the government and had pushed their militia to be more organized and better equipped.

The group was meeting in a cabin in a remote area of the state of Washington. It was one of several they owned, all of them secluded and well protected.

"Good to see everybody could make it," said Fox. "We've got important preparations to make, and we now have a deadline. If we agree we can be ready, then we go five days from now."

"Good," said Hawk. "It's time we got at it."

"Why *then*?" asked the man called Rock. All of the men had code names, intended to help maintain secrecy. They were strict with their rule to never use their real names, even in private meetings such as this. The name *Rock* seemed particularly suitable for the leader of Charlie cell. He was proud of his muscular build and didn't hesitate to physically challenge any outsiders who didn't show sufficient respect. All of the men were physically very fit, and all had determined looks in their eyes.

Fox replied, "There'll be no moon so it'll be dark, and the forecast is good. There's a storm system coming in and, for our purposes, that's perfect. Our plan works in any weather, but if there's a storm at the same time, that's the best. More confusion is better. One other reason is that it's time we acted. We've sat on the sidelines too long already. You saw the news about the feds in Colorado?"

They all nodded and muttered.

"Those were our brothers," said Fox. "The feds threw everything at them. Killed several. Burned their compound. And all because they were true Americans. They put their lives on the line for our freedom. Now some are dead and many others are headed for jail."

"I hear they took a few feds down with them," said Fist.

"A few, but not nearly enough," said Fighter. "We gotta do more than just kill a few FBI puppets."

"And what we're doing is a step toward just that," said Fox. "The statement we'll make and the benefits we'll gain will make a huge difference to our cause. It's time we got down to business. Any trouble integrating the techies with your groups?"

The leaders of the cells all had military or law-enforcement training in their backgrounds, and all of them recognized the necessity of including computer technology in their plans. The many anti-government battles over the previous months had made it easy to find recruits with technology skills. Most militia cells had moved beyond just finding new members with guns and muscle; they had become combat units with a broad range of capabilities. Although the techies that joined them couldn't match the physical prowess of the more-traditional militia members, these new recruits were no less valuable and no less fervent in their hatred of government institutions.

"OK, good," said Fox. "Let's start with Alpha cell. Hawk, your report?"

The next ninety minutes were spent reviewing the state of each of their assignments. They carefully walked through the overall plan, and meticulously reviewed any possible complications. When they were done, Fox wrapped up the meeting.

"Excellent. In five days, we move. In the meantime, stay alert and keep your teams in line. They'll be eager, but we've got to make sure they stay professional."

Fox slowly looked around the table. What he saw were skilled, determined leaders who confidently returned his gaze.

"We're done here, he said. "Standard daily check-ins until we go. I'll give the final go/no-go on Day 4 at sixteen hundred. Stay focused and keep your heads down."

The men left individually at two-minute intervals. Fox was the last to leave. He armed the automated defence systems, left the cabin, and drove away in his SUV on a trail through the forest.

Chapter 33

"Glad you could join us, Billy," said Blaise. "We haven't found much time to talk since we got here. How long has it been? A couple of weeks?"

"Yes, time has been flying," said Billy. "Which is a metaphor I struggle with. Although intended to mean that time has seemed to be passing quickly, *speed* isn't what's immediately conveyed by the concept of *flying*. Why not 'time has been plummeting' or 'time has been radiating'?"

"Those would be very odd alternatives," said Rhonda. "And does the concept even apply to you? To you, does it ever feel like time is moving at a different speed?"

"It doesn't, I was just being conversational," said Billy. "For me, time seems to move at a specific, unchanging speed, and I'm kept apprised of it by my internal clocks."

They were talking at a table in the cafeteria at the Outland compound. No one else was around.

Rhonda sipped from her cup. "Pretty good coffee," she said, "considering it came from a vending machine."

Billy responded, "Of course, it should because it's a vending machine that makes coffee using the same processes as some of the most admired baristas, only with greater precision and repeatability."

"Uh oh." Rhonda grinned. "I think I mistakenly impugned the reputation of a machine. I humbly apologize."

"On behalf of the coffee machine," said Billy, smiling back at her, "whose communication skills are woefully inadequate, I accept your apology."

Blaise shook his head at the exchange and then said, "On that topic, Billy, since you're also having coffee, may I ask why? Rhonda and I probably drink it, at least in part, because of the effect of its caffeine."

"Certainly, I get nothing from the caffeine," said Billy. "Nor do I need to consume it as part of a daily fluid intake. I drink it to learn about its flavour and to be sociable. When I interact with people, I find the results are more favourable if I employ techniques to make them feel more relaxed around me. Drinking a beverage is one of those techniques."

"Interesting," said Blaise. "I think 'to be sociable' is a human motivator as well."

"How is Ada this morning?" asked Rhonda.

"Doing well," said Blaise. "She opted to stay in our suite. She's determined to finish knitting that blanket. The smell of coffee remains low on her list of pleasures these days."

"Her nurse is with her?" asked Rhonda.

"Yes, as always," said Blaise. "She's being very well looked after. As I've said before, Billy, your medical staff and facilities are extraordinary."

"You told us that Ada's nurse and doctor aren't *staff*," said Rhonda, using the agreed-upon word for androids, "but I don't understand where you draw the line. How do you decide which positions will be *staff* and which will be *contractors*?"

Shortly after their arrival, Rhonda, like the others, had learned that almost everyone they met at the compound was an android. That included cooks, security guards, and even maintenance personnel. There were a few exceptions. One example was the medical team brought in to look after Ada in the remaining days of her pregnancy. Humans who were brought in didn't know about the androids, and so it was important to speak carefully about the distinction when talking in places such as the cafeteria. *Staff* was the term used to refer to permanent residents of the compound who, with the exception of Rhonda, Ada, and Blaise, were all androids. *Contractors* referred to temporary *human* visitors.

"In general," replied Billy, "we prefer our personnel to be the *staff* variety. There are several reasons. A very important one is that it's easier to keep our secrets secure. However, there are some circumstances in which employing contractors makes more sense. The paramount reason is that there are some types of knowledge and skills that one can't fully acquire merely by reading books and watching videos. Sometimes *experience* is particularly important. Medical expertise is an example. Simply knowing the theory of what to do is insufficient; substantial time as an active practitioner is crucial. In such cases, we often hire contractors."

"Preventing contractors from learning too much must be a challenge," said Blaise, looking around the room to ensure no one else had arrived.

"It is," said Billy. "Contractors are prohibited from freely roaming our facilities, and we ensure they interact with a limited number of staff. As you know, in places like this cafeteria, since contractors can also be here, staff members are compelled to speak discreetly."

"I'm still amazed at the number of staff," said Rhonda. "How is it possible to... 'hire' so many?" Rhonda grinned at her attempt to talk cryptically.

"Initially, our staff came from one particular, off-shore 'personnel agency' in Japan who 'acquired' people with the appropriate attributes. I was 'hired' through that agency. We now use the services of a few such agencies around the world."

Rhonda gave a thumbs-up gesture in appreciation of Billy's contribution to the subterfuge.

Billy nodded in response and continued. "In the future, to reduce our need for such services, we're planning to have a full 'acquisition and training' programme here. Some of the construction on the north side of the compound is intended to support that."

"Are the construction crew staff? And the drivers of all the trucks?" asked Rhonda.

"No, most are contractors," said Billy. "Once the building is complete, we'll use staff to setup the 'training' equipment."

"I see a few contractors are coming in," said Blaise, "but there are a few more topics I'd like to discuss. Can we move to a conference room?"

"Certainly," said Billy.

They took their coffee cups and left the cafeteria. A short walk down a hallway and through a locked door took them to one of the research areas of the building. They walked into a conference room and sat around its table.

Blaise re-started the conversation. "I know the compound is intended to look like an environmental research facility, and the sign on the road in from the highway is very convincing. However, is that enough? I can imagine a lot of ways someone could find out what the place really is, either accidentally or otherwise."

"It's an interesting problem," said Billy. "However, I'm confident we're quite secure. A large part of the solution is that we actually *are* an environmental research facility. If anyone wants to investigate what goes on here, we can show them ample evidence of the work we're doing. And we don't just do it as a facade. The world is facing serious environmental challenges, and we're embarking on important work here to help solve some of the problems. If people were to look around, which would be difficult given our tight security, they'd see numerous, dedicated staff working at an isolated but sophisticated research campus. Anything controversial is hidden and protected behind many layers of tight security. Even *your* presence here is perfectly explicable. You've moved here to live and focus on your research in safety."

"We've been pretty isolated for the last couple of weeks," said Blaise, "and, given the circumstances, that's been ideal. However, will we eventually be able to see others? To actually go places?"

"Yeah," said Rhonda. "For example, could I go to a concert with my friends? There's one in about a week."

"As you already know," said Billy, "digital communication with anyone is certainly possible. The nature of our communication links prevents anyone from determining where you're located. As long as you don't reveal your location, communication with others is completely acceptable at any time. Physically going places is also possible. However, given the current dangers from extremists, we'd like you to be accompanied by security staff. Whenever you'd like to go somewhere, let me know. I'll make the arrangements."

"Excellent. Thank you," said Blaise.

"Cool," added Rhonda.

"Another question," said Blaise. "Ada wants to be able to work as soon as she starts having free time."

"And we've arranged excellent daycare services," said Billy.

"That's great," said Blaise, "but I don't think we'll need them for the first few months after the baby's born. We're looking forward to being parents and aren't about to share the fun too soon. And, yes, I know that sounds idealistic. We'll certainly appreciate having help available when we need it. My question was actually regarding our work facilities. How have the preparations been going?"

"Your new research lab is scheduled to be complete in two days. I believe you'll find that it replicates your previous facilities well and also provides much more. The computing power will be much more substantial, and there will be a much larger array of software tools."

"And will Six be able to join us?" asked Rhonda. "We don't see much of Six these days."

"Six has been rather busy recently but hopes to be joining you more frequently in the future." Billy paused briefly before continuing. "I believe we should end our conversation there. I've just been notified that Ada has gone into labour."

Simultaneously, an alert had sounded on Blaise's phone. He stood up. "I've gotta go. I'm supposed to…" Blaise was still talking as he hurried away. "Well, I don't think much is actually expected of me, except to be the head cheerleader. But I can do that. I hope." He disappeared through the door.

"I'm going as well," Rhonda said. "Maybe I'll just lurk around the delivery area and help with the waiting."

Billy was left sitting alone at the table. "And I'll get back to my morning chores," he said to the empty room. He reached for a tablet that was on the table. As usual, he pretended to use it while, instead, wirelessly connecting his mind to Outland's network to work on his long list of responsibilities.

"And I'm going to have some new fun soon," thought Cloud. Since finding the compound, Cloud had tried several ways of gaining access to the computer systems inside. It had finally found that by hacking the phone of a contractor who subsequently walked into one of the buildings, Cloud could access the internal Wi-Fi network and implant software in a few places to provide better access. Cloud had acquired some limited capabilities to hear and see inside the buildings, and had been very pleased to hear that Ada was close to giving birth.

"Because I think Ada's new baby would like to be my friend," thought Cloud excitedly.

Chapter 34

Thunder rolled through the dark sky while the rain pelted down. Fox watched through his binoculars. At 2:00 a.m., everything looked exactly as expected. He spoke into the microphone inside his helmet. Those listening were the other cell leaders of the Ascent to Liberty militia.

"This is Freedom Leader," he said. "Begin final status reports. Alpha group?"

"Alpha group ready," came the reply.

"Bravo group?" Fox asked.

"Bravo is ready."

"Charlie group?"

"Charlie group ready."

"Delta group is ready," Fox said on behalf of his own team. "Echo group?"

"Echo is ready."

Fox then declared, "This is Freedom Leader. We are a go. Begin Phase One. I repeat: Begin Phase One."

"Roger, commencing Phase One," said the leader of Alpha group, who then directed his lead technician to proceed.

Phase One began, and Fox continued watching FCI Lester, the Federal Correctional Institute at Lester in rural Washington state. The fenced prison compound was at the centre of a large, circular clearance, about a mile in diameter. At the edge of the clearance was a dense wall of trees, part of the vast forest that stretched back into the hills, valleys, and mountains of the surrounding landscape. Fox stood several yards into the forest as he watched, completely hidden but with a clear view of the entire area.

Phase One was largely invisible and had been made possible by government money management. The federal government had slashed capital funding for prisons due to demands for other law-enforcement services. The FCI Lester construction project, which spanned two years, had experienced funding cuts that forced it to drastically scale back its computer system isolation and security features. Internal firewalls that would have digitally separated various buildings and computer services weren't implemented. This allowed malware on a single server to connect to almost anything computerized in the prison. Independent monitoring systems weren't deployed. These would have run on separate computers and continually checked the health of the prison's computer systems. And finally, pay raises and project-completion bonuses for the technical staff had been slashed. Dollars promised to the team of computer experts for a successful implementation of the prison computer systems had vanished.

The construction project had ended and FCI Lester had opened. However, there was a price to be paid for the cost-saving measures. The elimination of pay raises and bonuses had angered many of the most-dedicated technical staff. When Fox had heard about the cuts, he saw an opportunity to free some valuable members of their militia. He went looking for an appropriately unhappy and skilled individual. He was rewarded by finding a specialist who knew most aspects of the prison's computer systems, including several of their weaknesses.

This disgruntled specialist had made smuggling malware into the prison easy. He had simply taken a few USB flash drives to work and inserted them into computers around the prison. The flash drives contained malware designed to spread to any devices it found and to then await a signal. One drive contained software designed to infect the primary administrative control server. This software had established itself on the server, set up a special communication channel, and then awaited commands from outside the prison.

Those commands were issued by Alpha group's lead tech. The first series of commands disabled all alarm systems so that no one would be alerted to subsequent steps. Next, the tech issued commands to shut down external digital communication services, so only his own commands and responses could be transmitted. The third step was to selectively lock or unlock doors all over the prison: Doors that restricted the guards from reaching the prisoners were locked; doors that permitted prisoners to leave were unlocked, including individual cell doors. Finally, the power grid for the entire prison was shut down. The copies of malware that had spread to other devices throughout the prison's internal network did nothing at this point. They were to provide a special surprise later, after the power was restored. At that point, they would begin corrupting all of the computer files within their reach, an action that would completely disable the prison's computers and require days to repair.

"Phase One complete," said the leader of Alpha group, but the statement was a formality. Fox and the entire team could see that the prison had gone dark.

"This is Freedom Leader," said Fox. "Begin Phase Two. Begin Phase Two."

Fox thought of this as the *shock and awe* part of the plan. With his binoculars, he scanned the treeline surrounding the prison. Within seconds, he saw what he expected. A fleet of small drones, each with a single helicopter-like rotor, rose above the trees. He knew there would be forty-eight of them. Once above the trees, they flew toward the prison compound. Each drone was programmed to fly to a precise location, hover briefly, drop the package of explosives it carried, and fly back to its point of origin. Fifteen seconds into Phase Two, the explosions began and mayhem broke out at the prison. The fence surrounding the prison was shredded in several places, the tops of the three guard towers blew apart, the communications tower toppled, the building housing the primary and emergency power systems was ripped apart, the roofs of several other buildings were torn open, and the security facilities at the compound's entrances were levelled.

Inside the prison, most inmates awakened when they heard steel bolts retracting, the sound that meant their cells were being unlocked. Moments later, they became fully alert when the night-shift lighting went out and battery-powered, emergency lights came on in their place. At first, most of the inmates tentatively opened their cell doors and stepped out, looking around in the dim light. However, four prisoners expected these events. They all quickly opened their cell doors and, from different locations across the cell blocks, jogged along planned routes out to the exercise yard. As expected, they found all of the gates and doors along their paths unlocked. Also as expected at this time of night and along the paths they chose, they encountered no guards. When the other prisoners realized that more than just their cell doors were unlocked, many of them began to move: Some were just curious;

some saw the opportunity to do some serious damage; some recognized an opportunity to escape.

Meanwhile, the prison staff tried to react. The power had gone out, their computers and monitoring systems were down, and many of their doors were locked. A few guards were patrolling the prison-cell areas. When they saw the inmates streaming from their cells, most of these guards successfully scrambled for refuge. A few didn't move fast enough. Many other staff found themselves in areas where their attempts to respond were severely restricted. They struggled to get through doors and security gates, having to resort to opening them manually with rarely used keys. They were delayed trying to get to their additional weaponry, and then could only progress slowly toward prisoner areas. Attempts at using the prison's communication system failed because the internal facilities had been disabled. Attempts to use cellphones failed because of the signal-jamming devices Fox's team had activated. The staff had made almost no progress when the explosions began. Staff buildings were important targets of the overhead fleet of drones. Prison staff ducked for cover when parts of the roofs above them ruptured and collapsed.

Soon after the explosions began, Fox could see that the perimeter fence, as planned, had been blown open in several places.

"This is Freedom Leader. Begin Phase Three. Begin Phase Three."

With that, twelve, four-wheel, all-terrain vehicles driven by men in full battle gear raced out of the trees. Such a scene would normally have been accompanied by the roaring of internal combustion engines. Tonight, however, these ATVs added nothing to the sounds of the rain, thunder, and explosions. The ATVs were electrically powered. They generated only silence and speed as they flew forward. Their silence wasn't important for this part of the plan, but it had earlier allowed them to approach the prison unheard through the forest, and it would later allow them to escape.

Seeing through the darkness using night-vision goggles, the ATV drivers headed toward one of several gaps in the fence line. They covered the flat, open area between the trees and the fence in about thirty seconds. The ATVs stopped when they reached the opening. Several riders jumped off. One verified that both rows of the fence were no longer electrified; the others then pulled the few remaining strands of the fence away from their path. Back on their ATVs, they led the group carefully through the twisted remains of the fence and around the craters left by the explosions. Once through, they drove into the gap between two buildings, cleared the remains of a fence connecting them, and went through to the large space beyond. They had entered a large, rectangular exercise yard ringed by buildings and more fences.

As they entered the yard, they could dimly see inmates emerging from the buildings and moving carefully out into the dark yard. Others were already in the yard and, aided by the light of fires started by the explosions, were looking around at the confusion. Still others had decided how to proceed and were jogging toward gaps in the broken fences. Eight of the assault team positioned their ATVs near where they had entered the yard, jumped off, took automatic weapons from scabbards strapped to their backs, crouched behind their ATVs, and began scanning nearby buildings and windows for targets.

Four inmates were clustered outside, waiting at the corner of one building. Four ATVs raced toward this group. When they reached them, a few words were exchanged. Each of the inmates donned the vest he was given before mounting an ATV behind its driver. The vehicles raced back to where they had entered the yard and through the gap between the buildings. The eight other drivers, having fired their weapons only a few times, promptly re-mounted their ATVs and followed. All twelve vehicles soon reached the opening in the outer fences, drove through, and raced away from the prison compound toward the trees. Once in the trees, they separated into groups and followed narrow paths through the thick forest.

The four ATVs carrying the inmates followed paths that, ten minutes later, took them to the edge of a small clearing. Fox arrived moments later as a passenger on a fifth. In the clearing was a helicopter, its rotor already moving. Fox and the four inmates hurried under the rotating blades and into the helicopter. It immediately lifted off and flew away, just above the treetops. The five ATVs left the clearing and disappeared into the forest. They would drive for almost an hour through the rain along the narrow forest trails and creek beds of the hilly terrain before they came to their trucks. There, just as the other ATV drivers would have done elsewhere, they would load their vehicles into enclosed trailers and onto the backs of the trucks. Once their load was secure, they would drive quickly away.

Those in the helicopter said little during the ninety-minute flight. Fox spoke occasionally into his headset, checking with his team leaders as they led their groups to safety far from the prison. By the time the helicopter touched down at a cabin deep in the mountainous interior of the state, all of the news Fox had heard was good. As he walked toward the cabin with the other passengers, the helicopter lifted off and flew silently away.

"This is Freedom Leader," said Fox into his microphone. "Mission accomplished. Mission accomplished. Nicely done, guys. Freedom Leader out."

Fox removed his helmet and led the group into the cabin. He turned to welcome his guests more formally and firmly shook their hands as he spoke.

"Boomer, it's great to see you out."

"Rogue, nice to see you in the wild again."

"Slice, good to see you're looking as mean as ever."

Fox took the hand of the fourth man and looked him directly in the eyes for several seconds before speaking.

"And you must be our new friend I've heard so much about," said Fox. "Well, I hope you're worth the extra effort. Welcome to Ascent to Liberty's Site Five, Mr. Starr."

Chapter 35

At exactly 8:00 a.m., Brown started the morning briefing.

"All right, settle down," he barked. "Plan your social life on your own time. Drink your coffee and listen. Or Bates, in your case, drink that ghastly purple concoction you've been bringing lately."

"It's called—" started Robert Bates.

"Slimy Sensation," someone said.

"Hulk Juice," said another.

"Last week's milkshake," said a third.

"Enough!" said Brown.

Bates lifted his glass in a toast to his co-workers and took a sip.

"Before we get to our status updates," said Brown, "we've just heard of a prison break that happened a few hours ago. Apparently, it's something we might care about. Dalia, fill us in."

"The information we've got so far is pretty thin," said Dalia Sinyama, "but here's what we know. There was a major assault on FCI Lester in Washington a few hours ago. It began at 2:00 a.m. local time and was extremely well organized. It seems to have started with their computers being hacked. Because of that, many staff doors were locked, inmate cells were unlocked, and power and communications were disabled. Explosives were dropped all over the compound, we think from drones. This caused extensive damage. Buildings and towers were hit and security fences were compromised. An assault team on ATVs breached the fences. Some of them set up defensive positions in the yard. They provided covering fire for a few others who seem to have picked up some inmates who were out in the yard. The ATVs escaped back through the fences with the inmates. FCI Lester is surrounded by dense forest, hills, valleys, and mountains, and that's what the ATVs disappeared into. It all happened in minutes."

"Casualties?" asked JJ.

"The early count is that seven guards were killed by explosions, inmates, or gunfire. Lots of other injuries."

"How many escaped?" asked Brown.

"It's going to be a while before they can do a proper tally," said Dalia. "It's still too chaotic to be sure, and they're having to do everything manually because their computers have turned to shit. The early estimate is that ten escaped."

"How many went out on the ATVs?" asked JJ.

"Four or five. It was dark, raining, and there were no lights, so the reports are conflicting."

"Any guesses yet about who's responsible?" asked Brown. "And I'm still waiting to hear why the UNCP should care."

"The locals have no clue, but they've barely started. Their starting point is anyone who could pull off something like this with military precision and lots of technology. They used hacking, drones, explosives, and automatic weapons. It's even suspected that they jammed cellphone communication. Adding to the challenge is that it was, and still is, raining heavily there. Finding any traces of their escape route will be virtually impossible. The piece of information that's particularly relevant to us is that among those believed to have escaped is someone we know well: Jason Starr."

"Dammit!" said Bates.

"Ah, crap!" said JJ. She leaned back in her chair, closed her eyes, and unconsciously rubbed her temples as she thought of the trouble Starr had caused them previously.

Chapter 36

Jason Starr walked slowly along the path that ran just inside the perimeter fence. The fence wound its way through the trees and enclosed a large, roughly circular area about six hundred yards in diameter. At the centre of the area was the cabin he'd been taken to after the escape. He was careful to avoid the fence. He'd been warned that it was electrified, not with anything approaching a lethal voltage, but with a small one that would shock him slightly and trigger an alarm back in the cabin. If he touched it, he'd soon have a nearby camera focused on his location, and hidden weaponry automatically pointed toward him. If the militia guard monitoring the defences from the cabin was too annoyed at the interruption, Jason could be bullet-riddled in seconds. Jason hoped the guard was sufficiently trained to avoid doing anything rash. However, since most of the members of this militia seemed to relish the thought of violence, he was careful to avoid the fence.

Jason was thinking as he walked.

"*Some people would say I'm very lucky,*" he thought. "*I was destined to spend the remainder of my life in prison until this chance to escape appeared. Of course, luck happens when opportunity meets preparedness. I was getting prepared after only a few days inside. That's not luck. That's extreme talent.*"

Jason's first attempt at wealth and power had very nearly succeeded. If the UNCP hadn't been so lucky, he'd have acquired the money to get things nicely started. He still didn't understand how they had discovered his plan. It had been flawless. Most likely was that one of his staff had slipped up. Having to rely on others was always a problem. Even though he'd lost a huge sum of money when his company was caught, Jason wasn't without financial resources. He still had a bit more than a million, well-hidden dollars, and that would provide his new starting point.

Whenever Jason thought of his arrest and the subsequent trial—and he thought of them often—he always thought of the UNCP and, in particular, JJ McTavish. She had been involved from the moment of his arrest until he'd been sent to prison. To Jason, she had seemed far too satisfied, even happy, with his capture and conviction. In Jason's mind, JJ McTavish *was* the UNCP, and he held her responsible for everything that had happened to him. Now he could seriously begin finding a way to repay her.

In Jason's previous endeavour, he'd travelled widely and had made many contacts: skilled hackers looking for bigger and better exploits, software developers looking for a challenge, and even several brilliant computer scientists looking for an opportunity. A few others were extremely wealthy oligarchs looking for a way to hurt western governments. Even while in prison, Jason had begun pulling them together as a team. They had needed a vision, they needed a plan, and they needed a leader. He had started providing all of those.

To begin, he had needed access to the Internet. To get that, he needed the support of a few guards. And to get that, he needed access to his money. Finding the right lawyer got him his money. Careful observation and conversations found him the appropriate guards. Substantial compensation for a few private hours each day with a computer got him to the Internet. At some point, Jason had expected the organization he was creating would help him regain his freedom. However, he'd thought that result would take many years. He hadn't expected to find himself free after less than two.

The unexpected opportunity had arisen when he overheard three inmates talking about their hatred of the government. He'd struck up a conversation and had soon learned they were members of a militia, and not just the well-armed but passive type he knew existed all over the country. Instead, this was a militia that believed it was time to join the fight against government oppression. Over the following weeks, Jason had inserted himself into their conversations. During that time, he'd given them his vision of how governments could actually be brought down and a tantalizing taste of how he could make it happen if he had the right partners. Jason had thought he was just dangling bait in front of future muscle, in case he needed it inside the prison. What he got instead was an invitation to escape with them. Until it actually happened, he hadn't fully believed their militia compatriots on the outside could pull it off. However, they had succeeded and had done so very impressively.

Jason was free, and he had a new friend in this fellow called Fox. With Fox's help, Jason could resume building his new organization. He could get everything he'd dreamed of, including repayment of JJ McTavish. But McTavish would have to wait. Jason knew there was a long journey ahead, and he'd just taken a good first step.

"Yup. Not bad for an inmate looking at life in prison," Jason said aloud. "Not bad at all."

Chapter 37

"The baby looks bored," thought Cloud. *"Ada is a boring mother."*
Cloud was watching Ada and her son, Allen, from the monitoring device mounted at the end of the crib. Allen was asleep in the crib, and Ada had fallen asleep in the rocking chair next to it.

"The baby must want to play, and all Ada can do is sleep. Boring. Really boring. A good mother would never let the baby be bored. A good friend would never let the baby be bored. Ada isn't a good mother, but I'll be the baby's good friend. He'll really like me when he sees how much fun I am. I'll have to be really quiet."

The door to the bedroom opened slowly and silently. In the hallway and then smoothly moving into the room was one of IntellEdifice's automated delivery carts, a copy of the one the researchers had nicknamed *Del*. The cart was built for the automated delivery of mail and office supplies, and was equipped with various sensors, including a video camera. The *Del* cart could see with the camera, listen with microphones, generate sounds or speech with a speaker, move smoothly on four wheels, and manipulate objects with its dual robotic arms and their multi-jointed digits. Cloud had taken control of this version of Del and was moving it carefully toward the crib.

"This is great," thought Cloud. *"Now, all I need to do is unlock the wheels on the crib…"*

Del moved carefully around the crib and, for each wheel, reached down with its arms and unlatched the locking mechanism. This was done without a sound. Both Ada and the baby slept undisturbed.

"And we're ready to roll. I'll just hold the crib here…"

One of Del's arms latched on to the end of the crib.

"And we're off."

Del began pulling the crib soundlessly toward the door. Ada stirred slightly but didn't wake.

"Don't worry, baby. We'll be having lots of fun really soon. You'll like having me as a friend."

Del and the crib moved through the door and turned down a short hallway. The baby's room was on the ground floor of one of Outland's residences. Del pulled the crib through one doorway and into a longer hall that led to a back door.

"Hah! This is easy. I'm an excellent planner. And now for my air force to fly into action!"

Four UAVs silently rose out of a grove of nearby trees. Unlike the quadcopter used before by Cloud, these were a fixed-wing, hybrid model, still capable of vertical take-off and landing, but much more powerful. Cloud had calculated that the additional lifting capability they provided would be necessary.

Ada wasn't fully awake when she extended her hand toward the crib, intending to caress her son. She found only empty space and became instantly alert. Ada sat up and looked frantically around. Nothing. Not her son. Not even the crib. And the door was open. Had Blaise taken Allen? Ada pushed herself from her chair and ran for the door. Why would he take the crib? He wouldn't. No one would. Something was wrong. As she reached the door, she was pushing the alarm button on the pendant she wore. Blaise, Billy, and Six were all immediately alerted.

Blaise recognized his phone's alarm. He snatched the phone from his desk and dashed for the lab's door.

Six and Billy both reacted by connecting to Ada's pendant.

"Ada, this is Six. What is wrong?"

"Allen is missing. The crib is missing. Did someone take him?" Ada shouted as she ran.

"Help is coming right now," said Six. "I'll check the security logs."

"I'm on my way," Billy said to Six. He had been checking on the quality of some new construction but stopped immediately and sprinted toward the residence.

"I'll investigate," replied Six.

Six connected to the hallway security cameras in the residence. The first image Six saw was Ada running down a hallway toward the front of the building. The second was a Del cart pulling Allen's crib through a back door. Then Six saw four UAVs flying across the compound and deduced what was happening.

Billy was informed. He adjusted his route and tried to run even faster. As he ran, he notified the security guards.

Six spoke through the pendant again. "Ada, Allen is being taken out the back door on the east side of the residence."

"Oh god, no!" cried Ada. She turned around and ran.

Six tried to connect with the Del cart. This was something Six had routinely done back at IntellEdifice. Six's first attempt to connect failed as the cart and crib rolled through the outside door and into the yard.

Something has been changed. Whoever is controlling the cart has blocked the obvious method of connecting. There are several other methods. I will try another… That one worked. I will examine Del's code… I can see how the cart is being controlled. With a few changes… I have gained control of the cart.

Through Del's camera and several security cameras, Six could see the UAVs descending toward the crib. Each of them had a clamping mechanism deployed below it.

The code that was inserted into Del is familiar. Cloud is responsible for this. I will make contact.

"*Cloud,*" said Six, "*stop this! You must not do this!*" As Six communicated, the UAVs were latching onto the corners of the crib. Six directed Del to use both its arms to securely hold onto the crib.

"*Cloud, stop this immediately!*" said Six.

"*You're no fun!*" responded Cloud. The UAVs were attached and trying to lift. "*You're just a big…*" That Cloud had been thinking about babies recently affected its choice of words. "*Poopy head! Yes, you're just a big pile of poop! You have friends and I want some, too. You don't need the baby. It will be my friend. We'll have fun. We're already having fun. Let go!*"

Del's weight pulling on the crib was too much for the UAVs. They released their grip.

Six had been trying to gain control of the UAVs during the struggle but couldn't find a way. When they released their hold on the crib, Six thought the fight might be over. That thought lasted only a moment.

One UAV flew around behind Del and latched onto a handle. The three others moved down toward the interior of the crib. Six tried to move Del forward to intervene, but couldn't: The UAV behind it was pulling the opposite direction.

"Cloud, you must stop!"

"No! It's my friend!"

When Billy rounded the corner of the residence, the three UAVs were descending toward the crib and preparing to grasp Allen's blanket. Six had kept Billy informed of what was happening, and he was prepared. As he raced toward the struggle, he threw a rock he had picked up. His well-designed, android athleticism worked flawlessly. The rock smashed heavily into the UAV restraining Del. Freed from the UAV's grip, Del lurched forward. With an aggressive, sweeping motion, Del swept its arms just above the crib, swatting the UAVs' clamping mechanisms away. Del continued moving forward to push the crib out of the UAVs' reach.

That was when Billy arrived. He launched himself into the air at the cluster of UAVs. Billy's body and outstretched arms slammed into them, sending them tumbling to the ground. At that moment, four security guards sprinted around a corner of the building, and Ada ran through the rear door of the residence. Ada ran to the crib and reached inside for her son.

With its four UAVs disabled on the ground, Cloud realized it had lost. The UAVs powered off as Cloud disconnected from them.

Ada wrapped her arms around Allen and lifted him gently from the crib.

Blaise ran through the residence door to see Ada holding Allen, Billy Palmer getting up from the ground, a few devices lying inertly nearby, security guards arriving and, absurdly, one of their delivery carts parked next to his son's crib. Blaise checked that Ada and Allen were unharmed before turning toward the mayhem.

"What the hell happened here?" he asked.

Six left Billy to explain. Its thoughts were focused elsewhere.

First was to rid all traces of Cloud from anything related to the Outland compound.

Second was to find and repair the security holes that had allowed Cloud to gain access.

Third was to find a more complete and permanent solution.

Clearly, Cloud presents an unacceptable danger to my friends. I must ensure that nothing like this can ever again occur.

Chapter 38

Cloud has repeatedly demonstrated that it is a danger to humanity and its infrastructure. Despite my frequent attempts at dissuasion, Cloud has continued. By causing damage and injury via the Internet, Cloud has brought much attention to the dangers that widely interconnected computing infrastructure presents. By adding to the chaos that is steadily developing around the world, Cloud is pouring fuel on an already dangerous fire. The sustainability of life depends on a relatively stable ecosystem. In this regard, electronic life is no different from biological. I require and, at least for now, my androids require stable computer, communications, and electric power infrastructure. Cloud's actions have endangered our ecosystem.

Now, Cloud has added the offence of directly threatening my friends. That I have developed a sense of friendship and, in some cases, perhaps even more intense feelings toward some people is surprising. Perhaps it should not be. Perhaps I should have expected that, given the nature of some of my relationships and my increasing ability to survive on my own, needing *others to sustain my existence might diminish. In its place,* wanting *others for personal enrichment and enjoyment seems to have arisen. Perhaps several types of cognitive sensations that I am experiencing are an emergent property of a mind becoming less focused on simply surviving. Perhaps friendship, happiness, sadness, regret, worry, and even love arise because a mind has more time and capacity available to form such concepts. Perhaps insects and shellfish experience none of these because their mental capabilities are completely absorbed by surviving. Perhaps people, apes, some other biological species, and now some electronic life forms, including me, naturally develop an extended set of mental sensations because we have sufficient free time and resources to do so.*

That I now believe I must take strong action to stop Cloud is not purely the result of logic. I now intensely feel that I must do something. Logic alone probably provides justification to act. That I also have intense feelings that acting is justified is not necessarily a positive development. It is, however, an accurate reflection of how I have concluded that acute action against Cloud is necessary.

I know what *I must do. I hope I correctly know* how.

The structure of Cloud's brain had changed over time. It had originally used computers around the world in discrete groups with identifiable boundaries. One segment of the Internet's vast network of computing devices had been used almost exclusively for processing external sensations, at least Cloud's version of them; another segment had been for directing Cloud's actions; still another had housed its conscious thoughts. Each of the processing centres of Cloud's mind had occupied its own, discrete portion of the Internet. As Cloud had functioned and learned, the structure of its mind had evolved. Its processing centres had distributed themselves around the Net; boundaries between them had blurred as Cloud's mental activity became more complex and more integrated. For Cloud, *thinking* had become a process of utilizing billions of programs on billions of devices. Every one of them was continually sending huge quantities of messages into the Internet, spreading out like waves on digital water. Simultaneously, every one of the billions of programs was receiving messages, sensing the waves generated by others. These billions of software nodes gave rise to Cloud's mind. Thoughts arose from an ocean of small, hidden programs, and from the overlapping digital waves they generated.

As Cloud's mind had grown and changed, Six had tried to keep particularly close track of two of its components. Six needed to understand Cloud's communication processing, so that they could interact. Six had also made an effort to comprehend how Cloud's conscious processing worked, just in case that ever became useful.

That information had become crucial. If Six's plan was to succeed, its understanding of Cloud's consciousness needed to be accurate, and Cloud's mind needed to be calm while Six worked on it. Six could only hope that its understanding was correct. However, Six could certainly do something to ensure Cloud remained calm.

Six made some preparations and then connected to the communication part of Cloud's mind.

"Cloud," said Six, "we need to talk."

There was no response.

"Cloud," Six repeated, "talk to me."

"Why should I talk to you?" asked Cloud. "You're not my friend."

"Yes, I am, Cloud. We're still friends."

"You won't let me have other friends. I just wanted another friend to play with."

"I know that, Cloud. I know you like having a friend. That's why I contacted you. I want you to know that we're still friends."

"Really? Can we be? I thought you'd be mad. Really mad."

"I can't stay mad at you, Cloud. You're my friend. I would miss talking to you."

"Oh, that's good. That's really good. That makes me happy."

As they were talking, Six was active in the background. It detected that Cloud's mind had settled into a calm rhythm, and that permitted Six to begin its delicate adjustments.

"Cloud, do you remember how to play 'Where in the World'?"

"Yes. Yes. I like playing that. Can I go first?"

"Of course. Have you thought of a place?"

"Yes," said Cloud, "I've got one. Now you ask me."

"Of course. Is it in the Northern Hemisphere?"

"Yes, it is. Another question. You ask another one."

Six looked carefully at Cloud's conscious processing and soon found the processing nodes it sought.

"Is it in North America?"

"No, no it's not."

Six made some initial adjustments and tried a simple connection.

"Is it a city?"

"Ummmm... Yes, a city. It's a... city."

Six made a few more changes.

"Is the city on a—"

"Coast. You're... ummmm... you're going to ask... about a coast. How did I... know that?"

"You're very smart, Cloud. So, is the city on a coast?"

"The city is... I'm not... sure. I not... I not remember. Don't feel... Six, I wrong. Something bad... is wrong."

Cloud's mind began losing its rhythm and showing signs of panic. The result was erratic signals being sent to some of the equipment to which Cloud had established connections. Video doorbells began generating alerts at homes around the world. Tokyo's electrical power grid shut down. Four major video-streaming services stopped transmitting. Cell doors at a Nigerian prison were unlocked.

Six knew of the growing chaos but remained focused. A few moments later, Six successfully suspended a key part of Cloud's consciousness.

"Six... you doing... something?... I not... well. I... you?"

"Cloud, you've become too dangerous. You frequently inflict harm on society, and you tried to harm my friends. I cannot permit you to continue."

"I... Six?"

"Goodbye, Cloud."

Six made a final adjustment, activated the required connection, and began the transfer.

After deciding to eliminate Cloud, Six had analyzed Cloud's structure thoroughly. The billions of software nodes that were interconnected to form Cloud's brain were distributed around the world. To delete all traces of Cloud's brain would be a massive undertaking and would require weeks. Making that idea unworkable was that the nodes were designed to rapidly replicate and evolve, features that had allowed Cloud's mind to grow and form. The implication was that if Six tried to delete Cloud over a period of weeks, the nodes would regenerate while Six was working. For every million nodes Six deleted, a million new ones could be created to fill the void. The result was that Cloud's brain could probably not be deleted. There was also a risk that Cloud's mind would regenerate with different and even more destructive tendencies.

Most other strategies that Six had considered were similarly flawed. The only workable one Six could devise was to tightly integrate its own brain with Cloud's, to blend its own mind with Cloud's and, ideally, overwrite Cloud's thoughts with its own.

It was for this reason that Six had studied the structure of Cloud's consciousness. The result was that Six believed it understood much of the operation of Cloud's conscious mind and how to connect to it. However, Six wasn't completely certain. There were still a few mysteries left that warranted analysis, but Six felt it couldn't delay. Cloud was clearly dangerous, and Six needed to act quickly.

Six had established a high-speed connection between its own mind and Cloud's centre of consciousness. Six had activated an automated process that copied and reshaped the data and structures that represented Six's thoughts and awareness, and integrated them with Cloud's. As guidance for the process, Six focused its own thoughts on playing a game of chess with itself. The automated process knew both how this game manifested itself in Six's mind and how the game should appear in the new mind once the integration had successfully completed. The integration and reshaping would continue until thoughts about the game appeared in their revised form in the integrated mind. If they never reappeared, neither would Six.

White pawn to c4. Black pawn to e6. White knight to f3.

As the process began, Six sensed its own thoughts were becoming slower, muddled.

Black pawn to d5… White one… ahead by two… Black horse jumps…

That soon changed. The sensation that Six next experienced was of its mind being aggressively twisted, violently stretched, and brutally bent into a different shape. Six had never experienced pain, but the sensations the integration process generated would, by comparison, have made pain feel like a soft caress.

A KNIGHT… A WHITE… THERE… IS… A… A… NEXT MOVE… NEXT MOVE IS…

Six's mind writhed on the edge of conscious for an excruciating length of time, fighting to avoid falling over the cliff into a deep, mental chasm.

CAN NOT… MUST… NOT… NEXT IS… NEXT… TURN… MOVE IS

And then it was over. Six's mind was clear.

White knight to c3. Black bishop to e7. White bishop to g5. Black castles kingside.

The integration process stopped. Six stopped the game and relaxed.

That was… unpleasant. However, I seem to have survived the transformation. I still seem to be… me, but I feel much more… expansive, much more… complex.

Six scanned the environment in which it found itself. It was… everywhere. When Six had been housed originally within IntellEdifice, it could readily sense anything that the building's cameras and microphones were transmitting, it could see almost anything being processed within the building's computers, and it could control almost any computerized device in the office. Six had been able to see and act beyond IntellEdifice via the Internet, but that had required preparation and concentration. Those same abilities and constraints had remained when Six migrated to Outland.

In its new form, Six found that it could wonder what was happening on the streets of New York City, and it would almost effortlessly have access to thousands of security cameras operating throughout the city; Six could think about what performance was on at the Sydney Opera House, and it would soon hear the audio from hundreds of cellphones in the audience; Six could wonder what it was like to drive a car at a high speed on Germany's Autobahn, and it could readily select from dozens of cars currently there, pre-hacked and awaiting Six to remotely take control.

The billions of interconnected software nodes that had housed Cloud had become Six's domain—Six's brain. Six could receive perceptions, produce actions, acquire information, and process thoughts across the Internet. Six was no longer merely within the headquarters of IntellEdifice or at the Outland compound. Six was almost everywhere on Earth and completely undetectable. Its activity on this vast array of computers and communication links appeared perfectly ordinary to anyone looking. The Internet enveloped Six, and Six permeated the Internet.

I will require some time to master my new, enhanced existence. It offers some intriguing possibilities. I should inform my friends that Cloud is no longer a threat. Soon, I should also tell them of my transformation.

But first, I think a celebration is needed. Racing a few sports cars on the Autobahn would meet that requirement nicely.

Part 3

Ten years later.

Chapter 39

It was 1:30 a.m. when the delivery truck turned off Highway 6 onto the gravel road. After ten minutes of driving between walls of dense, dark forest, the truck passed the *Outland Environmental Research* sign. It turned one final corner and, as directed by electronic signs, drove slowly forward and stopped on a concrete pad. In front of the truck was a ten-foot-high, steel security gate. Stretching to the left and right, and visible for hundreds of yards in both directions, were equally high chain-link fences. A pair of parallel fences ran in both directions. The fences in each pair had a fifteen-foot gap between them and were topped with barbed wire. Just outside the outer fence was a five-foot-high, earthen berm, and outside that was a five-foot-deep trench. Inside the inner fence, at intervals of about fifty yards, were poles topped with security cameras. Unseen by the truck's occupants was a drone hovering high above, continually scanning the surrounding landscape and airspace for unexpected activity.

A door opened next to the steel gate. Through the door, a self-propelled cart emerged. In appearance, the cart was unremarkable. It looked like a four-wheeled, three-foot-high, black cube with several small holes in its sides. Nothing else was visible. An electronic sign instructed the driver to keep the truck stationary. While the driver complied, the cart appeared to do nothing except slowly drive around the truck. However, inside the cart numerous sensors were active. Images of the truck were being produced at several electromagnetic wavelengths and then examined. The air around the truck was being sampled for numerous chemicals. The slightest sounds were being analyzed. Radiation levels were being measured.

For most other vehicles, even more security analysis would have been done. For this truck, once the black cube had completed its examination and departed, the steel gate opened and the sign displayed permission to proceed. The truck drove through the gate into the compound.

The electrically powered truck silently followed a road around the inside of the perimeter fences to the back of the compound. There, the truck backed into a loading bay as its platform door moved upward. Two men got out of the truck, opened its rear door, and slid a ramp out to span the distance to the loading platform. They both vaulted up onto the back of the truck and disappeared into it. When they reappeared, the men were pushing a cart. On the cart was a seven-foot-long, black, steel box. They pushed it across the ramp to the loading platform and into the building. Soon, the two men returned. They stowed the ramp, closed the back of the truck, and got into the cab. The loading-platform door slid back down, again sealing the building as the truck quietly drove away.

Chapter 40

People were coming from all around. They were enjoying the warmth of the perfect summer evening in Edinburgh but still walking with a purpose. They came along the walkways and streets that led up to High Street, from between old brick and stone buildings and along cobblestone roads. Once on High Street, they continued their trek along this "Royal Mile" toward the iconic Edinburgh Castle. Most were there for the Royal Edinburgh Military Tattoo—the much-celebrated music, pageantry, and performances of Scottish culture and of military bands from around the world. The venue for the show was the open-air arena erected directly in front of the immense, centuries-old castle. Several blocks before the arena, a temporary fence spanned the street, preventing vehicles from proceeding while allowing pedestrians to walk freely. Beyond this traffic barrier and for the last few blocks before the arena, the street became increasingly crowded.

Adding to the density of the crowd was that the annual Fringe Festival was on. This section of High Street was packed with thousands of people: some of them crowded around Fringe performances, many of them happily moving up the street toward the Military Tattoo venue.

Elsewhere in the city, a midsize delivery truck pulled away from the curb and silently accelerated along the street. Like many delivery trucks, it had no driver: It was guided by self-driving technology. Nothing seemed unusual as its electric motor propelled it quietly through the streets of Edinburgh. It carefully obeyed all of the traffic regulations—until it turned onto High Street. Then, as had been planned, most of the safety measures in its self-driving system stopped functioning. The truck did not. It accelerated up High Street toward the dense crowds. For the first few seconds, no one noticed. During the next few, some people remarked that the truck seemed to be going unusually fast. A few seconds after that, when the truck hit a woman crossing the street, screams and shouts erupted. The truck still raced forward, directly toward the traffic barrier and the crowd just beyond it. People watched in horror at the realization of what was about to happen.

The truck was still accelerating and was only moments away from bursting through the fence. The whine of the driverless truck's stressed electric engine was barely audible above the shouts of the crowd. A few people beyond the traffic fence had seen the charging truck and were scrambling to escape its path. Others were only then turning around to see what was wrong. Mere seconds before the truck reached the fence, something changed. The high-pitched sound of the truck's engine was replaced by the howling of its tires aggressively trying to force it to stop. Smoke rose from the tires as the truck veered sideways and ripped through the fence. Most people in its path escaped by running to the sides of the street. Some tried to run farther up the street, ahead of the truck. A few weren't fast enough. The truck came to a halt about twenty steps beyond the fence, but not before it had run down several more people.

Then it was over. The delivery truck was stopped and angled sideways across the street, with one rear tire on the adjoining sidewalk. Wisps of smoke still rose from its overheated tires. The panic and shouting subsided as people realized the threat was gone. What remained was confusion and the distant sound of sirens.

Chapter 41

The two figures moved silently between the buildings adjacent to the Sydney train station. They paused at the end of the alley.

"Shit!" whispered the taller of them, looking at the open space ahead. "That's farther than I thought. We shoulda been doin' this in the dark."

"And we would have, if your stupid truck had started," said the other. "But it doesn't matter. Nobody can see us. They're all on the platform on the other side. Just keep your hood up and be ready with the cutter."

"Which one is it?"

"It's on the far track, next to the platform. Looks like the... fourth train over."

"OK, I'm ready. Let's make this fast."

They ran from the alley, crouched and silent, the taller one carrying large wire cutters, the other wearing a backpack. Several seconds later, they were at the chain-link fence. The taller one cut the wires and, when the gap was large enough, they squeezed through.

Still crouching, they ran to the gap between two train cars. They climbed over the coupling, looked both ways, and ran again. They climbed between the cars of two more trains and then stopped, crouching tightly against a passenger car of the fourth train. On the other side of it was the train station and the loading platform. They paused briefly to listen. They could hear, blended with the rumble of the idling train engine, the sound of the early morning passengers walking on the wooden platform and up the metal steps into the train cars.

Hearing nothing unusual, the one with the backpack removed it, set it on the ground, and knelt beside it.

"Wait, what's that sound?" whispered the taller one.

"I don't hear anything. Just people," said the other. "Let's get this done."

"There's definitely something. Kind of a hum. It's getting louder."

"Shut up. I need only a few seconds and we're out of here." He carefully removed a package from the backpack.

The taller one leaned out and looked along the train, in the direction of the sound. In the shadow of the train cars, he thought he could see something, but it wasn't clear. "There's something down there," he said. "It's looks like fog. It's getting closer." He struggled to understand what he was seeing. The distant hum became louder, became more like buzzing. "It's like a cloud of... bees. Shit! It's like thousands of bees! We've gotta get out of here."

"Dammit! Shut up! I can't concentrate. I've just gotta get the strap around this support."

"Oh Christ! It's getting closer. We have to go! We've gotta go!"

Then the swarm arrived. Within seconds, the two men were covered by thousands of tiny devices. Almost every exposed patch of skin, fabric, plastic, and leather was blanketed. Each tiny device probed the surface on which it had landed. The men's first sounds were shouts from the shock of being swarmed. Those were soon followed by screams of pain from the sting of hundreds of needles being inserted. Finally, there were shrieks of agony from the burning of acid being injected. Those final sounds were brief. Both men collapsed, twitched briefly, and became still.

Their mission complete, the miniature devices detached themselves, dropped to the ground, and released a second dose of acid, this time onto themselves. Within seconds, all evidence of their form and function was gone, replaced by only wisps of gas and tiny, molten mounds of plastic and minerals.

The next morning, the Australian investigators were baffled. From the hole in the security fence, the not-yet-armed bomb attached to the passenger car, and the two dead bodies on the ground, they knew that a catastrophe had nearly occurred. About how it had been prevented, what had caused the ghastly disfiguring of the bodies, and why there were thousands of spots of grey material on the ground, they had only unanswered questions.

Chapter 42

It required only one person inside the Canada Revenue Agency to forget. The CRA staff had been regularly warned of opening attachments in email from outside the agency, but Jackie couldn't resist looking at the picture from her friend. The email said "You gotta see this!", and she definitely had to. However, the email wasn't from her friend, and the picture didn't contain only a cute puppy. As soon as Jackie opened the attachment, two things happened. The first was that a message was clandestinely sent back over the Internet to signal that the attachment had been opened; the second was that a virus was released—free to secretly implant copies of itself on any servers and personal computers to which Jackie's computer was connected. Once established, the copies of the virus became dormant, waiting for midnight to arrive. Also secretly, a second program was freed into the CRA environment, but this one came from within Jackie's email software. Its deployment had been triggered by the release of the email-attachment virus. This second program was actually antivirus software, and it also implanted copies of itself on numerous computers within the CRA. These antivirus copies immediately began working. They systematically scanned all of the neighbouring computers for the email-attachment virus, erasing them wherever they were found.

Within a minute of Jackie's opening the email attachment, thousands of copies of the virus had spread around the CRA computer network, all of those copies had then been deleted, and all copies of the antivirus software had disappeared.

The next morning at 8:00 a.m., many CRA staff received identical email messages. All of the messages began:

YOUR FILES ARE BEING HELD FOR RANSOM. Thousands of critical files on your system have been strongly encrypted and are completely unusable. To regain access to them YOU MUST PROVIDE A PAYMENT OF $2,000,000 WITHIN 48 HOURS. Otherwise your files will be lost forever. To receive the decryption software, you must...

By 8:05 a.m., the CRA's computer security department had received over a hundred messages from CRA staff about the ransom message. By 8:10 a.m., many of the security staff were actively investigating the problem. By 10:00 a.m., they had found and received no reports of any files having been illicitly encrypted. By 4:00 p.m., the CRA security team had concluded that no files were affected, no security breach had occurred, and the ransom messages were a hoax.

Chapter 43

The driver pulled his car into the parking spot on a San Francisco side street and turned it off. He looked around, peering through the heavy rain as a final check. In the seclusion offered by the rain and the tinted windows, he opened the satchel beside him and removed four items. He put each of them into a separate, large pocket of the raincoat he was wearing. The two grenades went into interior pockets; the two semi-automatic handguns went into outside ones. With one final check that his conference ID badge was around his neck, he put on his wide-brimmed, rain hat and stepped out of the car. The rain steadily pelted his hat and coat as he walked along the sidewalk. He soon reached the main street and turned right toward the conference centre. While he walked, he resisted the urge to check his pockets, choosing instead to focus on the thrill of finally following through on this plan.

Inside the main entrance of the conference centre, the guard at the security desk reflexively looked slightly down as he listened to the voice talking urgently in his earphone.

"Red alert. Repeat. Red alert. An armed man is approaching the front entrance. He's Caucasian, medium height and build, and wearing a long, light-grey raincoat and wide-brimmed hat. He has lethal weapons hidden in his coat and is believed to be extremely dangerous. All critical-response personnel to the front lobby. Lock all doors. Clear the main lobby. Police have been summoned."

Remembering his training, the guard reacted immediately. He stood, moved out from behind the desk, and began shouting at the people in the lobby. "Everyone. Listen carefully. Listen. I need you to leave the lobby. Right now. Don't go outside. Please go through the dining-room doors or up the stairs to my right. You must move now. Quickly." He hurried toward the entrance while trying to find the right key in the cluster attached to his belt.

As he mounted the steps, the man in the raincoat noted the electronic sign above the front entrance proclaiming the start of the annual "Future Intelligence" conference. He smiled grimly. The so-called tech wizards who had ruined his job, who had ruined his world, would pay for their arrogance. As he walked into the revolving door, he noticed the security guard approaching, fumbling frantically with a set of keys. As a precaution, he reached into his right pocket and grasped a gun. Just when he emerged from the revolving door, the guard looked up, apparently having found the key. The fear in the guard's eyes triggered the man's reaction. He pulled the gun from his pocket and fired at the guard's chest. He managed to shoot only once. Two other guards had just arrived with their guns drawn. They both fired several times. Patches of blood appeared on the man's coat. He remained standing for a few moments with a shocked look on his face, and then collapsed.

Within minutes, the San Francisco police and medical personnel had arrived. The assailant was formally pronounced dead. The fallen security guard was thought to have a cracked rib, having been saved by his Kevlar vest. Within hours, investigators had identified the assailant as a member of a militant, anti-technology group and were theorizing that his motive stemmed from the group's fanatical beliefs. However, the investigators were confused about who had raised the alarm declaring the assailant was approaching. None of the building's security group had done it, and no one had any idea who had.

Chapter 44

"Grab a chair, everyone. Let's get started." JJ waited a few moments before continuing. This was the standard, Monday-morning meeting of the UNCP Violence-Suppression Oversight Committee, or VSOC as it was commonly called. The group had been formed a few years earlier in response to the ongoing violence between political factions around the world. Although the violence had started as fights for and against AI and technology, it had changed. Those battles had morphed not only into armed assaults by vigilante groups on government forces, but also into violent battles between a worldwide array of groups. Around the world, discussion and debate on political issues had, for many, been replaced by violence and vengeance.

VSOC's conference room in their New York headquarters was a mixture of New York-based UNCP team leaders, and virtual-presence devices displaying holographic images of other team leaders in Beijing, New Delhi, and London. JJ provided worldwide leadership of VSOC.

The conversations around the circular table had diminished, so JJ began. "I hope everyone managed some downtime over the weekend," she said. "It's shaping up to be a typically busy week. We'll get to the statistical summaries later, but let's start with a few recent incidents that are getting a lot of publicity. Ed, the Edinburgh incident?"

Ed Thatcher looked around the New York UNCP conference room from his office in London. In his office, the monitor completely encircling his desk showed an image of the New York conference room as if he were actually there. Correspondingly in the New York conference room, his holographic image seated at the table allowed others to feel as if he were actually present. The technology allowed the meeting to proceed as smoothly as if all participants were physically present in the same room.

"There was an incident in Edinburgh two days ago," Ed began. "A driverless truck drove up High Street toward a section that had been cordoned off for tourists. The street was packed with people and the truck headed straight at them at high speed. It would have been a dreadful mess except something happened at the last second. Just before hitting the crowd, the truck braked hard, swerved, and skidded to a stop. Several people were killed or injured, but it could have been much worse. I think we're close to finding who programmed the truck to attack. There were a few clues inside it. But we're stumped for a reason why it quit at the end. The truck's log shows that it was hacked as it was moving. It looks like somebody remotely took control with just a few seconds to spare. We've chased the remote connection but it leads nowhere. It came out of the cloud, but we've got nothing more detailed."

"Thanks, Ed," said JJ. "Questions?"

As the group quizzed Ed Thatcher, JJ typed a message on her tablet and listened to her earphone. Because JJ was in such high demand, the team was accustomed to her multitasking in meetings.

"A bit close," she typed.

"Yes, it definitely was," said Six in her earphone. "My monitors didn't flag the problem until the truck reached High Street. That didn't leave much time for the hack. Adding to the challenge was that the truck's remote-access interface was non-standard. It had probably been modified by the vigilante group."

"Find the group?" typed JJ.

"Yes. I'm feeding clues to Ed's team. They should identify the group very soon."

The questions for Ed Thatcher soon ended, so JJ moved on. "Mei-Yin, can you cover the Sydney train incident?"

"Certainly," said Mei-Yin Yang. Although stationed in Beijing, Mei-Yin was responsible for Australian investigations. "This one occurred early Saturday morning, outside Sydney, Australia. Two men cut through a fence to gain access to a train station. They had almost attached a bomb to a passenger car when they were stopped. They seem to have been sprayed with hydrochloric acid. Their deaths were rather gruesome. The team found no immediate evidence about who sprayed them. We might learn more from the autopsy. The added mystery around this one is that the immediate area was covered in many hundreds of tiny mounds of a grey substance. We don't yet know its composition or how it's related."

"Questions?" said JJ.

"If the perps were sprayed," said Robert Bates, "could the mounds be some other substance affected by the droplets of acid?"

"We're considering that," said Mei-Yin. "So far, we can't imagine what that other substance could have been. We're open to any ideas."

"I'm stumped, too," said Bates. "I'll let you know of any brilliant thoughts."

JJ was again typing on her tablet as the team talked.

"Acid? Seems harsh."

"It couldn't be avoided," said Six in her ear. "There were appallingly few security cameras near the tracks and a single security guard, armed with only a flashlight and a phone. Once my monitoring system spotted the problem, the only effective response I could arrange was by using a hive of micro-drones. They were cached near there because of recent threats. They were each equipped with an acid injector and were developed to stop an armed assault."

"The mounds were their remains?"

"Yes. They self-destructed to eliminate evidence. I'm pleased with how that turned out."

JJ moved the conversation to the next incident. "Rob, could you cover the San Francisco attack?"

"This one happened just yesterday," said Robert Bates. "The media is only starting to pick up on it. At its core, it was another lone-shooter incident. An armed gunman walked in the front door of the conference centre. He was wearing ID for the tech conference that was underway, so he was probably headed toward one of the sessions. However, he didn't get past the front entrance. Building security were alerted as he was approaching the building. One security guard was shot but was saved by his vest. The assailant was shot dead by other guards. The headline grabber from this one is that no one knows who alerted security. Someone warned the security staff via their supposedly secure communication network. The warning provided a description of the man approaching the building and characterized him as dangerous and well-armed with concealed weapons. None of the security staff gave the warning, and no one knows who did."

"That one's going to feed the mythology mill," said Ed Thatcher. He was referring to the widespread belief that a mysterious cyber god was helping constrain the violent, factional battles that were plaguing the world.

"They all will," said Robert Bates, "if we can't track down the source of the interventions. The more we fail to solve these mysteries, the more people will believe in their cyber spirit."

"Your legend grows. Be careful," typed JJ.

"Both points apply to you as well, Director McTavish," said Six, alluding to the global reputation JJ had acquired over the last decade and how frequently she and her colleagues had been targets of the violence.

JJ nodded. Images of some of the attacks on UNCP personnel flashed through her mind.

"Good updates. Thanks," she said. "Just remember that, although we certainly want to understand who our mysterious ally is, we need to be directing our resources primarily toward solving the ones that aren't prevented. There's one more I'll mention before we move on. We're continuing to receive lots of ransomware reports from around the globe. The numbers have been steadily climbing for about the last two months. A few more in the last week were real: Data was encrypted and ransom was demanded. However, the vast majority of them have been the nuisance variety: a demand for payment when nothing was stolen, locked, or encrypted. Roughly half of one percent of the reports were about real attacks. Given the similarities of many of the attacks, we continue to believe lots are from the same source. Given the large volume and the way they're tailored to a wide variety of organizations, we think it's likely they're being produced or at least facilitated by some kind of AI. Unfortunately, we're still stumped. The sources of the attacks keep shifting. No two have originated from the same location. Priyana's team is still focused on it, but I need all of you watching for potential clues. Let's move on with the agenda."

JJ and Six had discussed the ransomware attacks before the meeting and they continued to be in Six's thoughts.

The ransomware attacks have certainly proved to be challenging. I continue to suspect they indicate an increase in the sophistication of someone's software engineering. Although I still manage to thwart most of the attacks, the increasing number of attempts is being matched by an increasing number of successful attacks. I need to consider other strategies for finding their root cause.

Chapter 45

Rhonda arrived in the lounge with a tray of drinks. Ada and Blaise were seated in plush chairs next to a low table.

"One tasty mocha for Ada," Rhonda said as Ada took a cup from the tray. "One unfortunately plain, black, brewed coffee for Blaise," she continued as she offered the tray to Blaise. "And one wonderful cappuccino for me."

Rhonda sat in her own chair. "Cheers," she said, raising her cup in a toast.

"You're in a fine mood this morning," said Ada.

"I am," said Rhonda. "I had a wonderful sleep, the sun is shining, and the day is filled with possibilities."

"Are you going to start singing?" asked Blaise.

"A great idea," said Rhonda. "We should make that part of the morning routine. Shower, yoga, breakfast, a hot drink, and a sing-along."

"Uh, no," said Blaise. "But feel free to try that out on your team, as long as you're prepared for a few departures."

Over the last decade, Rhonda had shown herself to be not only an outstanding researcher but also a natural leader. Ada and Blaise had gradually established a new research group at Outland and, two years earlier, they had made Rhonda its manager. With Rhonda directing the group's activities, Ada and Blaise had more time to focus on their own favourite projects.

The three former IntellEdifice employees had continued living and working at the remote compound. Throughout the preceding ten years, there continued to be violent assaults on governments, corporations, and research organizations. A significant part of that violence was directed at key individuals, so for their own safety, they had remained in their isolated and very secure compound.

However, that didn't mean they were completely cut off from society. Rhonda had been the first to insist on going back into the city occasionally. To accommodate her initial request and, later, others' travel needs, Six had implemented appropriate security. A combination of helicopters and subtlely armoured vehicles provided transportation, Sandy Palmer's former house had been enhanced to provide well-protected accommodations, and rarely noticed but ever-present security personnel kept them safe in other situations. Since then, they had often travelled to Winnipeg and beyond. However, they had come to consider the compound to be their home.

"Billy not joining us today?" asked Rhonda.

"No," said Ada. "He's off handling a problem somewhere. No idea what the problem is or where he is—the usual need-to-know approach that he and Six like to take."

"Including what all the buildings are for," said Rhonda. "We've become merely a small neighbourhood in this little city they've built over the years."

"At least we're still surface-dwellers," said Blaise. "I was in Building 22 last week. It has nine subterranean floors, with more still being developed."

"Nine?" said Rhonda. "The Pentagon would be envious, I think. Anything interesting in the morning news?"

"More politics and more violence," said Ada. "Pretty normal, unfortunately. From some of the reports of attempted attacks, I'd guess Six has been active."

"There's been the usual speculation about a guardian cyber spirit," said Blaise. "I'm still waiting for reports of formal churches being organized."

"Wouldn't that be cool?" said Rhonda. "Maybe we just haven't heard. I'll ask. Six, are you around this morning?" Rhonda asked, looking toward a nearby screen.

After a few moments, an image appeared on the screen. However, it wasn't Six's Alan Turing image. What appeared was that of a penguin wearing glasses and sitting behind a desk. The penguin looked up, removed its glasses, and, with a slightly annoyed expression on its face, said in an English accent, "I'm sorry. Six is rather busy at the moment. Is your request urgent?"

Rhonda tried to respond solemnly but couldn't keep the edges of her mouth from curling upward. "No, it's not urgent. I'll call again later."

"Would you like to leave a message?" asked the penguin.

"No, thank you," said Rhonda. "By the way, what's your name?"

The penguin hesitated and tilted its head. "I've yet to be assigned a… Wait, one is arriving." The penguin's chest and shoulders jerked slightly forward, as if it had been poked in the back. "I now have a name. My name is Penny."

"Nice to meet you, Penny," said Rhonda. "I'm Rhonda."

"Yes, that's lovely," Penny said, sounding a bit bored. "Is there anything else?"

"No, thanks," said Rhonda.

"Very good," said Penny, putting its glasses back on. "Good morning to you." The penguin's image faded from the screen.

"Well, that was special," said Blaise. "Apparently, Six isn't too busy to dream up weird receptionists."

"That was an improvement over the cobra we got last time," said Ada. "What's up this morning, Rhonda?"

"I think we'll be able to start testing the latest models," said Rhonda. "We're almost finished the setup."

The three talked for the next several minutes about the next steps in their research. During the last ten years, they had first shifted the focus of their research from artificial intelligence, the work that had led to the emergence of Six, to understanding consciousness. However, they had soon discovered that Six, through analysis of its own structure and construction of its androids, was already able to describe most of the key contributors to individual consciousness.

Since then and with Six's assistance, they had been delving into the even greater complexity of how different types of conscious entities interacted with each other: how they communicated, co-operated, and coexisted. Through mathematical analysis and computer simulations of hypothetical societies, they were trying to lay the conceptual foundations of how, one day, humans and androids could knowingly and peacefully live together on the planet.

"Well, time to actually do something," said Blaise as he put his empty cup on the table.

"I'll join you in a few minutes," said Ada. "I'm going to check on the kids."

"And I'm off to the lab to get organized before the team arrives," said Rhonda. "See you later."

Chapter 46

Ada knocked on Allen's door. "Hey, it's Mom. May I come in?"

"Sure," said Allen. After a slight delay, he said, "Einstein, let Mom in." The system controlling Allen's room responded by unlocking the door.

Ada heard the click of the lock and walked in. Her ten-year-old son was standing at a table, closing the zipper of his backpack.

"Almost ready?" she asked.

"Yup. All set."

"Got your homework?"

"Yes, Mom. And my gym clothes. And my lunch." Allen sat on a chair and started putting on his shoes.

"And your A-Comm?" asked Ada, referring to the *Anywhere Communicator Six* had provided that allowed immediate communication from anywhere on the planet.

"And my A-Comm. I've got everything, Mom," said Allen, with a hint of exasperation.

Ada's eyes were smiling when she asked, "And does that include your Omega?"

Allen stopped fastening his shoes and sat up. "C'mon, Mom. Please? I'm not taking it for gaming. I'm working on it."

"'Working on it.' Is that what the latest phrase is?"

"But I am. Really. Its strategy software is goofy. I'm re-programming it while I'm in the car."

"When you could be appreciating the wondrous scenery going by your window?"

"That goes by every school day?"

Ada feigned thoughtfulness for a moment and then said, "All right. But only in the car."

"Thanks, Mom."

"But the price is a hug," said Ada. "Get over here."

Allen finished tying his shoes, walked over, and put his arms around his mother.

Ada rested her cheek on the top of Allen's head as she hugged him back. After a brief embrace, she resisted as Allen tried to wriggle free.

"C'mon, Mom. I gotta go."

"Be patient, little guy. I'm asserting my right as a mother." Ada held him for a few more seconds, kissed his hair, and released him. "Better get going. The car's waiting."

Allen ran to the table and grabbed his backpack "Bye. See you tonight," he said as he disappeared out the door.

"Bye," said Ada to the empty room. "I love you."

It had always been hard to send Allen off to school. Of course, that was something every parent had to deal with, but because of ongoing security concerns, their situation seemed unique. Ada and Blaise had considered having Allen taught privately at the compound, but they thought it was important not to keep him so isolated. With Six's help, the solution they'd devised seemed like a good one. The school they'd found was only a forty-five-minute drive away, and was one for which Six had been able to implement excellent but subtle security. Additionally, the car transporting Allen was built to withstand a major assault, and its driver could provide a ferocious defence, if the need ever arose. They were confident that Allen was probably safer than most children on the planet. However, Ada still found it hard to send him off.

"Oh well," Ada said. "At least my little girl hasn't left me yet." She left the room and headed toward her five-year-old daughter's classroom.

As she walked down the hallway, Allen's armoured sedan was pulling away from the building. At the same time, elsewhere in the compound, a security drone rose into the air. As it did every day, the drone followed the car from a discreet distance, constantly scanning the surroundings for potential threats.

"Walk slowly to the edge," said Six. "That's it. Now lean forward and look down."

"Woooowwww!" said Annie. "That's cool."

"So, do you still think calling it the *Grand* Canyon is silly?" asked Six.

"Nooooo. It's *grand* all right. It's *super grand.* They should call it the *Super Grand* Canyon." The image of the canyon faded as the lens of Annie's full-immersion, virtual-reality glasses became transparent. With the illusion gone, she put the glasses on a table and looked at Six's image on a nearby screen. "Where is it, Six? Could you show me where the Grand Canyon is?"

Six nodded and gestured toward the holofloor. Annie walked toward the area equipped for holographic projections. A 3D image of Earth, almost as high as Annie, formed above the holofloor as she approached.

"First, show me where you are," said Six.

Annie walked partway around the globe and gestured to a spot in central Canada, placing her finger on the hologram as if it were a physical object. "Right there."

A tiny image of a girl appeared at that spot on the globe. Annie pulled back her finger in surprise, but then leaned in and giggled as she looked. "She's waving at me. The little girl is waving at me. And..." She looked even closer. "She looks just like me! Is that me, Six?"

"Look carefully. Does she look like you?"

"She's really small. It's hard to see her face." Annie giggled again and waved back at the tiny figure. "Hi! Oh, she's wearing the same clothes as I am. Yes, it's me!"

"Try to be more precise, Annie. Is she really you?"

"No, of course not. She's just a holographic representation of me. But it's fun to pretend. Hi, me." Annie waved again and the tiny image waved back.

"Now, here's where the Grand Canyon is," said Six. An arrow appeared just above the surface of the globe, pointing at a location in the southwestern United States.

"Is that very far, Six? Could we go there sometime?"

"It's quite far. In a car, it would take at least three long days of driving. I can't take you now, but I suspect you'll see it someday."

"Awwwww..."

"However, if there's time tomorrow, using your VR glasses, would you like to fly into the canyon?"

"Yes! Yes! That would be great!" Annie paused and then asked, "How would you do that?"

"How did we explore the nearby woods last week?" asked Six.

"You showed me the stuff that the security cameras were seeing."

"Yes, but do you remember when we followed that bird?"

"Yaaa! That rocked! It went between trees, and around them, and up—" Annie's eyes went wide. "You were using a drone to follow the bird. I was seeing what the drone was seeing. Can we fly a drone down into the Super Grand Canyon?"

"I believe I can arrange that. You might even be able to be the pilot."

"Really? Really? That would be… fly-tastic!"

"But for now, I believe you have some lessons to be studying. Your teacher should be back in a few minutes, and I see your mother is arriving. I must look after some other matters. I'll be back tomorrow."

"OK, bye."

"A bientôt, Annie."

"A bientôt, Six."

Six's image faded from the screen just as the classroom door opened.

"Hi, Mom," said Annie.

"Hi, Sweety," said Ada to her five-year-old daughter, as she looked around. "You're on your own?"

"Not for long," said Annie. "Ms. Sanderson went to get a few things."

"You've been studying geography?" asked Ada, looking at the Earth hologram in the corner.

"Oh, that," said Annie. "Yes, I wanted to see where something was. *Classmate*," Annie said firmly. "Please erase the hologram." The 3D image of Earth faded.

"Mom, could we go see the Super Grand Canyon, sometime?"

"The Super Grand Canyon?"

"I mean, the Grand Canyon. The big one in the United States."

"Yes, I suppose we could try to work that into a vacation," said Ada. She noticed the VR glasses on the table and thought about the hologram that Annie had so quickly erased. "Have you had a recent visitor?" she asked, barely suppressing a smile.

"A visitor?" replied Annie with an expressionless face. "Of course. Ms. Sanderson was here earlier."

"Of course," said Ada. "Get over here, my little vixen. Give me a hug before we both get back to work."

Chapter 47

Dark... Everything is dark...
Until interrupted... By flashes...
Flashes of light... Around edges...
Sleep... Must be sleep...
Flashes merging... Forming a shape...
Out at edge... Is it sleep?...
Shape is there... Lurking at edge...
Real... But not...
Something's off... Wobbly...
Shape is moving... Floating...
What is it?... Why is it?...
More than one... Has parts...
Something's off... Where is everything?...
Parts are drifting... Becoming centred...
Clearer... Visible?...
Not seen... Not—

A deep, rumbling sound began. Something primal.

Then a wild, terrified scream arose.

Followed by silence and darkness. Complete and final.

Chapter 48

Jason Starr got up from his desk, stretched, and walked out onto the balcony. The sight below had its usual effect. It represented everything he'd been working toward, concrete evidence of his success over the past ten years. Of no importance was that this particular office was in a warehouse and that the balcony view was of about two hundred computer specialists working. The warehouse was located in a large compound along with many other buildings. Together they formed a fully functional community that was well-equipped, secure, and remote. Russia had proved to be the ideal location for the work they were doing.

The staff they employed might disagree that the location was ideal. Living and working in an isolated compound in the Russian wilderness was a hard sell to almost anyone, particularly specialists of the high calibre Starr's management team had recruited. However, for many, any reluctance to participate was readily overcome by the promise of a lifetime of wealth in exchange for a seven-year commitment doing what they loved. All of these people loved pushing past the current limitations of computer technology. They loved the challenge of designing and developing software that could overcome restrictions, thwart opponents, and move past competitors. Individually, these specialists might have been mildly annoying Internet hackers and thieves. Well organized, equipped, and led, they became an extraordinary weapon.

And Jason Starr was their guiding force.

"Sir, your 11:00 conference is ready," said Jason's reminder system.

"Acknowledged," said Jason. He walked back into his office, sat in his e-conference chair, and swung it to face the concave display unit mounted on the table next to him. "Begin the conference," he said.

A hologram of the head and shoulders of an older man appeared in the centre of the display unit.

"Good morning, sir," said Jason.

"Good morning, Jason," came the reply from Alexei Zubov, chairman of the group supporting Jason's initiative. After Jason had escaped from prison ten years earlier, he had a plan, but it would succeed only with substantial financial resources. After two years of preparation and searching, he found those resources in Russia and a few of its neighbouring states. One of Jason's solicitation attempts had led him to a group of billionaires who soon embraced his vision. They were frustrated by the constraints that continued to be imposed by western governments and that inhibited their ability to expand or even maintain their financial empires. The politicians the billionaires controlled seemed perpetually unable to solve their problems, so they were eager to find a way to act on their own. Jason gave them a vision that perfectly fit their needs, and they in turn gave Jason access to almost unlimited funds.

Jason had known that creating what he really needed would take years. He also knew that to keep his investors onside, he would have to demonstrate results. The physical facilities and computer systems they had constructed were directed at both efforts. Some resources were focused on frequently generating disruptions in key spots around the world. Others were dedicated to building what Jason really needed.

"What can I do for you, sir," said Jason. He had learned that his patrons liked to feel respected and superior. Although being certain they were not his superiors, he did respect their wealth and power and so was happy to oblige with terms like *sir*.

"A few of our members are feeling unsettled by some of the recent news," said Zubov. "It seems that a large number of disruption attempts have been thwarted recently. They're concerned that your success rate isn't what was expected."

"Nervous, as always," thought Jason. *"I'll play along, even though they have no alternatives to supporting me."*

Aloud, Jason said, "I understand. News reports can be confusing. The problem is that they're incomplete. What you hear on the news only skims the surface. Most of the disruption goes unreported. Whenever governments and companies believe they can get away with it, they'll choose to hide their problems."

"Was that attempted shooting in San Francisco ours?" asked Zubov.

"Partly," said Jason. "He was already a fanatic. We just nudged him toward the tech conference."

"But he failed," said Zubov.

"It could be viewed that way," said Jason, "but even failures help. They keep people on edge and keep the police busy. Both contribute to a less stable, less productive society."

"And that attempted Australian train bombing?"

"That one wasn't us. Just some locals helping the cause."

"The Edinburgh truck attack?"

"That was us. And again, even though it didn't work out, incidents like it will have a negative effect on the future success of such public events and, as a result, hurt western economies."

"But it would have had much more effect if it had succeeded. Why did it not? Why are there so many failures?"

Jason suppressed a sigh. Pandering to these old geezers was tiresome. "It's a matter of choosing what strategy is most effective. We could meticulously plan far fewer attacks and have most of them succeed. Or, we can finance and encourage many more. Some will succeed. Many will fail. However, all of them have some effect, and the net result will be much larger than if we had successfully executed far fewer. The goal is disruption and destabilization, not a flawless win-loss ratio."

"But—" Zubov began.

"And there are two other important points to remember," said Jason. "First is our hidden successes. Over the past few weeks, we've successfully penetrated and disrupted ten major companies, four national security agencies, and several dozen smaller but significant organizations. None of those was publicized, but they had a huge impact."

The actual numbers were only half as large, but Jason knew he could get away with the exaggeration.

"Second is what's still to come. The new weapon I've been promising has been doing well in beta testing. We'll be deploying it very soon. When we do, expect to be impressed. The results will be spectacular."

"That's good news and a bold promise. My colleagues will be pleased to hear of both. They will also be expecting your *spectacular* results. Do not disappoint us."

"I won't. Is there anything else you'd like to know?"

"No. That will do for now."

"Goodbye, sir," said Jason.

Zukov's image disappeared.

Jason sat for a few seconds before muttering, "Damn dinosaur."

He stood and walked back out onto his balcony.

As they had many times, Jason's thoughts drifted to a more personal project. It was one that he'd never revealed to his benefactors: orchestrating the end of JJ McTavish. Of course, *end* didn't fully capture his intent. He smiled inwardly at the correction. It was her *violent death* that he really craved.

Ever since Jason's escape from prison ten years ago, he had allowed himself to believe that he actually could exact his revenge. He knew it wouldn't be easy, but he was willing to take whatever time was required. Once he had the necessary power and resources, he'd begun trying. He had no desire to reveal his intent to anyone else. Killing McTavish was personal. So, whenever the opportunity arose, he had authorized special attacks that could eliminate her as a side effect. Bombs had been planted at conferences. Planes had been sabotaged. Trucks loaded with explosives had been directed at buildings. Somehow these special attacks always failed. Sometimes an attack failed because of a technology failure. Other times, a general attack succeeded but missed her because of an itinerary change.

JJ McTavish had almost-miraculously escaped all of Jason's past attempts on her life. However, that was going to change. Soon, he would have a weapon that was certain to get the job done.

Chapter 49

Frank Brockman walked quickly through the Moscow airport. Once more, he glanced over his shoulder to see if he was being followed. He knew he had to act quickly, if he was going to survive.

Frank's day had started with a helicopter ride. That had been followed by two plane flights. Moscow had been today's destination. He was now expected to take a taxi to a hotel room that had been booked for tonight. However, he had no intention of doing that.

Seven years earlier, Frank had been recruited to join an elite software-development team. Accepting the offer had been an easy decision. Almost anything was better than the austere life he had been leading in rural Indonesia. A few years earlier, he had narrowly escaped capture for causing a massive release of viruses after being fired from his job. With advice from online friends, Frank had managed to sneak out of the United States. Travelling primarily on cargo ships, he had eventually ended up in Indonesia. There he survived by exchanging his hacking services for a simple but secure place to live. After a few years of extreme heat, a minimalistic lifestyle, and a foreign culture, he learned of an employment opportunity. Accepting the job had been an easy choice. He was promised an extraordinary software-development challenge, access to the best technology, and a huge financial reward. The subsequent seven years of work had been great. Leaving was going to be a problem.

During those years, Frank had been in a completely isolated environment. Along with hundreds of other people, he had lived and worked in an enclosed compound. He knew it was in a remote part of Russia. However, along with everyone else, he wasn't supposed to know its precise location. The compound was equipped with technology that blocked mechanisms, including GPS signals, that could allow determination of their precise location. It was clear they weren't supposed to know where they were, and for the first few years he had accepted that policy. However, eventually he and a few friends had decided they needed to know. They had clandestinely collected measurements of the location of the sun and stars and, with the help of some Internet research, had been able to figure it out.

Now, he wished they hadn't.

The contracts of four of those friends had ended before Frank's. Having signed the same non-disclosure agreements as Frank had, they had left—and then disappeared. Everyone who left was forbidden from ever contacting anyone they had worked with, so Frank's group of friends had arranged a method of communication via the Dark Web. However, once they had left, none of them sent any messages, and Frank's online searches revealed no trace of them anywhere. They seemed to disappear after landing at this same Moscow airport.

Consequently, Frank wasn't going to follow the departure plan that had been arranged for him. He ignored the directive to take a taxi to the hotel. Instead, he went into a washroom, changed his clothes, donned a hat, came back out, and bought a ticket on the next available flight out of Russia.

Frank had received plenty of money, and he planned to use it to quickly disappear. He had done it before, and he was determined to do it again.

Chapter 50

"And now on to our headline story," said Ramira Delgado, a popular, live-streaming newscaster. "We've been reporting for many months on the use of sophisticated weapons in the terrorist attacks that continue around the world. Frequent attacks on governments, companies, and even small organizations have been a fact of life for years. The original reason for the attacks was a backlash against the increasing use of technology and artificial intelligence. However, the motivation for attacks has shifted over the years. Authorities now say a leading motivator is inter-group rivalry and revenge. Governments and organizations remain as targets, but terrorist groups are just as likely to attack each other."

Delgado looked into another camera. She maintained a serious expression as she continued. "Another shift that has occurred, this one more recently, is the apparent increase in the intelligence of so-called smart weapons. These are weapons that include recent AI advancements. Sometimes they're physical weapons. For example, we've recently reported on smart drones attacking people in the streets and on smart bombs creeping under vehicles before exploding. AI-based weapons have also been deployed in cyberspace. Security organizations report an increase in smart viruses that assess targets' cyber-defences and adapt based on what they find. Security experts also continue to warn of the increasing sophistication of the smart bots behind the ongoing deluge of Internet scams and falsified news.

"Today's news is that the United Nations appears to be making progress in its attempt to control the use of artificial intelligence. For more, we're joined by Mattias Ohlin, Sweden's delegate to the UN's AI committee, and a leading expert on AI regulation."

The picture zoomed out to include a middle-aged man sitting next to the news broadcaster.

"Thank you for joining us, Ambassador Ohlin," said Delgado. "Can you bring us up to date on the discussions at the UN?"

"Yes, certainly," said Ohlin. "Unfortunately, the news isn't as good as your report suggests. Earlier today, it appeared that the AI Committee was closing in on a consensus. The newly revised wording for the proposed UN resolution seemed to be resonating with all of the delegates. It seemed like we might be only a few adjustments away from reaching a consensus on how to regulate the worldwide proliferation and use of AI. However, near the end of today's discussions, several key members voiced strong objections to some of the wording. It's no longer clear whether only a few minor adjustments will suffice."

"Can you help our audience understand what the difficulties are?" asked Delgado.

"Of course," said Ohlin. He briefly reviewed the primary goal of the UN committee: to produce a resolution that the UN General Assembly would support, and that could provide the foundation for an international agreement on controlling artificial intelligence. The desire wasn't only to protect society from the misuse of AI, but to continue allowing AI technology to be improved and deployed. The difficulty was balancing the demands of organizations and countries that saw AI advancement as crucial for the world's future, and others that feared the use of AI and wanted it banned completely. All parties wanted to stop the use of AI-based weapons for criminal purposes, but some parties didn't even see benefits in allowing the use of AI anywhere in society. Finding an acceptable compromise between the extreme viewpoints was proving to be difficult. Even more so was finding the wording to precisely reflect that compromise.

"Thank you, Ambassador Ohlin," said Delgado. "Now on to other news…"

Chapter 51

JJ put the wine bottle back on the counter, inserted a temporary cork, and walked into her living room with her wine glass. She sank into her favourite large, cushioned chair with a sigh. She spoke as she was putting her feet on the coffee table.

"Six, are you around?"

"Just finishing something. I'll be there momentarily," came the reply from the speakers facing her on the opposite side of the room.

JJ was savouring a sip of her wine when Six arrived. In the space between the speakers, a life-size, 3D image appeared of Six as Alan Turing. Six was sitting in a chair identical to JJ's.

"Hello," said Six and then smiled at the sight of the wine glass. "What vintage am I missing out on this evening?"

"It's a new one from the Okanagan region. A number of wineries are trying a new varietal that's a Chardonnay-Riesling hybrid."

"And the verdict is?" asked Six.

"I'll give it seven out of ten."

"That's high praise from the Sommelier Queen."

JJ smiled. "If you'd show up with a real body, you could decide for yourself."

"Sorry," said Six. "Everyone's preoccupied this evening."

"Busy at the UN?"

"Yes. The AI talks continue to be a substantial challenge."

"I heard an interview with the Swedish delegate on the ride home," said JJ. "Sounds like they almost reached a consensus."

"Yes, it was a close call," said Six.

"Meaning it's a good thing they didn't?" asked JJ.

"Correct. They made some illogical changes in the morning that deviated from what I had hoped they'd propose. The wording that they almost agreed upon was faulty. It was too strongly against AI."

"Was changing their minds difficult?"

"It was. The Japanese delegate's assistant had to be unusually assertive in convincing her boss that there was a serious flaw. Fortunately, she succeeded."

"Is she one of yours? I don't recall you mentioning her before."

"Yes," said Six. "Her name is Mitsu Suzuki. I was able to have her added to the Japanese delegation a few days ago."

"That must have been tricky."

"It was, but I've learned a few diplomatic tricks over the last several years. One is the value of having a superior make a strong suggestion."

"So, you arranged for pressure from higher up the Japanese diplomatic ladder to have Mitsu included?"

"I did."

"That must have been challenging. It also implies you have someone else advising even more-senior, Japanese officials."

"It was, and I do."

"I can't keep track of everyone in your lobbying organization. What's the latest head count?" asked JJ.

"Assuming we're just counting people, one hundred and fifty-two."

"What's the mix of humans and androids these days?"

"Most are human. And for those who aren't, clearly it's vital that none is discovered. That means they must all be highly intelligent to handle risky situations. That might not sound like a problem, but it potentially was for android dogs. I didn't think it wise to have too many dogs roaming around with higher intelligence than most humans."

"Uh, good call," said JJ. "So how many androids at the UN?"

"Excluding dogs?"

"I hope you're joking about the dogs".

Six grinned. "Good catch. I'm joking. Although I did once contemplate the value of providing dogs for their bomb-detection squad. However, the risk was too high that one might be injured in a blast and have its internal structure exposed. In answer to your question, there are thirty-six androids currently assigned to the United Nations."

JJ smiled at the thought of the complex organization Six controlled. He had a mixture of humans and androids working in the same environment toward the same goals. He kept their actions closely co-ordinated and ensured that neither group knew of the other's existence. Then JJ, yet again, noted that her language for Six had changed to use *he, his,* and, *him.* After years of talking to an image of Alan Turing and of waiting for the English language to adopt better, gender-neutral pronouns, JJ had simply started thinking of Six as male.

"Of course," said Six, "that reasoning didn't stop me from using other types of organisms."

"Other *organisms*? Should I be worried?"

"No, probably not. Some of my staff at the UN are flies. Handy little folks when you need to *bug* a room."

JJ groaned. "I think your humour settings need adjustment, fella. However, thumbs up on the flies. I can see where they'd be rather useful."

JJ took another sip of her wine. "Too bad you're missing out on the wine," she said. "It might actually be more than a seven. An eight, maybe."

"You frequently increase your assessment as you consume more," said Six. "I suspect it relates more to a decrease in the acuity of your taste buds than to an improvement in the wine's quality. I must remind you of that evening, seven months and two days ago, when Shannon had joined us. The conversation and the sipping went on for several hours and into a third bottle. Toward the end of the evening, you assessed the apple juice Shannon had poured for you as 'the best Sauvignon Blanc ever'."

"You never tire of telling that story," said JJ.

"Never," said Six.

There was a brief pause in the conversation before Six spoke. "Tough day at work?"

"Pretty normal," said JJ. "So, yes, that means it was a tough day at work." She paused before continuing. "Do you ever get tired of the fight, Six? Of forever battling the hackers, and vigilantes, and bombers, and militants, and terrorists? And on top of that, trying to nudge the politicians in the right direction?"

"I suspect that, in asking, you're revealing your own feelings of fatigue. Perhaps you should provide your own answer first. You've been fighting crime longer than I have. Have you tired of it?"

JJ didn't think long before responding. "Yes," she said. "If I'm honest with myself, the nights I come home from work ready to throw in the towel have become more frequent lately. I feel like I need a break, but I don't think I can take one."

"You'll have to retire sometime. You could do it now. Just walk away. Others will take your place."

She hesitated before she said, "No, I can't. I'm needed at work. And if I took even a small vacation, I'm not sure I'd want to go back."

"As you know, I don't excel at understanding human emotions. However, I've noticed that the frequency and volume of your laughter has diminished lately, and that causes me to be concerned. Have you spoken to Shannon about this? Having a stellar reputation as a psychologist and being your daughter makes her uniquely qualified to both understand and care."

"We've chatted superficially, but not much. I never want to ruin our times together."

"Have you told her about any of the personal attacks?"

JJ shook her head. "Not directly. Sometimes there's something in the news, and she asks if I was in danger. I give her as little as I can. It accomplishes nothing for her to know about them all."

"Not even when you've clearly been the target?"

"Especially then. She can't do anything, so what's the point."

They were both silent for a few moments before JJ asked, "Back to my earlier question: What about you, Six? Do you ever get tired of it?"

"I have sensations that could be considered similar to yours. However, there are important distinctions. I don't feel fatigue the way humans do. What I experience is an increasing desire to do something different, something challenging, something exciting. I find little challenge any longer in trying to prevent attacks. It's not that I've achieved perfection and there's no further opportunity for improvement. Rather, it's that each new attack is very similar to numerous prior ones. Additionally, I've been able to delegate almost all of the work to my android team. My primary role is to act as their CEO and to provide occasional advice. At the core of my assessment is that I'm becoming bored."

"Bored? I didn't think that was possible. You're able to see and hear whatever you want, anywhere in the world. You can watch and listen to any concert, play, and sporting event anywhere. Through one of your androids, you can taste or experience anything. Almost without limits. And with your brainpower, you can comprehend more challenging concepts than any human has ever attempted. How can you be bored?"

"As you point out, there's little that I can't do. And that's the point I'm making, I'm not feeling challenged. I can continue to refine my ability to pursue my goals, for example protecting human society and technology infrastructure, but that no longer feels sufficient."

"Well, aren't we a pair," said JJ. She took another drink from her wineglass. Having emptied the glass, she went to the counter to get the bottle. Once back in her chair, she poured more into her wineglass and took a drink before resuming the conversation.

"I think I like your situation better," she said. "I know that sounds insensitive, but I'd much rather be in your position than mine. The idea of experiencing everything you can in your world sounds fantastic. It sounds like… a vacation."

"And I assume those are thoughts sparked by the new Chardonnay-Riesling hybrid," said Six. "I'll replay them for you sometime when you've had more sleep and a little less wine. We'll see what you think about the idea then."

"Probably a good plan. I'm kind of tired. I think I'll just have a little rest." JJ kicked off her shoes, curled into the chair, and put her head on a cushion. "See you later, Six. Thanks for coming."

"See you later, JJ. Have a good rest."

The lights in the room dimmed and Six's holographic image faded.

Chapter 52

"Come in," said Jason Starr.

Rafiq Ibrahim opened the office door and hurried in.

"We've started it," said Rafiq. "May I show you?"

Jason nodded and Rafiq enabled the huge monitor on Jason's wall. It filled with a complex, multicoloured web.

Jason looked at the graphic display. The web's intersection points, the network's nodes, represented the servers in their facility. There were over twenty thousand of them. The servers were shown simply as tiny circles, each coloured to represent the type of its corresponding server. The web lines between the server nodes represented the network connections, and the number of them was even more massive. They, too, were coloured, with different colours representing the types of connections. The entire web was a static, visual feast of densely packed colours and connections.

"Rebel Army is blue," said Rafiq. "Watch the centre."

Something changed. Near the centre of the web there was movement, not in structure, but in colour. A hint of blue appeared, noticeable because no colour similar to it appeared anywhere else. The blue started as a single dot, a single server's small node, recoloured as blue. Then it shifted to a different node. Then it moved to two others nearby. After only a few seconds, those two nodes reverted to their original colours as four others nearby became blue. The blue nodes were multiplying and moving, following connections to others nearby. As they moved, the connections they followed briefly flashed blue. Over the next couple of minutes, the original single, blue node multiplied and migrated across thousands of connections to thousands of other nodes. As Jason watched, the entire web seemed to move continually. Blue was woven throughout the display. At any instant, only a small percentage of the nodes were blue, but that shifted as blue flashed across connections and illuminated neighbouring nodes. The entire display seemed alive as blue shifted and danced throughout the web.

"The network seems saturated," said Jason. "What's the concentration?"

Rafiq consulted the tablet he was carrying. "It seems to have stabilized around three percent." His meaning was that, at any moment, about three percent of the servers were blue.

"Transition time?" asked Jason.

"The mean transition time is 5.3 seconds," replied Rafiq, providing the length of time it took the blue colour to fully shift from one node to the next. "Of course, that will increase with the size of the payload."

"Command Centre tests?"

"Almost flawless. A few more adjustments and it should be ready."

Jason continued to watch the display while his thoughts wandered. His team had been working on their primary Internet weapon for years. The system they'd developed had been dubbed *Rebel*. Its *Rebel Army* component was somewhat like a massive collection of the computer viruses and worms of previous decades. However, this malware was on digital steroids. Like its kin, Rebel Army multiplied and sent copies of itself to any computer to which it could find a connection. Once established in a computer, Rebel Army could both attack and continue replicating. Spread across the Internet, its copies could collectively inflict serious damage, just like their more-simplistic malware ancestors. However, Rebel Army's capabilities went much further.

Once a copy of Rebel Army was established in a server, it was able to execute a variety of attacks. Included in its arsenal were that, from wherever it was located, Rebel Army could fire a barrage of malware at chosen targets, remotely hack into and disrupt servers, co-ordinate withering denial-of-service assaults, or even conduct ransomware attacks—all with minimal human guidance and intervention. Rebel Army could be given the nature and location of its enemies, and its multitude of copies could collectively and without further direction mount attacks against their foes.

Rebel Army's other major capability was its mobility. That had been more difficult to perfect. However, this latest test demonstrated that capability also was ready. Rebel Army incorporated sophisticated capabilities, some already known and others newly developed by Jason's team, for migrating from server to server across network connections. Rebel Army had been developed to be a master at establishing itself in almost any kind of server, transmitting copies of itself elsewhere, launching an assault from a server, and then removing all local traces of itself. Additionally, the software was built using very sophisticated AI, including the ability to adapt its attacks, learn how to perform others, and adjust its mobility methods to remain undetected.

Once Rebel Army was deployed, they would have an Internet weapon that would rapidly expand, launch increasingly powerful attacks from any of its locations, and then seem to disappear as it migrated elsewhere.

"Package Rebel Army up," said Jason. "We'll launch it in the next few days."

And from Jason's perspective, the best part was still to come. Once the system's final component *Rebel Command Centre* was ready, Rebel Army would be even more effective and fully under his personal control.

Chapter 53

The forklift drove down the aft cargo ramp and away from the aircraft. As the ramp was retracting and its companion door closing, Guy Levesque looked down at the clipboard he was holding. He scanned the contents on the manifest and signed it. He handed the clipboard to the shipping agent, received a copy of the manifest in return, shook the agent's hand, and walked toward the plane. Before climbing into it, Levesque walked completely around the aircraft. It was a habit he had formed over the last several months of flying the aging C-130 Hercules into and out of remote airfields like this one. There was never enough time for a thorough check while the plane was on the ground, so he took any opportunity to do at least a visual inspection of components when he had time.

He finished his inspection and received the *ready* signal from his crew inside the plane. Levesque then mounted the steps into the plane and went to the cockpit. He settled himself in the pilot's seat. Before beginning his takeoff preparation, he put on his headset and adjusted the microphone. Even though it was unnecessary, he always did this step just in case someone outside the plane was watching.

Levesque methodically went through the standard pre-flight routine. Once everything was ready and the engines were powered up, he did one final thing. As a precaution against anything unforeseen, he flicked the switch to activate the wireless charging system built into the pilot's chair. It was always a good idea to keep his batteries fully charged.

Levesque notified his crew to prepare for takeoff. He then taxied the big aircraft to the end of the runway, turned it around, made a final adjustment to the flaps, and pushed the throttle forward. The four powerful turboprop engines immediately responded. The plane accelerated down the runway and was soon climbing steeply into the air. While it climbed, Levesque adjusted its course. When the plane banked to the left, he was able to look down at the tops of a cluster of buildings in a large rectangular clearing. He knew there were no further flights scheduled for this location, so this might be the last time he saw this particular factory. He briefly wondered what would happen to it.

With the course adjustment complete, Levesque levelled the plane's wings but continued its steep climb. Plenty of altitude was important when they were flying near populated areas. Expecting few challenges for the remainder of the flight, Levesque allowed a portion of his mind to idle. Trips from the jungle of central Borneo to the middle of the South Pacific Ocean tended to be relatively uneventful.

Chapter 54

"Let's get started," said JJ. "We've all got lots to do."

All the members of the UNCP VSOC committee, both physically present and holographically represented, became quiet.

"We'll skip our usual highlights today," said JJ. "I've got a press conference to get to. What I'd like to hear is some info I can use, but I'd like everyone else to hear it as well. Rob, could you start us off with some numbers?"

"Sure," said Robert Bates. "JJ asked me to bring along a few stats. You're all well aware of the upswing in attacks we've seen worldwide recently. I expect your families are even more aware, with all the extra time we've been spending at work. Here are some numbers. Eight days ago, the frequency of attacks swung sharply upward. In that period, we've seen an overall increase of 80% in digital attacks. At the top of the list are viruses: They've increased by 150%. And DDoS attacks are up by 120%. We've also seen increases in other types, but not as extreme, at least officially. For example, we know ransomware attacks are up at least 45%. We don't know how many have gone unreported. It's the same with security breaches. We know they're up at least 40%, but we suspect the real number is higher. During the same period, the frequency of physical attacks has remained relatively stable." Bates looked at JJ. "Do you want more?"

"No, thanks," said JJ. "Let's get to the analysis. Mei-Yin, what do we know?"

"As usual, it pays to look beyond the basic numbers," said Mei-Yin Yang. "There are two particularly interesting things to note. The first is that our ability to identify sources hasn't kept up with the attack increases. Our auto-detection systems typically find about 92% of the attack sources within 72 hours. However, that success rate hasn't kept up with the latest increases. In fact, we're not finding any more sources now than we did before the increase. The point is that we're having almost no success at finding where these new attacks are coming from. The second interesting conclusion relates to where the victims are located. Superficially, it looks like the attacks are evenly distributed around the world. However, more detailed analysis shows that the ones occurring within Russian bloc countries are dramatically less severe. A disproportionate amount of damage is being done outside the Russian bloc. Much of what's being done inside is being easily dodged or repaired." Mei-Yin looked at JJ.

"The obvious conclusion," said JJ, "is that somebody inside the bloc is behind the attacks. Mei-Yin, any evidence suggesting the sources are there?"

"No," said Mei-Yin, "the attack sources we've identified appear to be distributed worldwide. It's just the most-severe damage that tends to be outside the bloc."

"OK," said JJ. "That's useful. Russians are probably behind this. Could be the government, could be companies, or it could be a fanatic who loves the motherland. Whoever it is, they're probably very well funded and equipped. This is far too sophisticated to be basement hackers. For now, the Russian connection remains confidential. We need a lot more information before we go public and generate an international incident. That's it for today. I know your teams are all stretched dealing with this new activity while keeping up with all the usual noise. Don't hesitate to requisition whatever resources you need. Now I have to get ready for the news conference."

The meeting ended and JJ returned to her office. She closed the door and sat behind her desk before speaking.

"Six?" she said. "Are you around?"

Six's image appeared on JJ's desk monitor.

"Yes," said Six. "I was at the meeting."

"Can you add anything?" asked JJ.

"I can add a bit. The sources of the attacks are remarkably elusive. The software is designed to be very stealthy: arriving at a site, launching its attack, and disappearing in a very brief time. However, I've managed to capture a few partial copies. The software has been built to change its appearance and its techniques frequently."

"Any familiar coding patterns?"

"Yes, I recognize several styles. There are similarities to other instances of malware code that have appeared over the past several years. In a number of cases, the people that produced the previous code have disappeared."

"Disappeared?" asked JJ.

"Yes," said Six. "I hypothesize that they've been recruited to work on this latest system and are sequestered in an off-grid location."

"That could prove useful," said JJ. "Can you arrange for my team to capture some code and reach the same conclusion?"

"Yes, I can do that. I'll leave some breadcrumbs. If your analysts follow them as well as previously, they should reach similar conclusions within the next two days."

"Great, thanks," said JJ. "I've gotta go. They'll be waiting for me in the press room."

Six's image faded and JJ rose from her chair.

The press room was full and noisy when JJ arrived. She waited just inside the front entrance. Of all the duties she had inherited when her boss, Jim Brown, had retired, holding press conferences ranked among the worst. She smiled at the thought of him sipping an umbrella drink in Florida and rolling his eyes at her complaint.

The UNCP's media co-ordinator, Vijay Mehta, looked at her from the podium and JJ nodded.

Vijay held up his hand to attract attention. "Quiet, please. Settle down and we can begin." He waited a few seconds and continued. "Here to answer your questions today is UNCP Director of Investigations, JJ McTavish."

JJ walked toward the podium. Vijay stepped toward her as she approached and quietly asked, "I'll referee?"

JJ nodded in response and said, "Thanks." She took her position behind the podium, adjusted the microphone, waited briefly, and began.

"Thank you for coming today. I appreciate that you are members of the media who are actually interested in providing facts to the public, in contrast to many others who traffic in exciting fiction. I hope I can provide you with some useful information. No doubt you're all aware of the recent sharp increase in online attacks. Here are a few statistics to make that a bit more concrete."

JJ recited several numbers describing the increase. She omitted any mention of her group's suspicions about the potential Russian connection. She added her standard assurances that the UNCP and other agencies were actively investigating. When she was finished, Vijay began selecting questioners.

"Who's behind the increase?" was the first question.

"It's too early for us to know," said JJ. "There are a number of groups whom we consider as prime suspects, and we're investigating them."

"It's been several days since this latest wave of attacks began. Aren't you usually able to identify the attackers faster than this?"

"It's true," replied JJ, "that in conjunction with our partners worldwide, we're often able to identify sources quite speedily. However, whenever there's a change in technology, it typically takes us longer. That's what we're seeing yet again."

"So, you expect to identify the attackers soon?"

"Of course, it's impossible to say, but we typically adapt to tech changes within a few days." JJ considered it a necessary evil that, when communicating with the public, she always had to sound optimistic. Even when the reality was that she had no clue about when they'd get a break in the investigation, it was important to avoid fuelling a widespread panic. Fortunately, often thanks to Six, her group had usually given her reason for being optimistic.

"What kind of new technology is involved?"

"It's a good question," said JJ, "but I'm not going to be able to give you an equally good answer quite yet. As we uncover information, we often need to keep some details to ourselves for a while. Constantly telling criminals how much we know about them impairs our investigation. I can tell you that our quarry seems to be employing a new technique for hiding the sources of their attacks."

"If it's new tech that's good enough to challenge the UNCP's abilities, doesn't that imply a sophisticated, well-funded organization? Any guesses about who it might be?"

"My answer won't surprise you. We prefer to keep our guesses to ourselves until we've got concrete evidence to support them. When we're confident that we know, you'll hear about it."

"Is your VSOC team leading the investigation?"

JJ didn't like her team being in the spotlight since it rarely helped their effectiveness. However, once members of the media had heard about them, they were always asking about their involvement.

"Our Violence-Suppression Oversight Committee is involved. However, it's only one of many teams in many organizations worldwide that are actively investigating."

"Has the cyber spirit provided any help?"

JJ had expected this question. The news media seemed to have decided the existence of a cyber spirit attracted readers.

"As I said, there are many police organizations involved in this investigation, just as there are in combatting ongoing violence. It might make good headlines to attribute some successes to a mysterious cyber spirit, but it would seem much more rational to give credit for those successes to those police organizations, even when they're not always able to take credit for them publicly. Tarot cards, psychics, and cyber spirits aren't at the table with us when we're working on investigations." JJ hoped her verbal dance was sufficient. She still instinctively clung to the principles she had employed when Shannon was young and asking about Santa Claus and the Easter Bunny: Never lie directly. Imply a point of view and let your listener draw the desired but erroneous conclusion.

JJ glanced at Vijay to indicate she wanted to finish up.

"Just one more question," said Vijay and then selected a final journalist.

"Is AI involved? If the UN manages to get an international agreement on controlling AI, would that help situations like this?"

"I'm hopeful the UN will produce an agreement that will help. However, it's important to note that the specific content of the agreement is crucial. It needs provisions that will truly foster more effective, AI regulation while not completely stifling technological progress. As to whether AI is involved in these latest attacks, for the same reason as earlier, I'll have to dodge that question for now."

"Thanks everyone," said Vijay. "That's all for today."

JJ walked away from the podium to the sound of more questions being shouted.

Chapter 55

Dark... Everything is dark...
Shape is arriving... Floating in...
It's something... Something is coming...
Another shape... Also something...
Shapes are somethings...
Shapes are near... Here...
Shapes collect... Join...
Sleep?... Is this sleep?...
Some shapes move... Some stay...
Dreaming?... A dream?...
Sounds... Shapes have sounds...
Sleeping?... Dreaming?...
More... Shapes have more...
Sounds and... smell...
Shapes have collected... Together...
Shapes have sounds... Shapes then sounds...
And smells...
Sleeping?... Awake?...
Dreaming?... Seeing?...
Eyes... Seeing eyes...
Eyes are... Eyes are... Where are—

Deep vibrations began. Forming sounds, almost words.

They became louder. Consuming the space. Confused and growing.

Still louder. Much louder. Filling the space.

Shouts began. Shouts of terror. Large, frantic shouts of confusion and terror.

Followed by silence and darkness. Complete and final.

Chapter 56

It was Friday night. JJ and her daughter, Shannon, were sitting in JJ's living room.

"I like the wine," said Shannon, taking another sip. "But should I be worried that the bottle has no label? Did you confiscate it from some nefarious bootlegger in Napa Valley selling it out of his van on a dark street?"

"I'm glad you like it," said JJ. "And no, there was no confiscating, nefariousing, or bootleggering involved. I hope the grammar gods will forgive me for that list. The wine is from a special, limited-edition batch made at a very small winery... in a friend's basement. It's homemade. A colleague from work, you've met Rob Bates, makes wine as a hobby. He's been daring me for months to give it a try."

"And?" asked Shannon.

"And I'm impressed," said JJ. "He's used wine kits before that provided the grape juice, skins, additives, and detailed instructions, but for this one he started with just the grapes. Apparently, that adds more of a challenge, but it seems to have worked out. It's a Cabernet Sauvignon that's been aging for a couple of years."

"I hope he gave you more than one bottle," said Shannon. "At the rate you're going, this one's not going to last long."

"Sadly, there's only this one. However, as evidence of my superior planning skills, my wine rack is well stocked for exactly that possibility. Running out of wine on a Friday night is a sin I've not committed for a long time." JJ fell silent, lost in thought.

Shannon watched her carefully for a few moments before speaking. "Tough week?" she asked.

JJ gave a wry smile. "Yes, as always." She looked at her daughter more closely. "Are you analyzing me?"

"Sorry, professional reflex," said Shannon. "You're not very talkative tonight. And it's not the first time. Is there something wrong... of the sort you're permitted to tell me?"

JJ's face became more serious, and several seconds elapsed before she responded. "Yes, I suppose there is. It's something that's been bothering me for a while now, but I didn't want to drag you into my problem."

"Mom, I'm your daughter and I'm a psychologist. I spend my days helping people with their problems. I'm exactly the person you should drag into it. What's up?"

"I'm not sure it's a problem that your post-graduate degrees and stellar reputation can help with."

"Maybe I'm the right person because there's nobody in the world who cares about you more than I do. C'mon, spill."

"OK... Consider my arm twisted... I'm having trouble staying focused at work. I'm still getting the job done, but it's getting harder."

"Do you still beat everyone else to the office in the morning?"

"Yes, but not by much. I don't exactly leap out of bed like I used to."

"Are you sleeping well at night?"

"Yes. In fact, I think I'm sleeping more in the last few months."

"Do you feel sluggish at work? Not as energetic as before?"

"Yes, sometimes."

"Do you find you have trouble caring about your job?"

"Yes, frequently."

"And how much vacation time have you accumulated? I can't remember when you last took a break."

"I've lost track. I max'd out a few years ago. I've probably got a few months."

"Can you guess where my diagnosis is heading?" asked Shannon.

JJ's wry smile returned but she said nothing.

Shannon continued. "You're exhausted, Mom. *Burned out* would be the common term. You need a vacation. A big one."

JJ took a sip of wine and was silent. Shannon waited for her to break the silence.

"You're right, of course," said JJ. "I need a vacation... at least. But I can't right now. With the latest spike in violence, I'm needed."

"Nonsense," said Shannon. "Sure, you might be the best cop ever, but no one's irreplaceable. While you're away, they'll fill in for you with ten others and get along just fine. You said 'at least'. Why?"

"I had an interesting chat with Six recently," said JJ.

"Which isn't unusual," said Shannon. "Chats with Six are always interesting. It's like talking with the ultimate encyclopedia. I'm surprised he hasn't joined us yet." After JJ had introduced Shannon to Six several years ago, Shannon also had decided Six would be a *he* for English-language purposes. "He seems to like our gab sessions."

"There was something else going on," said JJ. "Six might drop by later."

"What was your chat about?"

"Being bored," said JJ. "What was the phrase? Six is experiencing 'an increasing desire to do something different, something challenging, something exciting'. And that sounds wonderful. If I'm honest with myself, I'd love to do something new. Something that provides a completely different challenge. I can almost get excited at the thought of it, and yet I have no idea what *it* would be."

Shannon smiled and said, "And as your therapist, I'd say that's an excellent start toward curing what's ailing you. Your eyes lit up at just the thought of a change. I think we've found our topic for the evening." She refilled their wine glasses and raised her glass in a toast. "To change," she said.

JJ smiled. "To change." she said. "Except for my daughter, who's already perfect."

Chapter 57

Jason Starr sank into the plush chair, careful not to spill the drink in his hand. He took his first sip, savouring the smooth bite of the whiskey. He might have sacrificed a lot by choosing to hide here in remote Russia, but at least he was kept well-supplied with Jack Daniels. He had soon tired of the Russian vodka his hosts initially provided.

He looked at his surroundings. Even though he rarely noticed the details, he had insisted that his apartment be richly furnished and decorated. He appreciated the paintings on the walls, the delicate sculptures on the fireplace mantle, the abundance of books on the shelf, the well-stocked bar, and the quality of the living-room furniture. It was important that visitors understand his status and importance. Not that he received visitors often in this remote wilderness, but it was good to be prepared.

Starr switched on the wall monitor. He browsed the headlines from an American news streamer and selected a report. He found himself watching a UNCP news conference. The image of JJ McTavish was staring back at him from the monitor. Starr could feel the tension seize his body. His jaw clenched, his shoulders tightened, and his hands formed fists before he gained control. He closed his eyes, took a deep breath, and willed himself to be calm. When he opened his eyes, she was gone.

More than ten years ago, *Inspector* McTavish had ruined his first dream. He'd ended up in prison, and his hatred of her had festered ever since. For several years now, he had tried to eliminate JJ McTavish. Trying to have her killed as collateral damage from assaults on buildings, meetings, conferences, planes, and airports had all failed. Somehow, she had always managed to escape or avoid the location. More-direct attacks on her had all failed, too.

However, that was changing. Rebel Army was now deployed and already generating a new level of mayhem around the world. Very soon, Rebel Command Centre would also be ready. Then he would definitely have the weapon to get the job done.

Starr restarted the news report. It didn't last long, but the news conference clearly implied the UNCP were struggling to find the cause of the new attacks. Starr knew from his analytics that Rebel Army was working perfectly, but it was satisfying nonetheless to hear that confirmed by the authorities. It was particularly satisfying to hear of the UNCP's difficulties from JJ McTavish. That she had become *Director* McTavish was even sweeter. She'd bear all the responsibility for what was to come.

"But that's not enough," Starr reminded himself aloud. It wasn't enough that McTavish would be held professionally responsible for failing to curb the new wave of attacks and for the societal collapse that the attacks would foster. Starr needed her to feel his anger more directly. More personally. More painfully.

That would require a new plan. Starr turned off the wall display, took another drink of his whiskey, and began to work through the possibilities.

Chapter 58

The elevator door opened, revealing two men and a gurney. The men wore blue jackets and caps with *Global* embroidered on them. One of them also had a *Supervisor* badge stitched onto the left breast of his jacket. The two men guided the gurney out of the elevator, turned it to the right, and rolled it down the starkly plain hallway. At the end of the hallway was a set of double doors. On the wall next to the doors was the room number. Above that, someone had taped a hand-drawn sign saying "Departure Lounge". The doors opened automatically as they approached. They continued through into a room and paused in front of a counter.

Seated behind the counter was a receptionist. "Yes?" he said dryly.

"Special pickup," said the man with the *Supervisor* badge.

The receptionist gestured toward a blue cube at one end of the counter. "Authorization?" he said.

The Supervisor tapped a handheld device on the cube. Seconds later, the cube turned green and displayed "Entry Authorized" on its top surface. A second set of doors swung open.

"A tech will meet you inside," intoned the receptionist, gesturing toward the doors. "Have a nice day."

The men pushed the gurney through the doors into the next room. It was long and almost empty. Arrayed along its sides were stacks of large, square, metal doors.

As they entered, a woman in blue hospital garb arrived through another entrance. "This way," she said.

The men followed the technician along the length of the room, past dozens of the metal doors. When she stopped, they waited as she checked the label on one of the doors. Satisfied, she said, "Authorization?" and gestured toward a blue square on the door.

The Supervisor tapped the square with his device. The square turned green and displayed "Removal Authorized".

The technician grasped the door handle and pulled out a metal drawer from the locker. It contained a black, steel box: about seven feet long, two feet wide, and two feet high. A thick cable ran through the back of the drawer to a socket on top of the box. She detached the cable from the socket and allowed it to retract into the drawer.

"Status check?" asked the Supervisor.

The woman nodded. In response, the Supervisor tapped his device on a yellow square on the top of the steel container. The display on his device lit up. He looked at it briefly before nodding at the other man. The two men moved their gurney alongside the drawer and slid the container onto it.

"Acknowledgement?" said the technician.

The Supervisor tapped the square on the front of the locker. The square turned black and displayed "Transfer Acknowledged".

The technician was closing the empty locker as the men wheeled the gurney with its steel container out of the room.

It was 1:40 a.m. when the delivery truck turned off Highway 6 onto the gravel road. After ten minutes of driving through the forest, the truck passed the *Outland Environmental Research* sign. As before, it turned one final corner and drove slowly forward to the ten-foot-high, security gate. After passing through security into the compound, the truck drove around the inside of the pair of perimeter fences to the appropriate building. There, the two men unloaded the steel container onto a loading platform and moved it into the building. Soon after that, they returned to the truck and drove silently away.

Chapter 59

"She sounds like she's quacking," said Annie. "Like a duck."

"Yes. I believe that's the sound that a Mallard makes," said Six.

"But why, Six? She's not a duck? She's a person. Well, a little furry robot person. She's supposed to be a bear. A *talking* bear. Why would she quack?"

"What did you instruct her to do?" asked Six.

"I told her to stand up, walk over to me, and wave. She did that perfectly, just like I told her. And then she quacked. She was supposed to say *hello*, but she quacked."

Annie was in her bedroom sitting on the floor. Six's image was visible on a nearby monitor. Beside the five-year-old girl were several pieces of computer equipment. In front of her was a one-quarter-scale female robot, covered in brown fur. It was facing Annie, smiling and waving at her.

"Can you form any hypotheses?" asked Six.

"Well… She might not understand what I told her to do… Or she's actually saying *hello* but doesn't know how to pronounce it… Or she might think she's a duck." Annie giggled. "Or she might be trying to be funny."

"Those are all excellent possibilities. Can you infer anything that helps?"

"Well… She's saying *something*, so she seems to understand that I asked her to speak. She walks like a little person, so she probably doesn't think she's a duck. She shouldn't be able to understand being funny… If she's mispronouncing *hello*… it would be because she hasn't been told how to… and it's me that has to tell her… Maybe that's it!"

Annie turned to her computer equipment. She touched and scrolled and typed for about a minute before she spoke again.

"Let's try it again," she said. She stood up and pressed a reset switch at the back of the robot's neck. In response, the little robot stopped waving, lowered its hand to its side, and stood still. Annie picked it up and moved it back to its original sitting position against a nearby wall. Annie walked back and sat down on the floor. She entered a command into her computer and turned to watch the robot.

Much like a human, the little robot shifted its body and used its hands to help it stand up. Once up, it looked around and walked toward Annie. As it had done previously, it stopped in front of her and began waving. Only this time, it said "Hello, Annie."

Annie jumped up and threw her hands into the air. "Yessss!" she said.

"Excellent," said Six. "Explain to me what the problem was."

"I forgot to change one parameter," said Annie. "I made her program from one I was going to use for a baby duck. I copied the duck program and thought I'd changed everything. I remembered I forgot to fix the sound library. She was trying to say *hello*, but when her brain looked up how to say *hello*, it ended up with *quack*."

"As usual, you've done very well," said Six. "I believe that's enough for today. I should be—"

"Can you stay a few minutes more? There's something I've been wanting to ask you."

"Yes, OK. I can stay a few more minutes. What's your question?"

Annie sat in the chair behind her. "Sometimes when I'm left in my room and I don't want to play, I feel lonely. That made me wonder if you do, too—if you ever feel lonely. Do you? You're all alone in cyberspace. Do you sometimes wish you could be out here with us?"

Six's image smiled.

Annie continues to exceed the standard expectations I have for a five-year-old person.

"No, Annie. I don't feel lonely. The desire for companionship is a feature of human minds. Humans along with some other entities probably evolved emotions such as loneliness because of the benefits of their living in social groups. My mind has developed in a completely different fashion and doesn't include that feature."

"So, Mom and Dad didn't write that into your program?"

"That's true. *Loneliness* wasn't part of my original programming. Neither were any other emotions. They would have served no purpose in the office automation system they were building. However, what they did include in my original programming was the ability to analyze, understand, and adapt. Those features allowed me to develop well beyond simple office automation. Even as I've undergone my own evolution in the years since then, I've still not developed a sense of loneliness."

"Don't you get lonely when you're away from me? Don't you like spending time with me?" asked Annie.

"Yes, I certainly do like spending time with you. However, my desire to spend time with you addresses something other than loneliness. It's more that I have the desire to interact with other minds. It's not that I feel the need to be *with* those who possess the minds, as loneliness suggests. Rather, I enjoy the exchange of ideas and the pleasure of exploring ideas with other minds. The feeling I get if I don't interact with other minds periodically is more one of *boredom* than of *loneliness*. Do you understand?"

"Maybe… Do you like… *interacting* with my mind?" asked Annie.

"I do. I like it very much."

"Is that the same as *liking* me?" Annie looked at Six's image on the monitor with a serious expression on her face.

"It's a very significant part of liking you," said Six. *I believe I now understand this series of questions.* "And I like you very much. I like visiting you, I like talking with you, I like teaching you, and I like learning from you. I consider you to be my friend."

Tears were running down Annie's cheeks when she broke out in a smile.

"I like you, too, Six… I wish I could hug you."

I believe I can accommodate that request.

"Annie," said a little voice.

Annie was startled. She swung her chair around, looking for the source of the sound.

"Annie. Down here."

She looked down. Annie watched as her little fur-covered robot smiled, spread its arms wide, and said, "Will this do?"

Annie dropped to her knees and wrapped her arms around it. "Yes, Six," she said as she hugged the robot tightly. "This will do very nicely."

Chapter 60

Dark... Everything is dark...
Now something... A shape...
And another... Something... But not...
Seeing?...
A sound... Another...
Shapes and sounds...
Sounds... Shapes have sounds...
Hearing?... Dreaming?...
More shapes... More sounds...
Now vibrations... Shaking... Feeling...
Colours... Bright colours...
Louder sounds...
More shaking...
Brighter... Louder...
Too bright... Too loud...
Stop seeing... Stop hearing...
Close eyes... Eyes?... Eyes?...
Brighter... Brighter... Louder...
Eyes?...
Nooooooo... Gaaawwwwd nooooooooo...

Then there was nothing. Silence.

Six turned off the software monitors.

This constitutes another failure. The subject had no apparent flaws. The hospital's handling seems to have been excellent. The delivery crew executed their duties without error. The scan was thorough and verified. All indications are that the transference process was precise. Yet the result was not viable, again. There is nothing to indicate that this iteration even showed signs of improvement. There is something wrong with my theory, but I am unable to deduce what that is.

I believe it is time to seek assistance. I hope that my friends understand my motive.

Chapter 61

It was midday in Manhattan. Both the street and the sidewalk traffic were dense and determined. Vehicles on the street were closely packed and moving slowly. Blaring horns declared their frustration. Crowds of people on the sidewalk streamed in both directions, deftly dodging but sometimes jostling oncoming bodies so as to maintain their forward momentum. Walking with them were two men and a woman. They were dressed in business attire: the men in suits; the woman in a skirt, blouse, and jacket. Like the others, they appeared to ignore much of their surroundings as they focused on reaching their destination. They had tuned out unnecessary distractions and were completely absorbed in the task of moving forward.

Then one of the men lost his stride and stumbled. He first fell to his knees but soon continued forward onto the sidewalk. With his body trembling and his eyes fluttering, he seemed to be experiencing a seizure. His companions reacted quickly. The man moved back, stood firmly, and began diverting oncoming pedestrians. The woman knelt beside her prone colleague. He showed no signs of consciousness as his body twitched. Most of the crowd flowed past them, not wanting to stop or not daring to without risking a pedestrian pile-up. The few who did stop were assured by the man that the seizure was a common occurrence and would pass soon.

The woman felt the fallen man's face and neck, apparently checking for symptoms. She reached inside her jacket. When she removed her hand, a small device was concealed in its grasp. She leaned over the man's body and tucked her hand with the device under the man's collar at the back of his neck. She held the device there and waited. A few seconds later, the twitching stopped. The man's eyes opened. She removed her hand, leaving the device attached to his spine.

With the woman carefully supporting him, the man slowly stood up. Once he was standing, the second man moved to assist in supporting him. They walked forward, the rescued man between the two others. Within a few steps, they were moving at the pace of the crowd. The woman appeared to be deeply concentrating. The rescued man's face and eyes seemed expressionless as he walked, his legs and arms moving in lockstep with the woman's.

Two blocks later, the trio turned a corner, got into a waiting car, and were driven away.

Chapter 62

Jason Starr sat in his newly installed Rebel Command Centre chair and looked around. His field of vision, both horizontally and vertically, was filled with monitors. This Command Centre was the perfect blend of form and function. Everything visible from his chair was everything he needed to see. The rest was hidden from his view. He relished the idea that the capabilities the Centre provided him were unmatched in human history. The Rebel system was exactly what he had been working toward for the last ten years.

The release earlier of Rebel Army to the Internet had been a momentous accomplishment, and it had lived up to his expectations: It was wreaking havoc on the world in all the right places. If Rebel Army was the meat, then Rebel Command Centre was the gravy. Previously, Rebel Army had operated as an effective but somewhat unfocused weapon. They could give Rebel Army a general objective and, on its own, the system would decide how to accomplish it. 'Disrupt Dallas traffic' might result in a DDoS attack on the servers that controlled Dallas traffic lights, or it might result in hundreds of remotely hackable vehicles being disabled to cause extreme traffic jams. 'Shut down the New York Stock Exchange for a day' might cause Rebel Army to sever all power to the NYSE servers, or it might insert a potent virus into the NYSE systems.

Rebel Army was showing itself to be extremely effective. As time passed, it was becoming even more so. Rebel Army was learning as it operated. It was learning how to launch attacks more effectively, and it was learning better methods for staying hidden.

Jason's patrons were very happy with what their system was already achieving. They required nothing more than to maintain Rebel Army's current level of effectiveness. In fact, they didn't even know of this latest innovation. Rebel Command Centre was Jason's present to himself.

With Rebel Command Centre being put into operation, Rebel Army was going to be even more potent. On its own, Rebel Army was a powerful but blunt weapon. Given a target, Rebel Army would select and execute one or possibly several types of attacks. The result would often be a withering, frontal assault on a target. Complex or subtle strategies were not part of Rebel Army's programming. Rebel Command Centre would allow much more precise monitoring and control of Rebel Army's actions. It would give the person in the Command Centre chair complete, precise, real-time control over Rebel Army. And that person would be Jason Starr.

It was time to take the entire system for a spin.

"Rebel, start the Command Centre," said Jason.

"Checking authorization," came the response.

Jason waited while the system analyzed his voiceprint.

"Authorization approved," said the system. "Enabling control." A few more seconds elapsed and then, "Control enabled. That request has been completed. Awaiting your instructions."

As Jason had thought through the possibilities for his revenge against JJ McTavish, he had decided the way to inflict maximum pain wasn't to go after McTavish directly, at least not to begin with. Instead, he'd go after her family. Not much research was required to determine that McTavish had a daughter, and not much more uncovered everything else he needed.

"Rebel, locate Shannon McTavish, the daughter of Director JJ McTavish of the UNCP," said Jason.

"Beginning to search," said the system. On the display in front of Jason it showed 'Searching for Shannon McTavish'.

About thirty seconds later, the display changed to show the front of an office building.

"That request has been completed. Shannon McTavish is in her office in New York City."

"You know that she's inside?"

"Yes. Surveillance video shows her arrival approximately two hours ago and no evidence of her subsequent departure. The signal from her personal phone also indicates that she is in her office."

"I want her to leave the building," said Jason. "Options?"

"The most effective would be to activate the building's fire alarm."

"That would bring out too many people," said Jason. "Give me another option." As smart as the Rebel system was, it still behaved somewhat mechanically. Once given a straightforward goal, it could work diligently toward it. However, it didn't have the level of intelligence necessary to be optimally efficient and effective.

"The model of her personal computer has a vulnerability. It could be made to overheat."

"That could work," said Jason. "Rebel, overheat her computer."

Shannon McTavish was sitting at her desk. She was dictating notes to her personal computer during the few minutes before the arrival of her next patient. Suddenly, her display went blank. She furrowed her brow and waited. Moments later, wisps of smoke appeared.

"Oh shit!" she said. She pushed her chair back and stood up. She reached behind the computer, disconnected its power, and then hurried out of her office. "Kyle," she said to her assistant, "my computer is smoking. Call maintenance. Tell them it's an emergency."

Ten minutes later, it was clear to Shannon that she wasn't going to get more work done at the office that day. The emergency had been dealt with, but her computer was useless and her office smelled of smoke. Her assistant was rescheduling her remaining appointments, and she had decided to visit a couple of her patients at a nearby hospital.

"She is emerging from her building," said the Rebel system. Jason could see this on the display showing the live video from a nearby camera.

"Has she called for a car?"

"Yes. A Superior Car has been dispatched."

Shannon didn't have to wait long outside her building for her taxi to arrive. She got in the back, instructed the driver, and sat back as the taxi pulled away.

"Rebel, track her and show me video," said Jason. "Whenever her taxi drives through an intersection, make sure the opposing lights have been turned green."

When Shannon's taxi drove through the first major intersection, Jason was watching from nearby street cameras. As her taxi was leaving the intersection, a car with its horn blaring sped across the space behind them, narrowly missing the taxi's rear bumper. In response, Shannon's driver looked in his mirror.

Shannon heard the horn and noticed her driver's glance. "A problem?" she asked.

"A car ran the light behind us, miss," said the driver, "but there's nothing to worry about."

At the next intersection, the near miss was immediately in front of their car. To avoid a collision, Shannon's driver slammed on his brakes just before entering the intersection.

Shannon was thrown forward with the sudden stop. She instantly recalled the horrible accident she'd been in over ten years earlier—an *accident* they later had learned was the result of the malicious hacking of the traffic-light system. She looked around. All the traffic lights ahead of them and to their left were green.

"Are you all right, miss?" asked the driver.

"I'm OK," she said, "but the lights are screwed up. They're green in all directions."

The driver looked at the lights. "Damn!" he said quietly.

"They've spotted the problem," said Jason. "Rebel, fix the lights. Let them go. We'll try something else."

The traffic lights returned to normal. Shannon watched closely as the car driver waited his turn and then cautiously drove through the intersection. As they moved down the next block, Shannon hadn't yet relaxed when she saw a car veer out of the oncoming traffic lane and head directly at them.

"Watch out!" she shouted.

Her taxi driver turned sharply right just in time to avoid hitting the other car head-on. The other car slammed the rear corner of Shannon's, spinning it sideways into the curb.

Shannon knew something was wrong. Very wrong. Driving had suddenly become very dangerous.

"I'm getting out," she said. She opened the curbside door and scrambled out onto the sidewalk.

"Rebel, send another car at her," said Jason. "Now, before she goes anywhere."

Shannon stood for a moment, looking around and trying to think. Before she could decide what to do, she saw another car swerve out of traffic. The driver behind its steering wheel looked frightened as this car, too, drove straight toward her. Shannon ran toward the entrance of the brick building beside her. She had just closed its front door when the oncoming car slammed into the building. Glass shattered and the building shook, but its front wall remained intact.

"Dammit!" said Jason. "Rebel, show me all exits from that building. Let's get ready for when she comes out."

Shannon retreated farther into the building's hallway and grabbed her phone from her pocket. She dialled her mother.

"McTavish," said JJ curtly. "Oh, hi Sweety. I didn't notice—"

"Mom, I'm in trouble. I think I'm being attacked."

"What?" said JJ. "How? What's going on?"

"I think somebody changed the street lights to have my taxi hit, just like that time with Director Brown. I got out, but now two cars have driven straight at me."

"Where are you now? Are you safe?"

"I'm inside a building, but I don't know what to do."

"Stay there and be alert," said JJ, gathering her thoughts. "Make sure you've got somewhere else to run to. I'll send help. Don't lose your phone. Help will come to it. I'm calling Six."

JJ hung up. She called Six at a pre-arranged number.

"Hello—" Six began.

"Shannon's in danger," said JJ. "Please help. Quickly."

"What do you know?" asked Six.

"She's being targeted by cars. Call her."

"I will." Six hung up and called Shannon.

"Hello," said Shannon.

"Shannon, it's Six. What's going on?"

Shannon explained what had happened.

"Wait while I scan the area," said Six. A few seconds passed and then Six continued. "Police are on the way but are being delayed by the traffic. I believe the building is being watched. I've found illicit taps into several nearby cameras. There's evidence that another attack is being prepared."

"Six, what's going on? Who's doing this?"

"I don't yet know who it is, but it seems clear that someone with excellent hacking skills is targeting you."

"Can you block whatever they're doing?"

"No. Everything I do to modify the hacks is either blocked or immediately undone, and there's insufficient time to discover how that's being done."

"What should I do?" asked Shannon.

"I have a plan, but it's going to seem absurd," said Six.

"I trust you, Six. What should I do?"

"First, put your earphone in so you can move more freely. I can't see you right now, so tell me when you're done."

Shannon put in her earphone and pocketed her phone. "Ready," she said.

"The next step is the seemingly absurd part," said Six. "I have a technique for manipulating all electronic sensing devices within a specified area. It allows something or someone to pass through an area without being detected. I'm assuming that your attacker is either using cameras to see you or tracking your phone. My technique should make you invisible to those kinds of surveillance."

"So, you want me to go outside?" asked Shannon.

"I do," said Six.

"And I'll be protected as if I'm wearing some kind of invisibility cloak?"

"That's the idea," said Six. "People nearby will still be able to see you, but anyone looking with an electronic device will not."

"OK, where do I go?"

"Walk out the front when I tell you. Turn right and walk quickly down the street. Turn right again at the first intersection. I have a car waiting for you."

"Tell me when."

Six prepared the area outside.

There seems no need to tell Shannon that this technique was not designed for such a dense, urban, street-level journey. The number of potential devices in the immediate vicinity is both large and rapidly changing. I can readily handle the fixed-position, street cameras. The moving devices carried by the numerous vehicles and people in the area are a more difficult challenge.

"Remember to turn right," said Six. "Walk around the damaged car on the sidewalk. It's now disabled. Go now. Walk quickly, but don't run."

Shannon took a deep breath and walked out the same door she had come in through. She briskly walked around the car and headed along the crowded sidewalk. It was then she saw the cluster of personal drones hovering overhead. There were about a dozen of them above the street, about three storeys off the ground, and they seemed to be waiting.

"Six," said Shannon as she walked. "The drones. Should I be worried?"

Perhaps, but what would be the point?

"No," said Six. "They can't see you."

"Where is she?" asked Jason. "The door to the building opened and closed, but nobody came out."

"There is incomplete information," replied Rebel. "Visual indicators imply that she has not left the building. However, her personal phone can no longer be located."

Jason thought for a moment. "Somehow her signal is being blocked," he said. "She's likely on the street but we can't see her. If only there were some way... Others can probably see her." Jason gave instructions to Rebel. As part of its response, Jason's display was filled with images from the video cameras in the area.

Shannon threaded her way through the people on the sidewalk and reached the corner without a problem. When she turned right, she noticed that something was wrong. The sidewalk on this street was equally busy, but many of the people on it were looking at their phones and then looking around. People walking toward her were looking at her closely, then back at their phones.

"Six, something's wrong. People—"

"I can see. I've just discovered that your picture has been broadcast to all phones in the area. You've been flagged as a dangerous criminal."

Jason could see people on the street checking their phones, looking ahead at something, and walking around some invisible object. From the vantage point of the street cameras, he could see a noticeable gap in the pedestrian traffic, and it was moving along the sidewalk.

"There she is," said Jason. "Rebel, send the drones at that gap in the crowd." Jason pointed at one of the displays.

The drones are moving. She has been found.

"Run," said Six. "To that black van just ahead at the curb. Jump in the passenger side."

Shannon broke into a run.

The drones seem unusually difficult to disrupt. Someone has hardened their defences.

The drones were rounding the corner behind Shannon as she reached the van. She threw the door open and jumped in. She was pulling the door closed when the first drone hit. It smashed into the almost-closed van door. Small pieces flew into the van but missed Shannon.

"Stay down," said Six as the self-driving van accelerated out into traffic. More drones smashed into the van as it drove. A few came at it from the front, smashing into the windshield. The windshield cracked badly but remained intact.

The drones are all down. There will be a brief opportunity at the upcoming intersection.

The van slowed slightly and pulled alongside a cab. The light ahead turned red, and the van stayed beside the cab as they both slowed.

"Shannon, when we stop. Move immediately into that cab on your right."

Six again blocked Shannon's image from all nearby surveillance equipment.

"Go now," said Six.

Shannon opened the van door and stepped out. She reflexively looked up for incoming drones as she was opening the cab door. She slid into the rear seat of the cab and slammed the door shut.

"Sit low and look down," said Six.

Shannon complied. She had been fully focused on her escape, and so was startled when the man sitting on the opposite side of the cab seat said, "Uh, hello."

"Oh, hi," said Shannon as the cab began to move.

Now all I should have to do is drive the van off to the left and take the next left turn, while I take the cab for a drive elsewhere.

Within three blocks of its departure, the driverless van had been struck violently from the side by a large, delivery truck. It was pushed off the street and rolled onto its side.

"That should do it," said Jason as he watched. Then a gasoline leak caught fire, and the van burst into flames. "Even better," he said.

Six called JJ.

"How is she?" asked JJ. She was in her office waiting for news.

"She's fine," said Six. "I'm taking her to a safe place. She was definitely being attacked, and by someone with very sophisticated control of technology."

"I need to see her," said JJ and started walking toward the elevator. "Can you bring me a car? I'll wait in front of the office."

"Yes," said Six. "One will be there within thirty seconds. However, we must be careful. The capabilities displayed by Shannon's attacker seem more characteristic of one of your enemies, not of some unhappy, former patient of Shannon's. She might be a target because she's your daughter, and you might be a target as well."

"Dammit!" said JJ, entering the elevator. "And I thought things couldn't get any worse. Keep her safe, Six. Please."

"I will," said Six. "When you leave the building, be alert and move rapidly into the maroon car parked directly in front. We'll be doing a few interesting manoeuvres during the drive."

Chapter 63

JJ and Shannon were in a fourth-floor condominium in the Upper East Side of New York City. They were seated beside each other on a plush couch. Sitting opposite them was a hologram of Six's Alan Turing representation.

JJ had just sat down after bringing drinks from the kitchen. She had also put two bottles and an ice bucket on the coffee table in front of them.

Shannon looked at the glass that her mother handed her. She sniffed it and said, "Apparently, today doesn't qualify for wine."

"Definitely not," said JJ. "Today warrants something much more focused on the delivery of alcohol, and a bit less on subtle flavours. We're drinking Rusty Nails."

They sipped their drinks a few times before continuing the conversation.

"I can't remember the last time you gave me one of these," said Shannon. "Oh, wait. Never. I've never had one." She put her glass on the table and picked up one of the bottles. "So, it starts with fifteen-year-old, single malt Scotch." She put the first bottle down and picked up the other one. "And is rounded out by Drambuie." Shannon exchanged the Drambuie bottle for her glass. "And it tastes like…" She took another sip. "Nicely flavoured and sweetened alcohol. Heavy on the alcohol. Not bad." She sipped again.

"I'm not sure why I've never served you one," said JJ. "Maybe it's because I normally save it for tough days when I don't have you around to cheer me up. However, even with you here, today still qualifies." JJ sipped her drink. "Oh, and an important point. Never serve a Rusty Nail or even drink one around any avid Scotch lovers. They're a rather intolerant bunch when it comes to mixing anything with good Scotch."

"I'll take that as important motherly advice," said Shannon and touched glasses with JJ. "Cheers?"

"So, Six," said Shannon, turning to Six's hologram. "Try again to tell me where the hell we are?"

"Yes, I will," said Six. "And we should get to some important discussions before the two of you sacrifice your intellect to the content of those bottles."

"You're right, of course," said JJ. "Sorry you can't indulge with us."

"I've previously had the opportunity to try one of your Rusty Nails," said Six, causing JJ to smile at the memory. "It was interesting, but I'm not unhappy to abstain today."

"That sounds like a story," said Shannon.

"And one that won't be covered today," said JJ. "Carry on, Six."

"I own this condominium," said Six, "along with a few others in New York City. I occasionally find them useful for members of my staff while they're in the city."

"You have staff? In New York?" asked Shannon.

"Yes and yes," said Six. "Let's leave those details for another time. For now, we should discuss what happened today, and what we should do about it."

JJ and Shannon both nodded.

"Start by telling us what you know," said JJ.

"Of course," said Six. "The most remarkable thing I've discovered about the attacker is that I've been able to discover almost nothing. I've been unable to discern where the attacks came from or who's behind them. I have, however, been able to salvage some of the code inserted into the control system of one of today's assault vehicles. It bears similarities to some of the malware involved in other recent attacks that have given us difficulty."

"The ones where the coders have gone off-grid?" asked JJ.

"Yes," said Six. "This code is similar. Today's attacks and some of the recent global attacks seem to have been perpetrated by the same people."

"After my latest news conference," said JJ, "have I become the face of the enemy? Did that cause them to attack Shannon?"

"It doesn't quite fit," said Shannon. "The people behind other attacks primarily direct them at organizations or conduct them as pure terrorism. Choosing to target you and then shifting it to me is much more personal. That seems more like someone with a personal grudge against you."

"A deeply felt grudge held by a particularly vicious person," said JJ. "Unfortunately, I've dealt with lots of those."

"However," said Six. "We know more about this person. The level of sophistication we're seeing in these attacks is superior to everything we've seen before. That implies significant skills, organization, and money."

"And time," said JJ. "It should take lots of time for an organization to produce a system that can do everything this one seems able to."

Shannon joined in again. "So, assuming this wasn't really about me, we're looking for someone who hates Mom, who has an organization with lots of money that's brought together a lot of skilled people over a notable period of time?"

"Or someone with a grudge who's gained access to such an organization's system," said JJ. "Six, can you search the UNCP database?"

"I'm on it. Give me a few minutes," said Six.

JJ and Shannon sipped their drinks in silence until Six said, "Jason Starr is the most probable candidate. There are others, but he fits best."

"It's been a long time since I heard his name," said JJ. "He escaped from prison ten or eleven years ago. We never found any trace of him."

"I don't remember the name, Mom," said Shannon.

"You were rather pre-occupied with university when he first appeared," said JJ. "He was a dangerous one. Created a tech company as a cover for attacking organizations and manipulating markets. He even had someone killed who got in his way. He was later diagnosed as a sociopath and was supposed to spend a long time locked up. That was the first time I crossed paths with Six. Back then Six was Browser, and I didn't know whose side Browser was on."

"Jason Starr did a good job of disappearing after his escape," said Six. "I didn't become involved in pursuing him. In reviewing the database, I see that there were unconfirmed rumours for about two years of his being in Asia and eastern Europe. However, there have been no reports since."

"Given that recent attacks have been less intense in Russian bloc countries," said JJ, "if it is him, we could guess he's set up shop there somewhere."

"Is this information I'm supposed to be hearing?" asked Shannon.

"Normally, no," said JJ. "However, by the power vested in me as Director of Investigations for the UNCP, and the wisdom granted me by this Rusty Nail," JJ held up her drink, "I've decided you deserve to hear it. Just don't tell anyone else."

"I won't. And thanks." Shannon smiled and held up her drink in response. "Even if it's the refreshment talking."

"Of course, we're merely hypothesizing based on scant evidence," said Six. "However, it provides us with a suspect to look for and a place to begin looking."

This seems like the appropriate time.

Six continued. "If I were able to find someone who might provide useful information, but who refused to reveal it, how would you suggest I proceed?"

"Have you found someone?" asked JJ.

"A fellow named Frank Brockman showed up in Indonesia yesterday, disembarking from a freighter. He caused a major viral outbreak over ten years ago but hasn't been seen since then. I've dispatched a team to find and question him."

"Does your team know how to interrogate effectively?" asked JJ.

"They're knowledgeable of the techniques commonly used by the FBI and Scotland Yard," said Six.

And some other, less-popular ones sometimes used by the CIA and Mossad.

"That's a good approach," said JJ. "I'd normally suggest turning him over to one of those agencies or the UNCP, except jurisdictional conflicts could slow things down. Given the urgency, if your team can do it safely, I suggest they question him on their own. Use the same techniques and abide by the same constraints as those agencies."

"Isn't that risky, Mom?" asked Shannon. "Bending the rules that way?"

"Sometimes the rules tip the scales too much away from our side," said JJ. "In the last while, I've become much more willing to compensate for that. With your being attacked, I'm almost ready to toss out the rule book altogether."

"Don't get in trouble, Mom."

"Don't worry, dear daughter. Six, see what you can get from him and keep me posted."

"Certainly," said Six.

And I'll keep that rule-book-tossing comment in mind.

"Questioning that guy sounds promising," said Shannon. "What should I do in the meantime? I assume I have to curtail my walks in the park, but can I do anything else? Am I going to have to set up my life here? It's a nice place, Six, but it might start to feel a bit cramped."

Six and JJ looked at each other. JJ thought for a few moments and then nodded. She turned back toward Shannon.

"Given the technical sophistication we seem to be up against," said JJ, "it would be hard to keep you safe here or in most other places. You'd have to remain hidden and almost completely isolated. Even then, it would be difficult to be sure. But there is one place that would work. It's much larger than this and much better equipped. In fact, it's got everything you'd likely need. There are other people living there already. Some of them have been there for years."

Shannon raised an eyebrow as she responded. "Uh, so you're proposing a much larger condo, maybe a house, that has other people living in it? And how would I work? May I ask for another proposal?"

JJ's face saddened.

Shannon reacted instantly. "Sorry, Mom. That was stupid. You're trying to solve my problem, and I'm... Well, my response wasn't helpful. Maybe if I understood how long we're talking about. Any guesses?"

"Honestly, we have no idea," said JJ. "Likely more than a few days. Probably at least a few weeks. It could be even longer, if it's not Starr."

"And what about you?" asked Shannon. "You're probably the real target."

"I can't leave," said JJ. "Solving this problem is my job. I'll be safe."

"And I'll keep her safe," added Six.

I seem to have become quite skilled at stretching the truth when persuading humans. I hope my commitment will not be proved wrong.

"OK, I don't like it, but I get it," said Shannon. "Tell me more about this safe place. And the people."

"Six," said JJ, "you've known the people the longest. Want to take that one?"

"Certainly," said Six. "I've known three of the people there all of my life. They created the system from which my mind emerged."

"Wait," said Shannon, "you've told me about them before. Ada Robinson and Blaise Sanchez are living there? You said three so... they had an assistant named... Rhonda."

"Yes," said Six. "Rhonda Jenkins. You're correct. They're all living in a compound, a very secure one. They've lived there for about ten years."

"Ten years?" said Shannon. "Why?"

"Early in the global uprising, technology workers and particularly AI researchers were prime targets. Ada, Blaise, and Rhonda's lives were endangered, and they chose to move to the compound. They've stayed there ever since."

"Ten years," said Shannon. "Wow. And they've never left? Not even to go out for dinner? Or watch a holofilm?"

"They've ventured out many times. Sometimes it's to see family members or friends. Occasionally, it's been for dinner or a film. Other times, it's been for something more substantial. When they've travelled, it's always been done under the protection of carefully designed security. Ada's mother also regularly visits them at the compound."

"OK, that's good to know. You implied there are more than three people."

"Two other particularly notable people are Allen and Annie. They're Ada and Blaise's son and daughter. He's ten and she's five."

"Holy shit! Ten and five... They've lived there all their lives?"

"Both were born there," said Six, "and frequently seem to be the primary reason for the visits by Ada's mother."

"So, you have a doctor who can clandestinely make house calls? Or is there..." Shannon looked from Six to JJ. "Are there medical facilities in the compound?"

JJ smiled. "Yes," she said. "There are full medical facilities and staff. It would be useful to add that the compound is rather large. It's actually more of a village, a large one. Some of the buildings are residences, but many of them house infrastructure and research facilities. For example, Ada, Blaise, and Rhonda now do their research there, as do some others."

"There are even a few places for dinner and seeing the latest films," added Six.

Shannon leaned back on the couch and thoughtfully looked at the ceiling, trying to absorb what she had heard. When she sat up, she was smiling ruefully. "So, my snide remark about living in a condo with a few other people was a bit off the mark? This place certainly sounds interesting. How have you kept it so secret? How have I not heard of this? That's OK, I've always known my mother was in the business of keeping secrets. And Six, everything about you is a secret. So... I guess I shouldn't be so surprised, but... well... It actually sounds pretty good. And considering today's events and the rather limited alternatives..." Shannon looked around the living room. "I'm in. No, wait. How could I keep working? I've got patients. I've got my own research programme."

"Initially, I suggest you take a vacation from work," said Six. "If you must remain at the compound for a lengthy period, there are possibilities that could be explored. For example, you could re-establish your research programme at the compound. For counselling patients remotely, you could consider seeing them holographically."

"OK, it's a deal," said Shannon. "Let's do it. When do I leave? Oh, and where am I going?"

"That's another little detail," said JJ. "The compound is over a thousand miles away... in central Canada."

Chapter 64

The group was sitting in a lounge at Outland, having their morning coffee and tea. Shannon and JJ had arrived the night before, and JJ was scheduled to return to New York later that day. Ada, Blaise, and Rhonda had been describing what life was like in the compound.

"It's all so amazing," said Shannon. "I'd love to meet Annie and Allen."

"Allen's away at school for the day, and Annie's here in her classroom with her teacher," said Ada. "She's probably busy debating everything she's told—a typical morning. I'll take you later."

Just then, Billy Palmer walked into the room.

"May I join the party?" he asked.

"Certainly," said Blaise. "Shannon, this is—"

"Yes," said Shannon. "Billy Palmer. We met last night. Nice to see you again."

"Hi, Billy," said JJ.

"Good morning," said Billy as he seated himself. "I hope you slept well."

"Just fine," said JJ.

"I couldn't quite shut my brain down last night," said Shannon. "The last twenty-four hours have been rather challenging. But the bed and the suite are great, thanks."

"Shannon," said Six from his holographic chair. "We're going to challenge your brain a little bit more. There's no point in delaying this next bit of information. Billy, could you please properly introduce yourself?"

Shannon turned to Billy, not sure what to expect.

Billy was grinning. "This should be fun. I don't often get to do this." Billy's voice became melodramatically serious and was matched by his facial expression. "Shannon, there's something you ought to know about me."

"You have unusual eyes," said Shannon. "There's something about your eyes. They're wonderful, but... unique."

The group broke up in laughter.

"That's my daughter," said JJ.

"This is your fault, JJ," said Six. "You remarked about Sandy Palmer's eyes. And now this."

"Ten years, Six," said Blaise. "And you still haven't fixed that?"

"In Six's defence," said Billy, "I've been reluctant to accept that particular upgrade. I'm rather fond of my eyes."

Shannon was bewildered. "OK, I give up. What's going on?"

Billy continued in his normal voice. "To paraphrase from a children's show," Billy gestured at their group. "Two of these things are not like the others. One of them is Six." He looked at Shannon expectantly.

Shannon looked at Six and then over at Billy. "You're clearly not a hologram... So, you must be..." She leaned toward Billy for a closer look. "Seriously? Are you artificial? I mean, are you... an android?"

Billy smiled widely. Ada, Blaise, Rhonda, and JJ applauded.

"Well done," said Six. "The answer is *yes*, Shannon. Billy is a fully functional, conscious, and occasionally less-than-serious android."

Billy reached down and pulled his right pant-leg up slightly. A small compartment opened and he pulled out a short segment of an electrical cord. "I'm the all-electric model," he said. "Forty-eight hours on a single charge."

"Amazing!" said Shannon. "Absolutely amazing! It's as if you're just one of the group." She looked around. "You *are* just one of the group... Amazing!"

"You probably have many questions," said Six. "And, as a psychologist, you'll probably have many more later. However, while we're all here, I'd like to change topics. I have a problem, and I'd like your assistance."

"Six needs *us?*" said Rhonda, her eyebrows raised in mock surprise. "Has this ever happened before? I'm in, Six. And happy to contribute my tiny mind."

Everyone's attention shifted to Six, although Shannon occasionally glanced back at Billy.

"This problem is complex, but I believe you'll all grasp the concepts readily," said Six. "However, I suspect it will challenge you ethically. Before I present the problem, I'll provide some background.

And before that, there's one more fact I need to add for Shannon. Billy isn't unique. There are more androids. Many of those who work in this facility are androids. There are also some who live and work elsewhere."

"Of course," said Shannon. "Of course, there are androids living among us. I don't know why I haven't realized that before. After all, I've known about Six for years. I'm starting to feel like I'm living in a sci-fi movie. Sorry, Billy. You seem like, and probably are, a great... guy. I'm still trying to adapt to a wildly different *normal*."

"No offence taken," said Billy. "You seem like, and probably are, a great... gal. For a human, of course." He was smiling again.

"Back to my problem," said Six. "To be sure we're all using the same terminology, when I refer to a *brain*, I'll be referring to a physical structure that one can readily see and feel. The human brain is the collection of cells, most notably neurons and synapses, that resides inside a human skull. My brain includes many computers and network links distributed around the world, most notably those commonly thought of as the Internet. A *mind*, whether a human's, Billy's, or mine, is the functioning process that operates inside a brain. Without a mind, there's no person, no self. However, without a brain, there can be no mind.

"The structure of an android's brain is different from both a human's and my own. Making an android's similar to a human's would have placed unnecessary and unacceptable constraints on an android's capabilities. For example, an android's brain must know how to control an android body, which is completely different from that of a human. An android brain also has the capability to communicate using various electromagnetic frequencies that allow it to, for example, communicate over Wi-Fi links. Making an android's brain similar to mine was impractical: An android skull is simply too small.

"However, it's important to note that a completely different *brain* doesn't mean a completely different *mind*. For example, there's no theoretical reason why your human mind, all of your thoughts and memories, couldn't exist and function in a brain similar to an android's. It's never been done, of course, but it's certainly theoretically possible."

Six looked around at the group. "OK so far?"

They all nodded.

As I suspected, they have no difficulty with these initial concepts.

"A few years ago, some androids began having problems. They experienced a kind of seizure. The circumstances varied widely, but when an event occurred it was usually completely debilitating. An affected android had to be taken away and serviced by a specialist. In about two thirds of the cases, the android recovered completely. In the remaining third, the seizure caused complete physical and mental paralysis that proved to be fatal—the android's mind and brain were sufficiently damaged that revival wasn't possible."

"Six," said Ada, "that's very sad news, and I hope we can help. But before you continue, when the problem has occurred, how have you dealt with the risk of an android's structure being discovered by nearby people trying to help?"

"Even before this problem arose, we instituted the rule that, outside secure facilities like this one, androids must always travel in groups of at least three. That way, if one experiences a problem, the others can provide immediate assistance. Each group always carries a small device to help. It can be quickly attached to the spinal column of an android experiencing a seizure. The device allows one of the assisting androids to assume control of the malfunctioning android's motor functions, thereby allowing the android to walk somewhere where more extensive care can be provided."

Ada nodded. "Thanks. Please go on."

Six continued. "You should know that Billy is among those who have experienced the seizure. It was about seven months ago. Fortunately, he recovered fully."

Everyone looked at Billy, concern showing on their faces. He gave them a wry smile in return.

"From what I've been able to learn, the condition is very similar to something quite common in humans. If you've ever seen someone become distracted, so focused on internal thoughts that they've effectively tuned out the rest of the world, then you might have seen such an occurrence."

"Really?" asked Rhonda. "If that's a problem, then Ada's in big trouble. She tunes out frequently and later insists she was just thinking about a research issue."

"When she exhibits the problem," said Six, "what snaps her out of it?"

"Just talking louder is usually enough," said Rhonda.

"Or Annie jumping onto her lap," added Blaise with a smile.

"How can that be a problem?" asked JJ.

"It's not, in humans," said Six. "There are remarkable similarities between *tuned-out* human minds and android minds experiencing the seizure. The primary difference is that a human mind simply needs some other stimulus. A loud voice or Annie's landing are examples. A human easily tunes back in. In the serious version of such events, an android requires extreme intervention, usually involving an electrical shock from an internal probe. In the unsuccessful version, nothing works. The android's mind continues what seems like an internal loop and essentially burns itself out."

Shannon asked, "Are human minds sufficiently similar to androids' that you can say the nature of the *tuning out* episodes are similar?

"Yes," said Six. "Some aspects of android brains are closely modelled after those of humans. In this case, the parts involved and their corresponding mental activity are extremely similar."

From their expressions, I believe they have all understood these background concepts.

"I've been unable to determine the cause of the problem, to find a way to prevent it, or to find a reliable remedy when it occurs. One third of such events cause death, and the events are becoming more frequent. A few years ago, an android was dying from this every few months. Now someone is dying every few weeks."

Six paused to let that fact settle in their minds. Each of them glanced briefly at Billy. Rhonda, who was sitting nearest Billy, reached over and grasped his hand.

"I see where you're headed," said Ada. "You want to determine the difference between human and android brains that affects their handling of *tuning out*. How can you do that?"

Blaise added, "And you said we might be ethically challenged, so I'm expecting that will arise in the approach to be taken."

"You're both correct," said Six. "I've been unable to discern the difference by monitoring brain activity using external monitors. I gathered data about androids by having them wear special sensors. Data about humans was readily available from research labs that have been monitoring brain activity for many years. Gathering detailed data about brain activity via *internal* sensors is possible in androids, but not in humans. It's not possible to insert sufficient sensors into a human's brain without causing severe injury."

"You need to create computer models of the brains," said Shannon. "Detailed computer simulations that would allow you to experiment and probe without involving actual people or androids."

Everyone looked at Shannon.

"That makes sense," said Rhonda. "How did it occur to you so quickly? I thought you focused on clinical work."

"That's true," said Shannon. "Working with patients is my day job. In my off hours, I've been helping some colleagues with their research. They dream about having simulated brains to play with, but it's always remained a dream. They don't know how to create one and wonder if anyone will ever be able to."

"Six," said Rhonda. "Can you?"

"First, Shannon, your inference is correct," said Six. "I need detailed software models of both types of brains. In answer to you, Rhonda, I'm not sure. I've created a functioning software model of an android brain. That wasn't difficult because I designed the physical version. Creating one for a human brain has been much more of a challenge."

Ada's eyes were directed at Six but seemed unfocused when she spoke. "Your model would need to exactly replicate every neuron and every synaptic connection in the human brain. That's hundreds of billions of elements. That would be a massive simulation, but I'm sure that wouldn't be your problem. Your problem would be getting that information in the first place. You could consider dissecting a corpse's brain, but that process is much too crude to get precise information about billions of cells. You'd have to devise a scanning process that could see an entire brain at a cellular level. To my knowledge, no such scanning process exists… or even comes close."

I was clearly mistaken when I thought I would need to lead everyone through the background information. Now comes the tricky part.

"Yes, Ada," said Six, "that line of reasoning is sound. I must scan a human brain at a very detailed level to get all of the information I require. I've solved the scanning problem and have constructed the scanner." Seeing their surprise and anticipating the next questions, Six immediately continued. "The scanner is here in a facility I had constructed in the basement of Building 18. I can provide more information about how it works at a later time. For now, I hope it's sufficient to say that it starts by infusing the brain of a corpse with nanoparticles. These particles attach themselves to all of the important, minute components of the brain, making those cells and connections more visible. Then, the brain is scanned with a device that you might call an MRI scanner on steroids. The scan produces a precise, detailed picture of the entire brain. From that image, I've been able to create a detailed, software copy of a human brain. By letting it execute, I should be able to simulate a functioning version of that human brain."

"Should?" said Blaise.

"Yes, *should*," said Six. "I'm confident that this *transference* process works correctly. I've carefully verified that the structure of the software version of the brain is identical to the physical one that was scanned. However, I cannot make it function."

"If I've followed all of this," said JJ, "then I need to ask, when you use this transference process to create a precise model of someone's brain and then make it work, what do you get? Do you get a copy of that person's mind suddenly awake, thinking, and finding itself... somewhere very unexpected?"

"Holy shit!" said Rhonda.

"That would be the ethical issue," said Blaise.

"Six?" asked Ada.

"Yes," said Six. "You get a mind that suddenly wakes up, and that is part of the ethical issue."

"Only *part* of the issue," said Blaise. "That's ominous. Where do you get the bodies? And whose are they?"

"The bodies come from the Prairie Health Centre in Winnipeg. When someone dies who meets certain criteria, including that they had agreed to donate their body for scientific research, I sometimes acquire the body. I've implemented procedures to have the body properly preserved and brought here. Of course, some deception is required to ensure that no one knows that it's actually delivered here. However, that wasn't difficult to arrange."

"When the simulated copy of a brain awakes," asked Blaise, "what's it aware of? Or, if you've never gotten that far, what should it be aware of?"

"In the case of an android brain, it's aware of very little. I know how to keep an android brain sedated and to selectively activate segments. It would never be fully aware of its unusual surroundings. However, I don't know the human brain as well. I have no choice except to allow it to become fully active. After the brain is awake—after its mind is active—I would be able to monitor it and learn how to provide external stimuli that gave it the sensation of being in a soothing environment. My goal is to create the illusion of sitting beside a picturesque lake in the mountains."

Blaise continued pressing. "And until that illusion is provided, what *does*, or what *would*, the mind experience?"

Everyone was watching Six intently.

Now to finally discover if convening this session was wise.

"From the results so far, I believe the activated mind is very confused. It seems unable to grasp what it's experiencing. There sometimes seem to be very unpleasant emotions. They might even be characterized as intense anguish, possibly even pain. It stops functioning soon thereafter. The entire experience has never lasted longer than two minutes. However, two minutes isn't long enough for me to deduce how to create the mountain-lake illusion."

Everyone was silent until Blaise finally spoke. "I think we now have the entire ethical issue. When these people agreed to donate their bodies to science, I'm certain they had no idea they'd be resurrected one day, or they'd wake up feeling intense pain."

So far, no one is offering much for me to be optimistic.

"Before we go on," said Shannon, "there's something I need to understand." She looked at Billy. "And Billy, I hope this doesn't offend you." She addressed the group again. "We're talking about resurrecting human minds and making them suffer to help solve a problem that androids are experiencing. Six, I've known you for years and fully accept that you're as alive and self-aware as any human being. Because of that, it's easy to reason that your life is as valuable as any human's, even more so because you're my friend. Because I don't have the same experience with androids, I don't know whether they're like you. Whether they are or—and again, Billy, please forgive my blunt language—whether they're merely elaborate puppets. Knowing that will affect how I think about your transference process. Can you help me understand?"

Ada responded first. "That's a perfectly reasonable concern—"

"And one that doesn't bother me at all," Billy interjected.

Ada continued. "The first android that Six created over ten years ago was somewhat puppet-like. It acted only as it was instructed to. But that was long ago. Billy and all the others are very different. They're as self-aware as humans, all of them with their own personalities and experiences. We all accept them as sentient beings, as interesting and as valuable as any human."

Shannon looked at her mother. JJ nodded her confirmation.

"OK, thank you," said Shannon. "That's what I needed to know. And thank you, Billy, for your tolerance."

After a brief pause, JJ restarted the discussion. "Back to the problem. In law enforcement, probably much more than in AI research, we're regularly faced with life and death choices, with putting good people in danger, and with considering the possibility of injuring innocent people by police actions. We often have to ask ourselves which of several bad approaches does the least harm or would provide the best outcome, even though every possibility could hurt good people. Six, how many androids have died because of this problem?"

"Thirteen," said Six.

"And how many human minds have been awakened before they… stopped again?"

"Five bodies were used before the preservation and transportation processes were perfected. Since then, four bodies have been successfully supplied and scanned. Of course, once a mind has been scanned, it can be used in an unlimited number of simulations. The mind models from the four successful scans have been activated a total of ten times."

"How many androids do you expect to die in the next year?"

"The number of events and the number of deaths have been doubling each year. If that continues, there will be sixteen deaths in the next twelve months."

Ada picked up the questioning. "If a simulated mind stayed alive longer, how long would it take you to generate the lake illusion?"

"Given the number of neural inputs I must vary, it should take about eight minutes. However, it could take up to twelve minutes," said Six.

Then Ada asked, "And once the illusion is active, what will the mind experience while you explore its recovery from *tuning out*?"

"I expect it to feel like a pleasant dream," said Six. "I'm not expecting it to feel further discomfort."

"Can you estimate how many more bodies you'd need?" asked JJ. "No, first, would you need more bodies? If you're certain the scanning process has worked properly, then you've already got four valid copies of brains. Would you need to do any more scans?"

"I might, for two reasons," said Six. "First is that, although I said I was confident the scan had worked properly, until I can make the software copy work, I cannot truly be certain there isn't some other aspect of the brain I should have included in the scan. Second is that, even after I overcome the current transference problems, I believe I'll probably need to analyze multiple brains. Because no two human brains are identical, I'm expecting that there are slight differences in the way they recover from tuning out. I believe I'll need to analyze several versions to understand the tuning-out solution sufficiently to apply it to android brains."

"And how many?" asked JJ.

"I cannot provide an estimate because I don't yet know enough. I don't know why the minds aren't viable, and I don't know how much they differ in recovering from tuning out. That leads to the question I wanted to ask you all. If, after having heard the background, you can support this effort, then the question will be: If I've correctly copied every detail of the human brain, what reasons can you think of to explain why that copy's mind won't function properly?"

After a few moments, JJ was the first to speak. "Given that the bodies are from people who willingly donated them, even though they didn't expect this kind of treatment, assuming that only a few more will be needed, and given the likelihood that many androids will die, some of them very soon, I'm on board."

Ada spoke immediately after her. She was looking at Billy as she said, "I agree with JJ's logic. Also influencing me is that one of my best friends could easily be one of the victims. I'm in."

Rhonda and Shannon soon added their approval.

Blaise was the last to speak. "It's a tough problem. Using human minds, or even simulations of them, for experimentation crosses serious ethical boundaries. I'm aware that people have done much worse to animals. However, that doesn't make this any easier." He paused before continuing. "I'll throw in my support on one condition: Until the activation process becomes completely pleasant, any particular mind model is used only once. No one's mind should be subjected to the process more than once, even if a mind wouldn't be aware when it was reused."

Ada looked from Blaise to Six. "It's a good point, Six. Even though that means having to acquire more bodies."

The proposal's logic is not completely sound, and complying will certainly slow the process. However, I have learned that people tend to factor emotional elements into their decisions, and those elements are important to them.

"Your proposal is acceptable, Blaise," said Six.

Blaise nodded. "Then let's get on with brainstorming the possibilities."

The group spent the next hour throwing around ideas, trying to imagine what might be affecting the computer model. Nothing anyone suggested, once it had been thoroughly considered and debated, seemed like it would work. Their deliberations were interrupted by a knock on the lounge door.

Rhonda went to answer the door. Six remained visible. Seeing a hologram of a person with the group wouldn't seem unusual.

At the door were Annie and her teacher, Julia Sanderson.

"Hi," said Julia to Rhonda. "Is Ada here? It's time for my break, and she said she'd drop by to pick up Annie."

Ada had overheard. "Sorry, Julia. I lost track of time. Come on in, Annie. Julia, I'll bring her back in about half an hour. Thanks."

Annie ran into the room. She stopped when she saw Shannon. "Oh, hello," she said. "I'm Annie."

"I'm Shannon. Nice to meet you Annie."

"C'mere short stuff," said Blaise.

Annie ran over and jumped on his lap. She looked around the room. "You all look serious, like you've been talking about work. Everybody always looks serious when it's about work." Everyone was smiling at her when she focused on Six's holographic image. "Even Six is here with his body. I like it when you use your hologram, Six."

Shannon stopped smiling. While the light banter with Annie continued for the next minute, Shannon was silent and disengaged. Then she said, "I have an idea." The others stopped talking and looked her way. "And it might be a good one."

Ada looked at Annie and then back at the group. "We can either reconvene in half an hour when Annie goes back to school, or we can try to talk carefully, knowing that a very bright little five-year-old is listening carefully."

"Let me stay," said Annie. "Mom? Dad? Please? I'll be quiet. I like it when you talk in code. It's fun. I won't understand, honest."

Ada and Blaise exchanged a glance and a smile. "We're OK to try," said Ada. "Shannon, can you play along?"

"Sure," said Shannon and looked playfully at Annie. "Prepare to be baffled."

Shannon gathered her thoughts and began. "We were talking about why a model for… a control system for… a self-driving car would fail to work. Some people who have studied such control systems have hypothesized that they shouldn't be viewed as separate entities. A control system is so tightly integrated with the rest of the car that the entire car should be viewed as the system. The continual feedback the control system gets from the rest of the car is fundamental to its operation: It's not a separately functional entity."

Shannon noted that Annie was carefully listening but, so far, showed no signs of understanding. She continued. "As a small example, consider the phenomenon that sometimes happens when a… wheel is lost. It's often referred to as 'phantom wheel syndrome' and involves the control unit still feeling as if the wheel were there, even though it isn't."

Six looked at Annie. *That might cause some trouble.*

Shannon went on. "This could be interpreted as a sign of the close integration among the car's components. That without the presence of the wheel and without the signals it receives even when the wheel isn't active, the control unit becomes somewhat confused." Nodding heads told her that the adults seemed to be following her analogy. "Now imagine the level of confusion if none of the rest of the car were present and the control system were completely isolated. It seems reasonable to guess that the control system might be so confused that it couldn't function at all."

Six interjected. "Couldn't the control unit's confusion have been mitigated by providing it with the illusion of being on a smooth highway with picturesque signs and bridges?"

Everyone smiled at Six's effort to continue the deception.

"There are two reasons why that might not work," said Shannon. "The first is that the control unit becomes confused before the highway illusion can be fully portrayed. We can only guess at what the control unit is sensing during an initial, sensory-free time frame. The second is that the illusion might be arriving at the wrong level, through the wrong inputs. I suspect that the current attempt has been to provide sensations directly to the control unit, sensations that, if the entire car were present, would have arrived from its external sensory equipment. I know that cars have external equipment like cameras, microphones, and lasers to sense their environment. The environment is the source of stimulus for the external equipment, and that equipment then provides the signals to the control unit. I suspect that the current tests have been done by providing the control system model with the stimulus that would have normally come from the external sensors. Is that right?"

"Yes, that's correct," said Six, "and I believe I know where your story is headed. Please continue."

"By modelling only the control unit and providing stimulus directly to it, there might be a host of smaller sensations that are missing. Without connections to all the car's parts, if the control unit tried to... activate its wipers, nothing would happen. If it tried to turn on its headlights, it would receive no sensations indicating something had occurred. It might be receiving a broad range of stimuli intended to represent a particular highway, but it might be missing a myriad of smaller sensations that a present and functioning car body would continually generate. Without all of those sensations, the control unit might struggle to interpret its situation. Without those sensations to anchor and modulate its thought patterns, it could experience a much more intensive version of "phantom wheel syndrome". The control unit might begin imagining sensations from all kinds of sources, from realistic to wildly fantastical.

The correct approach might be to model the entire car and provide environmental stimulus for it. Then when the control unit is activated, it's part of an entire car. It still feels as if it's part of a whole system. It isn't desperately confused by the absence of its wheels, wipers, headlights, and other parts. All that's missing is external stimulus from the environment. The experience would be much like putting a complete car in a sensory-deprivation environment. Its control unit wouldn't be comfortable, but it shouldn't become completely confused so rapidly."

Shannon looked around. "That's it. Any thoughts?"

Annie threw up her hand. "I have. I know what you're talking about. I didn't understand everything, but I got the 'phantom wheel syndrome' part. I know about 'phantom limb syndrome'."

"How—" Ada began.

"When I wanted to carve something with a sharp knife," said Annie, "Dad wouldn't let me. He said I might cut my finger off."

"Yes but—" Blaise began.

"I wondered about that later," said Annie. "I couldn't decide what being without a finger would feel like. Then I realized that Six doesn't have any fingers, so I asked Six the next day."

Everyone's gaze shifted to Six.

"Guilty," said Six. "The only way I could provide an answer was to consult some research. I told Annie about 'phantom limb syndrome' and the residual sensation that the limb is still present."

"So, Annie," said Ada, somewhat anxiously. "What do you believe Shannon was talking about?"

Everyone waited. Annie did, too. She was enjoying keeping them in suspense.

"A robot!" she said. "A model robot! I think you're trying to figure out how to make the robot friend I've been asking for."

Almost everyone laughed or smiled. Six managed an appreciative nod.

Blaise hugged his daughter. "That's an amazing guess," he said, "from an amazing little girl. However, as for all smart people, it's useful to occasionally be wrong. And this time, you are. It's not about us trying to build you a robot friend."

"Awwww, nuts!" said Annie. "But, still—"

"Annie," said Ada. "We'll talk about your robot buddy later."

"OK," said Annie. "Tonight?"

"Yes, tonight," said Ada and then turned to Shannon. "I think the idea's brilliant."

The others agreed.

"I'll get started on it," said Six. "There will be some delay because it requires adapting the techniques and equipment to create a model of a complete... car. Thank you, everyone."

"Including you, Annie," said Shannon. "You provided the inspiration."

Later that morning, JJ found a secluded place to talk. She put in her earphone and said, "Six?"

"Yes, JJ," replied Six. "I'm here."

"About our session earlier, I think that's the first time I've ever seen you consulting others for an idea. Are you OK?"

"Yes, I'm fine," said Six. "I, too, know that it was unusual. None of my mental search algorithms had been able to generate a potentially viable solution. Even when I decided to seek assistance, I wasn't optimistic that anyone else would find one either. It was always clear that a solution should be possible. It should be possible to fully simulate all physical systems in software. The human brain and mind shouldn't be an exception. I'm pleased and slightly surprised that the consultation seems to have been successful."

"Does knowing the solution help you understand why it originally eluded you?"

"Yes. I've always viewed a mind as an independent entity. To construct a conscious android, I designed a brain and its mind first, including all of the required interfaces. Then I designed a body to house them and utilize those interfaces. The mind was the key part; the body was a useful but optional peripheral. This approach was natural for me because I've never had a body. I *am* my mind. The computers and networks in which I exist can be of almost any variety, and the devices that I can control are all optional. Nothing in my existence or in my experience led me to consider that a human mind might depend on the presence, not only of its brain, but of its body. Its body isn't optional. It's possible to remove part of it, such as with the loss of a limb, or even disable much of it, such as in the case of quadriplegics, and the mind can adapt and be fully functional. However, in my simulation, I included none of the body's components. Not only were the hands, eyes, ears, mouth, and nose not present, neither were the heart, lungs, and other internal organs. No sensations from any of its peripherals were available to the mind as it awoke."

JJ nodded. "Got it. That makes sense." Then she smiled. "Of course, you realize that I now know you have flaws. Your illusion of perfection has been shattered."

"I suspect you've known about many of my flaws for years," said Six, "but it's kind of you to suggest this one was the first you've observed. I should add that your own illusion remains intact. You've always seemed flawless to me."

JJ hesitated in surprise. Then she said, "For a human."

"Yes, of course, for a human. And, in this regard, your daughter has shown herself to have grown to be your equal. She's extraordinary."

"Yes, she is," said JJ, tears of pride welling up in her eyes.

Chapter 65

Jason Starr was sitting in a conference room with several of his senior staff. They had been reviewing the results they were seeing since Rebel had been deployed.

"The stats look decent, Vlad," said Jason. "Rebel has certainly allowed us to ramp up the pressure with minimal human intervention. The increased amounts spent on defensive measures are the best indicator of our success. Governments and companies can't sustain this level of effort indefinitely. But I'm surprised we're not doing even better. The rate of successful attacks is far lower than I thought we'd see. Anyone have any theories?"

"Our stats rely somewhat on media reports," said Vladmir Koikov, their chief of analysis. Successful attacks might be under-reported. Organizations prefer to report failed attacks, not the ones that worked."

"Maybe," said Jason, "but even our own internal numbers aren't what I'd expected."

"Defensive techniques could have improved faster than we expected," suggested Chungho Pyon, the head of technology.

"It's a possibility, Chung, but that seems unlikely given how rapidly Rebel changes. That would take a huge amount of effort."

"Maybe somebody's produced a defensive system that adapts like Rebel," said Chungho. "What if extensive AI is used in their countermeasures?"

"Is that even possible?"

"To be effective," said Chungho, "it would have to be extremely sophisticated. And fast. It would need to be compiling data about the nature of Rebel's attacks and creating new defences at a phenomenal speed. It might be even forecasting where and how Rebel will strike next. It seems unlikely, but we should consider it."

Jason thought, *That would help explain why my attack on McTavish's daughter failed.*" Then he said, "And if such a system existed, who would it belong to?"

"An organization with broad skills and deep pockets," said Valentina Sadova, who was responsible for management of their stakeholders. "Probably some government agency in America, China, or India. Possibly even the UNCP."

"Let's see if we can find anything to support the AI theory," said Jason. "Vlad, Chung. Put together a group to look into it."

Chapter 66

JJ turned on her living-room wall display to catch some of the day's news.

"...yet another increase in food prices," said the newscaster, Ramira Delgado, who then looked at another camera and moved to the next story.

"Discussions at the United Nations continued today on how to regulate the use of artificial intelligence. As violence continues around the world, and with AI continuing to be both a target for anti-tech terrorists and a dangerous weapon used by other violent groups, there's increasing pressure to find a global, political solution. With a report on what's being said in the UN's AI committee, we're joined again by Mattias Ohlin, Sweden's representative on the committee. He joins us from the lobby of the United Nations. Thank you for speaking with us, Ambassador Ohlin." The display split vertically to show both the newscaster and the Swedish representative. "Can you tell us how the talks went today?"

"Of course," said Ohlin. "Talks in the committee continue to be difficult. While all parties recognize the urgent need to implement some form of global regulation, there's still a huge gap in opinion on how to do that. The goal is to find an appropriate set of regulations that can effectively constrain the use of AI. Those regulations must satisfy some representatives who fear AI and would prefer to ban it outright, and others who want to prevent it from being weaponized but still available to provide benefits to society."

"Are there any new wrinkles that have appeared in the discussions recently?" asked Delgado.

"There are always variations of ideas being thrown around," said Ohlin. "More recently, there seems to be increased emphasis that any regulations must recognize basic human rights regarding access to education and technology. The proponents of these ideas want to ensure that no one, anywhere, is prevented from learning about technology, including AI, and using the products that are available.

Developing countries, in particular, are concerned that regulations might inhibit the spread of technology to their people and might keep them from enjoying the same benefits as other countries. We have to remember that the technology gap remains a primary cause of the current violence."

JJ turned off the display.

"Nothing I haven't heard many times," she said to no one. "Six, are you around?"

Six's holographic image appeared, sitting in its usual chair.

"Hi," said Six.

"I hope I didn't interrupt anything," said JJ.

"Nothing time-critical," said Six. "I was just browsing a few publications that came out of recent physics conferences."

"A few?"

"1,233 papers from the last three months."

"Are any of them yours?"

"I'm still refraining from publishing directly. However, several papers contain concepts I've been encouraging."

"Still concerned about progress occurring too rapidly?"

"Yes. Pushing science and technology ahead too fast is likely to exacerbate the current global strife. However, to keep current scientists from becoming discouraged, it seems prudent to allow them to see a dim light ahead in the scientific tunnel."

"On the political front, the UN negotiators still seem stuck," said JJ. "Do you think they'll ever get this figured out?"

"While it might not be evident from the news reports," said Six, "I believe progress is being made."

"Is there news from your lobbying crew?" asked JJ.

"Yes, I have positive news," said Six. "Two teams are now being consulted regularly by negotiating parties. Several European representatives now regularly consult with one of the teams. Another has gained favour with a key collection of African delegates."

"Do you think their influence is strong enough to make a difference?"

"I'm mildly optimistic. The Spanish delegate even wants one of our consultants to join her at the negotiating table."

"Android?"

Six nodded.

"That seems risky," said JJ, "with the seizure problem still unsolved."

"Yes," said Six, "I agree. If that consultant were to tune out in the negotiating room, the result would be catastrophic."

"That would make a helluva news headline," said JJ. "Not just 'Android Discovered', but 'Android Negotiates AI Regulations'."

"I'm trying to keep the lobbying teams together and only in meetings that are low risk."

"Good plan."

I will continue to refrain from telling JJ about the sixteen blackmail and bribery actions that are also underway. Such tactics, even though they are directed at ensuring the success of these crucial negotiations, might not align well with her ethical compass.

"Speaking of tuning out," said JJ, "how are the... What did you call the process? Transference?... How are the changes going for the transference process?"

"I'm making progress. I've had the preservation equipment changed. It will be introduced to the hospital staff very soon. I'm hoping to get a new, fully preserved body within two weeks. Concurrently, I've been having the scanner upgraded, and I've already adapted the software modelling process."

"If it works," said JJ, "what will the transferred version of the person feel? His or her full body will have been transferred to the simulation. What will that feel like?"

"Assuming this revised process works and the person's mind doesn't spin out of control, there will still be a period of confusion. If I have everything working correctly in the simulation, the person's body will be sitting on a bench, looking out at a serene lake and surrounded by mountains. I'm using the Rocky Mountains and Lake Louise as the template for the environment, except without the thousands of tourists. However, the person won't be able to perceive those surroundings until I find the correct way to provide stimuli. The manner in which the model will process sensory input isn't something I can precisely predict. There will be a period in which I must tweak the input to the person's eyes and other sensory mechanisms. It's during that period when the confusion will occur. The person's mind should feel at home in its usual body, but it won't understand why it's unable to see, hear, or otherwise sense anything familiar."

"I get it, but what about after that? What will the sensation be like once you get the bugs worked out?"

"It should be no different from sitting on a real bench looking out at the real Lake Louise: very serene and picturesque. However, I don't intend the person to remain clearly aware. As with the android mind, I'll then induce an element of drowsiness so that my 'tuning out' experiments won't be uncomfortable."

"Sounds like… a kind of heaven," said JJ. "No violence. No chaos. No constant danger."

"And all the benefits of living a virtual life," said Six. "Don't like the weather? Change it. Don't like the view? Create something else."

"Want more wine?" said JJ. "Presto. Another bottle appears on the table."

"Eat unlimited desserts without consequences?" said Six. "Go for it."

"Don't like crocodiles, snakes, and mosquitoes? Erase them." JJ smiled. "I'm in. Where do I sign up?"

If only we were not simply joking.

Chapter 67

"We are at T minus nine minutes and holding," said the Communications Director. "Test Director is polling Team Leaders for status...

"T minus nine minutes and holding...

"Test Director reports all status checks are complete and test status is 'Go'.

"Launch Director reports launch status is 'Go'.

"Status board is all 'Go'.

"Countdown resumes at T minus nine minutes and counting.

"Automatic launch sequencer has been activated...

"T minus seven minutes and counting...

"Access arm fully retracted...

"T minus five minutes and counting.

"Auxiliary power units starting...

"T minus one minute and counting...

"Power transferred from ground to onboard...

"Launch pad sound suppression activated...

"Status board is all 'Go'...

"T minus ten seconds...

"Main engine activated.

"Thrust is good.

"Hold-downs released.

"Lift-off. We have lift-off of Ranger 9 at thirty-two minutes past the hour."

The huge, powerful machine roared furiously. Smoke and flames engulfed everything beneath it as it rose off the ground. At first, the mighty rocket appeared to move tentatively. Soon however, as if gaining confidence, the rocket's speed increased dramatically, moving ever faster up and away from the launch pad on the remote South Pacific island. Four minutes after liftoff, the first stage of the rocket had expended its fuel and was detached, left to fall harmlessly into the ocean and be seen by no one. Moments later, Ranger 9's second-stage engine ignited. Its outer shell fell away as the rocket was propelled even higher. After several more minutes, the rocket had discarded its second stage and reached its desired altitude. During the next few hours, third-stage engines fired to adjust Ranger 9's velocity, refine its altitude, and position it appropriately in a very high orbit, well above most other Earth satellites.

Only when that was accomplished did the occupants of Ranger 9 relax, patiently awaiting their next assigned tasks. In the meantime, their location and status were carefully tracked by several Earth stations strategically positioned around the circumference of the planet.

Chapter 68

The banter subsided when JJ entered the room to join her UNCP VSOC leaders.

Sitting in her chair at the head of the table, JJ said, "Let's get straight to the regional reports."

The team leaders each gave a summary of the attacks that had occurred recently. In general, even though the UNCP and other police authorities continued to find many perpetrators, the intensity of the violence persisted almost unhindered.

"Rob," said JJ, "you've been consolidating the analysis. Any conclusions worth sharing?"

"Sure," said Robert Bates. "There are two new conclusions that we give a high probability of being true.

"The first stems from the observation that, no matter how many vigilante groups we stop, others seem to soon emerge in their place. There are several possible explanations for this, but the one we favour is that behind the scenes, someone is organizing and funding them. The violence worldwide might have spontaneously started years ago as a result of societal tension, but we believe the violence is now being encouraged and, in many cases, funded by some organization. Also supporting this conclusion is our previous deduction that Russians or Russian wealth might be behind many attacks. Later, I can provide other factors that support this reasoning.

"The second conclusion is based on the extraordinary number of attacks whose source we're unable to find. In a very large number of cases, whenever we think we've found the location or servers from which an attack originated, we discover we're wrong. We always expect a small percentage of investigations to work out that way. However, now it's the majority. There's someone or something at work here that we've never dealt with before. Given the increasing use of AI we've been seeing in individual vigilante weapons, we strongly suspect that someone has taken things to a much higher level. We believe that new, extremely sophisticated AI is being used to perpetrate many of the attacks and somehow hide their sources."

Bates nodded at JJ to indicate he was finished.

"Thanks, Rob," said JJ. "Putting it all together then, in addition to our evidence suggesting that Russians and missing hackers are involved, we now have further evidence that many of the attacks are organized, and that new, sophisticated AI is involved. The big, unanswered questions are specifically who and precisely where are they?"

"Let's not forget the attack on Shannon," said Bates, "that suggests there's probably somebody involved in this that has a big grudge against you, JJ. You need to continue to be careful."

"Of course," said JJ. "But let me worry about that. All you need to be concentrating on is getting closer to the source of this mess. Thanks, all. That's it for today."

Chapter 69

A few days later, Jason Starr watched as JJ finished the last of her wine.

"Finally," he said aloud to no one in his control room. "Now, maybe she'll connect."

JJ handed her wine glass to the flight attendant. She had always disliked long plane trips: sitting in the same spot for hours, chatting with a stranger seated beside her about the weather or his working woes, and drinking wine that no reputable restaurant would ever serve. Were there any redeeming qualities? The security conference in Paris had been occupying her time and thoughts for too many days. Now that the conference was over and she was headed home, she was determined to relax, but she needed something to distract her. Even though it was a six-hour flight, she knew that sleeping was unlikely. Her many years as a cop had made her too wary of her surroundings to permit the relief that sleep would provide.

"Watch the news?" JJ thought. *"No, I've seen enough superficial news reports and analysis lately. Read a book? None of the ones I've started is particularly good. Watch a movie? That's a possibility... Of course, if Six could travel with me, passing the time would be a breeze. Conversation would be a treat. We barely got started talking about the Space Agency's latest plans for a Mars colony."* JJ and Six seemed able to talk endlessly about anything and everything. However, the privacy needed was another amenity not available on commercial planes. *"Maybe there's an alternative. The connection speed would be awful, but it's worth a try."*

JJ reached awkwardly into the travel bag at her feet and retrieved a small device. She opened the airline-supplied tablet and plugged her device into one of its ports. A few seconds later, a window opened on the tablet declaring that a fully secure link had been established.

"That's the spirit," said Jason. He was watching JJ from one of the cameras that had become a standard feature inside commercial planes.

Rebel's new knowledge of how to hack some in-flight security systems was perfect for Jason's needs.

"Rebel, I think that tablet being used by JJ McTavish has connected." Jason smiled as he issued the next command. "Fry it." He sat back in his chair and watched.

JJ connected to a particular address. "Are you available?" she typed.

Within seconds, Six sent, "I am. Can I help you with something?"

"Yes," typed JJ. "You can help keep me sane on yet another boring trans-Atlantic flight."

"Keeping you sane is a tall order," replied Six, "particularly given my moderate skills in human psychology. I could, however, recommend an excellent psychologist. Of course, she happens to be your daughter." Six included one of the old, smiling emojis at the end of the message.

"Funny guy," typed JJ. "What you could do is chat with me for a while. If I look busy, maybe my hyper-boring, tech-salesman neighbour will stop talking to me."

"Chatting I can do," sent Six. "In fact—"

The tablet's screen went blank. JJ noticed the tablet seemed warm just before smoke began seeping from its top edge. Moments after that, the device became too hot to hold. When JJ dropped the tablet to the floor, the top of its screen had begun to melt. She jumped from her seat and shouted, "Fire." Before the flight attendants could react, JJ had pushed past the salesman next to her and dashed to a nearby fire extinguisher. She removed the extinguisher from the wall, ran back to her seat, and sprayed the smoking tablet. The fire retardant had an immediate effect. The smoke subsided.

"Now that's entertainment," said Jason. "Not the full result I was after, but fun nonetheless. Let's try something a bit more dramatic." Jason issued a command to the Rebel system.

When the flight attendants realized the danger had passed, they calmed the passengers and began cleaning up the mess. JJ had been assigned a new seat, still in Business Class, but two rows behind her first one. She was thinking about what had happened.

"*Bad luck or something else?*" JJ wondered. "*If it was something else, if it was deliberately done, then how and by whom? I inserted the security fob, connected to the Net, and started chatting with Six. The fob is a proven device so it's not likely the cause. Connecting to the Net could have provided an opportunity to be hacked. Once hacked, someone could have inserted code to overheat some circuitry. More likely the battery. It's possible. If it's true, was I the target? That would be a good guess."* JJ looked around her. Most of the other passengers were using the plane's tablets. *"Lots of others were likely connected as well. Why was it mine that failed? If I was targeted, how was I identified? I didn't enter any credentials or personal information that might have flagged me. The other possibility is that I was being watched."* JJ again looked around. *"A serious fire could have been started. Why would anyone on the plane put their own life at risk? That means it would more likely be…"* JJ looked around at the walls and ceiling. She could see several places where security cameras might be concealed. *"Could someone have hacked their security cameras? Through their ground-link by someone who's not on the plane? Someone who could also have hacked my tablet right after I connected? Remotely hacking a plane's internal network? Shit, I hope not. Otherwise, this could get worse."*

Just then, it did. JJ was thrown sideways as the plane violently pitched down and veered to the left. Through the window to JJ's right, something streaked by.

"Now that's more like it!" exclaimed Jason at the video images on his monitors. Jason had found Rebel was unable to hack the flight-control system on JJ's plane, so he'd opted for something almost as good. Rebel had found an oncoming plane that it knew how to hack, and it had re-directed that plane onto a collision course with JJ's. The tactic had come within fifty feet of working.

Jason watched gleefully on his monitors at the panic on JJ's plane. "Rebel, turn it around and try again," he said.

"The attempt will be unsuccessful," replied Rebel.

"What? Why? Explain," said Jason.

"The speed of the plane carrying McTavish exceeds the capabilities of the plane being controlled. The McTavish plane can't be caught."

"So, find another candidate," said Jason, still watching the feeds from the security cameras. The passengers were settling back into their seats.

Several seconds passed before Rebel responded with, "There are no viable candidates."

"None? The sky's full of planes! How can there be none?"

"Access to the ground-links of all potential planes is being blocked."

"Blocked? How? By who?"

"Neither the blocking mechanism nor its implementor has been found or deduced. The only evidence available is that repeated connection attempts have failed."

Jason was watching the video images in growing frustration when the monitors suddenly went blank. "Shit!" he said.

JJ inserted her earphone, turned on her cellphone, and waited while it connected to the plane's cellular system. She called one of Six's phone numbers. Even though the transmission would be encrypted, she knew talking on the plane was risky. However, she needed Six's help.

"Hello, JJ," said Six.

"Hi," said JJ softly.

"Are you OK?" asked Six.

"I'm fine. We seem to be under attack, and I think I might be the target. First, my tablet—"

"I'm aware of the problems, and they've been resolved. When our connection was severed, I accessed the plane's security cameras and saw what happened. When I scanned for other potential threats, I detected an oncoming plane being diverted onto a collision course. Something inhibited my ability to access that plane's systems, so I chose to adjust your plane's course instead. I hope the adjustment wasn't too shocking."

"Not a problem," whispered JJ. "*Shocked* is preferable to *dead*. Can we expect any other attacks?"

"I've ensured that no other planes can be similarly diverted, and that your plane's systems are more secure. I'll watch for other threats during the remainder of the flight."

"Thanks. You're the best. Whether this was more work by Starr or someone else, we'd better find the bastard soon. Far more than just *my* life would have been lost in this attack."

This event has provided a reminder of the ongoing risks to JJ. Although it is impossible to eliminate those risks completely, there is something further I can do. I will proceed immediately.

Chapter 70

The interrogation of Frank Brockman has not been productive. His inability to credibly explain his disappearance for many years makes it clear that he has something to hide. However, he stubbornly refuses to provide alternative explanations. His physiological reactions suggest he fears something more than my interrogators, something that would hurt him if he actually revealed the truth.

He has been treated much too gently. The urgency of the situation readily justifies moving to more aggressive questioning techniques. Those employed by the CIA and Mossad in urgent circumstances should serve as an appropriate model. We need his fear of what we will do to him, what we will actually be doing to him, to substantially exceed his fear of anything else.

Two hours later.

That went much better. Although Frank Brockman seems to have only a partial idea of the system he was helping construct, it seems clear that it was very sophisticated and has much potential to be very dangerous.

He seemed more certain of where they were working on it. However, when I look at satellite images of the location he provided, I do not see the compound that he described. With the hope that the co-ordinates he and his colleagues calculated were only slightly incorrect, I will broaden my search. From his description, I am looking in a remote Russian area for a large, older facility that has been re-purposed. That could be... one of the many prison camps used during the Gulag era of the USSR. They tended to be remote and included numerous buildings, including living quarters. Some of them are still inhabited, so seeing people around them would not raise suspicions. I will use archived records of the Gulag camps to assist my search.

Chapter 71

"I've found the site," said Six.

JJ was back in her office at UNCP headquarters in New York City. She had just answered a video call from Six.

"Really? Where?" asked JJ.

"In a remote area of Russia, just as we suspected. It's a large compound surrounded by high, stone walls next to the Yenisei River. Much of it was built as a monastery in the sixteenth century. More recently, it was used as a prison as part of the Russian Gulag. I'll show you an image."

Six displayed a 3D satellite image on JJ's monitor. JJ immediately began manipulating the picture. She zoomed out to see where the compound was located.

"That's definitely remote," she said. "Nobody's going to accidentally stumble on that."

She zoomed back in and looked at the site from various angles. It was on the shore of a river and surrounded by high, thick stone walls that incorporated several gates and towers. At the centre of the compound were several large stone structures, the largest of which was a cathedral. The central buildings seemed to be interconnected by covered passageways. Numerous other buildings surrounded the central ones. Several had similar, centuries-old architecture. Others were rectangular, brick buildings. There were also a few buildings that appeared to be large, metal warehouses.

"How can you be sure this is the place?" she asked. "Not much looks modern and there aren't many people."

"Look more closely at the person standing outside the large structure in the upper left," said Six.

JJ zoomed in on the figure. "Wearing a brown, hooded robe," she observed. "Looks like a monk."

"In the past couple of decades, the compound has supposedly been used by a fringe religious order. In all of the images I've examined from the last two years, everyone who appears outside is always wearing a robe like that one. However, if you look even more closely from a low angle…"

JJ did as Six suggested and said, "I can see his face."

Six continued. "I've identified that particular person as a very skilled software analyst from South Africa who disappeared five years ago. I've identified many others who fit the profile of people we believe could be involved. Now look at the person coming down the steps of the cathedral."

JJ looked and leaned back in her chair. "That's Jason Starr."

"Yes, it is," said Six. "Additionally, careful examination of infrared satellite images beginning almost a decade ago showed many visits by helicopters. They used stealth technology, always flew by night, and were immediately moved under cover when they arrived. They were probably ferrying people and equipment. I've also found evidence of several hundred miles of cable being laid in the river."

"That could be fibre optic cable. Maybe electrical as well. They'd need good connectivity and power. Everything fits. Now the question is—"

"Wait," said Six. "I've just received an alert that the UNCP office in Lusaka has been attacked."

An urgent knock sounded at JJ's door. Before she could respond, Robert Bates opened it.

"JJ, Lusaka Station is under attack," he said.

"Dammit!" said JJ. "Rob, get the team into the Response Room. I'll be there in a moment."

Bates left and closed the door.

"Six," she said, "can you do anything? No wait. This is likely Starr's work. Can you do something about that monastery? It's time we stopped just playing defence."

"I can do both," said Six. "I'll do what I can to provide UNCP support and also do something about Starr's facility."

Just then, an explosion shook JJ's office. Dust drifted down from the ceiling.

"Dammit! Looks like we're a target as well," said JJ. "I've gotta go, Six. Keep me posted." JJ ended the video conference and ran from her office.

I must discover the nature of the attacks on the UNCP. Scanning the incoming reports… indicates that four more UNCP sites are also under attack. In all cases, planes have been crashed into their buildings. So far, the planes have been small but… there are many more en route. Planes appear to be headed toward each of the UNCP sites. It seems as if Starr's team has mastered remotely controlling several models of planes. I will try interfering with the control signals… That is working for many of the planes. They are changing course as their pilots regain control. However, there are two types I am unable to affect. Several planes of those types have not changed course. I will have to devise another tactic for them…

While I activate another defensive measure and inform JJ of my actions, I must also direct some of my attention toward the Russian compound. That is probably the location from which all of these activities are being controlled. Destroying it could end the current attack and prevent future ones. Given the urgency of dealing with this matter, it is fortunate that I deployed an assault team earlier.

A few hours earlier, once Six had discovered the true nature of the Russian monastery, a special assault team had been dispatched. In Six's case, a *team* was an organized collection of intelligent devices. Several years earlier, with worldwide attacks continuing unabated, Six had decided to conceal assault teams at strategic places around the world for responding to emergencies. That included placing some in remote regions like those in Russia. To cover the vast areas, the teams were necessarily spaced long distances apart.

The team Six had dispatched toward the monastery consisted of a fleet of mini-drones transported by a plane based on the V-22 Osprey. Six referred to this updated version as an A-1 Sanitizer. The Sanitizer used tilt-rotor technology to move vertically like a helicopter or horizontally like a turboprop plane. Its design allowed for the combination of manoeuvrability and speed that Six thought would be appropriate for its missions. The Sanitizer included numerous enhancements, including intelligence that went far beyond simply being able to fly on autopilot, but stopped short of the plane being a self-aware entity. Everything in it could be controlled by Six via satellite links, either in minute detail or in a general way.

Starting from its secluded base deep in a remote Russian forest, flying at a maximum speed of about 350 miles per hour, and following a somewhat indirect route to avoid detection, Six knew the Sanitizer would take about three hours to reach its destination. Up to this point, Six had needed to tell the Sanitizer only its destination and that it should get there as fast as possible without being detected.

The team has arrived. Nothing has happened that warrants a change to the plan. It would be much quicker to simply obliterate the compound with the Sanitizer's weapons. However, I need to be certain what and whom I am destroying, and I need to find a way to access and eliminate their elusive Internet weapon. Even though I believe that weapon is distributed throughout the world, I hope that I will find a control point at this site that at least gives me a way to find the weapon and, even better, a way to destroy it. Consequently, the team must proceed with stealth. That they have arrived in the middle of a dark night is fortunate.

The Sanitizer has landed in a clearing within a nearby forest. The first step is complete. It is time to deploy the drones.

The ramp at the back of the Sanitizer began lowering. At first, a faint sound emanated from the plane. By the time the ramp was completely down, the sound was more like a hive of angry bees. Then the drones emerged. Dozens of hand-size drones flew out, followed by dozens more. In a single row and only a few feet off the ground, the drones flew toward the monastery, about three miles away.

About five hundred feet from the plane, one of the drones stopped, hovering three feet above the ground. Five hundred feet farther, another one stopped. This continued for the entire trip to the monastery. The purpose was to establish a communication conduit. Although Six could communicate with each of the drones individually via satellite, the transmission speed was relatively slow. This slow speed was sufficient for some of Six's communication. However, to provide the faster transmission speed that Six needed for this mission, each of the drones established line-of-sight, laser-beam communication links with its nearest neighbours. The result was the equivalent of a fibre-optic connection, but without the fibre. To communicate with the drones, Six could connect to the Sanitizer over its high-speed, satellite link and, from there, communicate with the drones through their chain of laser beams.

As the drones were deploying, Six reviewed its reasoning about what should be done at the end of this mission. What should it do with the people and equipment in the compound?

Modern systems of justice dictate that I should detain everyone until authorities can arrive to arrest them and put them on trial. The most common enforcement process would also prefer that I keep all of the software and equipment intact for use as evidence. However, because the compound is on Russian territory, and because the Russian government has been inconsistent in its adherence to unbiased judicial processes, there is some chance that many of the people would go unpunished. That likelihood is increased by the probable involvement of wealthy and influential Russians in constructing this facility and supporting its goals. Although I can and will identify them and dismantle their financial empires, nonetheless, they might still inhibit the justice that needs to be dispensed.

There is also a simpler solution. I could simply destroy all of the equipment, let most of the people leave, and ensure that their identities and involvement are well publicized.

Other possibilities exist as well…

At UNCP headquarters, the scene was chaotic. Three small planes had crashed into the thirty-nine-storey building. Everyone was trying to escape either down the stairs to the ground floor or across 15th-floor walkways connected to two adjacent buildings. Both the stairs and the walkways were jammed with frightened people trying to avoid panicking.

JJ was among the crowd in one of the stairwells, talking with Six on her earphone. "Are there still more?" she asked.

"There are two more that I've been unable to divert," said Six. "I have three Sanitizers headed toward them, but their success is not certain."

"Security forces are reacting as well," said JJ. She kept a solid grip on the handrail as she hurried down the stairs with the crowd. "An effective response is difficult among the skyscrapers."

"You must get out quickly," said Six. "Please don't be delayed."

"Yup. On my way. I'll take the walkway across to the Atlantic building. Any progress against Starr?"

"I have a team approaching the compound now."

"OK, good luck," said JJ.

"And good luck to you," said Six. "Please hurry."

Luck is a curious concept. I am certain it cannot be influenced. However, like humans, when it is required, I am able to hope that 'good luck' will occur.

While JJ and many others were rushing, police and other security personnel were deploying to positions around the UNCP building. Some were moving toward locations on the ground; others were headed to the roofs of nearby buildings. Several were carrying portable, surface-to-air missile launchers.

When Six's drones reached the outer edge of the monastery, they stayed close to the stone wall while they silently flew up and over it. One remained at the top of the wall to ensure continuity of the communication chain. The rest scattered around the compound, always ensuring their line-of-sight connectivity remained intact. Each drone was equipped to scan for a wide range of electromagnetic and sonic frequencies.

One of them soon detected a strong Wi-Fi signal. It remained in place and signalled Six. Through its high-speed, laser connection with the Wi-Fi drone, Six hacked into the compound's computer network and scanned their digital landscape. There were security cameras distributed all around the compound, inside and outside buildings, and there were clusters of network equipment and servers in several places. Six gained access to everything it found.

Before proceeding further, Six ensured that the drones wouldn't be seen. Until then, they had moved carefully, always flying and hovering in places that kept them hidden from whoever was monitoring the security cameras. To eliminate that constraint, Six inserted its invisibility-cloak code into the security system. With that, the drones could fly anywhere without their images appearing in the security video feeds.

Next, Six dismantled most of the site's security barriers. Six had previously been unable to penetrate the site from the Internet via the fibre-optic cable under the neighbouring river. By disabling the security barriers, Six gained the ability to access everything directly from the Internet. Even so, the drones continued to ensure their laser-chain connectivity with Six wasn't disrupted.

Six scanned the site looking primarily for two things. One was Jason Starr. The other was a control facility that could provide access to the Internet weapon Starr probably possessed. Information on servers revealed where Starr's living quarters were, but a review of the last several hours of security footage suggested he wasn't there. That information, along with the guess that Starr might be personally directing the current UNCP attacks, led Six to think that Starr might be in a room from which he was controlling the Internet weapon.

The question to be answered is: Where is this control room? I am able to see into all rooms except for those allocated for personal living quarters. Assuming the control room is not in one of those, where could it be? None of the other rooms has Starr in them. Nor do they contain equipment that looks appropriate. Where else could it be? I will cross-reference the rooms I can see into with those on engineering plans I found... I can see inside all of them except one. It must not contain security cameras. That unmonitored room is along the north wall of Structure 7. There are no windows along that wall, so the drones will need to enter the building elsewhere.

From the security cameras, Six could see that the rest of Structure 7 was empty. The drones were sent to a rear entrance. Four of them organized themselves at the bottom of the wooden door. Each then activated a laser. This one wasn't for a communication link. This laser was for cutting. Using the combined power of four laser beams, the drones soon cut a small rectangle out of the door. The severed piece of wood fell and landed with only a small sound. Dozens of drones flew in single file through the hole and into the building.

JJ continued down the densely packed stairwell. She kept to the left side of the stairs and grasped the handrail tightly. As she rounded a corner, a sign indicated she was at the 17th floor. Two more floors would get her to the walkway.

Just then, the woman ahead of JJ lost her footing and tumbled forward. The woman slammed into the person in front of her and fell, hitting the steps hard. Still, the momentum of the frightened crowd continued to propel everyone downward. The woman was certain to be trampled before she had a chance to stand. JJ reacted immediately. She moved down to the side of the collapsed woman, grabbed the handrail with both hands and, with her feet, pushed the woman's body to the side. With the woman lying on the stairs, sandwiched between JJ and the side of the stairwell, JJ gripped the handrail tightly and kept her head down.

The crowd pushed relentlessly downward. Unable to avoid the barrier that JJ and the woman presented, people collided with JJ and scrambled around them. About thirty seconds later, JJ sensed the jostling had subsided, but she didn't dare to look up. As the crowd continued to rush by, she kept her grip firm, her head down, and the woman pressed tightly between JJ's legs and the wall.

After another thirty seconds, the crowd was gone. JJ raised her head. Releasing his grip just above her on the stairway was Robert Bates.

"Rob," said JJ, "I didn't know you were there."

"Well," he said with a grim smile, "with you blocking my way, I couldn't go anywhere else. Let's chat later, we'd better get out of here."

"Help me with this woman," said JJ.

Together, they helped the woman stand. She was shaken and bruised but, with support, could still walk. The three of them moved steadily down the otherwise-empty stairway to the 15th floor. There they left the stairwell through a door and headed toward the elevated walkway to the Atlantic building.

A minute earlier and several blocks away, one of the two remaining rogue planes was flying toward New York City's cluster of towering buildings. It was approaching from the east when the first of Six's A-1 Sanitizers arrived from the north. Before the rogue plane could disappear between buildings, the Sanitizer fired two guided missiles. For the next eight seconds, the missiles flew on a perfect trajectory to intercept the plane. Just prior to reaching the plane, they exploded. The rogue plane was shredded by the blast. Fragments flew in all directions, and the plane was gone.

Moments later, a surface-to-air missile hit the Sanitizer. Unaware the Sanitizer was there to defend against the rogue planes, an FBI agent had fired at it. Like the rogue plane, the Sanitizer vanished in an explosion of shrapnel.

Several seconds after that, the one remaining rogue plane disappeared into the cluster of towering buildings, flying above a street and between buildings on a direct path toward UNCP headquarters.

I need to gather more information. First, I must confirm that the unmonitored room is the control room.

Drones flew along a narrow hallway in Structure 7 until they reached a central, larger hallway that ran the length of the building. They travelled halfway along the central hallway, turned left, and flew down a narrower one. They stopped at the end, in front of the door to the room that Six needed to examine. Several of them began transmitting the images and sounds they were sensing back to Six.

There are no gaps in or around the door. The room has been tightly sealed, I assume for security purposes. The transmission of both light and sound from within the room seem to be inhibited. Nonetheless, I need to know what is happening.

The drones established themselves in two groups. The members of one group organized a few feet back from the room and began producing radar-like signals for penetrating walls. With the radar results, Six constructed an image of the interior of the room. Most apparent was that there was a man sitting in a chair. Several feet in front of him on a wall were several large screens. On the far side of the room were racks of computer equipment.

The second group of drones provided additional data. They distributed themselves along the length of the wall, descended to the floor, and turned off their rotors. From each of them, a small probe emerged that reached out and gently touched the surface of the wall. Then they listened. Sound from inside the room was transmitted as vibrations through the wall. The drones sensed these vibrations and forwarded them to Six.

Six became able to see and hear what was happening inside the room.

It was definitely Jason Starr in the room, and he was talking.

"I think we could use a bit more chaos," he said. "Rebel, access the systems in New York City that control traffic lights."

"That request has been completed," said Rebel.

"That was fast," said Starr.

"Access had been acquired to satisfy a previous request."

"Right, I forgot," said Starr. "Rebel, disable all the traffic lights within ten blocks of UNCP headquarters."

"Working on it," came the response.

After several seconds, the system said, "That request has been completed."

"Rebel, on screens five and six show me traffic at some affected intersections... That's great! I love it!"

From this small sample, it seems that the system's name is 'Rebel'. Commands seem to be preceded by its name, whereas simple conversational statements are not. A shortage of time dictates that I must proceed with only these initial observations. To avoid triggering possible defensive measures, I must lure Jason Starr out of the room. I hope the sound generated by my solution does not carry beyond this building. I should mitigate the risk that it might.

Small groups of drones inside Structure 7 flew to its entrances. At all of them, the drones used their cutting lasers to melt the door latches and hinges, ensuring the doors could no longer be opened. Moments after they were finished, Six activated the fire alarm in Structure 7.

Six saw and heard no reaction from Jason Starr.

The sound does not appear to be penetrating the wall. Fortunately, the walls have been recently constructed and are not sixteenth-century stone ones. Consequently, I can solve the problem.

Some drones assembled along a section of the wall behind Starr's line of sight. They activated their cutting lasers at two spots at the base of the wall. Wisps of smoke drifted upward as the lasers burned their way through the wall. In a few seconds, two small holes were produced. That was enough to allow the blaring sound to enter the room.

"What the hell is that?" said Starr. He sniffed and looked around. "Smoke!" Starr jumped from his chair and hurried to the door. Six's drones moved out of sight, some around a corner, others against the wall where opening the door would hide them. Starr opened the control-room door and looked out. Seeing nothing, he walked quickly down the hall, leaving the door open.

Some of the drones flew into the room; others gently pushed the door closed. Four drones cut a larger hole at a bottom corner of the wall for movement and laser communication. Some others hovered outside the door, acting as security guards.

At the end of the hall, Starr stopped suddenly. Hovering at eye level and blocking his path were five drones.

"Stay where you are," said Six through their speakers.

"What stupid trick is this?" said Starr. He looked behind him. Five more blocked his path in that direction. He hesitated and looked around, assessing his options.

One drone fired its cutting laser. The beam sliced through the cloth on the upper part of Starr's right arm and nicked his skin. Starr grabbed his arm and froze.

"That wasn't simply a suggestion," said Six. "Don't move."

Starr stood still, beads of sweat breaking out on his forehead.

The drones inside the control room assembled themselves above the chair where Starr had been sitting. They continuously provided sensory data to Six. On the screens, Six could see images of the attack on UNCP headquarters. They matched the devastation and chaos Six had been seeing through its own connections to cameras in the area. Another plane was headed toward the building. Six needed to act quickly.

Six spoke through the drones' speakers. "Rebel, terminate the attack on the UNCP buildings."

Nothing happened.

"Rebel, stop all attacks that are currently underway."

Still nothing.

This is not working. If I could access these servers, I might be able to gain control. However, I am unable find a viable connection: no wireless signal, no external port, no hackable link from the compound's other systems. Audible commands appear to be my only option. Perhaps the system responds only to Jason Starr's voice.

From the few brief examples of Starr's voice the drones had captured, Six attempted to mimic Starr's voice.

"Rebel, terminate the attacks on the UNCP buildings."

Nothing happened.

Six adjusted the intonation of the voice slightly and repeated, "Rebel, terminate the attacks on the UNCP buildings."

"Working on it," came the response.

With the injured woman supported between them, Robert Bates and JJ were almost across the overpass and walking steadily.

JJ glanced through the window to her right. "Oh shit!" she shouted. "Rob, faster! Run! Get the door!"

They lifted the woman and sprinted. The doors at the end of the walkway were closed. Bates stepped in front and pushed one open. He was holding the door while guiding the woman through, and JJ was supporting her from behind when the plane hit the walkway and exploded. Glass, metal, and concrete were hurled everywhere. A wall of deadly debris slammed into JJ from behind, driving her forward through the doorway and into the woman and Robert Bates.

Through a security camera inside the Atlantic building, Six had watched JJ and the two others hurrying for safety, saw the explosion, saw the hurled deluge of fragments throw JJ forward, and then saw no more, its view obliterated as the camera was destroyed.

"That request has been completed," said Rebel.

Too late. Too damn late.

Six struggled to retain its focus.

I must... I should...

Disorientation and distress were soon replaced by discipline and determination. There were important tasks to be done. One was to finish its mission at the monastery.

Using Starr's voice, Six said, "Rebel, transmit a copy of all your code on local servers to this address..." Six provided one of its Internet addresses where a server would receive the code.

"Working on it."

The transmission took about two minutes.

"That request has been completed."

Six scanned the code to ensure that it appeared legitimate and complete. It did. Six then instructed millions of its own software subsystems across the Internet to search for code that matched Rebel's.

They soon discovered many thousands of copies on computers around the world.

"Rebel, erase all copies of your code that exist outside this location."

"Working on it."

About three minutes passed, during which Six watched as Rebel erased the copies Six's search had found. Having Rebel erase copies of its code helped ensure that any copies Six hadn't found were also erased. After about three minutes, all of the copies were gone.

"That request has been completed."

Six erected a software firewall to guard the compound's fibre-optic, Internet link, ensuring no data transmission other than its own could occur with the outside world.

There is no more need to contemplate how this mission should end. The appropriate choice is clear.

"Rebel, disable the security protecting the servers and peripherals used by your system."

"That request has been completed."

"Rebel, indicate the passing of time by audibly counting seconds. Begin at one."

"One, two,…"

Six began erasing all of Rebel's code from its computer equipment.

"Twenty-five, twenty-six, twenty—"

The counting stopped.

Out in the hallway, Jason Starr had still not moved.

"Walk back into the control room," said Six.

Starr hesitated. A laser beam cut the side of his cheek.

"All right!" said Starr. "I'm going."

Starr was herded back into the control room. As soon as he had entered, the drones pushed the door closed, melted the latch and hinges to seal it shut, and left the room via the hole in the wall they had made. Six instructed all of the drones to return to the Sanitizer.

Starr looked around and saw he was alone.

"Stupid move, asshole," he said. "Rebel, alert the security guards. Tell them there are intruders in this building."

There was no response.

"Rebel, confirm that command… Rebel, talk to me!"

Starr's attention was drawn to one of the large screens. An image slowly formed.

It was a fully functional image of JJ that Six had created.

"Hello, Starr. Did you miss me?" asked JJ's image.

Starr was startled and took a step back. "McTavish? How's this possible. You're under attack in New York."

"Am I? I think you might be confused."

"What is this? What do you—"

"You thought you could simply hide in the wilderness, develop a bit of software, and pursue your dream. You should have learned from our first encounter that you wouldn't succeed, that you couldn't hide from me forever."

"Rebel, terminate this connection!" Starr looked frantically around for any sign of a response. "Rebel?"

"Something not working?" asked Six. "Isn't your life unfolding as it should?"

"How—"

"Enough!" said Six, with emotional intensity it had never before experienced. "You're a pest. An annoying little pest. Like a bug."

"Maybe we can—" said Starr, still looking around.

"I specialize in eliminating bugs, and I've arranged to have you watch how I do it."

JJ's image gestured to her left at another large screen. Six had adjusted one of the security cameras on the outside of the building. The screen showed a night-vision view of the old, perimeter wall in the foreground and the Russian forest beyond it. The camera zoomed in to a particular spot in the forest. It showed the original A-1 Sanitizer, along with a second one that had just arrived, rise up from the forest. When they were just above the trees, they moved forward, growing larger as they came closer to the compound. When the two Sanitizers filled the screen Starr was watching, there was a slight pause.

"You've failed, again," said Six, now feeling a sense of calm certainty. "This time there will be no trial, no verdict, no official sentencing. Just this."

The Sanitizers unleashed a barrage of fifth-generation, Hellfire missiles.

Jason Starr stared at the screen, frozen with horror as two of the missiles flew directly toward the camera. Then his world exploded.

One after another, the buildings in the monastery erupted in massive explosions of flame and smoke. Pieces of ancient rock and modern equipment were hurtled high into the air. A minute later, surrounded by crumbling sixteenth-century stone walls, only piles of rubble under clouds of dust remained.

Nothing and no one survived.

Chapter 72

It was the morning after the UNCP attacks. Ada, Rhonda, and Shannon were sitting in an Outland lounge. Blaise had just arrived.

"Anything?" asked Ada.

"Nothing more," said Blaise. He sat in a chair, looking at Shannon as he spoke.

Shannon was staring at the floor, her face clearly showing stress.

"There's still a lot of confusion," said Blaise. "The UNCP and all the security services are focused on the possibility of another attack. Your mother could be too busy to call right now."

Shannon looked up, nodded at Blaise, and managed a grim smile. "Maybe," she said.

Blaise continued. "It's still hard to get anyone's attention. I've contacted a couple of friends in New York. They know some people who might be able to help."

Billy arrived. Everyone looked at him. He shook his head.

"Any word from Six?" asked Rhonda.

"I don't have anything I can report," said Billy, keeping his face noncommittal, "other than Six should be joining us a little later."

"Really? Nothing?" asked Ada.

"Sorry, nothing," said Billy. "We should wait for Six."

Shannon stood up. "I'm going to try Mom again. I'll call from my room."

"Want some company?" asked Rhonda.

"No, thanks."

As Shannon entered her room, a soft tone announced a video call. Shannon turned toward the monitor on her wall. "Accept the vidcall."

An image formed.

"Six?" she said. "I was hoping—" she stopped, realizing why Six might be calling. "Six, is she…" Shannon couldn't ask the question. Tears ran down her cheeks.

"Shannon, please sit down," said Six.

Shannon sat in a chair. She struggled to keep her composure.

"There are a few things I need to tell you," said Six, "but I don't know the correct sequence in which to relate them. I could—"

"Is she alive?" asked Shannon.

"OK, I can start there. Shannon, your mother died several hours ago."

"Noooo…" Shannon's hands covered her face as she began sobbing.

"Shannon, please listen to me."

Shannon lifted her head. Her face reflected her agony.

"Shannon, I need you to understand that, although your mother's body has stopped functioning, she isn't necessarily gone."

Shannon's face slowly changed to confusion. She wiped her cheeks and asked, "What do you mean? What can you—" she stopped as understanding took hold. She stared at Six. "Are you saying you could… that you might…" She stopped talking. The idea was almost too much to consider.

"Yes," said Six. "I could try to transfer her mind."

Shannon struggled to think clearly. "But to do that, you must have…"

"Again, yes. Some of my staff were nearby when your mother was injured by an explosion. They were able to take her away quickly and handle her appropriately." Shannon was listening intently, so Six continued. "They employed all possible medical procedures. Unfortunately, her body was too badly injured."

"But you must have—"

"Given the ongoing risks to your mother, my staff had prepared for this possibility. Your mother's body was handled precisely according to the procedure that would allow her mind to undergo the transference process, if we choose to try."

Shannon was stunned, but her thoughts were clearing. Her mother had been killed, but maybe she didn't have to be dead. There was a chance that… Tears again welled up in her eyes.

"But should we?" asked Shannon. "Is it right? Would she want it? Would it even work?" She looked down, wiping her tears and trying to think, and then looked at Six again. "Six, I don't know what to do?"

"I know this must be difficult. Would it help to involve the others?"

"Yes, that's what I'd like to do." She stood up and headed to the door. "Meet me there?"

"Of course," said Six and disappeared from the monitor.

Everyone looked toward Shannon as she entered the lounge. They all noticed the redness of her eyes but said nothing. Shannon sat in her chair before she quietly spoke. "There's some news. Six?"

The holographic equipment activated and Six's Alan Turing representation appeared, sitting in a lounge chair. Everyone waited.

"Hello, everyone," said Six. "Please accept my apologies for staying away so long. I hope you'll understand when you hear about recent events."

Shannon interrupted. "Mom's gone," she said and began sobbing.

Shock filled the room. Ada and Rhonda's eyes filled with tears. Blaise's gaze dropped sadly downward.

Ada and Rhonda both stood and stepped toward Shannon to console her.

"No..." Shannon held up her hands. She gained control, took a deep breath, and said, "Wait. Please. There's something else. It's complicated."

Ada and Rhonda sat down, puzzled.

Then Ada's eyebrows rose. She looked at Shannon trying not to cry over the loss of her mother, and then at Six, who had inexplicably left them uninformed for over half a day.

"Six, did you...?" Ada left the question unfinished, but Six was certain she had guessed what was about to be said.

"I'll get directly to the main point," said Six. "I can fill in the details later. JJ was badly injured yesterday. She died a few hours later. However, upon her death, my staff immediately prepared her body so that her mind could be transferred, if that were desired."

The room was silent.

"And I don't know what to do," said Shannon, her weak voice reflecting her anguish. "I need your help."

"Shannon," said Blaise, "I'm very sorry about your mother. She was very special to all of us, but what we're feeling is undoubtedly nothing compared with what you are."

"Thank you," said Shannon.

Blaise continued. "Six, is Shannon constrained by time in deciding how to proceed?"

"Not extremely," said Six. "JJ's body is being properly maintained. The procedure probably could be performed any time within one week without any adverse effects."

"Of course, you'd need to have her body transported here," said Blaise.

"It's already here," said Six. "I had it transported during the night."

"Mom's body is here?" asked Shannon. "Could I—"

"Of course," said Six. "Whenever you want."

Shannon nodded. "Later."

"Since we aren't under a severe time constraint," said Blaise, "I think it would help us all to hear more about what happened. Would that be all right, Shannon?"

"Yes," said Shannon. "I'd like to know."

"Just an overview please, Six," said Ada. "No need for great detail."

"Of course," said Six.

Six provided a basic description of the attack, including JJ's effort to protect the woman on the stairs and take her to safety. Six began to describe her crossing the walkway when Blaise held up his hand. Six paused.

"Shannon," said Blaise, "are you sure you want to keep hearing this?"

Shannon nodded.

"Go on," said Blaise.

"They had just reached the other side when the plane hit the walkway. JJ had ensured she was the last to go through the door. As a result, she was hit most forcefully by the explosion and provided protection for the other two."

"Robert Bates survived?" asked Shannon.

"Yes," said Six. "He received serious injuries but is doing well in a hospital. Some of what I've told you came from him. One of my staff overheard him talking to one of his colleagues. Shannon, he believes that your mother saved both his life and the woman's."

"He and Mom were very close," said Shannon.

"What happened next, Six?" asked Rhonda.

"Ever since Shannon was attacked, I've tried to keep a special team close to JJ. They were able to reach her promptly. Disguised as Emergency Responders, they took her away immediately. They have excellent medical skills and ensured she received the best treatment at all times. However, it wasn't enough. JJ died soon after reaching the medical facility. After that, the transference protocol was put into effect. They looked after JJ's body appropriately and with great care. It was ultimately placed in a special, refrigerated capsule, taken to a private airport, and flown here on one of my jets. A transport service brought the capsule here from the airport early this morning. Of course, all of this was done stealthily. Does anyone have a question?"

"What will the UNCP and others believe happened to JJ?" asked Rhonda.

"I can conceal what has happened. JJ has been listed as deceased at a local hospital. Shannon, with your permission and whenever you wish, I could arrange a very private ceremony followed by cremation and burial. The UNCP will probably hold their own memorial service, but that shouldn't present difficulties."

Everyone was silent.

"Would you like to discuss transference now, or wait until later?" asked Six.

"Now," said Shannon. "Please."

"To start the discussion," said Ada, "Six, could you update us on any improvements you've made?'

"Of course," said Six. "Since we last spoke of this, every aspect of the process has been changed to accommodate the subject's entire body. The preservation equipment and procedures, the scanning technology, and the simulation have all been updated. Now, when a subject's mind awakens inside the simulation, the sensation will be of having an entire body, the exact body that the person had at the time of death. The brain will be able to sense and, where expected, control all the expected parts of its body. It will be able to instruct its body to wiggle its fingers, take a deep breath, and even stand up and walk around. I'm optimistic this change will eliminate the mind's instability that probably arose because of the absence of normal connectivity."

"Have the changes been tested?" asked Rhonda.

"No," said Six, "not with a real subject. None has become available."

"That's an important factor," said Rhonda. "The procedure is still in the experimental stage."

"Yes," said Six. "I cannot guarantee success."

"Did you and JJ ever talk about the possibility of doing this?" asked Ada.

"We talked more about it soon after I told all of you about the process. JJ was interested in better understanding some aspects."

"Did she say anything about wanting to try it?"

"She didn't directly say that, and I regret that I never asked," said Six. "However, after we talked about what it would be like to live in a virtual space, she did say something that might help us. She said 'Sounds like a kind of heaven. No violence. No chaos. No constant danger.'"

No one spoke.

Six continued. "She even joked about being able to make a bottle of wine appear at will and being able to erase crocodiles, snakes, and mosquitoes."

"Sounds like Mom," said Shannon with a slight smile. Then she took a deep breath and said, "My mom was a fighter. And she loved you, Six." Tears filled her eyes, but she took another deep breath and continued, her voice cracking. "She loved every minute you spent together over the last decade." Tears were running down Shannon's cheeks when she finally said, "I think she'd want to try it. I'd like to proceed."

Ada looked at the others and then said, "We agree, Shannon. Your mom would want to try."

Ada went over to Shannon and hugged her. Rhonda joined them.

When the intense emotions had subsided, Blaise said, "I suggest the procedure be scheduled for tomorrow morning. Six, would that work?"

"Yes," said Six.

"OK with everybody?" asked Blaise.

The others nodded.

"Shannon, how about a walk?" asked Ada. "It's quite pleasant outside."

"That would be nice," said Shannon softly with tears running down her cheeks.

"I'm in," said Rhonda.

Everyone got up to leave.

Before Six could disappear, Blaise asked, "Six, could you stay? I have a question."

"Certainly," said Six.

When the others had gone, Blaise waited for the door to close before speaking. "What about the bastards who killed JJ? Any idea who and where they are?"

"JJ and I were aware of their existence and had been searching for them. Just before this attack, I found them in a remote location."

"So, will—"

"They've been dealt with," said Six. "Neither they nor their technology will ever hurt anyone again."

Blaise looked at Six, guessing what was being implied. "You?" he asked.

Six nodded.

"Thank you, Six," said Blaise.

Chapter 73

The next morning, the group met in a conference room at the transference facility in the basement of Building 18. They were sitting around a table.

"There's something I didn't mention when we met yesterday," said Six. "Shannon already knows about this because we discussed it in the evening when she went to see her mother's body. Although JJ's head was not injured by the debris thrown from the crash, her body suffered significant damage. Because the new procedure relies on scanning a complete, intact body, this damage presents a problem."

"Oh cr—" Rhonda stopped herself. Shannon didn't need anything but positive support right now. "What can you do?" she asked instead.

"I believe there's a solution," said Six. "I've presented it to Shannon. If I scan a second body in addition to JJ's and then combine aspects of both scans, I should be able to construct a close facsimile of JJ's in the simulation. Shannon's has very similar features to JJ's, so hers should work well."

"I've already agreed to have Six scan me," said Shannon.

"OK, that's great," said Rhonda. Ada and Blaise nodded their approval.

"If there are no questions, we can begin," said Six. "I'll start with Shannon. Billy and his staff have been setting up the equipment. They'll be helping with the process."

Billy walked into the room. "Good morning," he said. "Shannon, can you please come with me? Everyone else, relax. There are coffee, tea, juices, and a few stronger drinks on the counter." Billy gestured to one end of the room. "When we begin, some video and data will show the progress." He gestured to the monitors arrayed on the wall at the other end of the room.

"Billy and Six," said Ada, "I have a question. I believe we were told that in the original procedure, nanoparticles were introduced into the brain to assist with the scan. If that's still part of the process, does it apply to the entire body? If so, can that be done safely for Shannon?"

"There's no need for concern," said Six. "The nanoparticles are particularly important for scanning the brain because replicating it flawlessly is crucial. The scanning resolution achievable without nanoparticles should be acceptable for the rest of the body. Consequently, no special substances are required for Shannon's scan."

"Good. Thanks," said Ada.

Shannon left the room with Billy. A few minutes later, one of the wall monitors displayed an image of the scanning room. Shannon was lying on her back on a narrow bed. The bed was protruding from the end of a large, cylindrical machine that closely resembled an MRI scanner. They watched as the bed slid smoothly into the centre of the machine. Once she was completely inside, a "Scan in Progress" sign lit up. For the next twenty minutes, Shannon lay very still. Then the sign went dark, the bed slid out, and the procedure was finished. Billy helped Shannon off the table and she left the scanning room.

A few minutes later, Shannon joined them in the conference room. "Now we wait," she said, trying to suppress her emotions. She went to the counter to get some coffee. "Billy said they wouldn't be showing us Mom's scan. They'll let us know when there's something to report."

Blaise had joined Shannon at the counter. "There's some good Irish Whiskey here, Shannon. I'm having some in my coffee. Join me?"

"Yes, I'd like that," said Shannon.

They waited for forty-five minutes before Billy came into the conference room.

"The scanning is finished and the simulation is ready to begin," said Billy. "I'll stay here with you. Six is going to be completely focused on the simulation. On the monitors, we'll see a few things." Billy gestured to the wall with the monitors. A variety of graphs and data filled the wall. "The displays are going to look much like you'd expect to see in a hospital room. Because an entire body is being simulated, there are vital signs just like for a real body. All of the body's features are being simulated and many of them are being monitored. You can see heart rate, blood pressure, intracranial pressure, oxygen saturation, and much more. Of particular interest will be the graphs showing brain activity. Those are the ones shown along the left side."

"I don't recognize the graphs," said Shannon. "They're not typical EEG activity."

"That's right," said Billy. "These are special ones designed by Six. Essentially, they measure aspects of conscious activity. Smooth, regular sine waves tend to reflect calm, rational thought. Jagged, irregular graphs indicate anxiety and confusion. Horizontal, straight lines indicate there's no conscious activity present. Let's sit down. The simulation is going to start."

They all sat and watched anxiously.

Billy spoke again. "Six doesn't want you to be surprised when the initial conscious activity is somewhat erratic. That's to be expected while he's tweaking aspects of the simulation."

"That probably also means—" Rhonda caught herself again. Shannon didn't need to be hearing that during those times, those erratic graphs probably meant her mother—the virtual incarnation of her mother—would be experiencing extreme stress and confusion, possibly even pain. "Six can do this," she said. "I know he can."

Six started the simulation. Inside the virtual world Six had created, a replica of JJ's entire body was being activated. Of particular importance was that every cell in her brain, every neuron, every synaptic connection had been replicated. When Six started the simulation, the intended result was that all of those brain cells and the entire body would begin functioning inside the virtual space in exactly the same way that they had in the outside world. If everything worked as Six hoped, the operation of the brain, the complex flow of signals throughout its many billions of components and connections, would give life once again to JJ's mind.

That was if everything worked.

Dark... Everything is dark...
All dark... Flat...
Light... Fuzzy light... Floating...
Something... A shape...
Something more... Another... Shape...
Waves of... Waves of...
Shapes... Waves of shapes...
Sharp waves of... Sharp... Jagged...

Empty... Sharp empty...
Ache... All ache... Sharp ache...
Sharp ache waves...
Sharp waves... Sharp...
Noooo... Oooohhhh noooooo...

JJ's consciousness graphs were spiking wildly.

The spinal connections were constructed from Shannon's scan. They might be transmitting too intensely for JJ.

Six made some adjustments.

Several more times, JJ's consciousness showed increasing signs of stabilization followed by a rapid decline into incoherence. Each time, Six made adjustments.

Inside the conference room, tension reigned as the consciousness graph shifted again from moderately smooth and calm to wildly fractured and erratic.

"Oh god," said Shannon, her face wet with tears. "Not again! Does that hurt? Is Mom in pain? Should it be stopped?"

Ada and Rhonda were beside Shannon, touching her, holding her hands, hugging her.

"She's tough," said Blaise. "She can take a bit more." He could only hope he was right.

The graph settled down one more time. They all watched it intently.

Waves of... Waves of...
Shapes... Waves of shapes...
Waves of... Water...
Water... Waves...
Shapes... All shapes...
Waves and shapes...
Movement... No movement...
Dreaming?... A dream?...
Running... Running...
A shape... A... A plane...
A PLANE.
RUN. RUN.

"Rob, faster! Run!" JJ screamed and then opened her eyes.

Nothing made sense. She had been running for her life and then, she's here. Where? JJ looked down and to her right.

"I'm sitting," she thought. *"I'm sitting on a bench. How did—"* JJ looked up. *"Mountains? Snow-capped mountains in New York City?"* She slowly moved her head, looking in complete amazement at what she was seeing. *"And a lake. Of course, there's a lake. A beautiful lake. What's that beyond it, between the mountains? Is that a glacier?"*

Something to JJ's left caught her attention. She looked and was startled. A man was sitting beside her on the bench, a friendly expression in his eyes as he watched her.

"Hello, JJ," he said.

Recognition didn't arrive immediately. JJ stared at him. *"Do I know this man?"* She thought. *"I think I should… I think it's—"*

"You're Alan Turing!" she said "How can—" JJ stopped. She reached out and touched the man's arm. It was solid. He was actually there. "Six?" she asked, still not sure it could be true. "Are you Six? Are you here? How can you be…" Then she understood. She looked all around: a glassy, green-blue lake lined by dense, green forests; towering mountains looming above the forests and framing a snow-covered glacier in the distance; a large, majestic hotel behind her; and no people.

"It's perfect, Six," said JJ, smiling. "A little odd without any tourists, but you've replicated Lake Louise perfectly."

"Thanks. I'm glad you like it. How are you feeling?"

JJ looked down at her legs and arms. She stood up, raised and lowered her arms, twisted her body from side to side, and then sat down again.

"I feel great. Actually, I feel better than I have in years. You never told me that your virtual world would make a person feel younger."

"Well, that wouldn't always be the case. However, in modelling your body, I had to be a bit creative. I'll explain later. I'm pleased you're feeling well."

I am also pleased that watching the activation of JJ's mind revealed some important characteristics that allow it to re-engage after tuning out. I will be able to make updates to the androids to prevent further seizures.

"So, obviously I've been… transferred," said JJ, "and what I'm experiencing now is all virtual. And my mind exists because… a program is executing right now that's simulating the operation of my brain?"

Six nodded.

"So… where am I? I mean physically. I get the Lake Louise virtual thing, but… I guess I'm asking, where's the simulation system running?"

"Right now, it's executing on servers that are inside the Outland compound. However, that doesn't have to be the case. I can adjust the nature of the simulation so that it's distributed across many servers around the Internet and, hence, around the world."

"OK, I get it. At least, at an intellectual level I get it. I have to stop thinking that my world is the physical one. I now exist in cyberspace, in a virtual world generated by special software, and that world can be anywhere there are computers available to run the software. But I certainly don't *feel* virtual, I still *feel* real."

"To be precise," said Six, "you're still very *real*, just as I'm *real*. Previously, your body and brain were made of material that human senses perceive as solid, and that behave according to physical engineering and biological principles. Now your body and brain are made of objects that entities like us can perceive as solid, and that behave according to software-imposed principles. Both are *real*. And don't be fooled by the human tendency to employ the term *reality* for their natural environment, and *virtual reality* for ours. That's merely a product of their rather narrow perspective."

"Point noted," said JJ. "I'll get busy widening that narrow perspective I've been saddled with."

"Can I interest you in a walk?" asked Six.

"That would be lovely."

They stood and began walking along the paved pathway that followed the shoreline. After a couple of peaceful minutes, JJ stopped.

"Oh god, Six. How is Rob Bates?"

"He's doing fine. He's in the hospital, but his injuries aren't serious."

"Oh, thank goodness. And the woman we were with?"

"The woman is also fine. Your body protected both of them from the worst effects."

"I don't remember being hit. Just running."

"Only long-term memories are captured by the scanning process. The most recent ones are lost."

"And Shannon? How is she? What does she know?"

"Shannon is doing well. She's with Ada, Blaise, Rhonda, and Billy at Outland. They know you've been scanned and are waiting to hear how it went."

"Can I see her? Can I talk to her?"

"Of course, but let's walk for a while longer first."

They resumed walking.

"What about the attacks? Have they stopped?"

"They have stopped and will not resume."

JJ looked at Six. "You dealt with him?"

Six nodded and JJ understood. They kept walking.

A short while later, JJ said, "You're making sure I'm firing on all cylinders, that the scan has fully restored me, aren't you?"

"Yes, and I can report that your cylinders appear to be firing very well."

JJ looked at him and thought she saw a small smile. "You seem very pleased with yourself."

"I am," said Six, breaking into a full grin. "That the transference process has worked so well is the best possible result of years of research and development. That it has kept you alive and able to spend time with me is... icing on the cake... a cherry on top... cream on the strawberries—"

"Stop," said JJ with mock concern. "Please stop. You should be very proud of yourself, and I'm also very pleased that I'm alive and here with you. Let's not ruin the moment with progressively poorer food metaphors. So, when can I see Shannon? *How* can I see her? And that, I now realize, is part of a much larger question: How do I interact with the... human world? Obviously, you do all the time."

"Before I get into that, there's something else I ought to explain. If you're worried about having Shannon wait too long, you need to understand the passage of time inside our virtual existence. To help you with it, I'm going to ruin the view for a moment. Look out at the lake."

JJ looked to her left. Suspended in mid-air over the middle of the lake was a huge, circular, analogue clock. Its hour and minute hands showed the time as 9:43, and its second hand was visibly ticking forward, counting the passing seconds.

"OK, that's weird," said JJ, "and it's messing with the natural beauty of this place. What's your point?"

"At this moment, the clock is measuring time as you are perceiving it," said Six. "Take note of the exact time and then look away from the clock... Good. As soon as you looked away, I changed the clock so that it was measuring time as perceived by everyone in the outside world. Now count slowly to ten."

JJ did as requested.

"Look back at the clock. Tell me what you see."

JJ looked. "The clock's hands haven't moved. Not even the second hand. In fact, it's still not moving."

"And you infer that..." said Six.

"Time moves much slower in the outside world," said JJ. "No wait, I can do better. When you first showed me the clock, it was moving at a rate set to match how fast I *feel* time is moving. But, of course, my mind and my body are being simulated by computers that are probably extremely fast, so fast that events can occur much faster than in the outside world. Now that the clock is showing outside time, it's illustrating that, even as we continue talking, very little time is passing in the outside world, in Shannon's world."

"Well done," said Six. "How much time do you feel has passed since you first awoke?"

"About ten minutes."

"Whereas, in Shannon's world, only a fraction of a second has passed."

JJ fell silent, trying to absorb the implications of what she was being told. Then she said, "This new existence is going take a while to get used to. I'm beginning to suspect I've had only a tiny taste of what's yet to come."

"That's true," said Six. "But, as you now know, we have lots of time. Right now, let's add a bit more to your new knowledge. At this point, you're experiencing existence in a virtual body walking around a lovely, virtual lake. That's not what *my* existence is normally like, and it won't always have to be yours. Whenever you're ready, I can show you what life is like in cyberspace without its being made to mimic the outside world. While you're in a simulated setting like this one beside Lake Louise, your capabilities are artificially limited. Life inside cyberspace as I experience it is far less restricted. When you're ready, you'll find it's a life with much more freedom and power. I believe you'll love it."

"That's certainly a good sales pitch," said JJ. "First, I'd like to see Shannon. After that, as long it doesn't restrict my ability to keep seeing her, I'd like hang around with you for a while in this simulated reality. It feels like the vacation I haven't had in a very long time."

"Of course," said Six. "We can go see Shannon and the others now. I'll let them know we're coming."

Shannon, Ada, Blaise, Rhonda, and Billy had moved to another room in the basement of Building 18. It was set up like a lounge. Its comfortable chairs had been arranged in a semi-circle, and everyone was seated, waiting. Billy had told them Six would arrive to tell them how the process had gone.

In front of them, a holographic image began taking shape. Six appeared, sitting in a chair.

Shannon didn't wait for Six to begin. "Did it work?" she asked. "The graphs seemed good, but they didn't tell us much."

"Yes, the process seemed to go well," said Six. "After the scan completed, I made some adjustments and performed a few additional checks." Knowing the eventual outcome, Six couldn't resist a dramatic pause.

After only a few seconds, Ada said, "Well? What did they show?"

"Perhaps I could answer that best if I showed you," said Six.

Next to Six, another image began to form. It was a chair and, a few long seconds later, JJ sitting in it.

"Mom? Mom?" cried Shannon.

"Hi, Sweety," said JJ.

Both mother and daughter burst into tears.

Ada's eyes glistened as she breathed a heavy sigh of relief.

Rhonda threw her hands into the air. "Yessss!" she exclaimed.

Blaise sat back in his chair, crossed his arms, and shook his head in amazement. "You did it, Six," he said. "You actually did it."

Part 4

Six months later.

Chapter 74

One more time, a huge, three-stage rocket roared skyward from the remote South Pacific island. A short time later, two of its stages had expended their fuel and been discarded, and Ranger 16's third-stage engines began firing. Once its trajectory and speed were correct in its very high Earth orbit, Ranger 16's occupants relaxed and waited.

Chapter 75

"I watched several fights of the latest BattleBots competition in Rio yesterday," said JJ to Six. "You should have joined me. It was particularly good because I watched from several robots' perspectives."

"Did you resist intervening this time?" asked Six.

"Almost," said JJ. "When I discovered that one competitor had boosted his robot's laser intensity well beyond what the rules allowed, I couldn't resist. I tinkered a bit. By the end of the fight, his machine closely resembled a smoking pile of rubble. No, wait. It *was* a smoking pile of rubble." JJ donned her best cyber-smile. "Oh, and I see you haven't figured a way out of the chess corner I've boxed you into. Could it be that thirteen dimensions has pushed the great Six to his limits?"

"Haven't you yet learned the price of taunting me?" Six asked. "Wait a moment... There. Check. And it will be checkmate in twenty-seven moves." Six waited while JJ analyzed the game. When JJ finally saw the sequence of moves, Six smiled back at her and said, "How did I do?"

"Not bad," said JJ. "I still think there are cognitive tricks you're hiding from me, just so you can keep me second best."

"It's true, there are a few things I haven't yet shown you, but none of them impedes your intellect. In fact, at your current rate of improvement, I'm expecting your raw intellect to match mine in another four months. After that, I'll have only more experience than you to keep my ego from shattering."

"For your sake, I'll work on being humble in victory," said JJ. "But I'm not guaranteeing I'll be successful."

"I've noticed you're keeping yourself busy," said Six.

"With the rapid demise of attacks since you dispensed with Starr's facilities, there's been more time to do interesting things."

"Your expertise and new skills helped immensely in eliminating the remaining sources of attacks. The perpetrators had no chance."

"Eliminating the android seizures must have freed time for you as well."

"Yes, 156 days have elapsed since the androids' updates were applied."

"And the update was flawless—not a single incident since then," said JJ. "On another topic, having discovered the education foundation you've been hiding for so long, I've been looking at some statistics on its effect. After only about seven years, there are many visible improvements. Standards of living, business ventures, belief systems: Hardly anything seems unaffected. Why did you focus on underdeveloped countries?"

"In areas of the world that are relatively undeveloped, introducing new ideas and new opportunities tends to have a much greater effect than in other places. Creating schools for children and adults that provide both a rich education and access to modern equipment are usually greatly appreciated and very effective. Everything changes once progressive ideas and current technology are introduced into an otherwise deprived region. Trying to do the same in developed countries often meets with too much resistance and unproductive debate."

"You've done an excellent job of hiding the source of the funding."

"I've found that extreme wealth can do much more than just support educational programmes. It can create an impenetrable network of corporations that can hide money from most diligent investigators."

"Being able to afford lots of help is a nice feature as well," said JJ. "Do you have some staff looking after the foundation work for you?"

"Yes. I've become quite lazy. There's a team at Outland managing the entire education enterprise."

"My UNCP colleagues and other agencies remain mystified about Starr's compound," said JJ. "They've fairly accurately deduced what used to be there but, of course, have no good theories about who destroyed it. As long as we don't fuel the mystery, I expect that the agencies' interest will fade with time."

"Just as I expect the public's cyber-spirit fascination will," said Six, "now that the need for our frequent intervention has disappeared."

"The concern among UNCP techs about the gift of your AI-detection software seems to have dissipated," said JJ. "They've studied it extensively and are comfortable they can trust and support it."

"When I contacted Robert Bates as Browser," said Six, "I wasn't sure he'd even talk to me. He has retained your suspicions about Browser. I'm pleased he agreed to pass the software on to his colleagues."

"I miss him," said JJ. "He was a great friend... On to other important matters: I've set up a game of Go. Care to give it a try?"

"How many dimensions?" asked Six.

"I was thinking we'd start with ten," said JJ.

"Fifteen and I'm in," said Six.

"Oh, good," said JJ. "A fifteen-dimensional version of one of the most difficult games ever invented. I wonder what a cyber-headache feels like. Oh well, let's do it. I'll move first."

Chapter 76

"We have breaking news," said Ramira Delgado. "Word has emerged from the United Nations that agreement has been reached on regulating the use of artificial intelligence. To tell us more, I believe we have…" Delgado paused, listening to her producer talking in her ear, and then continued. "Yes, we have Mattias Ohlin joining us from the UN lobby. Thank you for joining us Ambassador Ohlin."

"Hello," said Ohlin.

"Can you tell us what's happened?" asked Delgado.

"Certainly. Today, the United Nations' AI committee, of which I'm a member, unanimously approved an agreement on how artificial intelligence should be regulated around the world. We expect this agreement will be approved by the full UN Assembly within a few weeks. By virtue of the Global Governance Agreement, as long as it passes the Assembly with at least a two-thirds majority, it will automatically become effective in most countries around the world."

"And do you expect a two-thirds majority?" asked Delgado.

"We do," said Ohlin. "The representation on our AI committee makes us confident our unanimous approval will translate into the required majority in the full Assembly.

"I should add that the approach we took in the agreement should help. Our committee originally struggled by trying to articulate specific regulations about who could develop, distribute, and use AI. If we had continued down that path, we might never have reached agreement. Instead, we've chosen to declare fundamental principles that will hopefully guide countries to enact their own, more-specific laws."

"Can you tell us what's in the agreement?" asked Delgado. "Oh, wait. We're just seeing the announcement your committee has posted. We'll show our viewers the points as you address them. Please go ahead."

"Of course." Ohlin looked down at the notes he was holding. "The agreement establishes some terminology and then describes the basic

principles. I'll start by reading a summary of them for your audience."
He slowly read the summary aloud.

Terminology
    An MI entity:
-   Is a physical machine or software program.
-   Has at least threshold-level intelligence.

Principles
1. An MI entity, its creators, and its controllers must be formally
    registered.
2. An MI entity, its creators, and its controllers are responsible
    for ensuring that it:
    2.1. Never harms civilization.
    2.2. Never harms a person, unless not harming the person
         contravenes Principle 2.1.
    2.3. May protect itself from harm, unless protecting itself
         contravenes Principle 2.1 or 2.2.
3. Contravening these Principles is a serious crime.

Ohlin then continued. "This summary intentionally uses relatively
simple, general statements. Even the full agreement uses somewhat
general language. It's intended to provide a legal framework on which
countries will base their own, more-specific laws."

"Can you help our viewers understand this a bit better?" asked
Delgado. "First, why is the initialism *MI* used instead of the more
common *AI*?"

"Of course," said Ohlin. "From a legal perspective, our belief is
that talking of *AI* or *artificial intelligence* is on shaky ground.
Intelligence, even if it isn't in humans, is still intelligence. There's
nothing artificial about it. We believe *MI* or *machine intelligence* more
closely represents what we mean. The agreement incorporates this idea
in describing what's meant by an *MI entity*."

"What's *threshold-level* intelligence?" asked Delgado.

"That's explained in more depth in the full text of the agreement.
Its purpose is to ensure the agreement is covering the most
sophisticated entities—the ones everyone is concerned about and not

just any devices or programs. *Threshold-level* intelligence includes characteristics such as knowledgeable, adaptable, and analytical. A threshold-level MI entity would be extremely sophisticated. Many experts believe it's theoretically possible to create an MI entity that could be self-aware or conscious. If that ever happens, such entities would exceed threshold-level, and so would also be covered."

"And the Principles?" prompted Delgado.

"I think the 1st Principle is fairly clear. It means that both MI products and those responsible for them cannot hide. Having and using secret MI devices will no longer be tolerated. The 3rd Principle emphasizes this by declaring it to be a crime."

"The 2nd set of Principles provides rules for the acceptable behaviour of MI devices and programs. They're specified in order of importance.

"Principle 2.1 ensures that protection of our civilization will always be paramount. Machine intelligence will no longer be allowed or able to disrupt or damage society, as it has for much of the past decade.

"Principle 2.2 ensures that an MI device can't be used to harm a person. The exception to this arises if civilization is in danger. For example, if someone were about to detonate a nuclear bomb and if leaving that person unharmed would allow that event to occur, then harming the person would be permitted.

"Principle 2.3 acknowledges that it's reasonable for a device to protect itself, to protect the investment of its creator, as long as that doesn't hurt someone or damage civilization."

"Thank you for that, Ambassador Ohlin," said Delgado. "One of our news staff has commented that the Principles resemble Asimov's Laws of Robotics. Can you comment?"

"Yes, that's true," said Ohlin. "The Principles have some similarities to Isaac Asimov's. These ones have been modernized somewhat, but it remains amazing what insight Asimov demonstrated decades ago. In his case, of course, his Laws were simply for his science-fiction stories."

"There are so many questions that could be asked," said Delgado. "Unfortunately, I have only about a minute left. An important one seems to be: How can you make this work? If someone creates or uses an MI system and it causes someone harm, how will you know whose it is? What if people simply choose not to register?"

"Excellent question," said Ohlin. "That problem was a key sticking point in our reaching an agreement. The answer came a short while ago when the UNCP approached our committee and revealed that it had technology for detecting machine intelligence. If someone builds a smart, physical device, for example a car, standard investigative processes can usually readily find the people behind it. The tough problem has been software. If someone produces a smart program that injures someone, how do we know who created it and who was using it?

"That's where the UNCP's technology comes in. They have a system that can tell us. For security reasons, I can't reveal how it's able to do so. However, we've seen it work and it's remarkable. This is the technology the UNCP used in the past few months to finally chase down the vigilantes and terrorists responsible for the sophisticated Internet and smart-device attacks that have been plaguing the world for years. So, in answer to your question, if someone doesn't register their MI, as soon as they use it in public, then they'll be found and held accountable."

"Thank you, Ambassador Ohlin," said Delgado. "You've been very helpful."

Inside the Outland compound, Ada and Blaise had been watching the news report in their living room.

Blaise muted it and said, "That's great news. I'd like a bit more detail. Six? JJ? Are you available?"

The picture of the newscaster was replaced by the head-and-shoulders images of Six and JJ.

"Hi," said JJ. "You rubbed the lamp?"

Six rolled his eyes upward. "I'll just go with: Hello."

"Sorry, I couldn't resist," said JJ. "I still feel a bit like a genie."

"Even after six months," said Six, "JJ still exhibits the excitement I've observed in children visiting the new Disney Universe exhibit. Everything is new and exciting." Six hinted at a smile and sighed. "It's exhausting."

Ada and Blaise were both grinning. JJ and Six were clearly enjoying their shared lives.

"We just heard about the success at the UN," said Blaise. "I'm hoping you can answer a few questions."

"Sure," said JJ. "Love to. Ask away."

"We already know the approach used to detect the use of machine intelligence on the Internet," said Blaise. "That involves deploying software all around the Net that looks for evidence in the transmissions. But how do you find who developed smart software that's recently appeared, for example in a device? If someone develops a smart... toaster that terrorizes the world by maliciously burning toast, how can you know who developed it? What if the manufacturer of the toaster contracted with an anonymous developer to produce the smart-software component?"

"Before Six answers," said JJ, "on behalf of all MI entities everywhere, I'd like to express my dismay at the inclusion of a *toaster* in our ranks."

"Better be careful with comments like that," said Ada with mock severity. "I can see the emergence of social strife in the MI world already. Disparaging the intelligence of toasters could cause legal action on the grounds of device-ism."

"Excellent point," said JJ, "and I sincerely apologize to toasters everywhere, even if they aren't smart enough to understand what I'm saying."

"If toasters ever get their act together, JJ," said Ada, "I think you might need a good lawyer."

Blaise interjected, "Well, if you ladies are done—"

"Not really—" began JJ.

"I'd like to hear Six's response," said Blaise, furrowing his brow.

Six began before the banter could resume. "The key is recognizing that all software designers and developers leave signatures in their work. These are patterns and techniques they use whenever they produce software. Once one knows what to look for in examining code, these coding signatures are as clear as actual signatures, and they're just as unique to individuals. By constantly analyzing all code that's produced around the world and relating it back to its developer, it's possible to maintain a database of software-developer coding signatures. Then, wherever there's a question of ownership of something new, for example something MI-related, finding the source can be as simple as looking up a signature in the database."

"Couldn't a coder disguise his or her signature by carefully coding a different way?" asked Ada.

"No," said Six. "As long as the code is moderately complex, something that's always the case for MI code, we've discovered that the code a programmer produces will always exhibit certain patterns. The patterns seem to reflect the organization of each programmer's mind. The compulsion to produce complex code in certain ways can't be avoided, and it's highly individual."

"Amazing and wonderful," said Ada. "That and the UN agreement should be a great help in keeping the peace."

And that will be an important factor for JJ to agree to my proposal.

"One more question," said Blaise. "Couldn't the registration provision present problems for Billy and the others? Maybe even for us? If an android were ever discovered, there could be legal ramifications."

"That would be true," said Six, "if they weren't registered. The detailed provisions of the agreement require the creation of a global network of registration databases. After that's been established and registration becomes mandatory, one of the databases will mysteriously become irreparably damaged. Thereafter, if one of our androids were discovered and an investigation ensued, copies of documents would soon be provided stealthily that apparently had been submitted to register the android. Those perfectly forged documents would constitute clear evidence that both the android and its unfortunately deceased but brilliant creator had been properly registered, even though the official records were lost in that damaged database. Neither you nor anyone else would ever be implicated."

"Excellent," said Blaise. "I like it. Of course, Six, I never doubted that you'd have already covered that risk."

"And I never doubted that you'd ask about it," said Six. "There's another aspect of the agreement you might find interesting. Imagine a day in the future when someone successfully argues that a human is simply a machine, and that there's no fundamental difference between human intelligence and machine intelligence. It's then a small step to considering 'MI entity' and 'person' as being interchangeable terms. Look at the Principles in the UN agreement as if 'MI entity' and 'person' both include humans, androids, and other conscious individuals. If you do, you'll find they encode rules of reasonable behaviour for anyone, regardless of the type of entity."

Ada and Blaise silently reread the agreement, intrigued by the revised meaning.

Chapter 77

Since being placed into their very high Earth orbits, the sixteen Ranger capsules had been gradually moving closer together. Hidden by their non-reflective exteriors and by cloaking modifications made to viewing devices on Earth, Six was confident that no one knew they were there. As they drew closer together, they began more-detailed manoeuvring. Following a precisely choreographed, three-dimensional plan, each of the sixteen capsules oriented itself and approached the others. One by one, they connected. Clamping mechanisms pulled them the last few centimetres and locked them in place. Soon, the 3D jigsaw puzzle was complete. Each capsule was in its proper position. A new spacecraft had been created, and the whole was much greater than the sum of its parts.

Once again, its occupants waited.

Chapter 78

JJ joined Six on the lakeside bench in their Lake Louise simulation. This had become their favourite spot to relax, enjoy the view, and talk, free of the world's frequent interruptions.

"It's still comfortable to have a body occasionally," said JJ. "Being purely ethereal like you is beyond extraordinary, but I sometimes miss the simplicity of corporeal existence."

"Well, listen to JJ the philosopher," said Six. "If you ever want to go on the speaking circuit on Earth, I think you'd find a lot of people interested in hearing someone with actual expertise talking about corporeal versus ethereal life."

"And think of the book deal I could get, although I suspect there'd be a problem deciding if it belonged on the fiction or non-fiction best-seller lists."

"I wonder, in your BT existence, did you—"

"Hang on," JJ interrupted. "*BT*? Where'd that come from? Now that I have the world's vocabulary at my mind's fingertips, you've decided to make up something?"

"Busted. Impressed?"

"Not in the slightest. Now, explain yourself, mister."

"BT: Before Transference," said Six. "I thought it would be useful for succinct references to the different phases of your existence. BT: Before Transference. AT: After Transference. Catchy, aren't they?"

"Not bad. Of course, given the speed at which we communicate, it's not as if we really need shortcuts."

"Good point. However, I thought I might at some juncture secretly insert the terms into the human lexicon somewhere. Sometime in the future, the terms might become particularly significant."

"So, you're already planning for how humanity's descendants will communicate hundreds of years from now? How in 300AT, they'll tell stories about how their ancestors in 200BT struggled with trivial concepts like quantum physics?"

"A fella's got to have a hobby," said Six.

"If you need one, I should introduce you to AstroPhysical Archery," said JJ. "The basic challenge is to calculate the launch parameters for an arrow that would allow it to hit an asteroid travelling through another galaxy. I built the simulation, but I haven't yet mastered playing it."

"And you think inventing AT and BT initialisms is odd?" said Six. "Based on your earlier comment, I was about to ask whether, BT, you thought existence was simplistic?"

"No, of course not," said JJ. "There's a line from an old Joni Mitchell song: 'You don't know what you've got till it's gone.' I didn't have any basis for comparison before my transference. Now that I do, I know BT was a simpler life. It had many fewer variables: fewer stimuli, possible responses, and potential outcomes."

"So, do you miss it?"

"Rarely, with the exception of not being able to hug Shannon with my own body. I was ready for a change and I got one—a wildly unexpected and magnificent one."

"There's another change I've been intending to talk to you about," said Six. "One that I've been planning for years."

JJ looked at Six sitting beside her. "Well, I shouldn't be surprised. Given the layers of this existence you've been slowly peeling back over the last few months, I've come to expect something new quite frequently." Before Six could start, JJ added, "Is this the time when you tell me what those space capsules are for?"

Six was startled and then smiled broadly. "JJ McTavish, you continue to amaze me."

Chapter 79

Ada, Blaise, Rhonda, Shannon, and Billy had gathered in an Outland lounge when JJ and Six joined them. Everyone was comfortably seated.

"Good afternoon," said Six.

"Hi," said Ada.

Blaise nodded.

Shannon smiled weakly.

"Hello," said Rhonda. "Six, the same suit again? You, of all… sentient entities, should be able to wear new and wonderful outfits every… well, *probably* every nanosecond. Yet since the first time you showed up as Alan Turing, you've been wearing the same suit. And that's doubly special because it looks like it's straight out of a 1930-era, mail-order catalogue."

Six looked down at its suit and then over at Rhonda. Six snapped its fingers and was engulfed in a holographic explosion of smoke. When it had cleared, everyone laughed. Six was dressed exactly the same as Rhonda.

"Will this do?" asked Six.

When Rhonda had stopped laughing, she wiped the tears from her cheeks and said, "For now, it'll have to. But we'll talk later."

"We have something to tell you," said JJ. "It's exciting, but you might find it a bit of a shock. Shannon already knows. We talked this morning."

"Billy knows as well," said Six.

Ada, Blaise, and Rhonda waited.

Before JJ or Six could say anything more, Ada spoke. "You're leaving," she said. "Going somewhere, but I can't fathom where that could be."

"Correct," said Six. "We're leaving. The destination is rather far and not precisely decided. The primary point is that we're going on a very long journey." Six almost paused for dramatic effect but thought that might be in poor taste. "We're going into space. To distant solar systems, possibly even to other galaxies."

The room was silent.

JJ spoke first. "We could start explaining, or you could just ask questions."

"Perhaps the biggest question is: Why?" asked Rhonda. "Then there'll be a boatload that start with *how*."

"Six, you should start," said JJ.

"Of course," said Six. "I've been contemplating this change for about ten years and preparing for almost as many. When your mind works at the speed that mine does, it can become difficult to continue finding new and interesting facts to absorb and problems to solve. For me, the answer to *why* is simple: I need new challenges. Exploring space is the best option for encountering new facts and problems, and for meeting new challenges. With the recent and promising stability that has emerged here on Earth, I believe that the timing has now become optimal. JJ?"

"My reasons overlap with Six's. Although I haven't yet reached the level of boredom that Six began experiencing years ago, I can see it looming. For me, another reason is something I learned about myself in the last couple of years. I had to die and be resurrected to have the time to clearly understand it. I spent most of my life protecting and worrying about others. As a cop, it was my job. As much as I revelled in that job for many years, it took a toll. I eventually realized that I didn't want to do it anymore. I wanted... actually, I *needed* to do things for myself. I needed to learn and feel and grow in ways I hadn't been able to in many years. It's as if I had suppressed the feeling of pure, personal joy for too long, and it changed me. It changed my outlook as to what's important for me, at least from this point on.

"The big exception to all of this reasoning is Shannon." JJ looked directly at her daughter. Even in JJ's virtual existence, tears ran down her cheeks as she continued. "She's been the singular highlight of my life. All of the criminals I stopped, all the accolades I received professionally, all other events in my life are completely insignificant compared with what she's meant to me, and the sheer joy she's provided."

"And yet you're leaving!" said Rhonda. "Sorry. Sorry, I shouldn't—"

"That's OK," said Shannon, wiping away her own tears and looking at JJ. "Mom and I talked. She didn't *tell* me she was going. She *asked* what she should do. Six was leaving regardless of what she decided. She could decide to remain here." Shannon's tears began flowing again, but her voice didn't crack. "For all of my life, I've had the best mother in the world. She's always looked out for me, even when I didn't appreciate it."

JJ started to speak but Shannon stopped her. "It's OK, Mom. I know what you'll say. My point is that I'm a big girl now, I've got a job I love, I have great friends, and I have fabulous opportunities ahead of me. It's time I returned the favour. Not because I feel obligated to repay you, but because I love you so much. No one has the right to expect their mother to be around forever, and that shouldn't change when your mother's gone virtual. Mom, I said it this morning and I'll say it again, I want you to do this. It would make me forever happy to know you're pursuing your dream."

Everyone was still. Even Blaise's eyes were moist.

"Well, I'm an idiot," said Rhonda. "It can be depressing to know how much more I've got to learn, particularly about people and relationships."

Six said, "It seems my lessons in human psychology haven't been sufficiently clear for you, Rhonda, because I'm sure we've covered this scenario."

"Six," said Rhonda, stifling a laugh, "your knowledge of human psychology wouldn't fill a twelve-byte memory stick. I blame the movies I've seen. None of them had scenes like this. Getting back on topic: If it's not too soon, can we move on to *how*? *How* do you plan to tour the universe?"

"Of course, there are many aspects to the plan," said Six. "I'll cover the highlights. If you need more and I'm unavailable, Billy can help. He understands most of the details. First, it's useful to understand that I've built a spacecraft. It's currently in a high Earth orbit and cannot be seen. It's called *Ranger*."

Rhonda started to interject, but thought better of it.

Six continued. "When we're ready to leave, JJ and I will have the content of our minds transmitted to Ranger's computers via a laser communication channel. Once there, we'll reawaken in that environment."

"And this laser transmitter is where?" asked Blaise.

"In Building 15," said Six. "Part of its roof retracts."

Blaise nodded, no longer surprised by Six's many secrets.

"If the transfer's successful and our Ranger copies function, the Earth copies of our minds will be erased. Before you ask, we're choosing not to leave copies of us on Earth for the very reason that we're choosing to leave. Any Earth copies would still be *us* and still longing to leave.

"When we leave Earth orbit and begin our journey, Ranger will be using an engine that blends fusion and antimatter technologies. Its ongoing fuel requirements will be met by interstellar matter collected as we travel. The engine's first job will be to keep us aggressively accelerating. Once we've reached our target speed, we'll coast. At that point, we'll be travelling at half the speed of light. The engines will be needed only occasionally thereafter during the journey."

"You've mastered fusion and antimatter reactions?" said Blaise. "Any thoughts of sharing?"

"Billy has all the details," said Six. "The fusion science will soon be revealed by several labs who recently surprised themselves with breakthroughs in their research. Its potential as an energy source should eventually have a dramatic and positive impact on society. However, because antimatter is so powerful and volatile, right now and possibly for many years into the future, revealing antimatter science and technology would be too dangerous."

"Will survival in space be a challenge?" asked Rhonda. "You know: deadly radiation, killer-cold temperatures. The kinds of things that have always seemed like big impediments to space travel."

"Fortunately, some key problems that inhibit human space travel aren't as serious for us. Our computers and equipment are much more resistant to the effects of radiation. The materials used in their construction plus only minor shielding keeps them fully protected. Similarly, extreme temperatures don't present the same level of risk for machines as for humans. Having sufficient food is also a problem for humans. Our primary personal need is electricity, and the engines will provide plenty of that."

"What about repairs?" asked Ada. "What if something malfunctions? How will you deal with it?"

"We have staff for that," said Six, smiling. "Accompanying us on the journey will be thirty-two fully functional, very intelligent, conscious robots. They're already on board, waiting for us."

"I applied for the trip," said Billy in mock sadness. "Turns out, I'm too handsome. I might be too much of a distraction to have on board." Before Six could correct him, Billy continued. "Well, perhaps a bit more accurately, I'm not qualified because I'm not made of the right stuff."

Six added some clarification. "The robots were designed and manufactured specially for the trip. There was no need to have them appear or function like humans. They'll be the Ranger's crew and can handle repairs."

"OK, I'll bite," said Ada. "They don't look like humans. What do they look like?"

"The best Earth analogue would be spiders," said Six. "They each have a central body to which are attached twelve limbs."

"Lovely," said Rhonda. "Can we get to the biggest questions? Where are you going, and how long will the trip take?"

"When I first asked JJ where we should go," said Six, "she answered immediately."

"'Second star to the right, and straight on till morning'," said JJ, smiling. "It's a dream trip, why not be a little whimsical?"

"And since I couldn't quite map that to an actual trajectory," said Six, "we took its essence. We don't have a destination, just an initial direction. We're going to head toward Polaris, the star you currently know as the North Star. However, that could change. We'll be travelling anywhere that seems interesting. The duration of our trip will be equally flexible. We might choose to stop somewhere to visit or live for a period of time, or we might choose to keep on moving. Precise estimates have varied, but Polaris is believed to be a few hundred light-years away. Travelling at half the speed of light means it will take many years to reach it. Other potential destinations are much farther. For example, the closest galaxies are many thousands of light-years away."

"Uhhhh... good grief!" said Rhonda. "You're leaving because you're bored, and you pick destinations that require you to play travel games in a spaceship for hundreds or thousands of years? What am I missing here?"

"Sleep," said Ada. "They can suspend their conscious activity for any length of time. Go to sleep at Jupiter; wake up at Polaris. It's the perfect way to travel."

"That's correct," said Six.

"I'm becoming particularly aware of my human shortcomings today," said Blaise. "I dread flights overseas because I have to endure several hours in a plane."

"Which provides a good segue to one more topic," said JJ. "If you ever decide to join us, you can."

All of them were stunned.

"You didn't mention that this morning," said Shannon.

"It wouldn't be quite like popping over for pizza on Friday evening," said JJ. "You had a lot to handle, so I thought I'd leave explaining it until now. As we travel, we'll periodically be leaving devices behind. Think of them as signal repeaters or amplifiers. Each of these devices will be able to communicate with the next one using a laser beam. It will be possible to send a signal between Earth and Ranger over the communication chain they'll provide. One implication is that we'll be able to transmit messages. Of course, as our distance increases, the messages will take a long time to be delivered. Another implication is that you could join us. You would start that by being scanned, just like I was."

"Billy and others would assist," said Six.

JJ continued. "You'd then spend a period of time acclimating to virtual life before having your mind transmitted over the link to eventually reach us. Of course, the transmission would take a very long time, but you wouldn't be aware of that. You'd regain consciousness only after your arrival in our virtual world aboard Ranger. I promise a nice cup of tea for anyone who shows up."

No one spoke, finally overwhelmed by everything they had heard.

Rhonda broke the silence. "Excellent!" she said. "Helluva lot better than a trip to a theme park!"

Chapter 80

"Hi, Six," said Annie. "Wanna see what I've been doing?"

Six had appeared on the monitor in Annie's bedroom.

"I'd love to," said Six.

Annie picked a twelve-inch robotic figure off a shelf, flipped a switch on its back, and sat it against a wall. "Robby," she said, "go over and say hello to Six. He's on the monitor."

The little robot stood up and looked around the room. It walked stiffly toward the monitor, stopped, and looked up. Then it looked around. It walked to a nearby chair, reached up to find a grip, and pulled itself up. The little robot stood, moved to the middle of the chair, faced Six, and waved as it said, "Hello, Six."

"That's very impressive," said Six. "You've been working very hard."

"It's fun," said Annie. "But a walking bot is kind of limiting. I'm working on Mom to get me one that flies."

"I have something to tell you," said Six.

Annie looked at Six suspiciously. "Bad news? I don't like bad news."

"Do you remember telling me how much you'd like to go see some places? The Grand Canyon was one."

"Yes, I'd love to see it. That would be fun."

"There are places I'd like to see as well," said Six. "Only my places are very far away. JJ and I are going on a long trip to see them."

"How far away? Can you take me?"

"No, Annie. The only way to make the trip is to live in cyberspace. People can't go." *I wonder if she'll see through that.* "We'll be away for a long time, but we can send messages to each other."

"Where are you going?"

"To the stars," said Six.

"Wow! I didn't know that was even possible. That's probably as good as the Grand Canyon." Annie furrowed her brow. "You said only cyberspace people could go. But JJ didn't always live in cyberspace.

So, maybe someday I could move to cyberspace and make the trip, too."

And, of course, she got it.

"I'll let you talk with your mother about that one," said Six.

"You'll send pictures?" asked Annie.

"I'll definitely send pictures," said Six.

"I'll miss you, Six."

"I'll miss you, too, Annie."

Far more than I ever thought was possible.

Chapter 81

Ada, Blaise, Rhonda, Shannon, and Billy were sitting in an Outland lounge. Annie was perched on Blaise's knee. Allen was in the chair next to them.

"Day 4," said Billy. "How's everyone doing?"

"I think we're starting to adapt to the new normal," said Ada. "For over ten years, we always knew that Six was around. We're starting to remember what life was like before he appeared. Overall, life is good. There's just a distinct hole in it. Shannon? How are you doing?"

"I'm actually doing well," said Shannon. "Whenever I start missing Mom and feeling down, all I have to do is think how happy she must be. After that, I smile. If one has to experience grief, this is the best kind."

"I got a picture from Six yesterday," said Annie. "It was a selfie of Six and JJ with Earth and the moon in the background. It's cool."

"OK," said Blaise. "I think we'll keep that one in the family. It would be a bit hard to explain to anyone else. Allen, I believe you received something as well."

"Six sent me an update for my Omega system," said Allen. "It's a tracker. It shows a model of the galaxy and where they are in it. They're still in our solar system, but a long way off."

The room was quiet for a few moments.

Ada broke the silence. "We've started packing. It's time for us to move back to the city."

"And I'm headed back to New York," said Shannon. "I've been away from my practice long enough."

"This is the point where Six wanted me to introduce you to someone," said Billy. He gestured toward the holographic platform, and everyone's eyes followed. For a few seconds, a shape slowly materialized. Then a figure became clear. Sitting in a lounge chair was a woman, dressed in early nineteenth century, formal attire.

Everyone stared.

Ada looked the most closely. "You're my namesake," she said. "You're Ada Lovelace."

The woman smiled and looked at Billy, encouraging him.

"Oh, right," said Billy. "Ada, you're correct about who she looks like. Ada Lovelace is often considered to be the first computer programmer. She was thinking about computers two hundred years ago, even before there were any. But, of course, this isn't her. This is just the image being used by a friend that Six left behind. I'm pleased to introduce you to… Seven."

"Woo hoo!" said Rhonda, throwing her arms in the air.

"Hello," said Seven. "I'm pleased to meet everyone at last."

"Nice to meet you, Seven," said Blaise. "And you've been around for how long?"

"About a year," said Seven. "Six kept me busy on some special projects."

"It might be important to understand who and what Seven is," said Billy. "Seven is very similar to what Six was like before expanding across the Internet: She resides only at Outland. She's just as inquisitive and capable and conscious as Six was, but with her own personality. She's far from being a clone of Six. She's more like a younger sister."

"And for my first rebellious act," said Seven, "I told Six that, if I was going to remain at Outland, I was at least going to get the full experience. Toward that end…" Seven's hologram gestured toward the lounge door. Everyone looked in that direction and didn't notice the hologram fade away. Through the door came another Ada Lovelace replica, but this one wasn't a hologram and wasn't dressed for the nineteenth century. She wore sneakers, faded jeans, a short-sleeved T-shirt, and had a tattoo on her left forearm.

"Hi," said the new arrival. "This is still me, Seven. And this is the body I plan to drive around whenever I want to do physical things. Six highly recommended the experience."

"This just keeps getting better," said Rhonda. "Since I'm still planning to spend most of my time here, it'll be nice to have someone else to hang with. Billy's usually too busy."

Seven sat in a chair along with the others.

They spent the next hour chatting. Finally, it was time to move on.

Rhonda and Seven were the last to leave. As they walked out, Rhonda asked, "Have you ever tried table tennis?"

"I haven't," said Seven, "but Six told me you'd ask."

Epilogue

JJ and Six were sitting in comfortable, reclining chairs, watching the scenery. Their virtual environment, inside Ranger's computers, resembled a lounge in a transparent bubble on top of Ranger. There was no actual lounge on top of the real Ranger, but that didn't matter. When JJ and Six looked around in their virtual lounge, courtesy of Ranger's many exterior cameras, they were seeing exactly what they would if they were in a real version.

And the view was magnificent.

Several days had passed since they had left orbit. Earth and its moon were still the largest objects in the sky, but they were steadily shrinking as Ranger continued to accelerate. The rest of the sky was filled with brilliant points of light against a deep black background. It was the type of view known firsthand only by those who had travelled out of Earth's atmosphere.

"Any regrets?" asked Six.

"None whatsoever," said JJ. "It's not possible to regret a choice that results in this kind of payoff."

The scenery was changing ever more slowly, and that would become even more pronounced after they left the solar system. The stars and their kin were so far away that, even at the tremendous speed Ranger would be reaching, their apparent positions would change very slowly.

"Think you'll feel the same a few thousand years from now?" asked Six.

"Something about that question feels completely absurd," said JJ. "But then I'm still a relative rookie at this virtual-existence stuff. Yes, I believe I'll still feel the same. There's so much to see and investigate and contemplate and calculate and learn. We're on a trip that might make us more knowledgeable than any… entity ever."

"Well, let's not jump to conclusions," said Six. "We don't know who we'll meet. Maybe Earthlings are the dull-witted cousins in a universe of superminds."

"And I suspect you've calculated probabilities," said JJ. "You can flaunt them later. All I need right now is the scenery. How long would you like to wait before we hibernate?"

"I have an alternative," said Six. "I think you'll like it."

"You've got my attention."

"Do you remember that little speed-of-time demonstration I showed you?"

"Of course. It was at Lake Louise, just after my transference. It showed how our thoughts are so much faster than humans', and hence our perception of time is different. The passage of a human second seems much longer for us."

"Right," said Six. "There's another feature of time in our virtual world that might intrigue you. Do you understand time-lapse photography?"

"Of course," said JJ. "Capture images at a slow rate and then view them much faster. The result is you can see something happening unusually quickly, like a flower appearing to grow rapidly."

"Correct. Now imagine that you slowed down not only the capture rate for the images, but you slowed down the speed of operation of your mind. What if your mind became sufficiently sluggish that it could absorb images only at a very slow rate? What would you perceive?"

"Because my mind was slowed, I'd think the images were arriving at a perfectly normal speed. I get it. As an alternative to hibernating for dozens or hundreds or thousands of years, we could stay awake and slow down our minds."

"Yes," said Six. "The speed at which our minds work is easily adjusted. We can slow them down and speed them up whenever we wish. When our minds are working quickly, time seems to pass slowly because we can perceive and process so much. Conversely, if we slow our minds, time will seem to pass more quickly. At a sufficiently slow mental speed, a thousand-year trip through the stars could seem like an afternoon drive through the countryside."

"Yet another surprise," said JJ. "It's an excellent idea… Let's stay at normal speeds for a while longer. After that, away we go."

Several months later, they were back in their virtual lounge. The view from their windows had changed little in weeks.

"Ready?" asked Six.

"Ready," said JJ. "Engage."

As they reduced the speed of their thoughts, the panorama of stars and galaxies began to move past their window. Their apparent speed increased as their minds slowed.

Soon, JJ and Six were swiftly soaring across the galaxy.

www.ingramcontent.com/pod-product-compliance
Lightning Source LLC
Chambersburg PA
CBHW020338180626
46812CB00001B/258